STAN LABOVITCH

The Pedagogue

STAN LABOVITCH

The Pedagogue

MEREO
Cirencester

Mereo Books

1A The Wool Market Dyer Street Cirencester Gloucestershire GL7 2PR
An imprint of Memoirs Publishing www.mereobooks.com

The Pedagogue: 978-1-86151-712-8

First published in Great Britain in 2016
by Mereo Books, an imprint of Memoirs Publishing

The address for Memoirs Publishing Group Limited can be found at
www.memoirspublishing.com

The Memoirs Publishing Group Ltd Reg. No. 7834348

The Memoirs Publishing Group supports both The Forest Stewardship Council®
(FSC®) and the PEFC® leading international forest-certification organisations. Our
books carrying both the FSC label and the PEFC® and are printed on FSC®-certified
paper. FSC® is the only forest-certification scheme supported by the leading
environmental organisations including Greenpeace. Our paper procurement policy
can be found at www.memoirspublishing.com/environment

Typeset in 12/18pt Century Schoolbook
by Wiltshire Associates Publisher Services Ltd. Printed and bound in Great Britain
by Printondemand-Worldwide, Peterborough PE2 6XD

To my mother and father,
Jack and Ann Labovitch

About the author

Stan Labovitch was born and brought up in Leeds. After studying geology at Cardiff University, he spent two years as an IVS volunteer in Africa, an experience which inspired him to pursue a teaching career in Britain. It was here that he developed a passion for extra-curricular activities as a means of creating fully-rounded pupils. Known for his pithy letters to the national press on virtually every conceivable subject, Stan has drawn on his teaching experience to write his debut novel, *The Pedagogue*. He has a son and lives with his wife in Berkshire.

Contents

About the author

PART 1

Botswana

Chapter 1

It was the last day of the summer term at Beechwood School, a large comprehensive in the London borough of Hestwell. The staff room was resounding to the celebratory sound of teachers enjoying their AGM – Annual General Meal, with wine. No mistaking the euphoric atmosphere, so different from the morgue-like tenseness that marked the start of the school year in September.

Everyone was on a high. Beechwood had just been judged 'Outstanding' by the long-awaited Rottweilers from Ofsted, and for once everyone felt great. Even the uptight librarian Mavis, with the aid of several glasses of Tesco's half-price Pinot Grigio, managed to change the habit of a lifetime and grace her normally miserable face with a smile.

For Michael Zabinsky, this was a very special day; at the age of sixty-four he was finally hanging up his chalks and retiring from the noble profession of teaching. Thinking only of his imminent leaving speech, Michael wrestled with a slice of cold pizza and some oily lettuce leaves. He was unable to enjoy his lunch, preferring to fortify himself with copious helpings of *vin rouge le plus ordinaire du monde*. Although his once Bob Dylan-like black curly hair was now sixty-four shades of grey, when compared to some of his clapped-out colleagues he didn't look his age. His generous eyes and suntanned face radiated the same youthful optimism and mischievousness that had always been his hallmark. His appearance was more Hollywood than Hestwell.

The Headmaster began his address. It had been yet another successful year at the West London school, with the best exam results ever (as usual) and a successful Ofsted inspection to boot. In short, it was a vindication of his commitment to box-ticking and arse licking – or as he preferred to call it, leadership. As is always the case in big city schools, many teachers were leaving, so each one had to be given a send-off, a prezzie and a card.

Leavers were called according to their length of service. Michael watched as a series of young teachers who had only been at the school for a year or two, most of whom he'd seen but never known by name, were thanked for their services and given a bunch of flowers or a bottle of wine, and wished well in their future careers. Then came those who'd been around for over five years, who were allowed a short speech, a couple of gags and a few tears. And suddenly it was Michael's turn.

To the sound of heartfelt applause, Michael extricated himself from his seat and slowly approached the front of the staff room. He'd spent the last four weeks preparing this speech. He decanted his grubby notes onto the table. For many years Michael had dreaded this day, but as is so often the case on such momentous occasions, he felt incredibly confident and relaxed.

"I've been at this school for thirty-three years, more time than Nelson Mandela spent on Robben Island, but not as long as the Moors murderer Ian Brady, spent inside," he began. He paused to milk the response to this most witty and cool of introductions. "It all began nearly forty years ago in Botswana, when as a young and idealistic fresh-from-university volunteer, teaching changed from being a *vacation* to being a *vocation*. For the first time I experienced the unimaginable thrill of seeing a child learn. I will never forget the joy on the face of an African child called Nkomeng on discovering that mosquito larvae turned into mosquitoes. Yes, that's where it all began, a lifetime ago in Botswana."

As he climbed out of the 1970s steam train from Johannesburg onto the oven-hot platform of a ramshackle station called Gaborone, Michael noticed to his horror that not only was everybody black, but they all looked the same. So it's not just Chinamen, he mused. This was just the kind of stereotype, or was it prejudice, he'd spent his whole life trying to avoid. But far from being intimidated, the young volunteer just marvelled at the sheer exoticness of it all. "Shit!" he exclaimed. "I'm in Africa! Now how do I get to the school?"

The situation was saved by the timely appearance on the scene of a dusty Jeep straight from the 1970s TV series *Daktari*, driven by the legendary aid-worker and honorary *lekgowa* (white man), Sandy Coombes. Dressed in a blue safari suit, with long dishevelled hair and a handsome rugged sunburnt face, Sandy was clearly in his element out here; he looked every bit the colonial explorer. Michael was whisked at what seemed an unreasonably high speed, along the potholed dirt road to the village of Mochudi, some twenty miles from the capital.

As the Jeep rattled its way north, it created an impenetrable cloud of dust in its trail. Everything was so different, from the stunted acacia trees to the occasional glimpse of African *rondavels*. The searing heat blasting through the open windows induced a sense of timeless siesta. What an utter thrill to be in this new place, what an adventure.

And so to the village where Michael would be spending the next two years of his life. Sandy delivered his bright-eyed cargo to the gates of Moketse Secondary School.

It was January, so the school was on "summer" holidays and virtually deserted. Everything was dusty and hot. Michael gazed at the strange surroundings, his long hippy hair blowing in the heated afternoon breeze, sweat oozing out of every orifice and the sensation of burning on his anaemic European arms. The school campus consisted of modern prefabricated huts with corrugated roofs, which crackled in the summer heat and glistened in the blinding African sun.

A man shuffled into view and introduced himself as Wayne Fanshawe, a Canadian Mennonite. His face was pale and sickly-looking, his self-conscious movements suggesting a neurotic disposition. His shorts extended way over his white knobbly knees and he twitched nervously. His pale blue eyes had the mad, messianic look of a biblical prophet. He was known to the kids as *Menseke* – quicksilver – and he was to be Michael's new housemate; a match that was not made in heaven.

Among the other volunteers, "wacky Wayne" had a reputation for being somewhere between an off-the-wall eccentric and just plain crazy. His main driving force was the musings of radical educationalists Alice Bailey and Rudolf Steiner. He was very much into philosophical flagellation. On hearing of Michael's new housemate arrangements, Jim Kennedy, a huge long-haired, bear-like creature from the Midwest who looked more like an American football pro from the Michigan Wolverines than a teacher of mathematics, just rolled his eyes and said "Wow!" Like most of the Americans on campus, Jim was a spaced-out Peace Corps Vietnam draft-dodger who loved smoking grass. These guys were down on their country and seriously cynical about Nixon, whom they regarded as a duplicitous shyster. They couldn't wait to receive their weekly edition of *Newsweek* or *Time* Magazine, with the latest lowdown on the Watergate scandal.

In the days leading up to the start of term it got even hotter, and there was no relief from the rains that never came. Rain (*pula*) was fantastically important in Botswana. It was both a source of spiritual inspiration for songs and prayers, and a practical necessity; its life-giving water could make the difference between crops and a poor harvest, food or starvation. The "Pula" motif was worn on colourful shirts, and would become the new currency once the rand was discontinued.

Michael decided to explore Mochudi. Being young, headstrong and a bit stupid, Michael, like many a mad Englishman before him, walked off in the midday sun in what seemed to be the general direction of the village. Obviously there were no signs, just the gut feeling that he knew where he was going – which of course he did not. In his blue M&S shorts, tie-dye T-shirt and desert boots purchased from a safari store in Johannesburg, Michael trundled along the narrow sandy track, but he soon realised his mistake: he had forgotten to wear the floppy kibbutz hat he'd brought back from Israel the previous year. With the sun directly above – something he'd read about before coming out here – his scalp felt close to ignition. He began to feel light-headed and weightless and on the verge of delirium, something he'd only previously experienced on Kibbutz Mishtanah, secreted somewhere in the baking bowels of the Dead Sea rift valley. In short, he was fucked.

He collapsed beneath a stunted Mothlopi tree by the wayside. He had only walked a few hundred yards, but he felt certain he was going to perish, which was a pity because he'd only been in the country a day and hadn't taught a single lesson, or indeed met any of his pupils. He'd heard about homeostasis and how the skin and kidneys were supposed to prevent dehydration, but it didn't seem to be working for him.

As is often the case when one stops, one has time to observe and think. In his state of semi-consciousness our intrepid explorer began drinking in his surroundings. There was the all-pervasive sweet smell of burning wood from a hundred household fires. In this sweltering heat there were only a few villagers wandering about. Occasionally a barefoot young girl carrying a huge bucket of water on her head passed by and giggled.

"*Dumela raa*, are you all right sir? Would you like some *metsi* [water]?"

She had probably walked several miles from one of the many wells that supplied the village, her dead-straight back supporting the enormous load. He had read that ants could carry ten times their own weight, but humans? He wondered how such a little frame could support two gallons of water.

A few older ladies, babies strapped to their backs, hovered outside their crumbling mud huts, sweeping the yard with a dried grass brush while naked children played with each other. The village seemed to have no men. Everything looked so other-worldly, extra-terrestrial even, as the village dozed in its sleepy torpor. It was uncannily tranquil and peaceful, with only the sound of a few distant voices or birds and the hiss of the tropical breeze punctuating the near-silence. Michael luxuriated in the sheer otherworldliness of it all. He really was in Africa.

After maybe twenty minutes of helplessness, his strength gradually returned; it was like emerging from a sedative-induced deep sleep. Michael left the sanctuary of the tree and cautiously continued towards the village. He realised that the only way to survive such conditions was to imitate the villagers and walk very slowly. The purposeful rush of the north European was definitely not suitable here. And anyway, where was the urgency? Here in Africa where time wasn't money, there was never a rush. The sense of time or the lack of it was clearly one the biggest differences between the European and the African way of seeing the world. When in Rome, one had to adapt to the local conditions.

Crossing the bridge over the arid channel of the Mochudi River, the track opened into a wide *OK Corral*-style "Main Street" which sported a few primitive shops and the village bar. It was here that Michael would be spending much of his "quality time". Known to the local cognoscenti as the "Library", the village bar was like something out of the Wild West, a simple breeze-block building with a flat roof and a couple of poky rooms furnished with a few small rickety tables and wooden chairs. The walls were bare apart from a few strips of peeling paint, and there was absolutely no decor. From the wooden veranda one could drunkenly witness spectacular sunsets and watch the dusty world go by. Although the bar was extremely basic, it only attracted those who could afford the (by local standards) seriously expensive South African lager. Which meant *mekgowa* (whites), government employees and the Chief, who would chase away local riffraff when it suited him. The villagers were reconciled to drinking *chibuku*, a foul-smelling African beer brewed from sorghum, in their shebeens. This was a highly selective upmarket establishment.

The veranda was like a stage on which the daily theatre of life played itself out. On this hot January afternoon, as was so often the case, the chief was holding court to his loyal subjects; expatriate teachers, a couple of his cronies, and the headmaster of the poorly-equipped village school, Nkhosi. Chief Matlapeng 11 was the chief of the local Bakgatla tribe, respectfully known as *Kgabo* (monkey). He was the tribal factotum of the Bakgatla, to those who knew him. He was an immensely impressive and cultivated man of the world who in the 1960s had served as Botswana's US Ambassador. His youthful looks and formidable intelligence made him an instant hit with the ladies and enabled him to talk knowledgeably about almost anything. He could also drink everyone under the table without himself being in the slightest bit affected. And like many in those days, Matlapeng was also a chain smoker. He was Mochudi's link between its tribal past and the modern world.

In 1969 he had been called upon to announce the American moon landing to a gathering of the traditional village council, the *Kgotla*. One of his tribesmen had burst out laughing and said: "Are you trying to tell me that the Americans have reached the moon, *Kgabo*? Beat me if you must, but I cannot believe that there is a man on the moon."

Perched on the veranda and showing off her sunburnt little legs was Cathy Routledge, a short and feisty, highly-politicised lefty from Brighton who had a massive guilt complex about the white man's treatment of the black man. As a VSO English teacher, her role was to redress the balance by sleeping with as many black guys as possible. One of these was Tom King, a warm and softly-spoken Peace Corps from Alabama, who spoke with a pronounced southern drawl. He wore centuries of slavery and oppression on his sleeve. As a Development Studies teacher, his role was to redress this crime against humanity by indoctrinating his pupils with the injustices of colonialism and sleeping with as many white women as possible. He sipped a cool can of Castle lager.

Sitting nearby was an older man with glasses, Mr Tiro, who looked like an older version of Robert Mugabe. He was a local Mochudi maths teacher at the school, and like most state-employed Batswana he spent his leisure time getting sozzled on Western beer. Although rarely coherent, he exuded an endearingly world-weary humour and was probably the laziest teacher that ever graced the profession. He didn't give a fuck about the kids, which was amusing because his name, *Tiro*, means 'work' in Setswana. His favourite joke was about the bar being known as the Library. One popped in to read a page (drink a beer) or a chapter (several beers) in order to become educated (sozzled). He sometimes had to be surgically removed from the bar in order to give a lesson, even though he was still half-cut.

After introducing himself to the veranda dwellers, Michael entered the dingy bar and tried out his new language, Setswana, on Sam the barman.

"*Dumela rra.*"

Sam smiled, his bloodshot eyes scrutinising this just-off-the-plane, wet-behind-the-ears *lekgowa*, and continued chewing his matchstick.

"*Ee rra.*"

A couple of bleary-eyed locals in bare feet and torn clothes stared at him passively. Both were smoking roll-ups. Michael requested a can of beer, which Sam dutifully provided from the "fridge". Luckily the freeze-box was working today, so the beer was lovely and cold and thick drops of condensation were rapidly forming on the gleaming metallic surface. When there was no power, the fridge didn't work, but beer was still stored there and served warm. You took your chance.

Taking his can outside, Michael joined the other "readers". As he was hot and dehydrated, the beer took immediate effect. After the first exquisite, thirst-quenching sip, Michael felt instantly better. After two sips he felt great, and as the aluminium cylinder was emptied and the 5% alcohol – much stronger than English beer – got to work on what remained of his cerebral hemispheres, he began to experience a wonderful sense of relief and liberation. This would be the one time in his life that he would get pissed on a pint – and for only fifty cents!

As evening approached Michael began to giggle uncontrollably, much to the amusement of the well-read literary giants on the veranda, who had never witnessed such a wimpish performance.

Michael knew that the sun, *letsatsi*, rises and sets rapidly in the tropics, but the reality was, as always, more impressive than the theory. The setting sun seemed to drop out of the western sky, a huge orange fireball briefly swelling and glowing against a thin band of cloud and dust, before plunging below the horizon. Within half an hour it was dark. As the womb-like warmth of the dry evening breeze stirred a few discarded crisp packets and caressed Michael's already hot arms and face, the silhouette of Papane Hill against the diminishing evening sunlight was like watching the stage at the National Theatre dimming after a great Shakespearean performance. A sense of immense peace and well-being coursed through Michael's veins. Everything looked so exotic. This really was Africa.

The school campus was on a hill overlooking Mochudi. Unlike the crumbling village school Matlapeng – named after the chief – which looked exactly as one imagined an African school would be, Moketse Secondary was a purpose-built government school with an astonishingly modern appearance. It consisted of white prefabricated classrooms and expatriate-style houses for the teachers. It had a European look about it. Between the buildings there was no grass – just brown desert sand.

Each house was, by the standards of a squalor-loving graduate from England, almost agoraphobically spacious and generously fitted out with lots of rooms, with the ultimate luxury of running water. A large sandy garden enabled the teachers to be self-sufficient in giant green watermelons, so long as they were watered every day. At the end of each garden were the "servants' quarters", which were usually inhabited by a deserving pupil from the school, who, in return for free accommodation, watered the garden and was paid a couple of rand pocket money. On the roof of each house was a solar water tank, and when it rained, water would drain down the gutter into a massive metal cylinder which stored the fresh *metsi a pula* – rain water. In Botswana, *metsi* was precious. The silver-coloured aluminium roof expanded in the sun and crackled explosively at night, frightening the life out of new arrivals as it cooled down and contracted.

Michael shared a house with wacky Wayne; they were like a married couple – the odd couple – with Wayne playing the female role. He wore thin-rimmed glasses and squinted neurotically. Like most women, Wayne would fuss about the minutiae of cleaning the house and doing the shopping. He was highly strung and moody, frequently sulking when he couldn't get his way, like a woman. Michael didn't give a fuck about housework and tidiness, and had absolutely no interest in composing tedious lists of food that apparently needed to be bought each week from the supermarket in Gaborone. Where Wayne preferred to voraciously consume the alternative quasi-religious musings of Alice Bailey and Rudolf Steiner (he had the complete works), Michael was more interested in playing his guitar, sunbathing and drinking cheap South African wine.

Over the next few days the other teachers began arriving back from summer vacations spent gallivanting around southern Africa, so that finally everyone was assembled for the first staff meeting of the new term. The headmaster, Mr Seretse, an avuncular-looking chunky man with a shiny bald head of about fifty, was meticulously dressed in a dark blue cotton suit, and in spite of the unbearable heat, he wore a white shirt and tie. As was so often the case in Africa, African professionals looked more European than the Europeans. His eyes radiated an intelligent warmth and his bald black shiny head seemed to reflect the morning sunlight. He sounded like Nelson Mandela and frequently returned to his family ranch in the South African border town of Rustenburg.

Seretse welcomed some thirty or so teachers back to Moketse Secondary School and introduced the new staff. Michael, dressed in Marks and Spencer shorts, sandals and a short-sleeved green shirt, inhaled his new surroundings. The teachers were overwhelmingly young, gifted and white idealistic twentysomethings, fresh out of college. The Africans consisted of big Joe Maktum, a South African exile whose Xhosa name was pronounced with a Miriam Makeba-like *click,* a sprinkling of local Batswana and several Rhodesian refugees who'd escaped Ian Smith's white-supremacist regime across the frontier with the pariah state. The volunteers were mostly British VSO, Canadian Mennonites and American Peace Corps.

Periodically the headmaster sought clarification from his ginger-haired, mild-mannered, seen-it-all-before deputy Frank Johnson, a timetable guru and a consummate gentleman. As always, Frank, an English teacher from Romford who deferentially referred to the headmaster as "HM", was impeccably turned out in a colonial-style cream safari suit with long grey gartered socks and brown leather shoes. He was the only contract teacher on campus, which meant he could afford a posh blue Volkswagen Beetle with good suspension. He looked ancient but was probably about forty-five, and he could have stepped out of a Noel Coward play in Shaftesbury Avenue. Frank wasn't married, but had a "sister" in South Africa whom he visited each summer.

When Idi Amin evicted the Asians from Uganda in 1972, Michael had volunteered to help out at Stansted Airport and later on a refugee camp in Lincolnshire. It was here that he found himself teaching refugee children about Britain in a makeshift classroom and first dabbled with the possibility of becoming a teacher. But this was his first lesson in a proper school. And like an actor about to tread the boards before a new play, he felt nervous.

On entering his new form room, this Jewish boy from Leeds was met by a sea of black faces. To his great amazement and totally at odds with his fashionable-at-the-time liberal beliefs, the children stood up and gazed at this exotic intruder with wide, expectant eyes and in complete silence. Michael felt uneasy at this show of seriously old-fashioned and totally unnecessary respect. The pupils wore the school uniform of Moketse, and smelled of smoke.

Although this was meant to be form 2A, who would normally be 12 or 13 years old back home, Michael immediately noticed the huge variation in height. Some of the children were small and puny and looked like primary school kids; others were as tall as he was and looked at least as old.

"*Dumela* 2A, I'm your new form teacher, Mr Zabinsky, please sit down," he said. The pupils giggled at the funny-sounding name, but they answered as one, "*Dumela ticheri*," and sat down.

As Michael took the register he made the earth-shattering observation that the children in his class *didn't* all look the same; Mandrise, Batsile, Noah, Violet. "Present sir." There were as many variations amongst black people as amongst whites, which came as a big surprise. For a start some were much blacker than others, perhaps denoting a different tribal origin. A few, who obviously had European, probably Afrikaans blood in their family trees, were almost white. There was an albino child whose pink eyes and pink blotchy skin lacked pigment, and who, to protect himself from the merciless glare of the African sun, had to wear long trousers and sleeves and a peaked cap. Michael had seen albino mice before, but never humans.

Then there was the school uniform, which made the kids look cute: orange cotton dresses for the girls, brown shirts and shorts for the boys. Everyone had made an effort to be well turned out. But here again there were differences; some uniforms were spotlessly clean and new, others were frayed and shabby hand-medowns. Although every kid here was poor by Western standards, some were clearly poorer than others. And this was reflected in their footwear; some wore sturdy brown leather shoes, others went barefoot.

Of course the really hard-up couldn't afford to pay the necessary school fees in the first place and were condemned to a life of strenuous domestic work if they were girls, or looking after cattle if they were boys. In Botswana as in much of Africa, most of the work was done by women. Without education girls could look forward to a life of cooking, cleaning, pounding corn, fetching water, planting and tending crops and eventually marriage – if they were lucky. Or simply having lots of children – often with several men – who would then grow up and repeat the cycle, the meek inheriting the earth. Boys could look forward to a life tending cattle on the "lands" for weeks at a time, then, as they got older, passing on their not-so-industrious genes by siring lots of illegitimate children and retiring to some seedy shebeen, where they would spend their days drinking *chibuku* and smoking and generally sitting on their backsides doing fuck all. The Western concept of gender equality was anathema in these parts. Here education was a meal ticket to escape village life and better oneself, which usually meant getting a cushy job in the burgeoning civil service, as in all developing countries, and moving to Gaborone, where they would exchange a poky village mud hut for a poky brick box called a town house. This was deemed to be progress.

"Tebogo, Sophie, Nkomeng, Molefe."

"Present sir."

As the new teacher continued to take the register the class stayed silent – something that Michael would later discover never happened in an inner-city school back in Blighty. Thirty pairs of wide and expectant black eyes watched in amusement as Michael tried to pronounce their names correctly. David, Stephen, Emmanuel were familiar English names but Tschwenyana, Monthlanyani – Jesus! The class burst into spontaneous laughter, which as he smiled back in acknowledgement became raucous. These kids really knew how to laugh, loved laughing together, doing *everything* together. None of this suppressed individualistic European nonsense. The more he smiled the more they laughed. Their laughter was infectious and strangely liberating.

And then there was the hair. Africans have tight, black, curly hair, but this too showed variety and individuality. Some had their curls plaited into bold lines of black separated by railway lines of pink scalp. Some had frizzy afros, while others had combed their hair into sharp black punk-like spikes. Bizarrely almost every pupil had pens and pencils actually slotted into their curls, which gripped them tightly. How logical using one's hair as a pencil case. In fact the locals really did use their heads to hold stationery, to carry school books, and of course to carry enormous buckets of water several miles from the well. This in turn meant that in order to maintain balance one had to maintain a dead straight back, which in turn resulted in excellent posture. You couldn't slouch with a gallon of water on your head, and the hands remained free to waggle and wave, or whatever.

Although it was only eight o'clock in the morning – school began at the ungodly but eminently sensible hour of seven – it was already starting to feel hot as the sun delivered its immense energy, continuously generated by the nuclear fusion of billions of hydrogen atoms at its core, onto this insignificant thin-walled classroom somewhere on the African plateau.

On the first weekend after the start of term, Michael's neighbours, Canadian Mennonites Maggie and Bev, threw a pancake party on the Saturday afternoon. It was mid-January, which was supposed to be the rainy season. In theory low pressure over central Africa should be sucking hot moist air from the Indian Ocean over Botswana, but not for the first time, the rains had failed. And when the rains failed so did the crops, which meant hardship for the mainly subsistence farmers. The failure of maize and sorghum – the staple food of Botswana – to grow, meant poverty or even starvation for some. Pula was like moolah, the very currency of life. No rain meant no grass for the cattle – Botswana's main export – to feed on, which meant even more hardship. The fields were like brown dustbowls as the summer temperature was ratcheted up to thirty-five degrees Celsius.

Michael and Wayne squeezed through a crack in the fence between the two houses and entered their neighbour's back garden. It belonged to two female volunteers, which meant it was well-tended with neat rows of well-watered sweet corn, interspersed with some kind of exotic red flowers. A Motlopi tree in full fragrant flower offered some shade from the blistering sun. Most of the teachers turned up as well as the sharp-nosed, intelligent-eyed Dan, who had flown out with Michael and had the pleasure of being posted to the rundown village school, Matlapeng.

North Americans love pancakes. They have elevated pancake eating to the status of a quasi-religious ceremony to which they had an almost erotic attraction. For these people, pancake eating was better than sex. Back in England, pancakes were no big deal and were vaguely associated with the rather quaint tradition of Shrove Tuesday, when pancakes were meant to be publicly tossed, but not to North Americans. It was a type of sub-culture which enabled them to indulge their wildest culinary fantasies.

While Maggie and Bev manned the pancake production line, the guests could gorge themselves on a selection of sweet and sticky viscous toppings like maple syrup, honey, treacle and an assortment of colourful "jellies" – American for jam. For the more discerning glutton, lemon juice was available. Squeals of orgasmic fulfilment could be heard emanating from the stuffed or glued-together mouths of the more serious players. "Wow!" yelped Big Jim from Michigan, as he consumed a double pancake topped with maple syrup and honey. "Far fuckin' out!" cried Paul from New York, "Jesus H Christ," mumbled Josh, his wide eyes and dilated pupils feasting on the sheer abundance of the sweet-smelling sickly fare. He was well versed in this ritual assertion of American identity, honed to perfection in his rickety Rocky Mountain shack back in Washington State. The congregation of worshippers praised the Lord of Pancakes and thanked him for his mellifluous munificence. Who said God didn't exist?

As the afternoon progressed, the heat intensified further; only the exceptionally low continental humidity stopped it becoming unbearable. Iced soft drinks were replaced by the more thirst-quenching and instantly-inebriating refrigerated beer from Johannesburg and white wine from Stellenbosch. Michael had noticed in Israel that when the air approaches body temperature the skin recognises a familiar state of equilibrium, a soft, knowing sensation like being in a warm bath or a foetus floating in its mother's warm-blooded and protected womb.

When the pancake mix ran out, the feasting stopped. Michael was amazed to observe that while he'd just about managed to force down two syrupy pancakes, the likes of Josh and Paul had consumed six, and were still begging for more. With only a few slivers of sweet pastry in his stomach coupled with the day's heat which always seemed most oppressive just before sunset, the rapid intake of alcohol created an instant sensation of glorious delirium and ecstatic well-being.

As the enormous fireball of the African sun exited the evening stage over Papane Hill, the western sky glowed briefly orange and then faded into a purple blackness, like an electric cooking hob being slowly turned up to maximum and then suddenly turned off. The sound of a thousand bush crickets became increasingly audible as they warmed up for their nightly performance, like the percussion section of an orchestra rehearsing for an open-air concert in Central Park.

The dull beat of music drifted from inside the house. "Bring the stereo outside and turn it up!" yelled the blue-eyed Sadie, a stunningly beautiful party-loving Development Studies teacher from Maryland. Everyone fancied her, but she was allegedly promised to some military guy back home; Sadie was always going on about Charlie James.

It had become dark with unseemly haste, this being the tropics. Back home the transition from day to night could take two hours at the height of summer, and even then there was always a glow of light to the west until midnight and then a glow from the east as the earth rotated on its axis and reconnected with the dawn. But not here. By now everyone had retired to the veranda; some sat on seats, the more chilled-out sat on the floor in cross-legged meditation. Paul circulated a giant joint rolled from a bag of freshly-delivered best Botswana grass. Above, the intense blackness of the African sky – as black as the skin of its gentle people – was peppered with a billion stars. The veranda was illuminated by a portable electric light that had been plugged into an outside socket. As the soothing country-rock sound of The Eagles harmonised *"I've got a peaceful easy feeling, and I know you won't let me down"*, a steady stream of exotic insects was hypnotically drawn to the lamp, and perhaps the music. They had good taste. Enormous moths and armoured beetles crashed into the electron-induced luminosity as they hurtled in from the bush to a certain but glorious immolation. Others danced their dance of death around and around and around the bulb. The whitewashed stone wall of the compound became covered in a thick black vertical entomological carpet of what seemed like most of the one million or so known species of insect. There were the more easily recognisable termites, locust-sized crickets, delicate lacewings, ants, bugs and flies, as well as a myriad of hitherto unseen and brightly coloured varieties. A lizard darted across the wall as other invertebrates were drawn to the light. Voracious centipedes turned up for a free lunch, while huge spiders crashed the party unannounced and proceeded to gorge themselves on the smorgasbord of mobile insect life. It was like something from the Carboniferous.

Was it the heat, the alcohol, or had someone laced those bloody pancakes? The sight of so many insects was surreal; what one imagines one would see after taking a mind-bending psychedelic drug like LSD. And not only the sight, but the sound. A loud, crackling, buzzing sound pervaded the still hot, night air. If a thousand arthropods could appear in an evening, just imagine how many there must be out there; millions, billions, trillions? Where did they all live? How did they survive? How did evolution manage to come up with so many types? Or did God create them? And if so, why and for what purpose? There was so much hidden night life in this parched land.

The soul-wrenching beauty of Joni Mitchell's oh so sweet and sincere voice emanated from the stereo and deeply penetrated the emotional pores of the young teachers as they sat contemplating the meaning of their lives under the gaping black, star-speckled African sky. The moon had not yet risen to replace the sun's heavenly light. Joni's exquisite and haunting lyrics perfectly captured the yearning of idealistic youth and the mellowness of the evening, the very zeitgeist of 1973:

Born with the moon in Cancer
Choose her a name she'll answer to
Call her green and the winters cannot fade her
Call her green for the children who have made her
Little green, be a gypsy dancer.

Chapter 2

A month had passed, and Michael had fallen in love with the school and its beautiful children. The first rains had arrived as moisture-laden north-easterly winds from the Indian Ocean set off violent convection currents and generated giant towers of cumulonimbus. The comfortably dry desert air of the first few weeks had been replaced by an oppressively tropical humidity. Spectacular cloud formations transformed the forever blue firmament into an alpine skyscape of what looked like snow-covered mountain peaks. Towards evening a blackening horizon rumbled the first salvos of the thunderstorms and torrential downpours to come.

As in Britain, the colonial power that had created independent Botswana from Bechuanaland in 1966, the school day began each morning after registration with an assembly. Assemblies are a uniquely British institution designed to engender a sense of belonging amongst the pupils and supply the necessary moral fibre required to prevent spiritual constipation. Originally designed to transmit an essentially Christian message, they evolved with the advent of multiculturalism to inculcate a more general non-denominational morality. Here assemblies were *alfresco* rather than in the school hall and unashamedly Christian, with the pupils in their brown and orange uniforms sitting outside on the mostly warm sand.

Although the raison d'être of the Mennonites was firmly grounded in Christianity, the majority of the volunteers were secular sceptics who were wary of religion and any attempt to indoctrinate others with its unenlightened mumbo jumbo. In an age of radical free-thinking and personal emancipation, religion was regarded as a sinister tool of neo-colonialism, especially out here in Africa. And yet as is so often the case with strongly-held beliefs, they can be instantly undermined by the acid test of reality. Just as the believer must question his faith in God's creation when confronted with the overwhelming scientific evidence for evolution, so atheists and agnostics can be made to question their lack of faith on entering a beautiful cathedral or hearing religiously-inspired music by Handel or Bach. It is difficult not to be moved to by the perfect harmony of five hundred children singing a sweet hymn to God and the joy on their faces.

Like the rest of the volunteers, Michael was not a qualified teacher and was expected to teach science on the strength of a university degree in Geology, Botany and Zoology. Unlike schools back in Britain, there were no schemes of work, just the syllabus or a pupil text book. And there was little appreciation of the importance of health and safety or the concept of risk assessments. So most teachers made it up as they went along, some more successfully than others. On the positive side, the complete absence of accountability or interference from senior staff – there were none, nearly everyone left after two years – meant that these young but hugely enthusiastic amateurs were given an unrestricted freedom to innovate that they would never experience again in their teaching careers.

Freedom means the chance to make your own mistakes. On one occasion in early February, the sultry morning session was interrupted by the sound of an enormous explosion. Lessons stopped, and looking through the classroom windows screaming children could be seen running out of Josh's chemistry lab, closely followed by a white-faced teacher and palls of grey smoke. Apparently Josh Jefferson – a knowledgeable biologist but with little understanding of the physical sciences – had just performed the most dangerous experiment in the Cambridge O-level syllabus without trying it out first. Burning the pure hydrogen generated by reacting sulphuric acid with magnesium ribbon in a flask can only be done safely if all the air in the apparatus has been flushed out by the hydrogen. If the hydrogen is not pure, instead of burning harmlessly like a domestic gas cooker, it explodes violently: this was the very same phenomenon that would blow up the Space Shuttle Challenger in 1986, killing everyone on board.

Luckily the pupils were wearing goggles. The apparatus exploded upwards with a yellow flash and a bang, sparing the onlooking children serious injury but blasting a hole in the lab ceiling. On emerging from his lab, Josh shook his head slowly and smiled.

"Wow man, that was close."

This spaced-out, happy-go-lucky hippy from Washington State had not the slightest inclination of how his obliviousness to life as we know it had nearly led to his pupils being maimed for life by flying glass or blinded by acid. Not to mention his career being ruined. This experiment would be later banned in all British schools.

The children in 5B Biology were the oldest in the school and were being prepared for the most prestigious school exam taken in Botswana, the Cambridge Overseas O Level, reverentially known simply as "Cambridge". This was a bizarre piece of benign neo-colonialism in which revered names like Oxford and Cambridge conjured up fantasies of what one imagined it must be like to be British; something definitely to aspire to in this backwater of the modern world. In England this would be a class of boisterous sixteen-year-olds; here ages varied from sixteen to twenty-four. It was sobering to think that the tall, thin and very serious-looking Clarence was the same age as Michael. Two young men in 1973, who thanks to an accident of birth found themselves in the same room, but with totally different destinies and life chances; one a university graduate and teacher with the prospect of living to eighty and a stimulating and well-paid career back in London; the other a student, an overgrown schoolboy whose future in an underdeveloped country like Botswana was anything but certain and who would probably die of disease before he was fifty. Fate. Men are not born equal. Was this God's cunning plan, and if so why?

Michael's biology students, although poor by Western standards, were in their own way an elite. Their parents could not only afford the fees required to stay in education – some dropping out when the cash ran out – but they had also passed the Junior Certificate exam, the JC, after year three. In Botswana one could teach in a junior school with JC. Cambridge was a passport to success, to university, or to the relatively cushy and well-paid civil service. Education really was a meal ticket, the surest way out of material poverty. For this reason, and because of the deferential way in which they had been brought up, the students in 5B were incredibly polite, gentle and eager to learn.

Because of their natural deference to adults and those in positions of authority, it was difficult to get students to challenge the teacher's opinion or actively participate in class discussions. Unlike back home, pedagogues were highly respected godlike members of society, not figures of fun to be mercilessly mocked and lampooned. Children were used to sitting passively in rows and listening to the teacher, who it was assumed knew best. He was a learned person, a pandit, a Malamed – a font of all knowledge.

Unless that is, there was an unintended double entendre between Setswana and English. In a lesson on the nervous system, Mr Zabinsky was trying to explain the difference between motor and sensory nerves which were scientifically known as neurones. At the mere mention of the word "neurone" however, every face lit up and the whole class began to giggle uncontrollably. "The sensory neurones carry impulses to the brain and the motor neurones carry impulses to the muscles." Audible laughter. "Words like neurosis, neurotic, neurologist pertain to the nervous system." Screams of laughter, wails of laughter, *howls* of laughter. Tears began to flow. This was the other side of the coin: the ability to laugh loudly and unselfconsciously about anything that was remotely funny. The henpecked and long-suffering Russian-Jewish immigrant husband of Michael's formidable university landlady, Mrs Schneider, often quoted from personal and bitter experience: "Cry and you cry alone, laugh and ze whole vorld laughs wiz you."

Laughter, unlike sadness, is infectious. At the sight of this previously indolent group of children laughing uncontrollably, the teacher began to laugh uncontrollably himself; what a great feeling, what a release. Like a comedian, he knew that what made his audience laugh was the word 'neurone'. But why?

We've all been there; ostensibly formal occasions where straight faces are required – funerals, sermons, school assemblies. But the very formality and seriousness of the gathering means that a sudden noise, an innocuous gesticulation or phrase can cause spontaneous tittering combustion, which because of the surrounding crowd, is painful to suppress. And as like-minded eyes meet, the amusement is cranked up into group hysteria, infectious like *The Laughing Policeman*, hands cover mouths, eyes are screwed shut, breathing becomes difficult. You feel like wetting yourself. These are incidents one never forgets. So it was with 5B biology. *Nyo* is Setswana for a vagina – a cunt by any other name. This made-in-heaven double entendre broke the ice between teacher and students. The more the class laughed, the more the teacher laughed. And because this uncontrollable laughter was so enjoyable and therapeutic, the teacher went out of his way to mention the "n" word as frequently as possible. God, how these people loved to laugh. A strong bond was developing.

Another topic guaranteed to cause amusement was that old chestnut sexual reproduction. The mere sight of the male or female genitalia in text books, in all their glory, was enough to provoke a fit of the giggles, even without the embarrassment of having to pronounce the dreaded names – vagina, penis, testicles. It was a taboo subject, rarely discussed in public, very different from the West. People self-evidently had sex, but it wasn't endlessly alluded to like back home. Couples openly fraternised, but overtly touching or kissing was not part of their culture. Letting it all hang out was not an option here. For a Westerner it was difficult to crack the sexual code.

Some of the pupils were very bright. Emmanuel was an immaculately turned-out student whose clear black intelligent eyes signalled a rapid comprehension of the subject matter and a craving to know more. He had classically handsome African features; perfect poise, unblemished smooth black skin, instantly endearing politeness. His ambition was to become a doctor, a profession for which he was temperamentally well suited, an ambition that he was easily clever enough to realise. Emmanuel was quiet and modest, always coming top in exams. He would not show off by putting up his hand, but would always come up with the right answer when picked on by the teacher. He was the envy of everyone in 5B, especially the girls, who admired his manners and intelligence. He quietly and knowingly exuded the aura of a prince whose position was unassailable.

Cecelia Linchwe was different. She was a frail, sickly-looking girl, whose intensely penetrating sad and tearful eyes were redolent of suffering. Her complexion was pale brown and flecked, racially different from Emmanuel, more akin to a Hottentot or a Bushman, with possibly a hint of white blood in her ancestry. Like many in Botswana, she suffered from tuberculosis and had to endure bouts of weakness and breathlessness, sometimes being too weak to attend lessons. Because of this, she was shunned by some of her classmates who feared contracting the disease. She had missed a lot of schooling and was older than the rest; about eighteen. Like Emmanuel, Cecelia was deeply religious, which coupled with her long suffering made her look pious. But when she smiled it was the most beautiful and gentle of smiles, like the sun emerging from behind a dark cloud, bright, warm and life-giving. And as is so often the case, suffering makes one mentally strong and more determined to succeed. She loved biology, but her main passion was singing. Like all Africans she had a natural sense of harmony and rhythm and would readily burst into soulful song. She could instantly harmonise with any tune. When she sang her eyes closed and her head swayed. One could instantly see where negro spirituals and the blues originated.

The origin of African rhythm had long fascinated Michael Zabinsky. Through blues, jazz and soul, black music had heavily influenced pop culture and helped create rock and roll. But where did it come from? One clue was the daily ritual of pounding maize. On his winding walks through the village of an evening, negotiating his way to the bar, Michael observed that in every compound, women were pounding their staple food – maize or sorghum – into flour. A thick wooden pole was used to pulverise corn placed inside a tubular wooden bowl, like a giant mortar and pestle. The coarse flour thus produced would then be boiled in an enormous black pot on an open wood fire to produce a delicious porridge called *bogobe* or *phaletshe*, which was served with relish and eaten with the fingers. Although the pounders could be elderly, they were mainly young, fit, nubile girls, some with a baby strapped to their backs for good measure. They were often schoolchildren from Moketse.

The pounding, like all work in Botswana, was done by women and was communal. Western individualism just wouldn't work here. The children often said "we" instead of "I". As they pounded they laughed, and as they laughed they sang. This was logical, since the act of pounding was highly rhythmical, the flexible, wavelike, almost erotic swaying of the body followed by the plunging of the pole deep into the bowl. One thing led to another; the rhythmic motion led to the singing, the singing led to the rhythmic motion and instinctive singing in perfect harmony. The repetitive pounding was soothing, therapeutic, almost trance-inducing in nature. And hugely enjoyable. No need for expensive psychobabble or physiotherapy here. This was fitness and wellness *au naturel*, and without the rip-off fee. This was why the girls were so supple. It was the origin of African music.

Chapter 3

Every Saturday morning, Cedric the Mennonite, for a fee of fifty cents petrol money, drove his big white open-topped Toyota truck to Gaborone, the capital "city" of Botswana. This was a major event in the calendar of Moketse and enabled the mostly city-bred volunteers to escape the monotony of the school and the village for a day and reconnect with the thrills and spills of urban decadence.

After buses, open-topped trucks were the main form of transport in Botswana. Up to fifteen teachers would pile into the back of the white Toyota and sit huddled together, often covered by a blanket in the cool morning air. This weekly adventure took an hour to travel the twenty miles to the capital. Apart from the final stretch of newly-tarred surface, the journey involved negotiating a deeply rutted and potholed dust road, which became a brown and muddy swamp in the rainy season.

This was a perilous journey and sitting in the back meant that every bump and undulation was amplified and transmitted through the backsides of the hapless passengers, like the seismic waves from an earthquake passing through the earth's crust. Like so many coach drivers and drivers of other people in general, Cedric was a power-crazed sadist who loved frightening the living daylights out of his powerless victims by driving as erratically and dangerously as possible. Normally a fastidiously-dressed, God-fearing if somewhat pompous history teacher, when behind a wheel Cedric morphed into a demon who enjoyed terrorising his colleagues, watching them cowering and shitting themselves, powerless to interfere with this pathetic weekly demonstration of faux machismo.

After doing the weekly shop at what passed as a supermarket, the main pleasure was buying Chinese fish and chips in downtown Gaborone and then repairing to the centrepiece of the town, the President Hotel. From the veranda of the hotel one could watch the hot sleepy world of Gaborone go by whilst getting completely pissed. The sumptuous luxury of the President was light years from the primeval Mochudi bar. The colonial decadence of the hotel with its soft seats, ceiling fans and deferential black waiters constantly grovelling at your feet and kissing your arse gave it the feel of forbidden fruit. Here one could get sozzled on cold Castle lager and contemplate the unfairness of wealth and privilege whilst enjoying its benefits. The sight of expensively-dressed, perfumed women made one crave female flesh; a deliciously indulgent sadomasochistic pleasure which improved the more one drank. And this painful sense of unfairness was emphasised by the prices, which were affordable to ordinary *megkowa* and wealthy blacks, but prohibitively expensive, *obscenely* expensive to the ordinary Motswana. One could empathise with the plight of the oppressed victims of apartheid just across the border in South Africa. And of course Michael and the other volunteers in their shorts and Pula shirts, were on their side.

This was also a watering hole for Chief Matlapeng, who held court much as he did back in Mochudi. As the day got hotter, people disappeared from the streets below the hotel for their afternoon siesta. Occasionally a barefoot African mother with a baby strapped to her back and a child on either side passed by, carrying a huge sack of personal belongings on the way to God-knows-where.

At about four, the hottest part of the day, everyone assembled at Cedric's truck for the home journey. Most were laden with bulging bags and rucksacks filled with tinned and bottled food for the coming week. Several hessian sacks of delicious South African *namune* (oranges) were loaded onto the truck's floor. As the Toyota left the shanty-town suburbs of Gaborone, Michael always felt a sense of relief to be on his way back to Mochudi. Although he was a Jewish boy from Leeds with Catholic tastes, visiting the capital with all its attractions and temptations somehow felt impersonal and lonely when compared to the camaraderie and friendship of the school campus and the adorable pupils he taught. That was where he belonged. In contrast to the cool morning, the afternoon air was now oven-like and humid. Huge cumulonimbus could be seen building to the north and the first distant rumbles of thunder could be heard rattling across the vast acacia-covered African terrain. There was no better place to be on a sultry afternoon in February than in the back of a fast-moving, open-topped truck hurtling through the *veldt*. The sensation of hot air blasting one's exposed face and arms, long hair blowing in the wind like Neil Young at Woodstock, was both caressing and sensuous – like luxuriating in a hot jacuzzi, one of the most therapeutic feelings known to man. Feeling high. This was air conditioning, African style.

As they travelled, they sang the chorus of a road song Michael had written to immortalise those heady trips:

Oh we're riding along on a truck
I sure hope you have a lot of luck
Trees are flashing by
And we're feeling kind of high
One big family.

Those were the days of singer-songwriters. Everyone aspired to strum a guitar and compose songs. Like many, Michael thought he was Neil Young, Bob Dylan, Joni Mitchell, Cat Stevens, Paul Simon. These guys inspired a generation with their heartfelt lyrical voices and meaningful words about the lives they thought they lived and the world they thought they lived in. They captured the zeitgeist.

Sadie looked as radiant as ever, her peaceful blue eyes and golden sunburnt face communing with the sun god. Jim smiled knowingly and looked spaced-out, like he'd just had a joint but was high on the day. Wayne sat cross-legged, his pale thin features contemplating the meaning of life, silently meditating. It wasn't cool to talk; it was the *look* that mattered. There was nothing cooler than gently nodding your head, serene face and eyes gazing knowingly into the distance and looking meaningful, occasionally saying "Wow," or "Hey man."

As the truck continued northwards, it left a dense cloud of sand in its wake, James Bond-style, so that anyone following would be blinded and crash. Occasionally Cedric would drive into the foggy sandstorm created by the vehicle in front. Instead of waiting patiently for the dust to settle, the mendacious Mennonite was unable to resist the insane thrill of overtaking into the opaque unknown of the dense brown void ahead. This was great fun, because it meant terrorising those in the back, who would be thrown to their deaths if anything was coming the other way. He had them where he wanted them; begging for mercy. As in all developing countries, the roadside was littered with overturned vehicles, road accidents being the most common cause of death. In Israel more people were killed on the roads than in the never-ending wars with their Arab neighbours. Once again Cedric had demonstrated that his pathetic machismo was alive and well and in need of constant renewal.

But Cedric Scott was not the only danger to life and limb playing Russian roulette on the crumbling roads of Botswana. It was quite normal for open-topped trucks stuffed to the heavens with colourfully-dressed villagers, huge bags of maize and flour and a goat or two to meander precariously, often on the wrong side of the road to avoid deep crevices, on their journeys from somewhere to somewhere else. Carrying twice the recommended number of passengers, these trucks were dangerously unstable, while the driver very likely couldn't drive and was probably drunk, often toppling over or causing other vehicles to swerve out of their way. No seat belts, no drink-drive legislation, no breathalysers, no highway cops to stop you. Buses were even more scary. Too big and heavy and too old for the roads in the first place, buses were never less than dangerously overflowing with people either crammed like sardines into a space without ventilation or, or hanging from suitcases on the roof. The Western concept of road safety and personal space was unknown here. Life was much more of a fatalistic gamble. Nobody deluded themselves that they were immortal. Like bus drivers everywhere, they were often serial misanthropes, who like Cedric, had a constant need to demonstrate and re-demonstrate their machismo. And like bus drivers the world over, they were genetically programmed to overtake every vehicle in sight, especially each other. This was dangerous enough on the M4 motorway from Reading to London, but on an African road that was barely wide enough for one vehicle, the spectacle of two buses racing each other was the sort of hair-raising stunt best left to nightmares or black and white Hollywood movies with Buster Keaton. It was the stuff of the Wild West.

Turning right at Pilane, a small hamlet and railway station on the main line from Cape Town to Lusaka, they saw a rusty metal sign pointing vaguely in the direction of Mochudi. The wide pocked road to Francistown became the narrow pocked road to Moketse. It was always a relief returning home to Mochudi and the school campus where one lived and laughed and taught knowledge-hungry children about the nervous system. Clusters of brown rondavels appeared by the roadside and stretched up Papane Hill towards the *kgotla* to the west and "Main Street", where the usual suspects could be seen drinking and philosophising on the veranda of the bar.

The best time to return to Mochudi was at night, when the darkness created its own sense of majesty and magic. As one drove through the village one could make out the flickering fires in each compound scattered like twinkling stars in the sky and the occasional silhouette of a villager walking slowly home through the night's blackness, somehow managing to navigate and unafraid of being mugged. Unless of course it was full moon, in which case the contours of the village were revealed like a black and white negative, the outline of hills and trees and mud huts illuminated, the sandy paths reflecting the yellowy moonlight. And as one crossed the river which shimmered like quicksilver, the bright electric lights of the school came into view, standing out on the hill like an airport terminal floating above the darkness. Sometimes the moon shone so brightly through the pristine night sky that one could read one's weekly mail collected from Rodney Metzger's recently constructed letter rack in the staff room, without a torch.

Michael looked forward to reading the weekly dispatch from his dad, written in beautifully-curved fountain pen ink on the inside a sealed thin blue airmail letter. Michael's mother had passed away when he was young, so his father, Nathan, had raised his two strong-willed sons, Michael and Jacob, on his own. Every week Dad wrote a letter and every week Michael replied. Dad would describe the week's events in Leeds, what the weather had been like, whether Aunty Guggi or Aunty Tilly had visited him and the state of the garden. Sometimes Jacob visited with his American girlfriend Sally, and this was a real treat. On other occasions his eccentric brother-in-law, Abe Shufleder, came round with news of orthodox Jewish life in Manchester and the latest stories about Leeds United's performance in the football league.

As he read his father's letter under the huge, yellow, medallion of an African moon, the sheer exhilaration of the moment and this gentle loving letter written with typical humour, despite his father's physical infirmity and loneliness, caused Michael's eyes to fill with tears. He could feel, hear, smell his father through this most ancient form of communication, which expressed so much more than a five-minute telephone call; the ancient power of the word.

At moments like these his father felt so close, despite being separated by nearly a quarter of the earth's circumference. Here Michael was pursuing his youthful dream of travel and adventure in the prime of his life. His whole future was in front of him and there was his loving father, old and infirm, on his own in a semi-detached house in Cedarwood Avenue, Leeds. Nathan Zabinsky loved his two boys more than anything else; they were the very meaning of his life, the very reason for his continued existence. He had selflessly cared for his children after the premature death of his darling wife Hannah when the boys were eleven and nine, taking on the role of both mother and father. Every penny of his meagre pension was spent on his boys; every hope for his future was invested in their future. There never was a more devoted, self-effacing and loving father. Nathan had selflessly given his blessing to both his sons' need to travel even though this meant years of being on his own, of unbearable loneliness which probably broke his heart. And yet he never openly complained or showed resentment.

Feelings of guilt stirred under the moonlit backdrop of the school. Had he done the right thing? What right did he have to leave his infirm father alone? Was the burning ambition of youth sufficient reason to leave a loving parent, as so many had done before and his own children would probably do to him when their time came? For every son or daughter for whom the yearnings of youth propel them away from the loving embrace of their parents and their childhood home, there are mothers and fathers left lonely and isolated behind. For every explorer or immigrant or refugee, there is this yearning to be free.

On nights like this it was as if the gravitational pull of the full moon could somehow lift and transport distant sons and daughters to their parents, like the tide ebbing and flowing, returning water to remote beaches a thousand miles away. It was as if a parent could somehow be reflected across the world to his child; for it is exactly the same full moon that presides over Botswana and England, a sort of lunar communality. How appropriate that the ancients had attributed magical godlike powers to this giant reflective satellite of mother earth.

Chapter 4

What is it that attracts people into teaching? What is it that makes teachers stay in the profession? What is it that in spite of long hours, disruptive pupils and the constant barrage of criticism from parents and the media, keeps a teacher going? There is no doubt that long holidays and the prospect of decent pay and a good pension are important factors. For some it is a love of children, the camaraderie of colleagues and the satisfaction of achieving good exam results that counts. For others it is the high-octane excitement of the classroom, the chance of changing people's lives or to dabble in the great issues of our age like gender, race and politics. It may be the chance to show off one's thespian skills and give a performance, like an actor on stage who craves the adulation of his audience. Or it may be the intellectual stimulation of enthusing children with a knowledge of your subject. What really makes teaching special is the thrill of seeing a child learn.

The thrill of seeing a child learn is one of the most rewarding and satisfying feelings available to mankind. It is the joy that every parent experiences on seeing their child grow up and develop and learn new things, the first words, the first steps, the first catch of a ball. And like an epiphany, such things suddenly happen without warning and are instantly recognisable. Every child in class 2A knew that in the wet summer months mosquitoes appeared in swarms and invaded every house, every mud hut. Their high-pitched buzzing, near the top end of the human range of hearing, was impossible to ignore. Like vampires, they entered your room at night and drank your blood. But where did they come from and how did they miraculously appear each summer? What happened to them in winter?

Michael asked his kids to bring in bottles of water containing the little worms or wriggly things they'd all seen swimming around in discarded containers in their yards. Each bottle was then covered in cotton gauze and left in the lab. After a few weeks the children noticed to their utter amazement that the wriggly things had vanished and metamorphosed – like Clark Kent becoming Superman – into adult mosquitoes which could be seen flying above the water. They had never associated the larvae with the adults. The wide-eyed smiles of incredulity on the children's faces indicated that they viewed the transformation as something miraculous, as something akin to magic. Like a fairy tale in which the frog becomes the prince, or Cinderella's pumpkin becomes a coach, the thrill at seeing class 2A learn about the metamorphosis of an insect moved Michael to tears.

Like all children, the pupils at Moketse loved to imitate and send up their teachers. Every teacher had a distinctive characteristic which was immediately picked up by the kids and amplified, much as a cartoonist lampoons royalty and politicians in the daily papers. The Danish physics teacher Sven Windström was a case in point. He was unlike the rest of the volunteers, being beanpole tall, exceptionally pale and unfashionably short-haired. He looked very straight. However he knew his subject and Michael often had him explain the finer points of Ohm's Law and Archimedes' Principle to him.

Windström's problem was that whenever he pronounced his *s*'s he whistled. So his name became Mr *Windsssström*, his favourite composer was *Sssstraus* and he loved the sport of *sssssoccer*. For the kids this was a dream come true and like children the world over, they could not resist mercilessly mimicking his whistle in class. As if to emphasise the universality of child behaviour, they could be cruel as well as loving and didn't know when to stop. They thought it was hilarious; Windström didn't. By European standards these were the most deferential, gentle and polite kids on earth. But being young, inexperienced and a bit of a geek, the tall Dane was given a hard time. Even in Africa, children instantly sniff out a weak teacher as a lion sniffs out a sickly wildebeest, and poor Sven was there for the taking. He made the fatal mistake of taking the bait, got angry and began to shout. This caused him to glow bright orange, shriek in a high-pitched Danish voice and whistle even more emphatically. For a while his lessons were a living example of chaos theory. But eventually the pupils were won over by his passion for physics, and he in turn was won over by their vitality and began to love them.

As the days went by and the weeks morphed into months, life at Moketse continued to exhilarate and thrill the long-haired Jewish science teacher from Leeds who still thought he was Cat Stevens. How wonderful to be out here at the very epicentre of world events, with apartheid South Africa to the south, an illegal white-minority regime to the north east and the liberated black independent country of Zambia to the north. Or so it seemed.

Geography teacher Luke Mbrire and history teacher Albert Chipunza were two refugees from across the border in Rhodesia. They claimed to have been involved in political dissent against Ian Smith's racist regime, and like many of their countrymen, had sought sanctuary in neighbouring Botswana. Because they were authentic black Africans involved in the struggle for equality in Rhodesia, Luke and Albert were regarded as exotic revolutionaries in the mould of Che Guevara and Nelson Mandela, and reverentially regarded by the highly-politicised, left-leaning white volunteers. These were real rebels.

Luke was a short, stocky and very black-skinned *Shona*, with thick black curly hair and a gentle, quiet disposition. Like many Africans in this part of the world, his father, although a fully grown man, was a "house boy" in one of the many sumptuous white man's mansions that populated the affluent suburbs of the capital city Salisbury. Unlike the chilled-out *mekgowa*, he made a point of being always well dressed and was very popular with the pupils. He was a shy and sensitive man, with an endearing smile and a lovely sense of humour. He loved to laugh.

Albert on the other hand, also a *Shona*, was tall and gangly, with huge rascal-like eyes, a wide conversational mouth and an expansively thoughtful forehead. He was much more highly-strung and gregarious than Luke, and overtly political. But he was partial to the allure of drinking beer and readily succumbed to its charms. He frequently went AWOL in one of the seedier village shebeens. When he'd had a few he became sentimental and nostalgic, and when Michael played Paul Simon's "Mother and Child Reunion" on his acoustic guitar, overtly tearful. The song reminded this exiled boy, of the mother he'd left behind in Rhodesia. Neither looked nor behaved like revolutionaries. They were neither humourless, nor fanatics.

Being amongst such exotic creatures as Luke and Albert, greatly added to the magic and authenticity of being there. They helped assuage the white man's guilt feelings and justify living in an Anglo-American middle-class enclave on the outskirts of Mochudi. The mere fact that white and black people were harmoniously working, eating and laughing together in this most troubled corner of the globe, and as equals, greatly enriched one's sense of doing the right thing. There was something thrilling about being part of history, and by one's own actions helping to change, and yes create, a better world. This was how the young idealists saw themselves, untainted by the cynicism of middle age.

Drinking and singing together on hot humid summer evenings enabled people of different colour and culture to embrace each other in the broadest sense of that word. The darkness somehow broke down the barriers that were the everyday reality for millions on this vast continent. A flash of brilliant fork lightning tore its way through the night sky and struck an acacia tree in the distance. It burst into spontaneous yellow flames which lit up the darkness like an exploding fire bomb. On such nights the air was filled with swarms of winged termites emerging from the sand like ejaculated gametes for their nuptial flight, their brief moment of aerial passion before hurtling to the ground *in flagrante* and losing their wings. This was surely an ancient metaphor for the primordial need to breed, the need to freely love and caress another being, irrespective of race or colour. When the Isopteran orgy was over, the sand was covered by a myriad of discarded termite wings, like dead bodies strewn in the mud of the Somme. Amongst the carnal carnage wandered solitary insects who had not managed to mate, wandering aimlessly over the winged debris having failed miserably to pass on their selfish genes, waiting to die.

It was on these magically mellow summer evenings that Michael would sometimes sit alone on his porch, wearing only his shorts, and strum his acoustic nylon-stringed guitar while reflecting on this most unlikely location in the cosmos. The sheer richness of daily experience enabled him to enjoy the most creative period of his life, readily and easily composing meaningful songs about his existence in the style of Bob Dylan and Joni Mitchell – or so he thought. He sang sweetly and effortlessly, with all the passion and profound yearning of youth gushing forth from his inner soul. He sang about the beautiful child Naledi – the star – whose big eyes and lovely smiling face had so enchanted him.

Little big eyes
Don't be so shy
You are young and lovely
Till the day dies.

He sang about the peace and contentment, the very zeitgeist that so many strived for in those days, and which he had unexpectedly found in this tiny unremarkable corner of the anything but dark continent of Africa.

Oh these lazy days of soft contentment
Are around me now
Feel my tension go away without a sound
And I will watch the sun go down
On Papane Hill
My life is like a butterfly
Nectar on my tongue
Flowers all around me
I will drink every one.

He composed songs eulogising those memorable trips in Cedric's truck, and sang about the sheer joy of being alive, at last.

Peace has come to me at last
Erased confusion from my past
I'm so glad that I've survived
I'm so glad that I'm alive.

And it was on such emotionally charged evenings that Michael thought of his family. His mum had been taken from him when he was eleven, his first encounter with death. Where was Hannah Zabinsky now? Was she watching over him? Would she approve of a boy who'd been lovingly raised in a Jewish home and had attended Hebrew school, eating a non-kosher goat stew in Botswana? How much had her short illness-ridden life affected him, made him what he was today; how much of her essence was in him now? She had died aged forty-six, of a brain tumour. She'd been sick for months, but nobody expected her to die: parents don't die until they're old. Dr Samuels had no idea that his quack prescriptions for nausea and vomiting were utterly useless in arresting the cancer that consumed her brain and eviscerated her soul. He remembered his mother taking him to infant school on his first day at Grove Road, her long black hair, her dark ruddy complexion, her reassuringly loving face. He remembered the sadness of seeing her go, and the joy at seeing her radiantly familiar face at the end of that first long day at school. He remembered Mum's delicious home-made chicken noodle soup, her laughter, her lighting the Sabbath candles on Friday evening. And he remembered his darling mother in her blue and grey checked nightgown being taken in a state of delirium to St James's hospital on July 9th 1960, never to return.

Back on Main Street, life went on in the village bar. The learned habitués of the Library continued to dedicate themselves to the selfless pursuit of knowledge and the study of ethanol. The usual suspects imbibed their if-you-were-lucky cold lager on the veranda, contemplating the meaning of inebriated existence and watching the world go by their viewing platform. They looked like the figures from Raphael's "School of Athens" depicting the great philosophers of ancient Greece. As usual Chief "Aristotle" Matlapeng was holding court with the perpetually plastered headmaster of the village school, "Plato" Nkhosi, and the equally wasted Man from Moketse, Mr "Socrates" Tiro, who looked on unconsciously. Michael, Jim, Mike and Dan, made up the quorum.

Nkhosi, a short and sickly morose-looking Motswana with red bloodshot *chibuku* eyes, was, as usual, blaming society for his personal and not inconsiderable problems. The world was incurably corrupt, which explained everything from his inadequate salary to his poor health and under-resourced school. Like the chief, he smoked continuously, but unlike the chief, he was unable to remain coherent and sober after consuming six cans of lager; more a case of *in vino confusionem* than *in vino veritas*. His latest rant was about the bribery of local villagers with blankets by the ruling People's Party in lieu of their vote in the forthcoming elections. Why hadn't more been done to upgrade his clapped-out school? Why was his salary insufficient to support his hopelessly indulgent lifestyle?

Because he was black and local, Nkhosi received a lot of sympathy from the white teachers – especially the women – who would frequently buy him a drink to assuage their guilt. He was yet another victim of white colonialism, so one could understand his need to drown his sorrows every night in the bar and neglect his wife and children, not to mention the school. Such characters were common in Botswana: black civil servants for whom the only way to celebrate their newfound wealth was to drink themselves to death. So much for being the *nouveau riche noir*. A whole generation of the young gifted and black, lost to the bottle.

Chapter 5

As the South African Railways steam locomotive slowly puffed its way out of Gaborone station in August 1973, Michael wondered what his first trip to Cape Town had in store. Having completed his first two terms at the school, it was time to explore this vast continent. Like so many aspects of life in southern Africa, travelling on a steam train in the 1970s was like a throwback to a bygone age. The continent had become a retirement home for decommissioned European steam trains, a veritable trainspotters' nirvana for those nerdish enough to sport an anorak on the Tropic of Capricorn. It was a thrill to be once again reunited with these stylish, noisy, smelly work horses of the Industrial Revolution. The nostalgic smell of filthy coal-generated steam; the soothing *clickety-clack* of the wheels moving over the track; the exhilaration of sticking your head out of the window and feeling the hot wind blast your face beneath a sign saying, "Do not expectorate". What the fuck was that all about? It was a typically pompous over-the-top way of warning people not to spit out of the window. But who was educated enough to understand this colonial-style Victorian gobbledegook? Certainly not the illiterate blacks, and probably not the barely literate white, thick-looking, thick-sounding Boers either.

In southern Africa trains had four classes: First and Second for whites, Third and Fourth for blacks. This was in-your-face apartheid, modelled on and inspired by the British class system and perverted by the South Africans. Being white – albeit of the bronzy suntanned kind – Michael reluctantly dumped his rucksack in second class where a corridor linked individual compartments with sliding doors, just like those in *Murder on the Orient Express*. He felt uneasy about not being allowed to sit in the much cheaper and less comfortably upholstered third class as he could in Botswana, not being allowed to identify with the natives and get the self-righteous, martyr-like buzz that comes from feeling one was defying the establishment and making a stand against the systematic humiliation of the black man by the white. He did not like playing their filthy racist games. He was young and idealistic, with rebellion in his waters.

All southbound trains from Botswana pass through the sleepy South African town of Mafeking, scene of the famous Siege of Mafeking between October 1899 and May 1900. To pass the time whilst waiting for his connection to Cape Town, Michael took a stroll through the spacious whites-only suburban streets of this quiet backwater, the once bloody site of a crucial British victory and turning point in the Boer War. The owner of the town's open-air swimming pool, on meeting a fellow white man who he assumed would agree wholeheartedly with his racist views, offered Michael a cup of tea and took pride in explaining how his army of black workers maintained the cleanliness of his beautifully-manicured pool by not allowing any blacks to swim in the water and contaminate it. "It's a gut kantry," opined the swimming pool owner in that unmistakably thick Boer accent.

After taking a nap under a tree in a whites-only park, Michael rejoined the train for the next leg of his journey. Travelling the remaining 1400km to Kaapstad on a South African railways "express" train would take the best part of a day. Travelling anywhere on this continent seemed to take a day, irrespective of distance, setting off in daylight, travelling through the night and arriving at dawn. The monotonous bush scenery of Botswana and the Transvaal on southern Africa's Highveld gradually gave way to the lush mountainous and wooded scenery of the Cape Province, taking in the diamond town of Kimberley on the way.

Michael was joined in his 1960s sliding-door carriage by a couple of British volunteers from Zambia travelling back to Blighty via Cape Town after a year's VSO and a shy but pretty female student from Jo'burg, returning to the university town and world famous wine-growing region of Stellenbosch to study viticulture. As they travelled south-westward through the Orange Free State and into the North Cape, they feasted on the endless sunlit expanse of the African plateau, a landscape of large opulent Boer farms interspersed with barren African villages. And as always in this part of the world, the conversation immediately got political. The pretty blue-eyed student, Nancy, whose soft, curvy perfumed features were impossible to ignore, espoused the usual white line that the world had misrepresented apartheid and that the blacks were in fact well treated. Without the white man the blacks would have nothing; the shambolic and corrupt state of every independent African country showed that blacks could not be trusted to run their own affairs. They were different from us; their childish mentality was incompatible with the western ethos of hard work and efficiency. Her words were not spoken with venom; she had, like even the most liberal whites, been brought up that way.

Surprisingly, the two VSO volunteers seemed to know little about apartheid and readily sympathised with the views of Nancy. They had enjoyed their year in Africa – shagged a few natives, seen a few interesting places – but were glad to be going home. They had not been overly impressed by the way Zambians ran their country. The government was corrupt, the railways were hopeless and the people were difficult to get along with. The volunteers lacked Michael's driving sense of injustice and idealism, showing little empathy with the plight of the downtrodden black African.

There's something wonderful about getting sloshed in the bar of a fast-moving train, hurtling along an endless track to some thrilling destination. It conjures up images of being on board the Orient Express before the murder. Train bars tend to attract sad characters who like to pour their hearts out to a fellow traveller; much better than drinking on a plane where you're strapped into a seat next to some sad boring bastard. On a train there's the freedom to circulate and select your quarry. And the journey is the goal, a metaphor for a life that's finally going somewhere, a sense of optimism that things are getting better.

Michael approached the bar situated next to the restaurant carriage, and ordered a can of Carling Black Label and some crisps from the stocky, clean-cut, indolent-looking Afrikaner barman. It was obvious that Michael, with his sunburnt face, long hippy hair and that general air of otherness, was not a South African, so as a sort of exotic curiosity he was instantly invited to join a group of Afrikaners sitting nearby. White South Africans were extremely friendly and hospitable to fellow whites. Unlike their snooty English counterparts, Afrikaners would readily open themselves up to a stranger and engage in conversation, especially if it involved justifying and praising their grubby country with its warped political system. They had an enormous chip on their shoulders about their pariah status as an apartheid nation, and like insecure children, craved to be liked by the outside world.

The group, most of whom were worse the wear for drinking continuously since boarding at Kimberly, had gathered around a well-groomed man in a light brown suit and cravat called Selwyn, who seemed to be holding court. He was probably on his fourth or fifth double whisky and wobbled unsteadily on his seat.

"You know Michael, this is a groyt kantry," slurred Selwyn, anxious to reassure himself that his godforsaken country really was great. "It is a privilege to sit next to you sir, let me buy you a drink."

"Thanks mate," said Michael, gratefully accepting the chance of a free drink. "I'll have another can of lager please."

"I would never sit next to a *kaffir*," the old Boer continued. "If a kaffir sat next to me I would tell him to fucking move. The white man has made this kantry what it is, created it from nothing. The black man is fucking lazy, he doesn't like work. All he thinks about is getting drunk." He poured himself another double whisky. "He likes to skive. He has the mentality of a child. He can't think for himself. He has to be told what to do. He cannot be trusted, Michael."

Selwyn viscerally hated his fellow Africans. The more he drank, the more he hated. Michael had never met anyone with such a deep-seated hatred for a fellow human being. And this was the thing: to a fellow white he was polite, generous and decent; he would do anything for you. And yet this very same man could simultaneously vilify and hate someone just because of the colour of his skin, in much the same way that a Nazi could gas some Jews in the morning, play with his children in the afternoon and make love to his wife at night.

The train plunged down the steep wooded slopes of the great African plateau and arrived in Cape Town at dawn. Michael woke from a troubled sleep spent slouched uncomfortably against a cold window to find a completely different landscape awaiting him. Instead of the endless bush of Botswana, a vast expanse of expensive white villas spread northwards towards the imposing green slopes and brightly illuminated, all-domineering presence of Table Mountain. Already a vast army of Lowry-like black and coloured stick characters were streaming into the city from the townships to commence their daily routine of feathering the white man's nest with their menial labour.

The bus to the youth hostel surprisingly had whites and non-whites travelling together, in great contrast to the strict racial segregation of Johannesburg. The passengers were mostly Cape-coloureds, whose hybrid complexion was noticeably paler than the black Africans of Botswana. The atmosphere on board was palpably more civilised, with people of different races even smiling at each other. Clearly apartheid in Cape Town was much more liberal than apartheid in Jo'burg.

The whites-only youth hostel, "Stan's Holt", was situated in an exclusive white suburb on the outskirts of the city, high above the Indian Ocean and surrounded by luscious green forest. To the east the imposing silhouette of Robben Island, where Nelson Mandela was incarcerated, was just visible, and to the west the imposing flat peak of Table Mountain could be seen though the pine trees. This was easily the most impressively-situated youth hostel Michael had ever encountered. It was more like staying in an alpine hotel. The other hostellers were an assortment of weedy-looking British backpackers who were ending their trans-African tour in Cape Town, and a motley collection of muscular and sporty-looking Aussies and Kiwis who were here to surf the massive waves on the Atlantic side of the bay.

Once a week, a local Jewish couple, Moshe and Esther Silverman, came round to the hostel recruiting young people to share a Sabbath meal with them in their comfortable middle-class home in the Sea Point area of the city. Apart from straightforward hospitality, their motive was also political: like all South Africans they were acutely aware of the way the world portrayed apartheid and wanted to justify their country to foreigners. There may be no such thing as a free lunch, but Michael volunteered immediately along with a couple from Manchester and an Aussie surfer from Sydney.

The lucky four were picked up at six by Moshe and driven for about a mile to their not-so-humble abode. The Silvermans were both doctors, and their opulence was reflected in the spaciousness of their house overlooking the bay. They had two young kids, Rebecca and Joseph, who were playing upstairs in their room. Their pictures were everywhere, two beautiful well-nourished kids with lovely smiles and bright intelligent eyes. Moshe and Rachel regarded themselves as white liberals and were staunch supporters of Helen Suzman, the Jewish leader of the Progressive Party who tirelessly fought against racism in parliament.

This being 1973, healthy organic food with lots of brown rice and nut sausages was served on a low table, with the guests sitting around cross-legged on colourful bean bags and cushions, hippy-style. The tiled floor was covered in a huge zebra-skin rug, with African curios like drums and wooden sculptures dotted around a large room furnished with rattan chairs and low comfortable sofas. Large scented candles produced a soft shadowy light, and with Pink Floyd playing in the background, they created a calm meditational aura. On the walls hung a print of Picasso's "Dove of Peace", a couple of Kandinskys and several original-looking oil paintings, presumably by local black artists. Faded sepia photos of sternly-dressed Russian and Polish grandparents reminded one of the Jewish immigrant ancestry of this family. A photo of Golda Meir hung above a sideboard which housed two Sabbath candle sticks and a silver menorah.

A variety of exotic fruit juices and white South African wine helped stimulate the taste buds and lubricate conversation. After the hosts had introduced themselves and each guest had given a brief resume of his life, Moshe and his wife tried to engage the hostellers in a discussion about South Africa. What did they think of the country? What did they know about apartheid? How did it compare with the rest of Africa? Both the Manchester couple and the Aussie were apolitical and loved it out here; beautiful scenery, hospitable people and much cleaner and more civilised than the rest of the continent. They knew little about apartheid and regarded it as a local matter that was none of their business; they hadn't witnessed any outright brutality.

Only Michael had issues. He hoped that the Silvermans – whose hospitality had been much appreciated – would not take offence, but as a passionate teacher of black African children in neighbouring Botswana, he had a natural empathy with the oppressed and disenfranchised victims of apartheid. Every time he saw a black or coloured child begging barefoot in the street, he thought of what he regarded as "his" children back in Botswana. When he travelled through a township he felt viscerally sick at the sight of such poverty and degradation. Seeing all the menial work being done by blacks insulted his intense youthful sense of fairness; he could not be seen fraternising with the enemy. You Silvermans could never afford your opulent lifestyle without cheap and expendable black labour. As Jews whose ancestors had suffered pogroms and centuries of anti-Semitism, you should know better.

Moshe and Rachel squirmed a little but managed to put on a tired smile. They had heard all this before, although never so passionately put. They tried to justify their position as all South Africans do. Yes, things were unfair, but conditions were improving, and anyway, much better than those in the rest of black Africa where corrupt Oxford-educated, Sandhurst-trained despots milked their own country and lived in palaces while their own people starved. As liberal whites, they did what they could to challenge the system. They refused to have black servants like all their neighbours, and as doctors working in the townships, they were able to relieve the suffering of those very people Michael felt so passionately about. If we weren't here they would die. They were not responsible for the actions of the Nationalist Party who created apartheid in the first place; Prime Minister Vorster was no friend of theirs.

On the day before his return to Botswana, Michael sat on the golden sandy beach at Camps Bay watching the enormous Atlantic breakers crashing onto the shore. The sea air was exhilarating and his head swirled like the foaming ocean with thoughts of his visit to the Republic. And that invitation to the Silvermans' troubled him. On the one hand Moshe and Rachel were part of the problem: as representatives of the ruling white tribe, their opulent lifestyle would have been unthinkable without the privileged status bestowed upon them by apartheid. It was ethically and morally wrong that a white minority government should rule the black majority whose destiny it was to serve them. Protesting that they didn't support the ruling National Party and that they didn't employ servants was a cop-out: if they really hated the system so much they would either leave, or try to change it. But if they left, who would look after their patients? Maybe start a revolution, civil disobedience; but how? What could two people do? It's easy to criticise others and take the moral high ground, but how would Michael have behaved if he too had been born into that milieu? We are all victims of our birth. What did the affluent middle classes of Hampstead do back home to help the underprivileged black underclass of Brixton? Apart from sanctimonious talk and writing indignant letters to the *Guardian*, were they really prepared to relinquish their privileges and redistribute their wealth? Were they really that bothered? Hasn't history taught us that revolutions are bloody affairs and that every revolution devours its children?

As Janis Joplin sang before overdosing on drugs, "Freedom's just another word for nothing left to lose," and the Silvermans had plenty to lose. They were self-evidently decent people who tried their best to lead an honourable life, and yet they were the enemies of progress, or so the left would have us believe. For all their protestations, they propped up a disgusting system which discriminated in favour of whites and against blacks. Unlike those liberated children back in Botswana, a black kid in South Africa had next to no chance of getting a good education and fulfilling his potential. He could never dream of becoming like Moshe and Rachel's two highly articulate children, Rebecca and Joseph, bright, confident, well-clothed and well-fed, and with the prospect of almost certainly going to university in a couple of years and becoming highly paid, middle-class professionals like their parents.

As he gazed out to sea, Michael could just make out the misty silhouette of Robben Island where Nelson Mandela was serving out a life sentence for violently trying to change the status quo. What would he want the whites to do? What would he do if he were white? If all the whites left, wouldn't South Africa just become like every other black African country; independent, but poor and corrupt, with a basket-case economy that was totally dependent on Aid? Would apartheid ever end?

Chapter 6

As he stepped from the huge hissing steam train at Pilane Station, Michael felt he was home. Although it was four in the morning and very dark, the immense silence that descended as the train moved off to continue its relentless journey northwards to Rhodesia and Zambia and the scent of the bush and village fires was like a cow recognising its calf – reassuringly familiar. There was a warmth to the early morning air that was lacking in the more temperate atmosphere of Cape Town. Michael hitched a lift to Moketse in the back of a Toyota truck; what a relief it had been to hear those friendly words "*Dumela rra*" from the driver.

The school was dead quiet and deserted. The ever-present humming of the school generator had as usual been turned off at midnight, so the only sounds were the sounds of the night. In Botswana the night was soothingly quiet but never silent. Through the incessant crackling of crickets, frogs croaked and whistled and Joe Maktum's dog barked. Occasionally an insomniac cock crowed, mistakenly thinking it was dawn. Missing was the daily sound of children playing, shouting and singing, the sound of teachers teaching and children learning. In short, the sound of Moketse Secondary School, the sound of young black independent African lives being joyously celebrated and lived. There was no moon, but a billion incredibly bright twinkling stars welcomed him back to what had become his new home. How he'd missed the sound of those children, *his* children. Cape Town had been beautiful, but there was always that nagging feeling of unease, of guilt of complicity even at being in that freak land of apartheid. It was like a chronic illness that never went away. Here he was amongst people who although poor, had a strong sense of their own identity, a self-confidence that was missing in the Republic. In South Africa he had felt like a fraud enjoying the county's hospitality while at the same time lecturing others on the evilness of the system. The daily sight of one race subjugating another had been difficult to take and even more difficult to understand. Apartheid was like a disease that infected every mind, ever conversation, every action. It was a malaise that corrupted everything. It was the African elephant in the room.

It was the weekend of the annual football match between the teachers of Moketse, "The Hungry Lions", and the teachers of Matlapeng. This not-to-be missed spectacle was due to take place on the dust bowl of a soccer pitch in the centre of the village and was expected to draw a substantial crowd. It was early September and spring, that time of the year between the endlessly sunny and temperate days of winter and the hot humid sultry days of summer. Spring was a lovely time of year when the skies were still deep blue and the return of real palpable warmth sent the thermometer hurtling back up into the mid to high twenties, like high summer back home. It was so liberating to be once again able to wander around in shorts, T-shirt and sandals without feeling cold. It was fantastically calming to once again sit in the shade and imbibe the irresistible warmth of the day caressing your skin, like a lost lover now found. The sun was getting hotter, but the very low humidity meant that sweating was easy and one never felt clammy or uncomfortable. The brown barren bush was illuminated by a myriad of colourful blooms. Acacia trees were covered in fragrant little white flowers, and in the village the giant jacaranda was proudly flaunting its brilliantly purple flower power.

The Hungry Lions were, in spite of their fierce name, a cowardly crew. The team consisted of Brits like Michael who could play the Beautiful Game, knew a lot about it, and thought they were good but weren't, and Americans and Canadians like Paul, Josh, Jim and Wayne, who had never played soccer, knew absolutely nothing about it and cared even less. To them, football meant an American game in which two teams of heavily-armoured thugs kicked the shit out of each other. Then there were the black Rhodesians like Luke and Albert and local Batswana like Pheto, Lucas and Cornelius, who had been raised on the game and were, in spite of their abject poverty and putatively inferior nutrition, super fit. To make up the numbers and in the interest of gender equality, a few weedy girls like Julie and Cathy would also be allowed to play. A couple of extra-large pupils who were probably older than the teachers, were slipped in as ringers for good measure.

Matlapeng were somewhat disadvantaged by having mostly female teachers like Chloe and Brenda and the sickly Brit Dan, so they had to rely on the services of their semi-inebriated headmaster and a number of very athletic-looking "ex-pupils" who just happened to play for Mochudi in the village league. Rodney's high-achieving houseboy Simon was given the dubious pleasure of refereeing this unorthodox fixture.

The two teams assembled at four. It was difficult to distinguish the two sides because of the huge range of kit on display. Clothing varied from garish T-shirts to red Manchester United tops, not forgetting some lovely summer frocks worn by the girls. Footwear ranged from the sophisticated trainers of Big Jim Kennedy to the bare feet of the Moketse ringers. Some wore sandals, others wore flipflops. A few curious villagers had gathered along the line-in-the-sand touchline together with supporters from both schools.

This was not the massive crowd expected, which may have had something to do with the fact that four o'clock – the warmest part of the day – was siesta time, and that only mad dogs and Englishmen go out in the midday sun. It could also have been that the locals just couldn't be arsed to waste two hours of valuable Sunday drinking time watching a load of overfed white expatriate wankers making a fool of themselves.

In Botswana, nothing starts on time. Several of the players had failed to turn up, including the referee, so the match was delayed by thirty minutes. Many of the unfit, overweight players were already tired and thirsty when the game finally kicked off. Pheto, the Hungry Lions captain, dressed in what looked like Pele's 1970 yellow Brazil World Cup-winning number 10 strip, hoofed the ball downfield towards the Matlapeng goal. As the ball bounced wildly on the uneven sandy surface just outside the ill-defined penalty area, Big Jim took a wild swipe at it and missed, stumbling as he did so and leaving Josh free to collide with the ball and head it vertically and aimlessly into the air.

"Hey man, what happened?" exclaimed Josh, as startled as a batsman who's just been clean bowled in cricket. As the ball landed, Julie tried to intercept but tripped over her long white dress and fell crashing to the ground, arse first. Luke, the Bulawayo bombshell who had learned how to play soccer in his English-style school in Rhodesia, smacked the ball into the goals past the clueless Chloe, who was too busy fixing her unbuckled sandals to notice the shot.

"Gooooooooal! Gooooooooooal!" Wild celebrations along the touchline.

"Lions! Lions!"

Albert jumped on Luke's head, while Lucas gave him a humungous hug – until the ref blew his whistle. No goal. Both Wayne and Paul had been standing in front of Luke when he received the ball and unleashed his sizzler, both being completely oblivious to the niceties of the off-side rule. By half-time the Matlapeng "old boys" had transformed the game and were scoring at will, the Moketse goalkeeper, Albert, had long since lost the will to live.

"Hey guys, give us a chance!"

The hungry and very thirsty Lions were four-nil down. It rapidly became clear that only the poverty-stricken, undernourished Africans were fit enough to play football under these exceptionally hot and arid conditions. The affluent and well-fed *mekgowa*, were, to a man and a woman, completely knackered. They were also dry-mouthed, and as thirsty as desert rats. Dan was already puking violently on the touchline. "Oh God."

Michael's orange Pula shirt was soaked in hot sweat; Jim's normally pale face had turned bright pink and streamed with salty droplets. Wayne sat down near the centre-circle puffing and panting, breathing heavily and rapidly like a dog after a fox-hunt, looking puce and sickly. "Oh God."

The Matlapeng headmaster retired to the nearby village bar at half time and didn't return. Cornelius mysteriously disappeared as well.

How was it that black Africans whose sparse diet of mostly mealie meal and the occasional bowl of overcooked goat's meat with virtually no fruit or veg were fitter than Europeans and North Americans who had access to a balanced intake of every food on God's earth? How was it that people whose childhood had almost certainly involved hard, physical, often back-breaking labour, were so much stronger than those whose carefree childhood had been spent playing sport, pursuing their hobbies and having family vacations by the seaside? How was it that people who had virtually no access to modern medicine had more perseverance and strength than those who could enjoy every vaccination, treatment and medication on the planet? How was it that people who lived in mud huts, bathed in bilharzia-infected water and walked around without shoes could possibly run faster than those brought up in comfortable houses with central heating, electricity and piped clean water? Or were these just the privileged ones who had survived infant mortality and disease?

After the players had drunk copious amounts of bottled water during the break, the second half began. Moketse were down to nine players, Wayne refusing to continue on grounds of delirium and hyperthermia, Cornelius having done a runner. Matlapeng were even more depleted. With their headmaster Nkhosi having decamped to the bar and the two ringers sloping off with their girlfriends for a little afternoon delight behind an acacia bush, they were down to eight. This meant that the pitch now had vast areas of unguarded space in which anyone who got the ball could run more freely towards their opponent's end. The goal posts of course had no net, so it was sometimes difficult to tell whether a goal had been scored or not, which led to endless acrimonious arguments. The Americans still hadn't got the idea of this game and were prone to picking up the ball and running with it for a homer. The weedy girls were utterly hopeless at controlling or kicking the ball on the rare occasions that it came their way, and soon gave up trying. The searing heat was beginning to affect their complexions anyway. Pheto and Lucas, whose superior fitness was now more evident than ever, mounted wave after wave of attacks, and with the help of the two barefoot, extra-large Moketse pupils, they were able to score the four goals necessary to make it an honourable draw.

Most sport is an excuse to socialise, get drunk and if you are lucky, pull women. The putative health benefits of strenuous physical exercise are used as an excuse to justify the unhealthy pastime of drinking copious amounts of alcohol. And never was this truer than at the foolhardy fixture between Matlapeng and The Hungry Lions. The Hungry Lions were thirsty. It was nearly six when the game ended and the slanting sun's rays were still strong and blinding as evening approached.

For Michael, the end of the game could not come soon enough. He had spent the last hour in a dazed semi-conscious delirium, having long since given up chasing the ball or trying to tackle infinitely fitter players who ran like cheetahs closing in on an antelope. He had marvelled at the athleticism of his undernourished black colleagues. Michael had always fancied himself as a football player; he thought he looked the part with his knobbly knees and Stanley Matthews shorts. But even at school he had realised that he couldn't match the natural skill and physical prowess of the Gentiles. He could never understand why he got hot and tired so easily and sweat like a pig, or why he couldn't run around for ninety minutes or shoot straight. Now he knew: he had been blessed with the wrong genes. Jews had evolved to think and argue, not to play pointless Gentile games like football. It was no coincidence that Moses took forty years to cross the Sinai desert, when an ordinary bloke would have taken forty days. And even with the Egyptians in hot pursuit, the need to argue about the existence of God and worship the Golden Calf took precedence over survival.

The dishevelled and sweaty remnants of what had once been two teams trudged into the bar like Napoleon's eviscerated troops returning from Moscow, and ordered a round of ice-cold cans of Castle lager. Being Sunday the bar was doing good business and had attracted the usual suspects. As always the chief held court on the veranda, surrounded by a motley group of sad acolytes, sycophants and serial arse lickers. Mr Tiro sat slumped over a double whisky and looked as spaced out as ever. He was nearing nirvana. The diminutive features of the Matlapeng headmaster looked calm and serene, his bloodshot eyes gazing heavenwards as he greeted the sad fuckers, who unlike him, had not deserted the field of battle.

Michael jealously cradled a can of exquisitely cold lager and sat down exhausted next to Dan. He cast off his hot, sticky desert boots and allowed his sweaty feet to cool down in the gentle evening breeze. He just sat drinking and sweating, too tired even to talk after such an energy-sapping game. Sometimes words aren't needed; a communal activity like drinking suffices. Words can be superfluous to requirements, only looks are needed. Dan breathed deeply, closed his eyes in meditation and nodded appreciatively.

The rhythmically-throbbing sound of South African *gumba-*

gumba music emanated relentlessly from the bar's ancient battery-powered radio. A couple of buxom young women danced with each other barefoot on the warm sand by the veranda, half-crouched, with slowly swaying seductive buttocks in traditional African style, a can of beer in one hand, a cigarette in the other. Unlike most *mekgowa*, Michael's eclectic taste in all things enabled him to readily love this uniquely pulsating township music that one heard everywhere in the village. In Africa people don't quietly sit and appreciate loud music – they spontaneously get up and dance, and unlike in Europe, usually with members of the same sex. People dance everywhere – in the street or in the station, young and old, men and women, bums thrust out, arms held motionless in front as if trying to balance their body weight, moving imperceptibly from one foot to the other. It reminded Michael of a slow motion version of the waggle-dance performed by honey bees on the surface of the hive, indicating the direction of nectar to their fellow workers.

Chapter 7

After nearly a year of sharing a comfortable European house with Wayne at Moketse, Michael was seriously considering moving to the village. Things had been deteriorating for some time, and although this spacious Western accommodation was free and a stone's throw from the school, life with Wayne was becoming ever more tense and claustrophobic. Although *Menseke* was at heart a deeply sensitive and loving person, his clingy neurotic almost female nature was beginning to get on Michael's tits. It was becoming increasingly difficult to have one's own privacy, since Wayne insisted on sharing everything and doing everything together. Like an ersatz wife unable to contemplate her husband occasionally going out with his mates to the pub in order to preserve his individuality, *Menseke* was becoming increasingly possessive, with bouts of jealousy, moodiness and sulking. As often happens with married people, they realise after a while that they are completely different from each other and have little in common.

Michael had secretly admired Peace Corps guys like Josh,

Paul, Mike and Jim for having their own authentic African mud huts in Mochudi. So he rented a lovely little rondavel in the compound of the Kang family, situated deep in the village near the Zionist church, and some thirty minutes' walk from the school. It cost him the princely sum of two rand a month, or £1 sterling, so that for the first and only time in his life, he was able to afford the luxury of both a town house and a village house – as it were.

His new neighbour was Mike Milton, a slim, clean-cut maths teacher from Alabama, who spoke with a southern drawl that was straight out of *Gone with the Wind*. Michael would sleep in the rondavel but still use his "town house" at the school to wash himself and spend his afternoon siesta there. His cleaning lady and maid Habile, was unable to understand why anyone would actually choose to live in a draughty, cramped and primitive mud hut. Europeans wanted to experience the life of African while Africans wanted to emulate the seemingly more desirable life of the European. Each civilisation believing that the other was superior, that the infernal grass was always greener.

Michael's rondavel was about the size of your average hotel room, but without the usual en suite facilities. It consisted of crumbling mud walls, a smooth mud floor, a permeable straw roof and glassless windows which allowed in a flow of air rather than sunlight, which entered anyway through gaps between the roof and the walls. Furniture consisted of a rusty iron bed and a rickety wooden chair. So this was how Africans lived; how cool to be living the simple life of a real African. It was said that mud huts were cool in summer and warm in winter, with numerous ventilation vents enabling lizards and frogs to enter and leave the hut freely and enjoy its ambience and shelter.

Having "gone native", Michael at once felt part of the village, which apart from the bar, Mr Aphirrie's fat cake store and the long walk from Moketse to the bar, he barely knew at all. What the villagers thought of this long-haired, suntanned, Pula-shirted white man living in their midst was another matter. Could they remotely understand or comprehend his decision to go native? Did they regard him as yet another patronising Westerner – a spy even – an intruder who didn't know his place? Someone who's birth, wealth and privilege prevented him from ever becoming a fully paid-up card-carrying African?

Just lying on his bed at night he could hear the sounds of his neighbours talking quietly to each other, sitting cross-legged around a wood fire in their yard. He was beginning to understand Setswana, occasionally catching the odd word or two of a language which at night sounded increasingly gentle and lyrical. *Ee*, "yes" and *nnyaa*, "no" being the most frequent words uttered. Were they talking about him? Conversation was dominated by the men, with the occasional sound of a woman, and even more rarely a child. There was a strict pecking order in these families. He could smell the fragrant smoke emanating from his own kraal and those in the vicinity. Sometimes a dog barked or a cock crowed. The sound of insects was ever-present, and when the rains came, a high-pitched chorus of whistling frogs from the nearby river drifted through the village on high frequency waves. Sometimes there was the rustling sound of a lizard moving across the floor or walking along the uneven mud walls. On Fridays, the perfectly-harmonised and passionately-sung hymns from a highly-religious congregation of men, women and children in the nearby church brought tears to the eyes and a lump to the throat. Hairs stood on end as if to ensure better reception. The sound of cars or planes – or indeed any machines at all – could not desecrate the sanctity of the evening.

Whenever one taught space travel to children in London or Botswana, the first question asked was always: "How do astronauts go to the toilet?" And so it was in the village, where none of the houses had flushing toilets or running water. In the morning before leaving for school, Michael simply relieved himself in the nearby bushes, gazing nonchalantly in no direction in particular as one does in a public urinal so as to appear cool and disinterested.

The serious business he left for the sophisticated plumbing of his "town house". But where did the villagers go? He had once visited the primary school perched on Papane Hill, and noticed the nearby cliffs covered in children's excrement, like the guano one sees in a coastal bird colony. As he stood outside the door of his "country house", he observed the daily trek of Moketse children on their way to school, like a line of wildebeest following a well-worn migration route across the Serengeti. In fact, even before he got up he could hear the excited chatter and laughter of children as they argued and joked and celebrated being young and alive. He recognised many of the smiling black faces of his children as they trooped by in their distinctive orange and brown Moketse uniforms. Some had shoes; others went barefoot, stopping occasionally to remove a thorn from their horny epidermis. They had no satchels as kids do in England, but carried, pens, pencils and rulers in their tightly curled hair and books on their heads. This ensured they had good posture, since this ingenious method of carrying school equipment could not be achieved without a straight back.

Michael waved at the children as they passed by, shamelessly milking the moment by doing an exaggerated imitation of an African dance with full backside protruding – which always evoked howls of laughter.

"*Dumela ticheri*," he called.

"*Dumela Xabo,*" they replied – the self-styled Xhosa Africanisation of his surname, Zabinsky.

One of the joys of being a child, and indeed being a teacher, is that young people are usually happy and cheerful. And like the *favela* children of Rio, the old stereotype that materially poor kids appear happier and more carefree than their wealthy Western counterparts seemed, in that daily stream of smiling and joyous faces, to be overwhelmingly true. Was it simply that poorer people had less to lose, and that having lower expectations of life made you less prone to the disappointment that comes with under-achievement? And again, the stereotype that the poor are more charitable than the wealthy seemed to be true as well, and probably for the same reasons. It wasn't just a racist construct that portrayed "the natives" as being content. Were all stereotypes essentially true? Many of these children would have risen at dawn to fetch water and carry out household chores before joining the long and winding road to the school on the hill.

One of Michael's neighbours was little Sophie Kefentse from year 1 and her elder brother Simon, who spent term time living with the mentally unhinged and crazy-eyed head of science, Rodney Metzger (the butcher), at the school. Both kids had incredibly smooth and unblemished shiny black skin, resulting in almost perfect Greek god-like complexions. They were stunningly handsome. Sophie was one of Michael's favourite pupils, and her bright inquiring eyes and endearing personality had bewitched him from day one. It was love at first sight – in the purest platonic sense possible. Until this point he hadn't realised that they were brother and sister, having never seen them together before. But now the family resemblance was striking; funny old thing, genetics. Simon was well known as the brightest and most deferential kid in the school. He seemed to have everything going for him – good looks, politeness, as well as natural intelligence. He was even good at sport, taking advantage of his perfectly-proportioned athletic body to become captain of the school football team. *Mad Metzger* had de facto adopted Simon as his own son, taking him under his grubby wings as the "great black hope". He even planned on taking him home one day to see his crazy Midwest family in Minnesota during the summer holidays.

Sometimes Michael returned to the village after a function at the school in the dark with Mike, his nearest rondavel-dwelling *mekgowa* neighbour. He marvelled at the effortless way the more experienced, lightly-built Peace Corps man from Alabama could navigate the narrow sandy pathways at night, in what seemed to Michael like pitch blackness. He soon realised that even on a moonless night, the stars gave out sufficient light to guide them home, like migrating birds returning to Europe after wintering in the southern hemisphere. When the moon shone, everything was illuminated. After a while, Michael's newly-acquired night vision enabled him to recognise an intricate network of shiny tracks branching through the village in every direction, like an infra-red map. As they walked down the hill away from the school, they encountered black silhouettes who greeted the two teachers with "*Dumela rra, tsamaya sentle.*" How the hell could they recognise them in the dark? It seemed that just as one could recognise the reflective surface of a whitewashed hut, so it was possible to recognise the reflective features of a white man. *Mekgowa* glowed in the dark.

On one occasion, the two "natives nouveaux" encountered what looked like a drunken villager collapsed on the floor. Michael and Mike tried to help this *chibuku*-smelling individual to his feet, but he immediately slumped back. They tried again.

"*Dumela rra, o kae?*" asked Michael.

"*Eh, eh, eh,*" were the only words to emanate from the man's vomit-impregnated mouth. Like a scene from Laurel and Hardy, the two teachers held up the old drunkard like a stuffed dummy, each supporting one of his spindly arms.

"Will you be OK, *munna?*"

"*Eh, eh,*" mumbled the now visibly older man dressed incongruously in a shabby jacket torn at the seams, without a shirt, and wearing soiled baggy trousers. This was pure slapstick, classic Tower of Babel stuff. The man slumped over Mike's shoulders and began to urinate warm steamy fluid over Mike Milton's leg.

Chapter 8

Back at the school, preparations were underway for the arrival of Botswana's biggest band, The Originals. Michael's obvious lack of organisational skills had been noted by the powers that be, and he had been asked to chair that most august of bodies, the School Entertainments Committee. Every month this group would meet to discuss the organisation of events and activities to entertain the pupils, many of whom were boarders. It was Michael's first and last experience of being in charge of a committee, and he rapidly realised that all the fun poked at committees rang true – they were dreary talking shops for nerds.

The committee consisted of four teachers and two student representatives. Michael tried to be proactive, but every suggestion he made was immediately undermined by the other teachers, who could not organise a piss-up in a brewery themselves, yet took a perverse delight in using the most fatuous arguments imaginable to pick holes in each idea. Mostly they had no suggestions of their own, or if they did, they were completely impractical or unrealistic, or both. Charging the pupils a small entry fee to help pay for events was controversial, because most of the kids were deemed to be poor even though their parents were able to pay school fees. And anyway, in the utopian socialist world they inhabited, money was an evil capitalist construct – everything should be free. Heated discussions took place in which the merits of a seven cent over a ten cent entry fee were passionately discussed. Nothing was too petty, nothing too trivial; the committee was a platform for philosophical flagellation and mental masturbation. What do we mean by mean? What have the Romans ever done for us?

The student representatives usually had no opinions of their own, or were too shy to put them forward; they had not been raised to have original thoughts and certainly not to express them. They were merely there to watch the Western democratic process in action.

After much soul-searching and gnashing of teeth, the entertainment committee of Moketse Secondary School finally agreed to invite Botswana's hottest group, The Originals, to play at the school on Saturday night. Apparently Lucas knew the lead singer in the group and would have a word with him over the weekend.

Having taken an eternity to come to a decision, the problem now was the delegation of responsibility for the physical organisation of the event. Who would collect the money? Who would man the doors? Who would print the tickets? Who would organise publicity?

Endlessly discussing the minutiae of the concert was one thing, but actually volunteering to get off one's arse and do something was another. This was the age-old problem of translating abstract theory into practice. Committees were supposed to be the oil that lubricated the wheels of democracy, in which power was delegated from the centre to small groups of consenting adults, who would then – or so the theory goes – make informed decisions. After sitting through hours of mind-bogglingly tedious discussion, going round and round in circles and letting everyone have their four penny-worth, one could understand the attraction of a benign dictatorship. Committees seemed to attract tedious, boring, petty people who made one lose the will to live.

Michael had "talent-spotted" The Originals at a disco in Gaborone the previous month. They consisted of two Batswana and two South African musicians who played a mixture of township jazz and black American soul music. What stood out was their ability to work a crowd, but they were also talented and could really play. They were not your usual Saturday night pub group that performed every weekend in the seedier recesses of Hammersmith or Fulham. They had apparently released an album entitled "Phefo ya Foka", which means 'the wind is blowing', almost certainly cribbed from Dylan's "Blowing in the Wind". It did not mean 'Phefo you fucker'. The album was allegedly selling well in the townships of South Africa, where they had money, record players and even electricity. Their songs were even being played on *Seromamoa Botswana*, Radio Botswana. They were seriously big cheeses in these parts, so it was something of a coup that they were coming to little old Moketse Secondary School, for a fee of 50 rand.

The money was collected by charging pupils 10 cents (decided at an extraordinary meeting of the entertainments committee by a majority of three to one, with two abstentions) and the teachers two rand, which in 1973 was worth about one pound sterling. In the event over two hundred children turned up, resulting in a profit for the school of two rand and seventy cents.

On the day of the concert – a scorcher in October – the main hall was prepared to create a stage at the front and a row of chairs around the perimeter where people could rest between dances. A little table was set up near the entrance where extremely watery orange juice and fat cakes could be purchased for a cent. The two student representatives, Victor and Nkomeng, manned the doors and were told only to let in people from the school who had tickets. Unbelievably for Botswana, the band arrived on time at six, and proceeded to unload their junk from a white Toyota van and set themselves up on stage. Mokgosi, the local Mochudi member of the band, greeted Michael and the entertainment committee effusively, his nicotine-stained teeth showcasing a chilled-out rock musician's smile.

"*Dumela rra, dumela mma, o tsogile jang?*"

"*Ke kgale re sa bonane*" – long time no see.

"*Ee, Ee.*" Exaggerated African handshakes all round, the local equivalent of the American "Gimme five!"

The children began arriving early for the seven o'clock show. First to appear were the school boarders, who only had a few yards to walk, but a steady trickle of kids gradually emerged from the village, and soon it became a torrent. The pupils were very excited, many having never seen a live band before. Their faces glowed with anticipation as they talked and laughed out loud. It was touching to see how many of the children had really made an effort, with a new hairstyle or a specially made printed-cotton dress, despite their limited means. The only ones to turn up in their normal rags were the white teachers, who didn't believe in "dressing up". It wasn't cool.

It rapidly became clear that although most of the pupils had tickets, they had also brought along their little brothers and sisters, who did not. Then there were the village undesirables who turned up for a bit of action, much as they would at a school disco in England. The committee, in spite of its long and acrimonious deliberations, had failed to see this coming. Michael had to personally step in and help the beleaguered Victor and Nkomeng at the door. Once the concert started, the two students immediately deserted their post and disappeared unceremoniously into the crowd to join their friends, leaving good old muggins Michael to man the barricades for the rest of the evening with the volunteered help of Luke and Albert. Being Rhodesians, Luke and Albert were less likely to capitulate to the mob than their more sentimental and soft-headed European and North American counterparts. But as is always the case with undesirables, they wouldn't take no for an answer, and hung around the whole evening mooching and smoking and generally looking hard. Groups of unticketed pupils were equally impervious to requests to go home, preferring to stay around in the expectation that the doormen would eventually wilt and relent. They could wait.

The hall was now rapidly filling up, with excited groups of Moketse children congregating in same-sex clusters, tapping and swaying to the background disco music that could just about be heard above the relentless cacophony of surround sound. Most of the teachers were there, and even the God-fearing, no-nonsense matron, who mirrored herself on her eponymous "Carry On" character, usually played by Hattie Jacques, showed her proud and pious face. Even the headmaster and his most distinguished sidekick, the Right Honourable Mr Frank Johnson, dressed as always in perfectly pressed khaki shorts and white shirt, knobbly knee-length woollen socks and beautifully polished brown leather shoes, made a cameo appearance.

The Originals eventually came on stage only half an hour late due to "technical difficulties", which was code for the lead singer having had an argument with his girlfriend, who insisted on singing with the band in order to promote her flagging career, and two fused plugs which needed fixing. Also the extension lead wasn't long enough. As soon as they started playing, the background chatter stopped and was replaced by the incredibly loud and exhilarating sound that only the guitars and drums of an electrified rock band can produce. The walls and floor vibrated to the most popular music in the history of mankind. They started off with The Temptations' "Papa was a Rollin' Stone", which everyone knew through radio Botswana, where it was endlessly played:

Papa was a rollin' stone
Wherever he laid his hat was his home
And when he died, all he left us was alone.

Everyone knew the words, so everyone sang along; pupils, teachers

– even the esteemed Mr Johnson. The hall heaved to the loud and pulsating beat, while over two hundred dancing bodies gyrated enthusiastically to this life-enhancingly vital music. In contrast to the West, boys and girls don't usually dance together or display obvious signs of sexual attraction in public, like holding hands and kissing. Boys danced with boys and girls with girls. More often than not, people just danced in their own space, swaying slowly, tilting forward with arms held out like stiff chicken wings, backside protruding provocatively, feet gently moving up and down rhythmically like someone trampling grapes to make wine. Sometimes one dancer would approach another and perform what in the animal kingdom would be described as a courtship dance; face to face or bum to bum, neither face showing emotion or expression, each concentrating on the dance with half-closed eyes and slightly swaying head. And then uncoupling to dance near someone else.

While the disgruntled mob outside rued their "unfair and unjust" exclusion from the ball and indulged in pathetic self-pity, inside the concert rocked. Unlike school discos in England where pupils often stood around shyly in groups, giggling and watching, here everyone danced exuberantly, expressing their natural rhythm and zest for life. As is always the case on such occasions, the teachers could not resist showcasing their John Travolta-like dancing skills, like parents at a family party, leaping and swivelling with gay abandon, wildly and uncoordinatedly on their own or with the pupils. The difference was that whereas back home children would cringe at the sight of their sad arthritic and "past it" parents or teachers making fools of themselves on the dance floor, here it was regarded as perfectly natural – you were given respect. In Botswana everybody danced; young and old, fat and thin, chief and peasant. It was one of the most endearing parts of their culture, and Michael, being a natural exhibitionist, shamelessly mimicked it.

As the night rolled on, the intense heat and sound drove groups of revellers outside to take in the relatively fresh evening air and cool off. The doormen had long since scarpered, so some of the remaining unticketed exiles were quietly smuggled back into the hall by their friends. Of course Michael saw what was going on, but turned a blind eye because the function was going so well, and anyway, he felt sorry for them. Maybe they couldn't afford the entry fee any more than they could afford to attend school, and also, what right did he have to come to Africa and impose a ban on local people attending their own entertainment? Was he being liberal or naive? Was his sense of fair play and a natural sympathy with the underdog and the dispossessed, clouding his judgment?

As ten o'clock approached, the concert was drawing to a close. All the extremely dilute orange juice had been drunk or evaporated and the fat cakes eaten. Those remaining held hands in a huge circle to sing the last song of the evening loudly together:

> *When a man loves a woman*
> *Can't keep his mind on nothing else*
> *He'll trade the world*
> *For the good thing he's found*
> *If she is bad he can't see it*
> *She can do no wrong*
> *Turn his back on his best friend*
> *If he put her down.*

Listening to the beauty of this world-famous ballad by the black American singer Percy Sledge – the poetry of the lyrics, the heartfelt passion with which the song was being played by the band – and a hall full of black schoolchildren and black and white teachers from every corner of God's earth, brought tears of joy to Michael's eyes and an overwhelming sense of happiness that he was alive and a witness to this moving expression of human togetherness.

Chapter 9

꒰꒱꒰꒱꒰꒱

After a year in Botswana, Michael felt a contentment hitherto unknown. It had been one of the most exhilarating and fulfilling periods of his life. He loved teaching and he loved the kids; well, most of them. It really was a love affair in the broadest sense. He loved their natural beauty and their willingness to help, their politeness and deference, their willingness to learn. He loved the way they spoke English. "Please sir, my pen is refusing to work." "Please sir, my pencil case is refusing to open," confusing the Setswana *kea gana* with the English "to refuse". And "He's a funny person isn't it?" or "She's forgotten her books, isn't it?" confusing the Setswana *ga kire* for the English phrase "isn't it". Probably the most commonly made mistake in any language and a sure way of identifying a foreigner is the overuse of "isn't it." Or "Please sir, we are tired." "Please sir, we don't understand." The use of the word "we" when referring to oneself – probably due to the communal rather than the individual way the children were raised; their communal way of thinking and doing, instilled in them since birth.

Michael's love of strumming the acoustic nylon-stringed guitar and singing like his alter egos Neil Young and Cat Stevens was well known to the pupils, who would see him practising new tunes on the balcony of his town house after school. They would stop and watch and listen shyly from outside the garden fence, and he would invite them in to sing along. Africans are hard wired to sing and have a natural and uninhibited sense of harmony and rhythm. And they loved to sing; singing was as much a part of life as breathing and eating; just listening to and appreciating music "European style" was not an option. As he sang and strummed the three chords he had picked up from the *Bob Dylan Song Book*, the children instantly tuned in and began to hum and sway and voraciously learn the words of songs they had never heard before. Their effortless ability to perfectly harmonise, transformed a simple tune into the most exquisite group experience, like singing in a choir. Eventually his beloved form 2A, whom he loved like his own children, begged him to start a music club: "Please *ticheri!*"

Michael's most loyal disciples were Rose and her friend Tebogo. Rose was a small, thin and very earnest child who was probably undernourished and rarely smiled. She could not afford shoes but took great pride in her thin cotton school uniform. Hunger and heat made her eyes cloud over and sometimes she fell asleep during hot summer lessons. Her most important identity was being a member of Mr Zabinsky's form, which she took very seriously, and she regarded herself as the voice of 2A. Whenever she said "Please Sir, *we,…,*" she meant 2A. Academically she was very weak and usually came near the bottom of the class in tests and exams, but she had a heart of gold and never missed a lesson. Singing was her passion and the window to her soul, and along with her trusty, shy and somewhat nondescript friend Tebogo, she was the most loyal member of "Michael's Meistersingers".

So every other day after morning lessons and before the afternoon study and homework session for the borders, Michael's Meistersingers would gather under the porch of his house and sing. At the start it was only 2A, but gradually, as word got round,

others would appear and the group swelled to over twenty. He felt
like the Pied Piper, or should one say the Pied Guitarist, whose
music could magically enchant the children and lead them out of
the village and into a cave. Or so he thought. Although Michael's
repertoire was limited to songs that could be sung with only three
chords, it was amazing how many popular tunes this included. And
those songs that required more chords could easily be adapted to
a simplified three-chord version. Peter, Paul and Mary's "Puff the
Magic Dragon" fitted that bill perfectly, with nice simple words
about a dragon – it was supposedly about drugs, as in smoking a
joint –and a great chorus where every kid could join in and
effortlessly and perfectly harmonise.

Puff the magic dragon lived by the sea
And frolicked in the autumn mist
in a land called Honalee…

Then there was Olivia Newton John's version of "Banks of the
Ohio", which again had a chorus heaven sent for 2A's vocal chords:

And only say that you'll be mine
And in no other arms entwined
Down beside where the waters flow
Down by the banks of the Ohio.

Best of all was Ricky Nelson's "Garden Party" which was played
every day on Radio Botswana, so the kids already knew the words.
This song not only had a great chorus, but told the story of Nelson
being booed off stage at Madison Square Garden in 1971, because
of his long hair and new country-style songs:

But it's all right now
I learned my lesson well
You see, ya can't please everyone
So ya got to please yourself.

This song became synonymous with Michael's Meistersingers. It was overwhelmingly their favourite, and was performed by popular request whenever the group played together. Little Rose would harmonise with big Mandrise, a muscular and sporty boy who in spite of his short trousers and school uniform, looked like a man, and was probably much older than the others. He had that very low-pitched, almost baritone Lion's roar harmony so often heard in African tribal songs, which would harmonise with high-pitched female voices and the occasional ululation thrown in for good measure.

It was a wonderful feeling being surrounded by so many young people for whom singing was the most natural and unselfconscious way of celebrating life. Singing always unites people, and there was a palpable spirit of unity here that seemed more profound among people for whom the group is more important than the individual, and came easier to those with little material wealth to divide them. Not exactly an advantage of material poverty, but certainly a compensation for it. Spiritually, these kids were millionaires. Michael felt embraced by the warmth being radiated from these carefree black African children, much as a father does from his family – if he's lucky. He was almost as popular as Elvis.

Michael's group were the star turn at the annual variety show, organised of course by the ever-eager entertainments committee. The sound of five hundred Moketse pupils singing "The Garden Party" loudly and in perfect harmony with the group on stage was reminiscent of Woodstock, albeit on a slightly smaller scale. Michael began to understand the exhilarating feeling of adulation and the addictive sense of power and immortality that Crosby, Stills and Nash must have felt in 1969 in front of half a million adoring fans at Yasgur's farm. This was what kept bands on the road and indeed actors on the stage and teachers in the classroom, not the money; the human craving to be loved.

Then there was the concert at the village hospital, which was run by an austere group of German missionaries whose natural habitat was the moral high ground. Their views on race were identical to those of the Dutch Reform Church, whose twisted morality underpinned the whole edifice of apartheid across the border in South Africa. They were in no doubt that it was God's will, as revealed through Jesus Christ, that the white man should save and enlighten the blacks. Europeans were *de facto* superior to Africans. Doctor Ludwig Kurtwangler, a pompous and pious practitioner from Augsburg, scared the living daylights out of all who met him, including his own staff, but he was universally respected for his medical prowess. He had famously saved the life of a Canadian volunteer whose leg had been severed by a train at Pilane station when she somehow managed to slip onto the line. He had successfully amputated her leg using the most primitive instruments, rudimentary facilities and only the most basic standard of hygiene. The acid test of an African hospital was whether one survived.

Michael had once had a blood test there when he was sickening for tick bite fever, and had been shocked by the sight of an inexperienced child-nurse trying to pierce his vein with a blunt and almost certainly microbe-infested needle. He never received his test results from the lab in Johannesburg – they had mysteriously gone missing, lost in action, gone AWOL. For most villagers for whom there was no choice, hospitals were synonymous with death.

Michael's cunning plan was for the singers to meet at the hospital around seven and sing to a ward of patients. In the event only the ever-loyal Rose and her sidekick Tebogo turned up. The others had either forgotten or been prevented by their parents: It was a long *schlep* in the dark to the hospital, and for many the daily chores of fetching water and cooking took precedence.

So the self-styled Pied Guitarist and his trusty pupils, set themselves up in the "common room" – a space with a window, a couple of chairs and a broken wooden table – and awaited their audience. Unfortunately, as so often happens in Botswana, what one imagined was a firm commitment to appear at a certain place at a certain time was either forgotten, ignored or just not taken seriously, or all of the above. Like the African sense of time, the concept of pre-arranged appointments was utterly alien out here, extra-terrestrial even; *mañana*, *kgantile*, maybe never, whatever. Michael had personally been to the hospital to organise this selfless act of charity and interracial co-operation, but on the night of the concert the original contact was nowhere to be seen and nobody knew anything about the arrangement. In the event, a dozen or so sickly-looking, mostly elderly, thin and toothless patients dressed in standard-issue hospital rags like concentration camp inmates were ushered into the "concert hall" and seated on quickly improvised drinks crates in the "front stalls". They looked seventy, but were probably forty. The guitar strummed and the trio sang, and as they did so the patients clapped and began to harmonise with the music. On hearing the muffled sound of guitar strumming in their wards, nubile young nurses with sumptuous busts and ample buttocks began trickling into the room and stood at the back, hands over mouths, giggling. Some of them were ex-Moketse students who after a year's training were on the wards. More nurses, who presumably should have been on duty, deserted their posts and added their sweet young voices to the now burgeoning choir. The patients now laughed and smiled, their hollow eyes watering with emotion, their toothless grins expressing unrestrained joy and delight that illuminated their emaciated faces. For most, this was the first concert they'd ever been to. It was a magical moment of human goodness, playing for the sick, singing with his children and doing *his* part to make good centuries of white-black conflict and misunderstanding – or so he imagined.

Right in the middle of "The Garden Party", the door suddenly flew open and in walked Dr Furtwangler, his unshaven ashen face contorted with Teutonic anger and rage. The nurses and patients cowered and screamed and covered their faces in shame with their hands.

"Get out!" cried the mad German doctor, and everyone bolted for the door in an attempt to escape his wrath. Some were slapped as they forced their way past him; they had sinned and deserved a beating. This was the proverbial missionary position, whites on top. The makeshift concert hall was now empty and reverted back to its former status as a squalid unfurnished room with a window. Rose and Tebogo helped Michael collect his music and pack his guitar.

"Ow!" said Rose. "He has refused to let us play."

The children were too young to understand how white power worked here. Nurse Grünwald appeared and apologised for the behaviour of her boss; the nurses had deserted their posts and had it coming. And anyway, the doctor didn't believe in enjoyment, he believed in saving people in the name of Jesus Christ, Amen.

It was getting dark when the teacher said goodnight and thanked the two girls who had so loyally walked across the village and turned out to support him. Little Rose, her big eyes holding back the tears, said, "*Danke ticheri, ke tla go bolodisa*" – I'll accompany you part of the way home.

Chapter 10

The overwhelming, almost messianic feeling of doing something worthwhile kept Michael motivated throughout those two long years of 1973 and 1974 in the Republic of Botswana. Even in moments of loneliness six thousand miles from home, or when he could not always satisfy a young man's craving for sexual gratification, the unflappable conviction that his science teaching was helping to improve these poor village children's lives and that his mere presence as a white man in a black African country surrounded by racists genuinely helped improve human understanding kept him going. Such were the convictions of a young idealistic teacher in 1973.

But this was not so for all the volunteers. Most of the American Peace Corps were prone to periods of introspective naval gazing and depression. Unlike the British VSO teachers, who were mostly idealistically driven young graduates wishing to see the world and make it a better place, the Peace Corps were less clear as to why they had left the States. They tended to be deeply cynical, like most college-educated Americans at that time, about the United States and its war in Vietnam, and this cynicism spilled across the Atlantic like a toxic vapour, suffocating their natural optimism as negative emotions always do. They were endlessly going on about "that crooked son-of-a-bitch Nixon", as well as their equally corrupt –as they saw it – South African co-ordinator Gerry Frankel, an ambitious middle-class Republican career-apparatchik from Brooklyn. Some were draft dodgers, while for others a trip to Africa was a chance to have an adventure and tread water until they could figure out what to do with their lives. Americans were restless, self-critical and self-flagellating, even in those days.

Paul, Josh and Big Jim Kennedy fell into this category. After one year at Moketse, when that first rush of excitement and the thrill of being in Africa had passed and a return to the States seemed a lifetime away, they had become increasingly withdrawn, unshaven and morose, preferring to meet only each other in one of their rondavels of an evening to whinge about America and smoke dope; lots of dope. Setantana and Naomi – two well-endowed village girls of easy virtue, with whom virtually every white volunteer had by the end of two years relieved themselves – supplied the Americans with huge bags of the best home-grown marijuana, the best grass, the best shit that money could buy.

Every society has drugs which lessen the pain of being human and relieve the boredom of being alive. Drugs don't solve problems, but they can make them more bearable; unless they're addictive, in which case they can destroy both the user and his milieu. Be it alcohol, tobacco, khat, ganja or coca leaves, the evolution of a brain capable of contemplating the meaning of existence – *cogito ergo sum* – has meant that from the yet-undiscovered tribes of Amazonia to the sophisticated tribes of Europe and North America, to remain sane drugs must be taken. For some, culturally-specific drugs like khat-chewing amongst Somalis or ganja-smoking amongst Rastafarians can produce anaesthetised communities incapable of functioning or competing in the modern world, and doomed to destitution. On the other hand, it is doubtful whether

Western civilisation could have evolved without the consumption of copious amounts of alcohol. *In vino veritas.*

The disillusioned Peace Corps would sit in a circle on the cool clay floor of Paul's rondavel, cross-legged like meditating Hindu mystics, and "Pass the dutchie on the left hand side". Their gatherings had all the trappings of an obscure religious sect, but without the singing and chanting. To begin the ceremony, the three not-so-wise men would admire and pay homage to the latest consignment of grass piled high on the altar in front of them, and worship it like a sacred statue of the Virgin Mary or the Aron Kodesh in a synagogue.

"Wow!" said Paul, his eyes rolling, his pupils visibly dilating as he viewed the forbidden fruit, "just look at that."

"Far out," said Josh, "just feel it, smell it, touch it." He caressed the holy weed and let it fall through his long, spindly fingers onto the floor. Not bad for three consummate atheists.

To the transcendental, almost psychedelic sound of Carlos Santana's sublime electric guitar cadenza rising up from Jim's portable cassette player like incense during Holy Communion, a huge joint would be passed around the congregation of worshippers, each taking a large drag of the mystical marijuana, inhaling deeply and sleepily blowing out the blue-grey scented smoke into the stagnant air.

"Wow," said Big Jim, "this shit is fucking great." He was nodding his head meaningfully up and down as only Americans can. As the joint was circulated, the three became increasingly stoned and then mellow. It was during these sessions that the problems of male loneliness and sexual frustration – a man needs a maid – temporarily disappeared into the ether like the diffusing cloud of exhaled hallucinogenic breath.

In March 1974 an event occurred that would make the self-obsessed, pot-smoking Americans stop feeling so sorry for themselves: the death of a pupil. For most Europeans and North Americans, death is something that happens to other people, and when it does it usually involves elderly relatives or friends, not children. Michael recalled how the death from leukaemia of Jeff König in 1963 had so seismically shocked everyone. Jeff was a long lanky pupil at Abingdon Grange School Leeds, with the smile of an angel and the voice of a *chazan*. The school devoted a special assembly to his memory; everyone was in tears, and his close friends cried out unashamedly. Adults asked how this could happen to one so young, such a stunningly handsome boy who had all the girls chasing him and his whole life ahead of him? "Oy vey iz mir, with that voice he could have been a star!"

How could the Almighty let this happen? Modern medicine has allowed us to believe in our own immortality. But this is hubris, a delusion; in spite of the wonders of modern science, everybody dies. In Africa, with its lack of Western wizardry and knowhow, the death of a child was something that every pupil, often fatalistically, accepted as part of the way of things.

Victor Ramaphosa was a quiet and shy member of Michael's 5B biology class who when asked a question, just smiled. A short boy with a smooth black-skinned face, his straight nose and wavy hair suggested some distant European liaison. He was always superbly dressed and impeccably polite. It was said that Declan Murphy, a philandering English teacher from Cork who had taught at Moketse the previous year and now worked in Johannesburg as a director of something called "distance learning", had described him as a "brilliant actor" who had starred in the school production of Hamlet that he had directed.

People said, "Victor Ramaphosa, I can't believe it, he was such a lovely boy," as if this should have somehow saved him from the wrath of The Lord.

Victor's burial took place at the Roman Catholic church in Molepolole, Victor's home village, and a group of Moketse teachers were transported unceremoniously there in the back of Cedric's truck. Some, like Cedric, had put on "proper clothes" as a mark of respect, but Michael was adamant that his presence was more important than the deliberately non-formal orange Pula shirt, shorts and sandals he had chosen to wear for the occasion. Actions spoke louder than dress, or so he thought. The church was a massive, surprisingly modern-looking building, with a giant steel spire and large stained-glass windows which on a hot day allowed the intense heat of the summer sun to pour through and cook the congregation. This place must have cost a bob or two, mused Michael as the mourners piled into this edifice of European colonialism, this house of God, ostentatiously crossing themselves as they did so. So this was what African missionaries got up to.

The service was conducted by the rather pompous-looking Father Seamus O'Flaherty, a pink-faced missionary from County Wexford who, in spite of the heat, was dressed in full purple silk regalia and black woollen cassock, and with what looked like a black silk yarmulke perched precariously on his shiny bald head. As a Jew, Michael had never been inside a Catholic church in his life, and he stared in amazement at the sheer opulence of this hugely imposing building, probably costing millions and surrounded by the crumbling mud huts and rag-wearing, God-fearing inhabitants of Molepolole. It was as if a European church had been transplanted from rural Ireland into the African bush.

Michael looked around the packed church and observed the congregation. In contrast to a synagogue where everybody talks before, during and after the service, the church was reverentially, almost funereally quiet. Was it out of a genuine respect for the sanctity of the church, or a vestige of some ancient pre-Christian religion of ancestor worship with its deeply ingrained tribal superstition and a profound belief in the afterlife? Was it out of deference to the superiority of a white colonial religion introduced by missionaries, or was it all a sham? Was this silence, which was so incompatible with the uninhibited exuberance Michael had witnessed at the Church of Zion near his mud hut in Mochudi, due to fear or faith? Was it the other-worldly smell of incense and the stirring surround-sound of organ music? Was it just the pious performance of serial sinners, or a genuine deference to the Father, the Son and the Holy Ghost? Or was it simply out of respect for their deceased friend, Victor?

The overwhelmingly black congregation was led by the white Father O' Flaherty, supported by a posse of white spectacle-wearing Irish Nuns who sat piously on the front bench, looking very pale and devout. Michael recognised many of the faces of Moketse children who sat solemn-faced, avoiding eye contact. Even Cecelia was there. A row of white teachers sat near the back of the church, reflecting the stain-glass filtered sunlight like patches of melting snow on a dark hillside in spring. Victor's brown, flower-covered wooden coffin was prominently displayed on a pedestal below the altar in front of his grieving family.

The priest uttered perhaps the most famous prayer on earth, the Lord's Prayer, in his lyrical Irish churchy voice, praising a God who in *his* power and *his* glory, was unable or unwilling to prevent the death of Victor Ramaphosa.

Our Father, Who art in heaven
Hallowed be thy Name;
Thy kingdom come,
Thy will be done
on earth as it is in heaven.

It was a deeply moving service in which European Catholic hymns were proudly and loudly sung to the sound of goose-pimple-inducing, soul-penetrating European organ music, by the whole congregation in perfect African harmony. Even the cynical *mekgowa*, who didn't know the words and just mumbled self-consciously, were moved by the sheer passion of this irrational spectacle. The short life of Victor was praised by the priest and the mourners filed out of the church towards the cemetery.

The coffin was carried by Victor's best friends – Emmanuel, Mpho, Simon and Boitumelo – along a narrow dust track to a deep freshly-dug rectangular hole in the ground surrounded by a sea of gravestones and crosses that would be Victor's final resting place. A huge crowd of tearful mourners watched as the coffin was lowered by the graveside and opened to reveal the body of the deceased schoolboy.

Michael had never been to a funeral before. He hadn't even attended the funeral of his own darling mother, who in 1961 had somehow avoided God's power and glory and succumbed to a malignant tumour, not spotted by Dr Samuels; it had devoured her brain. He was deemed to be too young for such adult pursuits, but remembered waiting with his brother Jacob at his grandma's house in Mornington Avenue, Leeds, for uncle Israel, uncle Shimon, uncle Abe and his dad to return from the Jewish cemetery, the besoylem. He had always imagined that a *besoylem* was a bit like a bazaar where people bought and sold things, and could never understand why the men's ties or pullovers were cut or torn on their return. He had never seen a dead body before, but had heard stories from his Aunty Essie of the way Catholics liked to exhibit their dead. She had even been invited round to view the corpse of her Catholic neighbour, but had declined on religious grounds. A dead body was unclean, *treyf*. When a Jew died he was buried within twenty-four hours, not exhibited for inspection.

An orderly line of mourners filed past the open coffin to pay their last respects. Many of Victor's classmates were inconsolable as they looked upon their dear friend for the last time, respectfully crossing themselves. Some laid flowers on his body, some kissed his forehead and wailed uncontrollably. Even the boys, who in this culture were not expected to cry, cried. Victor was loved by everyone.

When Michael's turn came, he stared at the supposedly dead body of his former pupil. Victor didn't look dead. He looked as if he were just sleeping peacefully, his eyes closed, the serene smile on his still smooth, black, handsome face, standing out against the brilliant white satin robe he was wearing. The body seemed smaller than in life, as if one shrunk after death in order to fit into the coffin.

But seeing a real corpse did not make death any more intelligible. On the contrary, the face looked very much alive.

Death seemed unreal. Father Flaherty recited the Catholic prayer for the dead in his lyrical Irish accent.

> *God our father,*
> *Your power brings us birth,*
> *Your providence guides our lives,*
> *and by Your command we return to dust.*
> *Lord, those who die still live in your presence,*
> *their lives change but do not end.*
> *I pray in hope for my family,*
> *relatives and friends,*
> *and for all the dead known to You alone.*
> *In company with Christ,*
> *Who died and now lives,*
> *may they rejoice in Your kingdom,*
> *where all our tears are wiped away.*
> *Unite us together again in one family,*
> *to sing Your praise for ever and ever.*
> *Amen.*

Does one ever come to terms with the death of a loved one? Michael's mother had died in 1961, but he was no closer to understanding what had happened, that the loving being who had given birth to him, raised him and cared for him unconditionally, was no longer there. Intellectually one knows that the person is dead, just as one knows that every person dies, even oneself. One knows that every person who has ever lived has died, just as surely as ever person who will live will also die. We are mortal. The prayer was asking us to believe that our fate, our life and death, were in God's hands, and that when we died we would rejoice in Christ's kingdom; if we were lucky. How could any intelligent being believe such stuff when there was not the slightest shred of evidence? It contradicted all the laws of science, all reason. Returning to dust was just a poetic way of describing the carbon and nitrogen cycles. When a living thing dies it is attacked by microbes and reduced to carbon dioxide and nitrogen, which in turn re-enter the atmosphere from whence they came. Only in the sense that these molecules are endlessly recycled do we go on living. This was the very cycle that Michael had taught Victor before he became part of it himself.

And yet to a believer – and most of those present were believers – this prayer, this belief in the unbelievable, offered the immense comfort and hope of an afterlife. The possibility that we somehow go on living was hugely reassuring. When the priest had finished praying, the coffin was closed and the brown wooden box containing the earthly remains of seventeen-year-old Victor Ramaphosa was lowered slowly into the deep chasm in the ground. Each friend or loved one of the deceased schoolboy filed solemnly past the grave and shovelled a spadeful of hot brown sandy soil onto the wooden coffin that lay six feet below. Was Victor really in there? How could a body be in that box?

His best friend Emanuel, dressed in a smart black suit, white shirt and tie and perfectly polished black shoes, was the first to go. Piously he crossed himself. He was bravely holding back the tears, but his reddened eyes betrayed the heartbreak within. Cecelia, who was too distraught to participate, stood sobbing by the graveside, her sickly eyes swollen large and bloodshot. Some threw flowers onto the rapidly disappearing remains of Victor, while others howled in anguish or ululated. Each crossed himself piously. Michael stood by the grave and wept. Tears of sorrow and despair and utter incomprehension flooded from his eyes over that perpetually sunburnt face and dripped onto his sandals.

Chapter 11

Most of the children, like Michael in his second year at Moketse, lived in rondavels, mud huts which to the Western eye looked romantic and "traditional" but in reality were flimsy and soluble and easily damaged by the elements. Michael had personally witnessed the tinder-dry grass roof of a dwelling near the school bursting into flames after being struck by a bolt of lightning, and the sight of helpless women sitting outside the crumbled remains of their home, which had been dissolved and washed away by torrential summer rains, fatalistically accepting God's will. A sure sign that you'd "made it" was the construction of a proper brick house.

Two of the nicest kids in the school were the Chingwe twins, Boitumelo and Metse, who were utterly indistinguishable from each other to the naked eye. Both had handsome round faces with friendly enquiring eyes, and both were disarmingly polite and good at school. Michael had long since recognised his inability to remember the names of pupils, so identical twins posed a serious problem. When he encountered one he always plumbed for the simpler name Metse, having a fifty percent chance of being right. The twins' father had saved enough money from his demeaning job as a "boy" at the Witwatersrand university campus in Johannesburg to start building a proper breeze-block house in the kraal of his family home in Pilane. Michael had met Moeng Chingwe on the way back from Cape Town; like his sons he was polite and self-effacing, dressed in his standard issue "boys'" uniform of blue shirt and shorts to ensure that he looked like a boy rather than the father of two strapping teenage lads.

A group of teachers had been invited to the inauguration of his new house, and Cedric duly obliged with his trusty truck. The truck arrived at the Chingwes' kraal as the sun was setting, and was greeted by the beaming faces of the twins. It had been blisteringly hot, but it was Friday, so no school tomorrow. The kraal consisted of two "family-sized" mud huts and what looked like a partially demolished building – the site of the new house. The teachers were offered a bowl of *bogobe* with goat meat relish by two young girls – female versions of the boys – and the normally unaffordable cans of warm Castle lager. No expense was being spared here to honour the guests by this most generous but still very poor family. Michael enthusiastically gobbled down the delicious porridge, while Paul and Julie stoically masticated and swallowed the white stodge with supercilious ear-to-ear grimaces.

The parents emerged from the larger rondavel, the diminutive head-scarfed mother stooping shyly behind the very much worse-the-wear-for-drink father. "*Dumela raa, dumela maa, o tsogile jang*? "said Michael deferentially. "*Ee.* "

Mr Chingwe, dressed in a badly-fitting and ripped pair of trousers and crumpled second-hand jacket, was completely pissed. The comical sight of the semi-conscious father of the twins stumbling across the rubble-strewn kraal reminded Michael of the pathetic drunkards who used to gather every Saturday night at closing time outside the rough pubs in downtown Leeds. He was the very caricature of the old soak so mercilessly portrayed in West End farces or in television sitcoms, and had evidently been drinking *chibuku* all day at the local shebeen. The teachers looked on uncomfortably as Mr Chingwe attempted to speak, his bloodshot eyes staring nowhere in particular, managing only to mumble an incoherent mixture of broken English and Setswana.

It was getting dark as Boitumelo and Metse contemplated the sad spectacle of their dear father as he gazed, but failed to focus, on the crowd of Moketse teachers gathered to celebrate his new dwelling. Watching an inebriated worthy making an ass of himself at an auspicious occasion is the very stuff of comedy, and Michael almost bit his tongue trying to suppress the urge to scream with laughter. Several cans of lager were beginning to loosen him up too.

Metse stepped forward, his eyes welling up with angry tears, and held his father's unsteady body close to him. "What my father is trying say," he said in a broken voice, "is that you are all invited to eat and drink with us on this special occasion in our lives. It was always our dream to build a stone house."

As the teachers politely applauded, they began to realise for the first time just what this house meant to the family. Moeng was so proud of his accomplishment that he had celebrated in the only way he knew – getting completely wasted on foul-smelling African beer. And the twins accepted this: he was their dad, and that was how dads celebrated.

And just what were they celebrating? In no sense had the house been built. What the teachers witnessed was the grey breeze-block outline of three rectangular rooms, with no furnishings whatsoever and without a roof. This was just the beginning, and when funds allowed, the house would be completed – one day, they hoped. In Botswana you don't hire a builder – that would be impossibly expensive – you build your own home. Every brick in the house, and indeed its very foundations, had been put in by the sweat and toil of the twins and their father.

In a scene bordering on farce, the guests were taken by

Boitumelo and Metse, in the dark, on a guided tour of each cell-like "room". As the half-moon rose over the bush, the silhouette of the new house resembled a derelict and haunted house from a black and white Hitchcock movie. The moon illuminated the visitors, whose ghostly shadows were projected against the bare walls like figures in a lantern theatre.

On the truck back to Moketse, Michael regretted his behaviour. In laughing at the drunken man, he had mocked him and underestimated his achievement. The house meant security and protection for his family. It would still be very basic by European standards, with no toilet or bathroom, and when complete each room would house five or six family or extended family members. Cooking would still be done outside on a wood fire as before. The evening would have made an excellent "Play for Today" in which a white middle-class audience of *bien pensant* luvvies would raucously laugh at the drunken father and cry at the hopelessness of his situation. But for Mr Chingwe and his beloved twins, standing pathetically amid the half-completed building site, the evening represented hope for the future and progress. Another five years working as a "boy" in Johannesburg would enable his dream house to be completed – he dreamed.

Chapter 12

As is the way with time, the second phase of an adventure goes by faster than the first. Time speeds up as you get older. Like climbing a mountain, the journey to the top is slow and arduous, the journey down rapid. For Michael, that first year in Botswana seemed endless. Everything was so new and exotic, every day a fresh and thrilling experience.

Those back home were real enough, but six thousand miles away on the other side of the world. He remembered his father waving him goodbye from a freezing cold platform 14 at Leeds City station, flat cap and black coat, breath condensing in the frosty January air, bravely holding back the tears as his eldest son left him yet again to pursue his dreams. For Michael, life seemed to stretch out never-ending in front of him; for his already sick father, he wondered whether he would still be alive to see his beloved son return. Liberally interpreting Einstein's theory of relativity, for Michael, whose life was conducted at close to the speed of light, time would pass more slowly than for his more sedately-paced father. Michael would age more slowly than his father, having inadvertently discovered the secret of almost eternal youth – or so he thought.

Time cascaded by. Days became weeks, weeks became months and the seasons inexorably changed from summer to winter and then to summer again. In many ways Michael's almost messianic zeal to teach was dependent on the knowledge that he would soon return. The prospect of moving on subconsciously kept him going. If there was no way out things would have been different. Like a prisoner doing a two-year stretch for robbery, he will be more optimistic than a man doing life for murder with no prospect of an early release for good behaviour. You could see the light at the end of the tunnel.

The daily but rapturous routine of teaching those educationally-hungry children science was punctuated by weekend parties in which the music played and the wine flowed, and there were trips to Mozambique, Rhodesia and Zambia. For a few rand, Michael could explore the continent, even on a volunteer's salary.

After the sadness of Victor's death, the annual game of softball came as a welcome relief for all. Having demonstrated beyond reasonable doubt that they were utterly hopeless at soccer, the North Americans felt the need to restore their credibility and national pride. And what better way to do this than through the game they had all loved and played since childhood – softball. Fondly mentioned in so many of Philip Roth's books about his childhood in Newark, New Jersey, softball was the user-friendly version of baseball, through which almost any *schmo* could make believe he was the next Babe Ruth or Joe DiMaggio hitting a homer for the New York Yankees. Previous American volunteers had ensured that the school was well endowed with a full set of softball gear. To the Brits this was a Yankee version of rounders, usually played by young schoolgirls in flimsy gym slips that used to titillate the boys: instead of a hard wooden ball, there was a soft leather one. They could not understand what the big deal was with this game; but for the Americans it was a serious business.

The school softball field consisted of a huge patch of gravelly orange sand carved out of the bush, just beyond the children's boarding quarters. About the size of a soccer pitch, this large sandy square sloped from left to right and was bordered on three sides by stunted acacia trees. The dimensions of the playing area were meticulously implemented from the Peace Corps manual by Jim Kennedy and Mike Milton, who regarded themselves as the self-styled custodians of this most American of sports. The home plate and pitcher's circle were marked in the sand, as was the infield boundary. The three bases consisted of white homemade sandbags. Mike and Jim had been coaching kids after school since the moment they arrived. Like a couple of religious evangelists, the word of the Lord must be obeyed and spread. The children of Botswana must be made to see the error of their ways (playing soccer) and be converted to the one true sport, softball – the very cornerstone of the American way. Whenever one mentioned softball, their eyes clouded over and watered and their pupils dilated. As they nodded their heads knowingly, they had that faraway look and the unshakable certainty of the religious nutter.

Having already selected a bunch of aspiring "Yankees" from years four and five, the motley assemblage of teachers had to be organised into a fighting force capable of defeating the school. They must beat the school team at all costs, or what was the point in playing? None of this wishy-washy British fair play bullshit about participation and enjoyment and may the best team win; none of this defeatist nonsense about losing a game honourably. What sort of limey bollocks was that? The whole purpose of sport was to win. The very serious and focused look on the normally chilled-out faces of the North Americans contrasted with the "I don't give a monkey's" looks on the faces of the Brits when they played their national game, soccer, against Matlapeng last term.

Twenty-four hours before the big game, the Brits and Rhodesians, who had never played softball in their lives, were given a crash course in how to master this somewhat idiosyncratic sport by their Yankee colleagues. Michael and the others tried not to giggle as the rules were painstakingly explained to them by the poker-faced Jim and Mike. Apparently, when you stood on the home plate, each batsman had three chances to hit the ball so long as it was deemed a strike – which was a ball pitched between chest and knees. You had to stand legs akimbo, holding your bat straight at arm's length, and look as if you meant business. If you hit the ball you must run to first base, and if you missed three times you were out. Hence 'three strikes and you're out'. If you hit the ball hard enough you could run around all the bases and score a home run. If you managed to hit it beyond the outfield, that was the best thing a softball player could do. The outfielders wore giant gloves, and if they caught your almighty slog you were out. They were there to spoil your day.

The game took place after school, on a Friday in October. The cloudless days and cold nights of winter had given way to the still sunny but warmer days of spring; perfect softballing weather. The two teams appeared at four o'clock along with a hundred or so children who had gathered by the touchlines. The pupils wore yellow shirts and looked like a team. The teachers wore a selection of makeshift kit, with the Americans sporting peaked caps and dark sunglasses to emphasise their coolness. Mr Seretse turned up in his neatly-pressed light blue safari suit, together with his sidekick Frank Johnson, dressed as always in a perfectly-ironed white cotton, short-sleeved shirt and long baggy brown shorts. A fifty cent piece was tossed and the pupils elected to field.

The teachers lined up to the left of the home plate like excited children waiting for sweets, self-consciously giggling and chatting as they did so. First up was Paul, wearing a pair of batting gloves for extra grip. A short stocky guy from Brooklyn, he had grown up under the aura of the New York Yankees, although any similarity to his childhood heroes Babe Ruth and Jo DiMaggio ended at him having two arms and two legs. He looked confident and determined, and slightly fierce as he approached the home plate. As he gazed around, his thin-rimmed spectacles bobbed precariously on the bridge of his sunburnt nose. "Goo on Paul!" cried the Americans, "show em what you're made of."

"Goo on Paul, the guy with the funny drawl," barracked the Brits, completely missing the serious nature of this life and death encounter.

Mpedi the catcher, clad in protective face mask, bulletproof vest and oversized leg guards, crouched intimidatingly behind the batsman, looking for all the world like a giant wasp, ready to sting. The tall, handsome and very athletic-looking Molefe Molefe, known colloquially as Molefe squared, approached the pitching ring and composed himself. He was a consummate all-rounder with the best voice in the school choir, and all the girls loved him. And of course he was the natural choice for head boy. He had an air of royalty about him, which oozed confidence and greatness. He pitched the ball violently towards Paul's torso. "Ball!" cried sexy Sadie, the blond bombshell of a match umpire.

The next pitch was in the strike zone and duly dispatched over Molefe's head for a run to first base. "Safe!" shouted sexy Sadie, smiling salaciously as she did so.

Next up was Big Jim Kennedy from the state of Michigan. Styling himself on the Detroit Tigers' greatest ever player, Ty Cobb, or just The Cobb, Jim believed that he too was a fearless player with a mean streak. Big Jim meant business. Like all Tigers' fans, he recalled the 1907 season when The Cobb had scored a batting average of 0. 370, which enabled his team to win the American League title for the first time in their history. The Cobb had scored 117 home runs in his career.

Jim surveyed the field of play and allowed himself a self-satisfied nod of the head.

"Go Jimbo, go!" yelled Josh.

"Come on Mr Kennedy!" cried the school cheer leaders.

Jim smiled at the row of teachers waiting in line to bat and the children cheering along the touchlines, cocking his head as he did so. Molefe looked Jim in the eye and pitched.

"Strike one!" yelled the umpire.

Molefe pitched again – perfect speed, perfect position for Jim to fully swing his bat from behind his immense shoulders with all his Michigan might, his Samson-like long hair stirring in the warm spring breeze. The ball flew off the wooden bat and high over third base, bouncing once before leaving the outfield.

"Home run!" squealed his Delilah, Sadie, a huge smile betraying her close friendship with Jim and her thinly-disguised support for the teachers' team.

"Yo Jimbo!" cried the Americans.

"Jimbo schmimbo!" countered the Brits.

Now it was the turn of the Brits to make arses of themselves. Julie looked bewildered as she hopelessly missed three perfectly-placed strikes and was out. Each time she swung her bat wildly, completely misjudging the trajectory of the ball and nearly decapitating the catcher twice in the process. Her hand-eye co-ordination left something to be desired. She hadn't played any ball sport since she was ten.

"Oh dear!" she exclaimed, as she trotted back to the touchline.

Little Cathy Routledge didn't fare much better. Her short-sightedness ensured that she couldn't really focus on high velocity projectiles, and not being very strong, she was barely able to lift the bat high enough to connect with the ball as it flew by.

"Strike two!"

Her third attempt somehow collided with the softball, much as randomly-moving molecules will eventually collide with each other according to the laws of particle physics, and edged it ignominiously into the hands of Nkomeng at second base.

"Out!"

At least the boys could get a cheap thrill staring lustfully at her white knickers as she stretched helplessly skywards.

"Fuck you!" she opined.

Next to approach the home plate was the red Pula-shirted Michael, his mane of black curly hair stirring slightly, his incredibly handsome and suntanned face surveying the dustbowl before him.

"Goo on Xabo!" cried his fan club gathered along the perimeter of the pitch, their orange-brown school uniforms blending chameleon-like with the semi-arid surroundings.

"Show em how it's done, Zabinsky," shouted Big Jim in his slow Michigan drawl, carefully pronouncing each syllable, Za-bin-sky, more in hope than conviction.

Michael grinned at his well-wishers, his gloved hands clasping the bat purposefully as he feigned a couple of stylish mock shots swiping virtual balls into the outfield and scoring an imaginary homer. This was his big chance to prove his prowess as a sportsman and demonstrate that his crash course in the art of softball the previous day had not been in vain. As he prepared to receive Molefe's first delivery, his mind drifted back to an inter-house rounders match at Turbot Road primary school, Leeds, in 1960. Then as now, Michael fancied himself as a lean, mean hitter of the ball, believing that because he thought he looked the part, it must be so. Certainly when it came to looks, the others appeared pale, pimply and anaemic when compared to his perpetually-healthy outdoor complexion. Then as now, he felt destined to score a spectacular match-winning goal in football, a six in cricket or a rounder in rounders, and fantasised about impressing the girls with his superhuman achievement; especially Avril Rosen. In 1960 it had been his house, St George, against St David. He remembered smashing the ball out of the playground over the high wall into the school garden, and hearing the loud crash as the ball mortared the school greenhouse in a direct hit. Mr Brownfit, the school gardener (known to the pupils as Mr Brownshit) was not amused, but everybody else was. Everyone had cheered as Michael ran round all four bases to claim his rounder, whilst wallowing in the adulation of the smooth-skinned and deliciously vulnerable gym-slipped girls whom he was destined to save.

"My hero!"

Even the great Gareth Jones, Turbot primary's best ever athlete, who in spite of his sickly looks and lanky gait had captained the school rugby and cricket teams and held the Yorkshire under-eleven 400m record, was impressed.

"Are you ready, sir?" asked the so-polite pitcher Molefe Molefe, on noticing that Mr Zabinsky had drifted off on a tangent and was not fully *compos mentis*.

"Take it away Molefe," responded the startled teacher, abruptly returning from his childhood to the present.

The first ball was pitched hard at the batsman's face, bodyline style, causing him to duck and avoid injury.

"Ball!" yelled the umpire.

The second ball was pitched menacingly close to Michael's torso.

"Ball!" repeated Sadie.

Ball three was a perfect strike. Michael's youthful 20/20 vision saw it coming and his body switched to automatic. Two hours of training had programmed him to connect with such balls. He swung the bat around the back of his neck and thrust it forward towards the incoming missile. Ping! The bat connected and forced the ball high into the cloudless blue Botswana sky. He started to run towards first base. After orbiting the solar system several times, the softball hurtled downwards, accelerating at a rate of ten metres per second squared towards Planet Earth.

"Strike!" called the umpire as the ball began its elliptical descent towards the outfield in the direction of Nkomeng and Batsile as they ran blindly towards each other. *Wham*, the two girls collided at full speed. *Kapow*, they knocked each other to the ground, leaving the way open for Michael's hit to reach the ground and land defiantly on the sandy surface.

Michael ran jubilantly to second base and then third. Mosimane, meanwhile, retrieved the ball from between the two dazed outfielders and hurled it to Mogapi on the home plate. Michael, who had taken his chance, now found himself stranded between third and fourth. Mogapi, who like virtually everyone else on the field had collapsed with uncontrollable laughter at the slapstick spectacle being played out before them, was in no state to catch the incoming throw. The ball went through his outstretched hands and landed with a thud on his oversized big toe.

"Ouch!" Yet more laughter.

"Run!" shouted the by now seriously excited Sadie.

Not for the first time, Michael noticed that the only really universal humour was slapstick. Each country had its jokes, its clever subtleties and witty innuendoes that enabled those in the know to laugh. But slapstick was universal. It had the power to unite in laughter people of different races and religions, whose culture might otherwise have been impenetrable.

Instead of the recommended seven innings, which would have taken forever, both teams agreed to play two so that everyone got to bat twice. The teachers won the game by four runs, thanks to the accumulated experience of Jim "The Cobb" Kennedy, Mike "DiMaggio" Milton and Josh "Babe" Jefferson, despite spirited performances from Molefe squared and Rodney's protégé, Simon. There were the usual teenage arguments about whose fault it was and that the bat had "refused" to hit the ball properly. As afternoon became evening and the sun's heat slowly relinquished its grip on the closing day, the softball stadium reverted to being an empty dustbowl of a school sports field in Botswana. The noise, excitement and laughter of the afternoon's encounter was replaced by the eerie silence and tranquillity of the African bush, punctuated only by the call of a weaver bird and the morose moaning of a goat. The fragrant scent of the bush replaced the smell of adolescent sweat. As the crickets warmed up for their evening concert, the only sign of the day's events were the footprints in the sand and the markings of the softball field. And of course the usual litter; plastic water bottles, a couple of pens and colourful sweet papers strewn across the playing surface. And a used contraceptive.

Chapter 13

There were many more communal activities in which the teachers and pupils of Moketse Secondary School willingly shared their lives. There were debates in the school hall, talent competitions, film shows and concerts. There were trips to the mining town of Selebe Pikwe and a slaughterhouse near Lobatse, as well as the annual school choir competition in Gaborone, which Moketse always won.

Among the teachers there were parties, affairs and an ill-fated wedding between Rodney Metzger and Bev Crosby that lasted precisely two weeks. There were trips to Lesotho and Swaziland as well as birthdays and soirees at each other's houses. There was Christmas and New Year and the celebration of Botswana's Independence Day on September 30th. There was the General Election in which the president, Sir Seretse Khama, turned up at the village with his cavalcade of black limos and body guards, to make an election speech at the *kgotla* in front of what seemed like the whole of Mochudi. School was cancelled, and the children were escorted into the village to witness the democratic process in action.

But those two exotic years in the southern hemisphere were nearly over, and Michael's thoughts were increasingly turning to home. At the beginning time had stretched out infinitely before him, but now that his African adventure was coming to an end, it seemed like a dream. Unlike the locals, who like most people were trapped in the mundaneness of their daily routines, Michael was well aware that his *joie de vivre* and perpetual optimism, was very much related to his freedom to hop on a plane and disappear back across the globe to Europe. Unlike the villagers, who were lifers, he had a get-out clause.

What had he achieved here? How had he changed? How had he changed others? What would be his legacy? Would he be missed? What would become of his beloved pupils, Cecelia, Emmanuel, Sophie, Naledi, Violet, Batsile, Noah, Rosemary, Mpedi and the rest? Had he taught them anything worthwhile? What had *he* learned? What would become of his fellow teachers – Josh, Paul, Big Jim, *Menseke*, Dan, Chloe and Sadie, and the rest of the volunteers? Would he ever see them again? Would he ever return here? What would he do back in England? What would become of the drinkers at the bar? What would become of his neighbours in the village? What would become of the chief? What would become of *him*?

As he walked back to his country house for the last time, Michael savoured the night-time sounds and scents of the village once more; the incessant beat of *gumba gumba* music complementing the shrill staccato of the crickets and the dulcet conversation of villagers talking and laughing round their fires. The silhouettes of mud huts and the ghostly shapes of people could be seen against the backdrop of a clear, black, starry starry night. The unmistakable shape of the Southern Cross hung above the antipodean horizon, its stars glistening brightly like the Christmas lights that would right now be adorning the streets of central London. For it was once again December and the night air felt warm and soothing as it caressed Michael's youthful skin for the last time, as if to say, "Please don't go." The perfumed aroma of the darkness intoxicated his very being, the sweet smell of burning acacia wood and smouldering marijuana wafted through his nostrils.

As he crossed the rotting wooden bridge that rattled and swayed precariously every time a truck went by, he was greeted, as so often before, by a deafening cacophony of squeaking, whistling and pulsating frogs making whoopee in the swamp below. This seasonal rendition of nature's watery noise was as much a part of the summer symphony as the millions of crickets that individually rubbed their legs and wings together like the string section in a great orchestra. Unlike at the start, when the night seemed so impenetrably dark and foggy, Michael was now able to navigate by starlight like the locals along the narrow, winding, sandy tracks that led him back to his primitive abode.

As he approached the lopsided mud hut that had been his home for the last year, the rising full moon cast its magical shimmer over the surrounding houses and yards of his immediate neighbours. As he approached his village dwelling, he noticed a plate of mealie-meal with relish and a piece of chicken on his doorstep. This must have been a parting gift from the Kang family in whose yard his hut had been built. They were all asleep by now.

Michael sat down at the entrance to his abode and tucked in greedily to this simple but delicious meal. Tears welled up in his eyes as he sat alone in the warm, tropical moonlight. The Kangs could not afford this meal. It illustrated yet again the unbridled generosity of people who had nothing. The poor share everything and remain poor; the rich hoard their wealth and become richer. Food tastes better when it is given selflessly and from the heart. This meal, so lovingly prepared, moved Michael deeply. It reminded him of the piping hot chicken soup his mother had spoiled him with when he came home from school each day. That was before cancer wiped out her loving life force, leaving two young boys motherless and a husband without a wife.

He had not expected anything like this. He felt like a prince. As he savoured the exquisite taste of African porridge with relish for the last time, his last supper, he deliberately tried to take in the moment so that he would never forget it. His eyes took in the illuminated surroundings like a cameraman filming a set. He tried to store for eternity the sounds and aromas of this sultry summer evening in Botswana. As he sat on his doorstep, dressed as always in his shorts, sandals and a colourful Pula shirt, his long wild hair emphasising his youthful chilled-out credentials, he wondered whether he would remember this magical moment when he was back in Blighty. Would he ever visit these simple, God-fearing people again, or would the fast flow of his new life swallow up and erase these memories as a torrent wipes away all traces of a flooded village?

The next day Michael vacated his rondavel and returned to the town house on the hill to pack and prepare for his imminent departure. *Menseke* paced around nervously, quite unable to cope with the impending loss of his part-time housemate. He looked pale and frightened, like a winged bird, as he tried to comprehend the cataclysmic events unfolding before him. Wayne Fanshawe was hurting inside, but he could not display his true feelings. He was strangely withdrawn, trying to put on a brave face but failing miserably. His face was like a barometer which never lied about changes in life's atmospheric pressure.

Since his move to the village Michael had grown fonder of his housemate, as often happens when two people separate from each other's clinging presence. Living alone had made *Menseke* stronger and more self-sufficient, although he still looked neglected and in need of a friend. He was now able to tie his own laces and cook himself a goat stew. Crazy as he still was, Wayne was a loving, caring human being and Michael would miss him.

The school campus was as it was when he first arrived on that hot January afternoon in 1973. Like then, the rains had not yet arrived, and each day saw a ratcheting up of the temperature and the humidity as the north-east wind once again directed its hot steamy flow over the great African plateau. The academic year was over and the students had gone home; most to their mud huts in Mochudi, others to their families as far away as Francistown and Maun in the tropical north. Of the remaining teachers, some had already gone on holiday, exploring the delights of southern Africa, while others preferred the tranquillity of their own gardens without the noise of screeching children disturbing their karma.

Michael wandered around the campus of Moketse Secondary School for the last time. Everything was so quiet and still, save the murmur of the hot summer breeze blowing between the classrooms and the sound of weaver birds defending their hanging nests and feeding their voracious young. The playground, once throbbing to the excited voices and laughter of happy black African children, was eerily silent; just hot red sand swirling in the wind. The classroom where he had taught 5A about the nervous system and the lab that Josh had nearly blown up were empty and silent; only the ghosts and memories of the hundreds of children he had taught and loved remained, like faded words on a gravestone. The school hall, where debates and concerts and variety shows had given life to the school community and to the village in general, was empty and bare, the actors and audience long gone. The dusty school field where children and teachers had played softball and the crowd had cheered them on was devoid of all human life. Only the footprints in the sand remained, like fossils reminding us of what once was.

Michael stood tearfully in the scorching sun, taking in the scene that had been his home for the last two years. Two of the most exhilarating and fulfilling years of his life, years in which so much had happened, were coming to an end. He recalled the myriad of faces and names, the sound of the choir singing in perfect harmony, the way the children spoke: "Please sir, my pen is refusing to work." The way they had screamed with laughter on hearing the word 'neurone' and the sheer joy and adulation when a thousand clapping hands had applauded his singing of The Garden Party with his guitar and the 2A Meistersingers. The headmaster had asked him to stay, but Michael knew his time was up. He missed his father, and anyway two years was enough. Like a reveller at a party instinctively knows when he's had the right measure, one more drink and the evening is spoiled. More can mean less.

On December 15th 1974, Michael left Moketse in style. That most well-mannered Englishman abroad, the Right Honourable Sir Frank Johnson MP, had offered him a lift to the airport in the luxury of his blue Volkswagen beetle. This was VIP treatment, but the least a polite English gentleman could do for a fellow countryman. Michael loaded his possessions into the boot, which unusually was at the front of the car. He didn't have much – just a rucksack and plastic bag full of "soft furnishings" consisting of a pile of soiled socks and underwear, and of course his collection of colourful Pula shirts. He also loaded a small African drum that he'd bought for the princely sum of thirteen rand in a Gaborone curio shop, and his trusty guitar. This was probably the only car in Botswana with proper suspension, which ensured extreme comfort and gave the effect of levitating rather than bouncing over every crater in the road like Cedric's truck. It was the same car that had driven Paul away when his sister had been killed in a road accident in upstate New York and he had to return for her funeral.

As he glided out of the school complex, no one was around to see him go. Life had already moved on; everyone was replaceable, even those like Michael who had imagined they were not. Out of the school campus for the last time and onto the dirt road to the village. The grubby sign at the school gate announcing 'Moketse Secondary School' still hung limply, its hand-written words worse the wear for those two extra years of wind and sand erosion and the relentless power of the sun. Over the bridge and past the football pitch and the bar where he had spent so many thoughtful evenings contemplating the meaning of life, aided and abetted by several cans of lukewarm Castle lager. The usual suspects were strewn about the veranda, but they didn't wave. He could just make out Mr Tiro-beer in one hand, cigarette in the other as usual through the darkened windows of the blue VW. Life for them had also moved on, if you could call it a life.

The village flashed by as in a surrealistic film, brown rondavels as far as the eye could see. Mothers with babies on backs brushed their compounds, girls pounded corn and naked children played with the chickens just as they had on the day he arrived and probably always would. Here too life had moved on. Out of the village and left at the Pilane junction towards Gaborone. Gliding past the barren rocky landscape, still baking in the sun, shepherd boys tending their goats and stunted acacia trees poking out of the barren bush. On to the shanty town suburbs of the capital and then further to a small airfield on the outskirts of town which went under the pompous name of Gaborone Airport.

Frank stopped outside the perimeter fence and Michael unloaded his crumpled belongings. The two men shook hands in the only way possible for an emotionally-stunted gent like Mr Johnson – formally.

"Good luck Michael, and send my regards to the Queen," said Frank, smiling ironically. He looked every bit the meticulously-turned-out old colonial he had been when they were first introduced.

"Thanks Frank, it's been a pleasure knowing you," Michael said, looking the elder man in the eye and shaking his hand warmly. Not wishing to cause a scene – stiff upper lip and all that – Frank got into his car and was gone, forever.

Michael surveyed the scene and noticed a small crowd of well-to-do-looking people gathered on the baking hot sand. The airfield thermometer showed thirty-four degrees in the shade. Presumably they were also waiting for the connecting plane to Johannesburg, which was due to leave at three. White South African officials in khaki safari suits checked each person's documents – the whites with respect, the blacks with indifference. He was about to follow the rest onto the tarmac, when he noticed a lone, slightly stooped figure approaching the airport. It was Cecelia Linchwe, who had walked the mile from Gaborone in the merciless afternoon heat, to say goodbye. She looked weak and frail, but beneath those long-suffering black eyes, Michael recognised a stoical pride and a profound beauty.

"*Go siame ticheri, tsamaya sentle*," she said, trying to hold back the tears already welling up in those big, beautiful, sad eyes that had suffered so much. "Did you really think I'd let you go without saying goodbye?"

Michael embraced her flimsy shaking frame tightly with both arms, his long black hippy hair covering her wet face as they cried unashamedly together. "*Go siame* Cecelia, *tsamaya sentle*." He kissed her perspiring forehead.

The volunteer teacher reluctantly extricated himself from the clinging embrace of his most loyal pupil. He gathered his rucksack and drum and guitar, and slowly shuffled his way towards the queue of passengers already boarding the small turbo-prop plane. As he stood on the scorching black tarmac, on Botswana soil for the last time, he saw Cecelia's tearful face pressed up against the airport fence, waving. He climbed the mobile steps and entered the cool, air-conditioned cabin. A blonde, busty, blue-eyed South African hostess smiled invitingly and showed Michael to his window seat. There were about forty other passengers on board, mostly white expatriate businessmen in open-necked shirts and linen trousers, and a few well-to-do blacks in dark suits, dark glasses and jazzy ties.

The three o'clock plane to Johannesburg began to taxi towards the short apology of a runway, only two hours late. The engines whirred, the propellers rotated frantically, and the aircraft powered its way down the tarmac and took off to the north. Banking steeply, the plane tilted its silvery glittering wings and turned south towards the capital of the apartheid state.

From his window seat Michael saw the tiny airfield below diminishing as they gained height, and the lonely, shrinking outline of little Cecelia Linchwe, still waving below. From the air he could recognise the sprawl of Gaborone disappearing into the distance, and to the north the mud huts of Mochudi, just tiny brown specs now, where two years of his life's story had unfolded, vanishing like the credits at the end of a film, into the dusty African horizon.

As the plane ascended to 20,000 feet, a few vigorously-bulging cumulus clouds generated by the African sun below, caused turbulence as powerful convection currents buffeted the plane. Over the endless sunlit expanse of the South African Highveld plateau, the border between Botswana and The Republic of South Africa was impossible to make out, the brown bush of one country merging imperceptibly with the brown bush of the other. Borders; just arbitrary man-made lines in the sand, but marking the boundaries between totally different societies. A few small settlements could be made out, an occasional golden field of insect-infested crops, the outline of a winding and potholed dusty dirt road.

The excitement and anticipation of going home to see his father and brother again and all those he'd left behind was tempered by the sadness of leaving those beautiful African children, *his* children, in Mochudi. It was easy for him to up sticks and go; they were for the most part trapped in their restricted lives with limited horizons below. What would become of them? How would they survive without him? Each person on the plane sitting anonymously belted into his or her seat had their own story to tell, each with his own dreams and aspirations. Nobody really knew what the past meant or what the future had in store. Just like those simple villagers on the ground, the life of those rich enough to fly was mostly at the mercy of fate.

PART 2

Somersby

Chapter 1

Michael's first day at Somersby High School in Ealing, west London, was a shock to the system, a veritable baptism of hellfire and brimstone. It was like a spacecraft re-entering the earth's atmosphere at too steep an angle after a long trip to Mars, burning up as it did so, its protective heat shield unable to withstand the white hot temperatures generated as the craft plunged through the dense air earthwards at a speed of over seventeen thousand miles an hour. He had secured this job after expressing an interest in teaching in a multi-ethnic school to the head of VSO, Nigel Winchester, at his debriefing in the voluntary organisation's squalid headquarters situated in the very multi-cultural East End of London. After what he considered a unique experience teaching real black children in the African bush, his talent would be wasted in a school of well-to-do, most probably racist whites. He did not trust the white man.

Michael needed a school where his revolutionary zeal would be appreciated and where he would be able to save as many oppressed non-white souls as possible. At the interview, conducted over mince pies and sherry at the end of the Christmas term in 1974, the festively merry headmistress, Mrs Barnes, had described the post as "challenging". When he opened the laboratory door to let in class 2X general science, the pupils ran past him, shouting and screaming as they did so, like a stampede of wildebeest migrating across the Serengeti in the pursuit of food and water. Nobody would sit down or stop talking. An indolent, gormless-looking character called Lee Crumlin, chased his mates Francis and Stewart around the room, *Tom and Jerry* style. "Come here, you hairy cunt!" shouted Crumlin, as he hurtled past the teacher's desk like the mad fucker he was.

Others contented themselves with making paper aeroplanes from the piles of A4 paper left lying around from the last lesson, and chucking them at each other. One boy, a West Indian called Winston, spent the whole "lesson" vandalising his desk with a brand new compass bought for him by his long-suffering mum for the new term. Flicking chewing gum around was another pastime enjoyed by this most delightful group of young people. And when the lesson was over, having learnt absolutely nothing, the pupils ran out of the classroom screaming and shouting and gyrating, just as they had done on the way in. They were the class from hell.

How could these children be saved from their capitalist oppressors if they behaved like monkeys and refused to listen to their teachers? Michael was confronted with the age-old dilemma of the idealist: reality got in the way. And disillusion led to cynicism. It had been different in Africa where the children had been the gentle and grateful recipients of education, respecters of their elders and of teachers in particular. For them, education was their meal ticket to a successful life. But things were different here. It seemed that the suburban working classes of Ealing had no interest in work, or at least school work. Before going to Botswana, Michael had imagined that children out there would be wild and natural, like an exotic species. But the real savages were here in London W5. Nothing that he had learned as a teacher at Moketse

Secondary School had prepared him for this. It was like confronting a new alien life form, a teenage mutant from the sewer. Many of the pupils at this godforsaken pile of sixties bricks and mortar were the children of semi-literate and semi-skilled white East Enders who had been displaced from their natural dockland habitat by "progress" and somehow ended up in an educational desert known as Greenford, where there was no tradition of reading books or going to university whatsoever.

The remainder of the school cohort consisted of stroppy West Indians, and perhaps the only significant group of academically motivated kids, the Asians, whose strong family and religious background enabled them to flourish in spite of the school. There were also a few bright, university-bound white middle-class kids whose ideologically left-of-centre parents were prepared to sacrifice their precious offspring on the altar of the local comprehensive in order to prove that socialism really worked. A significant proportion of the white working-class kids and West Indians came from one-parent families, so when they arrived at the school gates, they brought all their anger and frustration with them. They had issues which fucked them up.

Michael had arrived back in London at a time of great social change, a time when the police had weekly running battles with the thugs who supported West Ham and Millwall, and loud and rebellious punk rock music was replacing the make-love-not-war generation of the Sixties. Jonny Rotten, lead singer of the irreverent Sex Pistols, was inciting both anarchy and apathy among the younger generation.

> *I am an antichrist*
> *I um un anarchist*
> *Don't know what I want*
> *But I know how to get it*
> *I wanna destroy passerby*
> *Cause I wanna be Anarchy*
> *No dogsbody.*

And

Don't ask us to attend
Cos we're not all there
Oh don't pretend cos I don't care
Oh we're so pretty
Oh so pretty
We're vacant.

Social comment maybe, but of the calibre of Joni Mitchell or Bob Dylan it was not. So it was not too surprising that with all this nihilist nonsense on the airwaves, the pupils at Somersby High were bolshie rebels. Punk rock stuck two fingers up to authority, and so did the kids.

After teaching the most polite and motivated black kids in Botswana, Michael was amazed by how different the black West Indians were from their African brethren. Almost every one was an emotionally-disturbed troublemaker – or so it seemed – with a chip the size of several universes on their shoulders. The patience and conviction of the most ethnically friendly, bend-over-backwards-to-please socialist was tested to destruction. Was it nature or nurture? After all, most West Indians originated from West Africa, not Botswana. Many ascribed it to racism, but the picture was much more complex and nuanced. Lacking the rich cultural history and sense of identity of the children at Moketse with their strong family structure, these sons and daughters of the ancestors of slaves were like rudderless ships sailing aimlessly on the high seas of life. West Indian culture was a confused hotchpotch of African myth and the vacuous ganja-fuelled musings of Rastafarianism, an exuberant Caribbean carnival which ill-prepared them for the norms of British society. Many of these children came from split, fatherless families, with no tradition whatsoever of academic achievement, so it was no surprise that they rebelled in school, occupied the bottom sets and were many times more likely to be expelled than their white peers. Nationally they achieved the lowest exam results of any ethnic group, hardly ever went to university, and were seriously overrepresented in care homes and prisons.

The problem was that the increasingly powerful race relations industry in the mid-Seventies blamed everything on racism and actively encouraged West Indians to adopt a victim mentality and blame the whites. This flawed philosophy, which became the default position of the left, was ultimately counter-productive, since it undermined any sense of personal responsibility among black children for their actions, and was the biggest single reason why the problem was never solved. The new social experiment of multiculturalism and the insidious forces of political correctness were beginning to make it impossible to criticise this fashionably monolithic world view for fear of being branded a racist, and resulted in black kids wallowing in a whirlpool of self-pity from which they could not escape; feeling sorry for themselves and blaming society.

And yet West Indians excelled at sport, which became both a cliché and a stereotype, and like most stereotypes, it was largely true. The left of course refused to accept this, blaming as usual racial prejudice and a racist media. Sports Day would have been unthinkable without the sporting prowess of young, gifted and black athletes, and nationally Nottingham Forest's Viv Anderson and Leyton Orient's Laurie Cunningham were two black footballers causing a stir in the English league.

Michael's youthful idealism was being seriously challenged here, by the very people he was supposed to save. How could these black children be so different from the ones he had taught at Moketse? A disillusioned, disappointed idealist readily becomes a cynical reactionary. The political pendulum swings imperceptibly from left to right, and this is exactly what happened to many well-meaning teachers and eventually drove them out of the profession. But it was not only the blacks. There were also the children of the emerging white underclass, kids for whom school was a complete waste of time because they already had the promise of a job in their dad's roofing business, or working with a plumber friend of a plasterer friend of an uncle. Or so they thought, because in reality their world of decently-paid unskilled labour was already becoming a thing of the past, and they were much more likely to end up on the scrapheap of unemployment, and if not them, then their abundant, increasingly illegitimate, children. As Bob Dylan kept reminding us, the times they were a changin'.

These kids had the misfortune to be born at a time of great technological upheaval, when the social mobility of the sixties and early seventies had already dried up, and those like Michael, who could jump the class divide, had already cut and run. They were increasingly being left behind, like the last dinosaurs before the age of mammals, as an unemployable underclass, unable to evolve. And since school was deemed irrelevant, they spent the whole five years of their secondary education being as bloody-minded and confrontational as possible. As the disciples of Jonny Rotten, their de facto commitment to anarchy made life hell for the teachers and made learning for the other pupils almost impossible.

To fulfil her promise of the challenge alluded to at interview by Mrs Barnes, Michael was awarded the worst class in the school as his tutor group. Being part of the X Band, 3X4 consisted almost entirely of emotionally-disturbed, low-ability children, many of whom were on special needs and qualified for free school meals. They had the reputation of being a bunch of illiterate delinquents and serial liars, who would as soon mug you as pass the time of day. During their first tutorial, they nicked five pounds from the class dinner money and stole his marking pen. They were a class of moral vacuums. In keeping with the delusional leftist thinking of the day, the X band would later be rebranded the A band to make them feel more positive about themselves. A – top, was better than X – bottom, or so the educational establishment thought. In reality it made not a toss of difference.

Chapter 2

In order to get through to these disaffected, bloody-minded and unteachable brats from the educational wasteland that was Somersby High, Michael reverted to that tried and tested solution to this problem, extra-curricular activities. He had discovered in corridor conversations whilst on break duty that many of the worst kids in the school were obsessed with what Michael had previously regarded as the most boring pastime on earth – fishing – as if to emphasise their otherness from himself and challenge his high-minded, middle-class educational principles. Very shrewdly Michael befriended one of the school's most notorious thugs, Lee Westbury (why were they always called Lee?), who was not only crazy, but needless to say crazy about fishing. The theory was that if you indulged a pupil's out of school interests – no matter how unsavoury or vulgar these might be – there would be payback; a sort of peace dividend, with better discipline, better exam results, and more respect in class. Extra-curricular success would translate into the curricular. Or so he thought. It was a Faustian pact that seemed a good idea at the time.

This being the Seventies, SMT agreed to provide ample school funding to subsidise a coach trip to the Ruislip Lido and money for prizes and engraved fishing trophies. Within a week Michael had recruited a rogue's gallery of thirty academically-challenged odd bods and a few relatively normal types, all of whom were mad about fishing, for a trip on Saturday December 7th. After paying a token quid (free dinners naturally excluded) pupils had to meet outside the school gate at eight am.

On December 7th, an unseasonably well-developed zone of high pressure in Russia had decided, just for the hell of it, to flood Western Europe with freezing cold continental air. It was a typically crisp and frosty pre-Christmas morning, with a stiff east wind and the thermometer hovering around zero: Christmas of course, would be mild and wet as usual. When Michael finally arrived at 7.45am from his squalid flat in west Ealing, after the usual delays on the Central Line, a huddled group of children and parents had already gathered at the school. They reminded him of the passengers in *Dr Zhivago*, waiting for a train somewhere on the Russian steppe, clad in thick coats, gloves and boots and with dense clouds of white condensation bellowing from their mouths as their hot moist breath met the cold and dry Siberian infusion.

For the first time in his life, the thug Lee Westbury had arrived early for school. Like most fishermen he looked ridiculous, wearing a silly woollen hat, black duffle coat, and a huge pair of highly-polished bovver boots which he had no doubt used to kick in a few heads or doors. He had all the kit: state of the art carbon fibre rod, a box of hooks and other vaguely threatening paraphernalia, and a large plastic container filled with a seething mass of ugly, wriggling, smelly maggots.

"Mawning sir," he said in his cheeky Jack-the-Lad west London accent, his pale butter-wouldn't-melt-in-my-mouth face belying the nutter below. He didn't usually say good morning. "Fuck off you cunt," was more his style.

Among the early arrivals was the rather posh-looking Clarence

Waterman and his adoring mother Betty. Although Clarence was in the bottom sets for everything, this didn't seem to worry him. He was always cheerful and a surprisingly polite and good-natured lad who never did his homework. Naturally the other kids took the piss out of him. His mother, who was a member of the Somersby PTA, meant well and thought the sun shone out of her son's delicate little bottom. She was one of those eccentric, liberal, middle-class parents, who took an interest in everything her little diddums did.

At eight o'clock the bus had not yet arrived. The freezing group of aspiring fishermen waited cheerfully in their drab outdoor clobber, excitedly exchanging exaggerated fishing fantasies and stories of the one that got away. Some had bought huge hampers of food which they had already started to consume. Crisps, chocolates, cans of coke. It was extraordinary how small and unthreatening these normally bolshie kids looked. School uniform seemed to somehow magnify even the smallest child and make him assume a more rebellious and confrontational demeanour.

The coach finally turned up half an hour late. It was driven by an angry-looking middle-aged unshaven misanthrope called Bill, who obviously hated children and resented not only having to work on a Saturday but having to work at all. In short he was a typical coach driver with a chip the size of several galaxies on his shoulder. He didn't apologise for his lateness. As Michael loaded the kids on board, the coach driver scowled at the chirpy children and warned them not to make a mess and that he wasn't going to take any nonsense.

"Nice to meet you Bill," mumbled one of the pupils, Kenny Wiggins, ironically.

Once the register had been taken and the pupils had safely stored their bulky kit so that no one was in danger of having their eyes poked out by a protruding rod or their trousers ripped open by a hook, the coach set off on its maiden voyage to the Ruislip Lido. On arrival at the lake, after a journey in which the coach driver had refused to put on the radio and had complained about "that fat coloured kid at the back" laughing too loudly, the pupils collected their possessions and spread out along the extensive perimeter of the Lido. Although it was ten o'clock in the morning, the air was still numbingly cold, and a band of grey mist hung over the partially-frozen water like smoke on bonfire night. Leafless horse chestnut trees lined the water's edge, pale shadows of their summer selves, and a few ducks waddled along the bank squawking loudly at this unexpected invasion of west London yobbos. Just as well that fish were cold-blooded.

The Lido offered the usual anglers fare of roach, bream and perch, with rumours of a giant pike that had recently been reported in the *Angling Times*. The *Angling Times* was one of those nerdishly boring papers that flourish in Britain and occasionally pop up as this week's guest publication on *Have I Got News for You*. It was a bit like *Playboy* magazine, except that instead of pages of delicious photos of scantily-clad women, it featured page after page of what must have been, to the fisherman, erotically-dripping nude fish being held aloft by grinning goons in wellies with headlines like, "George Winkelthorpe from Wakefield bags another whopper." As with most publications, it reflected its readership: in this case thick and boring and with the imagination of a remedial trout. As allegedly Britain's most popular participatory sport, this meant about three million seriously sad fuckers, most of them married men with lots of gormless children, spending their Saturday afternoons by some dreary river in the hope of catching a slimy fish which they would then throw back. What was the point? Michael didn't get it-yet.

This being a fishing competition, the serious contenders like Lee Westbury and Gary Withers positioned themselves as far from the others as possible, using their "vast experience" to select the spots where their piscine prey were most likely to hang out. This was a serious business, with big money prizes available for the heaviest fish and the biggest catch, and cheap plastic trophies as consolation prizes for the likes of Terence Waterman and Kenny Wiggins, who were unlikely to catch anything, but nevertheless had made the effort to turn up on a freezing cold Saturday in December. In keeping with the educational zeitgeist of the day – prizes for all – under no circumstances should a child be confronted with its own uselessness and be deemed to have failed. Prizes for simply being there.

To stop himself getting bored and to keep himself warm, Michael spent the morning session wandering along the one-mile perimeter of the Lido to see how everyone was getting along and to make sure that nobody had fallen in the icy waters. As he surveyed his troops, he was struck by how quiet and calm they all were. Kids who would normally be wasting taxpayers' money fucking around in a classroom, disrupting lessons and being as obnoxious as possible, were sitting quietly and peacefully, concentrating on the near-impossible task of catching a fish, and above all exercising a patience that they had never shown back at school or in their own free time. As a caged animal behaves aggressively in a zoo but less so in the wild, it was as though transferring normally belligerent children from the confines of the classroom to a more natural habitat enabled them to express their humanity more fully. It was difficult to believe that they were the same academically -challenged kids who wallowed so hopelessly in the X-band. Not only did they sit patiently for hours on their improvised fishing stools, they chatted calmly with each other, even laughing occasionally like normal children.

Michael was moved by this transformation. Kids who had made his life, and the life of every other teacher in the school hell, were now behaving impeccably, showing both respect for each other and for their teacher. As he surveyed these born-again children, *his* children, he felt an enormous sense of love and affection for them. "Hallelujah, brothers!"

David Brand, a boy with a fair, clean-looking complexion, well-combed light brown hair and warm sympathetic eyes, was the only top set kid on the trip and greeted Michael with his usual "Hello sir, how are you?" Normally taught separately from the rest of this lot, and almost certainly destined for a good university, he nevertheless seemed completely at ease here, fraternising with the underworld. Like most of the other contestants, David had brought an enormous hamper of food which he was now busily consuming; he was already on his fourth cheese and chutney sandwich. Although he had not yet caught anything, or even experienced the slightest hint of a bite, he remained positive. To keep himself warm, he had lit himself a fire using the small twigs and branches that littered the ground, and although this was almost certainly prohibited, it showed the sort of common sense you'd expect from David Brand.

"Great day sir, and thanks for taking us," chirped Dave cheerfully, his colourless face indicating just how cold he was. But he didn't complain; his upper lip was already far too stiff for that.

A hundred yards further on, the rather portly Kenny Wiggins sat on his collapsible canvas chair and stuffed himself with Mars Bars and smoky bacon crisps. Every so often he reeled in his bait and replaced it with a fresh wriggling maggot which he enthusiastically impaled with his hook. Perhaps due to his considerable reserves of subcutaneous fat, or his thick black anorak and red woollen hat, he didn't seem to feel the cold and refused to wear gloves.

"Hello sir, I've just seen the most beautifully-coloured robin perched over there on the fence," he said, his rosy cheeks just visible through the cloud of white condensation emanating from his continuously masticating mandibles. In school he was hopeless at biology, quite literally not knowing his anus from his humerus, but here he knew the name of every bird and plant, as well as the identity and anatomy of all the fish thrashing around in his partially-submerged net.

"Look sir, this striped olive-coloured one with a spiky dorsal fin is a perch," he said excitedly. "They're carnivorous so you can use ordinary maggots to catch them. Some people eat them."

Was this the same Kenny Wiggins who stared blankly in science lessons, showing no interest in anything? Was this the same Kenny Wiggins who tore pages out of his book and scribbled obscene graffiti on his desk? Was this the illiterate kid from 3X4 who enjoyed flicking paper pellets across the classroom and never, not ever, not even once, had done his homework?

Meanwhile master-angler Lee Westbury sat motionless at the far end of the Lido, his halo just visible in the dim winter light, positioned as far from the other mere mortals as befitted a global player of such distinguished calibre and renown. But all was not well with the chosen one. For some reason he'd been unable to catch more than a couple of risibly retrograde roach, despite his state of the art equipment and legendary experience. He stared listlessly into the icy, muddy-green water, his bloodless pimply face and thin blue lips making him look even more unsavoury than usual.

"How's it going Lee?" asked Michael nonchalantly, trying hard to suppress an almost overwhelming sense of *schadenfreude* at this far-too-full-of-himself upstart's bad fortune.

"Not much luck today sir," the master-angler said philosophically. "Sometimes the cold weather makes the fish a bit listless, them being cold-blooded and that. They're not like us sir, able to function at any temperature. They don't bother to hunt for food when the water's too cold. Sometimes these things happen, that's the way it goes sir. You've got to be patient sir, but thanks for organising it."

Although Michael didn't have the pleasure of teaching Lee, he realised that the boy was universally hated by those who did. He was regarded as a rude, bolshie and generally unpleasant piece of work. And yet here on the shores of the Ruislip Lido, Lee was different. It was as though an aquatic environment was his natural habitat, and like any animal in its natural habitat, its behaviour was more natural. This wasn't rocket science – it was stating the bleeding obvious. It was the sort of thing he taught every day about polar bears in the arctic and zebras on the African savannah, so why shouldn't it apply to humans?

Michael began to see Lee differently. He felt ashamed of his premature judgment, prejudice even, about this sad-looking teenager, who in spite of his obvious disappointment had managed to do something he could never do in the alien environment of the classroom – be modest, courteous and patient. Lee had said "sir" more times in a single conversation than he usually managed in a week. Hell, he had actually managed a conversation! And he'd shown a surprising understanding of the biology of a fish.

Michael wondered whether he could somehow harness this propensity for fishing to improve the lad's academic performance in school, and who knows, maybe even pass science at O-level. And then A-levels and university; Lee Westbury PhD, Lecturer in Aquatic Biology at the University of East Anglia. Or was this just the wishy-washy musings of a young idealistic teacher, fresh from the African bush? Could the likes of Lee – and there were many of them at Somersby High – only function in their natural environment, like the fish they so passionately pursued? In school, was Lee both literally and metaphorically like a fish out of water?

As he watched Lee carefully select yet another smelly maggot in a final attempt to catch something, his last throw of the line so to speak, Michael was overcome by wave of sympathy, love even, for this pathetic ungainly specimen before him, dressed in all that ridiculous clobber. Unlike the epiphany of the mosquito larvae in Botswana, where he had experienced the thrill of seeing a child learn, here he was experiencing the thrill of learning himself.

"Without you Lee, there would have been no fishing trip, so thanks for that," said Michael, trying hard to suppress the tide of emotion welling up in his eyes. "It's been a pleasure taking you, Lee." And it had.

By the time Kenny Wiggins was declared the winner with five roach, three perch and a bream, it was starting to get dark and the mercury had once again dipped below zero. As the cold but happy pupils boarded the coach, the first frost was forming on the shrubs next to the lake, which was now covered by a thick grey layer of freezing fog. When the coach finally reached Somersby, it was completely dark, even though it was only five o'clock. The fuzzy lights of Watersplash Lane were trying in vain to penetrate the foggy air and a few Christmas lights twinkled through the still uncurtained windows of the surrounding houses. The cold seemed to have shrunk the pupils, making them look even more vulnerable than before. As each kid, most of whom had caught nothing, disembarked the bus, a cloud of condensed breath said, "Thank you sir, it's been a great day. When can we do this again?"

After taking the Central Line back to Ealing Broadway, Michael stopped off at Franco's fish and chip restaurant. Having nothing at home, and not wishing to return too soon to his primitive and lonely digs, he often came here after school. For a couple of quid they provided a massive portion of delicious battered cod and a humungous portion of deep-fried chips, milky tea, bread and butter.

He had just ordered when a short West Indian boy in a black parka and wearing a QPR scarf pulled up a chair and sat down opposite him. Roy Partridge was one of the most obnoxious pupils in the school, with the reputation of being a compulsive liar and virtually unteachable. He never smiled, and delighted in wrecking every lesson he attended. He had been suspended from lessons more times than any other pupil and was on the verge of being permanently excluded – the politically-correct term for being expelled. He looked shifty, but his innate ability meant that he was in the "L" band and on course to do eight O – levels, including Latin, physics and further maths. His bluish lips and watery eyes suggested many hours out in the cold.

"Hello Roy, what on earth are you doing here?" spluttered Michael, unable to fully grasp the scenario that was unfolding before him.

"Hello sir, I've just returned from the match. Mind if I join you?"

Suppressing the urge to tell him that he would rather dine with the devil and invite him to fuck off, Michael said, "Sure Roy, no problem."

Roy avoided eye contact as usual and pretended to study the bit of ketchup-encrusted card that passed as a menu. A short, chunky Spanish-looking waitress shuffled up to the table, and like his teacher, the pupil ordered a large cod and chips, with mushy peas. This was the first time the two had agreed on anything.

"What you doing 'ere sir?" asked Roy, still averting his eyes and rocking his head from side to side as if it were attached to his body by a spring.

"I've just returned from a fishing trip with the school," said Michael, still grappling with the surrealism of having dinner with the pupil from hell. "Just thought I'd warm myself up with a bit of grub before going home. What brings you to these parts, Roy?"

"I'm spending the weekend with my stepdad in Hanwell," muttered the boy, his head still bobbing around like a boxer trying not to be caught off guard in the ring.

As with the kids at the Lido, Roy looked smaller and less threatening in his civvies. If you had not known him as the bloody-minded shit from Somersby High School, you might have mistaken him for a quiet and unassuming youngster, a completely unthreatening teenager who could even have been your own son. Michael stared at the vulnerable child sitting opposite him. Was this the real Roy, or was this Dr Jekyll before the potion transformed him into Mr Hyde?

Two plates of steaming hot food appeared on the table, and the odd couple tucked in. Both were starving after a day in the cold, and they ate voraciously. Instead of flicking the food around the room with his fork, or spitting it on the floor as he would normally do in school, Roy ate like a gentleman, offering Sir the salt and vinegar and politely enquiring whether the meal was nice. He even put on a napkin and used his knife and fork properly, which, along with his impeccable table manners, he had obviously learnt from his parents.

"I love fish and chips," said Michael. "You can forget your poncey *coq au vin* or *petits pois*. Give me fish and chips and mushy peas every time."

"Me too sir, my favourite food as well, although I do like a nice burger. My dad makes great chips."

As with master-angler Lee Westbury, Michael marvelled at

this obsequious use of the word "sir", a word that never graced the lips of Roy Partridge at school. Michael watched the boy devour his meal and wondered what he'd been up to that afternoon. Presumably he'd been watching Queens Park Rangers playing Leeds at Loftus Road. There was always trouble when Leeds played – their fans had a reputation. Was he involved in any of the violence that always erupted at such games? Was his dining partner really a common football hooligan, one of the thugs one saw on the nine o'clock news? There was a slight bruise above Roy's left eye.

Michael studied the child in front of him and asked, "Roy, do you like school?"

"I love it sir, I want to be a scientist," the boy replied.

"Then why do you give us all such a hard time?" asked the teacher incredulously.

"Dunno sir," replied Roy. "It's just a bit of a laugh, that's what school's for, having a laugh. I'm an attention seeker, sir. I like it when the others laugh at me."

For the first time ever, Roy was making eye contact with a teacher. Roy had kind sensitive eyes, the sort you would want your own child to have. But there was also a sadness. What made this kid tick? How could he be such a swine at school yet so gentle outside? Was it the natural habitat thing? Could people like Roy and Lee only be normal in their natural habitat, which lay outside the school gates? And why the sadness? Was Roy yet another victim of a broken family, mum during the week, dad at weekends? Was his aggressive, mad, animal-like behaviour at school a cry for help, a cry for love? What would Freud have said? Was Michael's attempt at armchair psychology anywhere near the truth, or was he just grasping at wishy-washy straws? Would Roy's behaviour in school now improve because of this evening's chance encounter, pupil and teacher dining with each other at Franco's Fish and Chips in Ealing Broadway? Or would he drink the potion and be just his abnormal self on Monday morning, pissing everyone off, getting sent out, learning nothing; just another black kid, failing at school, another black statistic?

"Gotta go now sir," said Roy, pulling his chair out and looking sideways at his teacher. The eye contact had gone and his head was once again bobbing from side to side, preparing himself for the next bout in life's never-ending confrontation. "Have a nice evening sir."

As Roy walked slowly towards the door, his QPR scarf flapping behind his black parka, Michael shouted, "Take care Roy, see you on Monday." The boy kept moving and in a second was gone into the black frosty night. For the second time that day, Michael felt love for a pupil he had previously hated.

Chapter 3

In contrast to Botswana, where in what seemed like a lifetime away the daily thrill of teaching enthusiastic, wide-eyed African children had kept him going, here at Somersby it was the other teachers. It would have been impossible to survive the daily diet of abuse and violence; bogus fire-alarms and opened water hoses; stink bombs and low-flying missiles, without the comfort of other battle-weary combatants.

With a staff of over a hundred, there were plenty of like-minded young teachers who sought each other's company. The staff room was like a huge social club, where lonely twenty-somethings could meet and flirt and exchange horror stories from the front. Michael would never go home straight after school. In fact he would do anything to avoid returning home prematurely and sober to his depressing bedsit in west Ealing. Instead he would usually meet up with a group of fellow imbibers at what became their club, the Red Lion, for ethanol therapy – a pint or three of Courage Directors after work. On weekdays it was not unusual to see a line of ten Somersby teachers queuing outside the pub, waiting for the doors to open at five-thirty. On Friday, drinking was usually preceded by a couple of hours of vigorous badminton in the school gym to build up a thirst and justify even more drinking. Sport was always a cover for ethanol anaesthesia.

The Somersby teachers usually occupied a corner of the pub near the recently installed and newly invented space invaders machine. It served as a reminder that life, and teaching in particular, was a never-ending conflict in which only the fittest survived. The electronic sound of interstellar warfare, punctuated even the most raucous evening.

Ping! Ping! Ping! Ping!

Peter Bradley, a fashionably-dressed, thinly-spectacled Cornishman from Penzance, sat next to Sammy Bell, a dog-eyed TD teacher from Carmarthen who always wore a grey suit that made him look forty instead of the twenty-five years he claimed to be. Barney Paisley, a muscular gentle giant of a PE teacher from Guildford, who was reputed to be shagging the sex-crazed Hazel Finch from science, would hold court with his latest joke about Pedro the Bandit. Usually arriving later than the others because he was head of art, John Levin had the reputation of being the school's Casanova from whose lascivious spell no young female teacher was safe. He was a serial seducer who all the male teachers looked up to and studied his style with incredulity. Known simply as Pan, after the boy who never grew up, John was of indeterminate age, but clearly older than the rest.

On Friday nights after the usual session in the Red Lion getting tanked up and playing space invaders, the drinkers repaired to Willy's Wine Bar in Ealing Broadway. In mid-seventies London, when wine bars were becoming fashionable, Willy's was the hedonist hotspot to go. Every Friday evening it was heaving with beautiful people hoping to get laid after consuming several bottles of fizzy pink Lambrusco. It was a *schlepping* shop. Seventies Ealing Broadway was rapidly becoming Bohemia Broadway. On the bar stood an enormous barrel of iced water into which the mostly gay-looking, tight-trousered barmen would place their opened but unfinished bottles after serving a customer.

On arriving at Willy's, Pan, his disciples in tow, dressed in his Cafe-des-Artistes, Toulouse Lautrec black fur coat, would immediately home in on one of the many groups of half-cut, highly-sexed female twenty-somethings like a heat-seeking missile, and commence his ritual courtship display. At the mere sight of a woman, Pan's face would light up like a high-voltage lamp, like a man on speed, his confident performance courtesy of copious amounts of that most powerful of aphrodisiacs – alcohol.

"Did anyone ever tell you that you were beautiful?" was his opening gambit, followed by the even more cringeworthy, "I'd love to paint your portrait nude."

Although he was nearly twice their age and balding with a wiry grey beard, the women at Willy's were powerless to resist his excruciatingly corny charms. Women love being flattered, all women, and John Levin was a master of flattery.

While the serial seducer mesmerised his quarry, Michael and Sol Denzel perched themselves at the bar right next to the wine bucket. Sol Denzel was a short and totally unreconstructed Welsh woodwork teacher from the valleys, who looked as if he'd just emerged from a coal mine. Like all Welshmen, he loved to drink, and for the first time in recorded history, he'd actually bought a bottle of wine and was sharing it with Michael. The beauty of the bar was that it made you feel you were in a Wild West saloon. Chatting to the bar staff knowledgeably and nodding knowingly at newcomers, you looked experienced and cool, and had first refusal at chatting up the highly-scented exotic birds that pressed themselves up against you as they piled in.

After pouring out the first two glasses of bubbling wine, Sol placed the half-empty bottle nonchalantly into the ice bucket. The problem was that in the deliberately-dimmed light of the wine bar, it was impossible to tell your own cheap bottle from that of the other, sometimes expensive bottles that resided there awaiting the next punter. So when a refill was required, Michael would stretch over the vitreous vegetation that had sprung up in the bucket and pull out a bottle of 1975 vintage Chablis. Oh dear! No one was watching, so Michael thought why not, and proceeded to pour himself and Sol a munificent portion of the golden French elixir before returning it to the bucket.

"Cheers Michael, this shit tastes fucking great," said Sol, who knew nothing about flash drinks like Chablis. The wry smile on his flushed face indicated that he'd cottoned on to what was afoot, and could see where it was heading.

"Cheers Sol, you ignorant Welsh bastard," said Michael, as he felt the cumulative effect of Courage Bitter, Lambrusco and Chablis coursing through his veins.

Peter Bradley and Barney Paisley appeared at the bar, taking a break from pissing themselves laughing at Pan's fornication master class.

"Allow me," said Sol, who was notorious for never knowingly buying a drink, as he plunged his grubby hand into the magic bucket and pulled out a recently-opened bottle of Rioja Reserva. "Red or white?"

"That's very magnanimous of you," said Barney with exaggerated poshness, wondering if what he thought he had just witnessed was really happening. "A large glass of red please."

"Me too," said Peter, a look of agreeable incredulity spreading across his ruddy Cornishman's face like a Mexican wave. He was thinking, "What the fuck's going on here?"

Sol returned the Rioja to the icy waters of the wine bucket and the four teachers lifted their glasses in mutual collusion and shouted, "Cheers!"

"This bucket is amazing," explained the increasingly unintelligible Michael. "It never runs out of wine. It's a magic bucket. It's like the miracle of the five loaves, or should I say the five bottles? I prefer a bottle in front of me to a frontal lobotomy."

Word of the magic bucket had filtered through the hot, smoky, hedonistic ether of the wine bar. Sammy Bell and Harry Knowles popped in for a top-up. Even Levin was finally lured away from his nubile harem of gagging-for-it women by the increasingly seductive sound of his mates raucously laughing and guffawing at the bar and obviously having more fun than he was. Such was the intoxicating power of getting pissed with the lads when compared to the relatively solitary and much more serious business of chatting up a group of prick teasers who probably weren't up for a shag anyway. In the presence of all these youthful and carefree people, Pan had to continually balance proving his Casanova-like success with women against the need to impress his mates with his ability to play sport, hold his drink and have a bloody good laugh like any other twenty-five-year-old.

At ten twenty, the last orders bell sounded and the wine bar began to spew its hot and smoky drunken contents onto the cold wet pavement outside. As Willy's emptied, a freezing cold draught could be felt chewing away at the balls of the Somersby teachers still stranded at the bar, who were still unable to decide whether they'd been dreaming or whether there really was such a thing as a free drink. Long after they had ceased believing in magic, the magic bucket was still filled with half-drunken bottles of fine wine. But had it all been a dream? The next time Michael returned to Willy's wine bar, the magic bucket had gone.

Chapter 4

In 1975, the year Michael arrived at Somersby, teachers had just received a huge pay rise, which meant that the average annual salary suddenly rocketed from £18,000 to £23,000. For a teacher used to living on a modest volunteer allowance, this was a fortune. Michael had never had so much disposable income in his life and this was also true for the other teachers, who for the first time in their careers were being paid like proper professionals.

And yet in spite of this windfall, teachers were not happy. Being paid more temporarily boosted morale, but pupil behaviour didn't improve and the job remained as stressful as ever. Every Monday morning the cover board in the staff room displayed a list of at least ten names – usually women – who for one reason or another couldn't be arsed to make it into school. This meant that those who did turn up had in addition to their normal workload to cover the classes of absent colleagues, which needless to say were the most unteachable bottom sets. The same names cropped up every Monday, and it seemed like some staff were on a de facto three-day week whilst being paid for five. Janet Kirrage suffered from school phobia, Hazel Finch had perpetual PMT and Sue Bateman had "personal problems" with her boyfriend and got stoned at weekends; every Monday the same names. Nobody complained, because in a climate of women's liberation, it seemed reasonable that female teachers should be allowed to piss everyone around and assert themselves by taking days off whenever they felt like it and for whatever outrageous reason they fancied. After hundreds of years of male oppression, it was quite justifiably payback time.

Names were important not just as a means of identification but because of their association. Roll-your-own chain smoker and scruffy art teacher Jon Dale and posh, la-di-da special needs teacher Giles Scott were both named after well-known racehorses. Barney often quipped how difficult it must be to successfully juggle being a teacher and a race horse. Whenever one of the horses ran, Barney would always put a couple of quid on them at Maurice's, the local bookmaker, saying, "You've got to support a colleague." And the funny thing was, both teachers actually looked like horses – Jon even smelled like one.

Perverse pupil names were another source of amusement among the young staff, who in order to remain sane, sought humour in virtually every aspect of school life, every character, every incident. Nothing was to be taken seriously; everything was fair game for lampooning and a wind-up. The parents of some of the worst pupils, in an attempt to deflect suspicion from their crooked offspring, had passed on deceptively benign names. Jerry Good was incredibly bad and Phil Sweet was a sour little shit. Simon Lawless on the other hand, positively wallowed in his name. He was lawless by name and lawless by nature. A moral vacuum destined to become a petty thief if he were lucky, he would never succeed in spelling the word "vacuum" as long as he lived.

Better known as the founder of Barratt Homes and Barratt's Liquor Mart, Doug Barratt was a good-natured and bald Mancunian, whose assemblies invariably centred on Spurs' longest ever serving star, Steve Perryman, who Doug had allegedly taught in the Sixties. "Steve Perryman, smashing lad." Although he was head of Lower School, his main passion was the school tuck shop: he was head of tuck. Every evening he'd sort out his stock of recently-arrived crisps and fruit fizzers in a tiny office next to the staff room. He would canvass staff opinion on his latest lines and depending on whether staff liked his new mushy pea flavoured crisps or not, he would mount a sales campaign in the school. He had no sense of irony and took every word literally.

"These crisps taste like shit Doug," joked Steve Pusey, noisily munching away at and thoroughly enjoying the aforementioned crisps.

"Do you really think so Steve?"

"No Doug, just fucking joking!"

The never-ending threat of rape and pillage, thuggery and buggery, was not restricted to the classroom. The corridors and toilets, as well as the playground and school gates, were all designated war zones where ancient scores and family feuds could be settled as un-amicably as possible.

The Bermuda Triangle is an area of tropical ocean between Miami, Bermuda and Puerto Rico, where planes and boats allegedly disappeared under mysterious circumstances and without trace. Somersby's "Bermuda Triangle", which was really a square, was no less dangerous and occupied an area of dark space between two long corridors connecting the main school entrance with the science labs. The square was dark because the 60-watt ceiling bulb was designed to illuminate a small bathroom or study, and the switch controlling it was either turned off or vandalised. It was enclosed by two sets of heavy wooden fire doors which had stopped the school burning down on at least three separate occasions. The danger lay in the nocturnal low-life that lurked in the dark recesses between the doors.

Because of its pivotal position, there was a well-trodden stream of human traffic passing through the triangle, like the wildebeest migration routes through the Serengeti. It was usually safe between lessons, although pupils who'd been sent out, walked out, or were simply out of lessons to "deliver a message" – code for getting rid of them for a few minutes – sometimes took a detour through the triangle, where they congregated like bats in a cave. At break time or during the lunch hour however, transit was severely restricted by the likes of Adelaide Samson, Junior Barstow and Derek Burnett, and their fellow mafiosi. Little year ones were obliged to pay a "toll" if they wished to avoid being punched, while others were ritually kicked or spat at as they passed through. Sometimes the fire doors were forced shut so that anyone trying to enter the space would crash into a hard wooden barrier at high speed. A common trick was for one of the "residents" to politely open the door and then smash it in your face just as you walked through. Many teachers avoided the triangle altogether, preferring to take a more circuitous route round the bike sheds. But those who dared ran the gauntlet of catapulted pellets, flicked chewing gum and a barrage of "Wanker!" from the indistinguishable silhouettes that jealously guarded their twilit subterranean netherworld.

There was always the smell of cigarettes or something stronger between the fire doors, and fights often broke out. Some of the cooler and more savvy teachers like Michael and the wine bar brigade had negotiated safe passage through the dark matter. Having a natural empathy with what were essentially loveable rogues – lower-set black kids with issues – they befriended the boys and agreed freedom of movement in exchange for immunity from prosecution: A mutually-amicable Faustian arrangement. Derek, Adelaide and Junior were after all reasonable lads. The only person capable of clearing the Bermuda Triangle was the school policeman and deputy head, Mr Stills. As soon as "Stillsy" was spotted, the dark space opened like the parting of the Red Sea, allowing Moses to enter Sinai.

This was a million light years from Botswana, but Michael could not deny enjoying a huge frisson of excitement at being on the edge of all this plunder and pillage. Like standing in the family enclosure at Elland Road and watching the violence on the terraces erupting around him. It was like being on the set of a never-ending Carry On film. Carry On Up The Corridor.

At least once a month there were big fights, or rumours of big fights, outside the school. Somersby had a long history of tribal warfare and the settling of ancient scores with neighbouring schools in Perivale and Ruislip. Sometimes the fight was waged between rival gangs from within the school. On the afternoon of Friday the twentieth of May 1976, rumours spread – there were always rumours – of a big rumble to be staged on the green opposite Watersplash Lane after lesson eight. The usual message was sent round warning pupils not to get involved with the prospect of expulsion if they did, and teachers were requested to be on duty at the end of the school day – just in case.

When Michael poked his head into Watersplash Lane, a huge baying crowd had already gathered on the green and were spilling out onto the road, much to the chagrin of the passing motorists, who swerved and swore and hooted hatefully. If ever one needed proof of our basic animal instincts, the school fight shows just how thin our veneer of civilisation really is. At the slightest whiff of violence, groups of normally peace-loving children are drawn hypnotically into battle like medieval zombies. As in *Lord of the Flies*, the jeering masses cannot resist the thrill of the kill. The mob mentality removes and excuses an individual's need to think for himself.

As he approached the periphery of what looked like a Category 5 cyclone approaching the coast of Florida and growing bigger by the second, Michael recognised many of his pupils, normally nice kids, who seemed to be thoroughly enjoying the festive atmosphere generated by this grim and primitive spectacle.

"Hello sir," giggled Cynthia Watson from 4L1 chemistry, dressed tidily in school uniform and carrying a big pile of homework under her arm. "You come to watch the rumble in the jungle?"

Stood watching the fracas from a safe distance, were a group of "mature" teachers in suits, shaking their heads sardonically and complaining about the state of modern youth and how standards of behaviour had plummeted since their day. "Today's kids have no respect for property or authority," opined Les Slater, who had himself witnessed the horrors and destruction of the last war as a British soldier in occupied Germany.

As Michael forced his way through the excited but benign outer rim of the storm, the crowd became increasingly male and angry. The innocent faces at the periphery had been replaced by those of the usual suspects at the core: the thugs and yobbos he met every day mooching around the school in their relentless pursuit of "bovver", forever scowling and looking for trouble – or worse. Phil Sweet, Jerry Good, Simon Lawless – they were all there, shrieking like madmen, the colour having drained from their faces at the prospect of adrenaline-powered action, and baying for blood like the hounds at a Sunday afternoon hunt in Berkshire who have just smelt the fox. The crowd resembled a swirling galaxy, with all matter being sucked into the immense gravitational spacetime at its centre.

At the event horizon, Michael witnessed two white kids kicking the shit out of each other, egged on by the screaming mob. Jeff Darrow and Tony Heaps.

"Kill 'im! Kill' im!" cried the brainless onlookers, who had long since parted company with their cerebral hemispheres and surrendered themselves unconditionally to their primitive animalistic instincts. Occasionally a boy broke ranks and hurled himself feet-first at one of the combatants to enhance his status as a serious player in front of his mates. Both fighters had torn mud-stained clothing and bloodied faces as they writhed on the ground, frantically cursing each other.

Michael's heart and adrenal glands responded homeostatically as he went into auto-pilot mode, and with no thought for his own safety or for how his actions might inflame the crazed madmen who now encircled him, launched himself at the warring factions and proceeded to pull them apart. He had never been in a fight in his life, never mind stopping one.

"Zabo! Zabo!" chanted the crowd. "You wanker, Zabinsky."

As he grabbed the stronger-looking of the two, Jeff Darrow, Tony Heaps, beside himself with anger, his bloodied eyes popping out and oblivious in his rage to what was happening, continued to throw punches, one of which collided with Michael's chin.

Another roar from the crowd, "Kill 'im! Kill 'im!" They were loving this. This was better than down Millwall. Using reserves of strength he had no idea he had, Michael grabbed Jeff with both hands and pulled him away from the now tearful Tony. As he dragged Jeff away, the crowd parted to let him through. What would have happened if they had not? Jeff continued to resist arrest, desperately trying to break free and finish Tony off.

"Let me fucking go!" he yelled. "I'll kill that cunt."

At this point, the now considerable group of spectating teachers closed in and started to disperse the crowd. Sol Denzel and Peter Bradley surrounded Tony, trying to console him and prevent his apparent death-wish to return to the fray.

"Go home, the fight's over," bawled Les authoritatively, the danger of personal involvement and injury having passed.

"Well done Michael," said John, who had just arrived on the scene. "I would never have had the guts to do that."

"You must be fucking mad Michael," opined Sammy Bell sarcastically. "You should have just let them get on with it and done us all a favour."

It transpired later that Jeff, being the vulgar son-of-a-bitch he was, had insulted Tony's stepmother, not for the first time, by calling her a slag. This had resulted in Tony challenging Jeff in the only way he knew that would afford him the satisfaction of defending his stepmother's honour: a duel after school.

Chapter 5

Every three weeks or so, Michael would swap the badminton, drinking and womanising of Friday nights and visit his dad in Leeds. He would either make his excuses or simply not show up in the Red Lion for pre-drinking drinks. As in Botswana, Michael continued to write weekly letters or postcards to his dad, who, having never re-married, continued to live stoically alone in his semi-detached house in Cedarwood Avenue. He would leave straight after school, and take the Central Line to Holborn and then the Northern Line to King's Cross. The six o'clock train to Leeds departed every Friday from platform eleven, and was crammed to the rafters with weekend trippers like himself returning home to visit their friends or loved ones.

In the mid-seventies, King's Cross was a heaving hub of humanity, and as the main London link with the north, perpetually busy. The area surrounding the station was drab and rundown, with a distinctly seedy feel to it as prostitutes and drug dealers plied their sleazy trade. This added a frisson of excitement to the journey – being on the edge of human degradation but not being part of it – unlike the poor sods who had to live there, who were mostly immigrants. And it was always raining. King's Cross seemed to be staffed entirely by little Ho Chi Minh-like characters with long goatee beards – and not just the men. They cleaned the platforms, served in the grubby cafes and attended the lavatories. They looked sad and downtrodden, with deferentially bowed heads and expressionless eyes, and hardly spoke a word of English. They were probably dreaming of back home – wherever that was. But what the fuck were they doing *here*?

Stations are very evocative places with all the comings and goings, emotional greetings and departures, and the thousand-and-one stories that lay behind each journey. Michael constantly imagined himself to be on the set of Noel Coward's *Brief Encounters*, where the lovers meet only in the station waiting room; or *Casablanca*, where Rick waits in a wartime rain-soaked Paris station for Ilsa, who doesn't show up. And it was no less so with the weekend special from King's Cross to Leeds City, arriving at nine if you were lucky. As each departure grew near, a long queue of luggage-laden passengers formed near the entrance to platform eleven, often merging imperceptibly with the queues to Edinburgh and Newcastle. The trick was to be at the front of the queue, so that when the West Indian guard opened the gates and clipped your ticket ten minutes before the off, you could sprint to the far end of the platform and get a seat before the less athletic passengers arrived. Luckily not many people reserved seats in second class. By the time the guard blew his whistle and the train slowly pulled out of the station, every seat was occupied, the corridors strewn with luggage, and the carriage exits crammed with people standing, sitting on their suitcases or just slumped on the floor.

Being January, it was pitch black and a sleety drizzle peppered the grimy graffitied windows of carriage F, like the final stages of a cheap carwash. As with all weekend excursions, the journey out was as joyous as the journey back was sombre. Each passenger bristled with the relief of finishing a week's work and the prospect of leaving the frenetic pace of London for the tranquillity of the sticks. Unlike London Underground, where commuters generally sat or stood in silence reading their papers, or pretended to sleep and generally ignore each other's existence, the passengers on the six o'clock to Leeds were available for conversation. This may have been due to the euphoria of escape, or the fact that many of the travellers were northerners, whose exaggerated accents loudly proclaimed their legendary propensity for candid conversation in contrast to their stuck-up and reserved compatriots down south. There was an eagerness to share their lives with complete strangers for an hour or two – something most un-British. It was not unusual for a six-pack of Tetley's or Newcastle Brown Ale to appear on the table, along with giant packets of Golden Wonder crisps and KP nuts to be shared and enjoyed by the spontaneously convened new group of friends. Decks of cards sprang up.

"It's good to be going back up north," said a middle-aged woman in a thick woollen jumper sat opposite.

"Aye," said Michael, in the faux Yorkshire accent he reserved only for these train journeys to Leeds.

As the train picked up speed, it rattled its way through the illuminated suburbs of outer London and then on towards strange place names like Stevenage, Peterborough, Grantham, Newark and Retford, places that were known only to him as nondescript towns on the line to Leeds, which he had never visited and almost certainly never would. Why on earth would anyone *want* to visit such places? A West Indian guard appeared and announced "Tickets please." There was always someone who'd lost their ticket or couldn't retrieve it from the bowels of their floppy bag or rucksack.

After the first "happy hour" of drinking warm canned beer and the exchange of wholesome northern life histories, conversation gradually died down as people ran out of things to say and tiredness took over. By Peterborough, long queues had started to form by the filthy toilets as passengers felt the need to restore their aquatic equilibrium by relieving themselves of their Friday night fluid intake. Like many, Michael gradually succumbed to that lovely warm, tipsy feeling that usually enveloped one on these occasions, and battled to keep his eyes open while trying to browse through the crumpled pages of the *London Evening Standard*. Aided and abetted by thick layers of winter clothing and the increasingly hot and stuffy atmosphere of a carriage whose rudimentary air-conditioning system had long since given up any pretence of extracting the excess carbon dioxide and moisture-laden breath from the overcrowded compartment, Michael nodded off. Thick condensation formed on the cold black windows and dribbled down the wall.

There is nothing more conducive to sleep – apart from reading a book or watching television – than a long train journey; they should be prescribed on the National Health as a cure for insomniacs with no known side effects. The rattle of the tracks and the warmth and wilful self-delusion of being on some exotic adventure, all contribute to the sense of wellbeing and security that are the prerequisites of a deep and peaceful slumber. Being vaguely aware of the waves of movement and the noise that accompanied intermittent stops, Michael woke up in Doncaster. This signified Yorkshire and home territory. Then Wakefield Westgate and finally Leeds City at nine fifteen – only a quarter of an hour late.

Whenever Michael came to Leeds, he was always overcome by a sense of nostalgia for his childhood, which like most nostalgia was a highly-edited cocktail of fact and fiction. He made his way through the sleazy, sleety streets adjacent to the station that lead to City Square, which was always populated by wild-looking drunken types and prostitutes, just like King's Cross. He headed down Boar Land, carefully avoiding groups of inebriated Leeds United fans shouting "You're gonna get your fucking heads kicked in," and on to the bus stops for north Leeds on Briggate. Almost immediately a green number twenty-one to Moortown appeared, which he boarded. He sat upstairs in his usual seat from childhood, seven rows from the back.

The bus trundled through the seedy suburb of Chapeltown, where grandma Shufleder and Uncle Israel used to live, and on to Moortown Corner where hordes of Jewish kids used to congregate after school to chat up members of the opposite sex and give a performance which asserted their ancient Biblical right to occupy this patch of hallowed ground. Much to the chagrin of the local residents, whose latent anti-Semitism was fully vindicated by these outlandish goings on.

As was so often the case in winter, the sleet of the town centre had turned to snow in the higher northern suburbs. By the time the bus arrived at his stop on Streep Lane, the pavements and rooftops had turned a wintry white, with only the road defiantly maintaining its black, slushy, freezing wetness.

He hopped off the number twenty-one as he'd done so many times before, slipping in the snow as he did so and wishing the conductor good night in an exaggerated broad Yorkshire accent. He then followed a well-trodden track down Cedarwood Drive, past Shmuel's bakery where he used to buy bagels on a Sunday morning and where, when he had a Saturday job there, he had once stood on a Swiss roll which Manny Shmuel had laid out to cool on the floor and later sold, past the red phone box which was their only means of communication, round the corner of Cedarwood Mount, and on to the slope that led to his ancestral home at number 29 Cedarwood Avenue, Leeds 8.

From the bottom of the street, Michael could just about recognise his house half way up the hill, a dull orange glow penetrating the drawn curtains like a distant lighthouse out at sea guiding him home through the snowy darkness, like the eternal light of the Aron Kodesh that houses the holy scrolls of the Torah in every synagogue. When his son was expected, his dad always left a welcoming light on in "the room" before going to bed. Cedarwood Avenue looked magical, like the Christmas card winters of his youth, real or imagined, as the snow blew around the street lamps, settling on the grass and pavements and walls, and on the road. He remembered the record winter of sixty-three when it had snowed for three months and he had sledged down the street covered in deep snowdrifts and hard-packed ice until March.

It was so quiet. As he traced the footsteps of his childhood in the ever-deepening creaking snow, every point in the street disclosed a memory. The lamppost where they used to play cricket; Martin's house at number eleven where Fanny Fisher paraded herself in the window in her dressing gown and permanently permed hair, like some tart in the Amsterdam red-light district; Monty's house at number seventeen where the flamboyant socialite Sally Fleischmann once stood, arms folded, extolling the genius of "My Monty" in a loud cockney accent, and on whose gatepost his dad had once revealed the magnificence of a barn owl that flew away as they approached it. What a thrill that was.

The orange gate of his house was half-open as usual, a broken hinge ensuring its default position. The kitchen light had been deliberately left on to illuminate the path and the garden, inadvertently exposing giant swirling snowflakes that danced excitedly in the easterly wind as they recognised and greeted this visitor from the south. Two bare lilac trees evoked memories of spring, when in full bloom – one white, one pink – they had perfumed the evening air with their intoxicating scent. The long snow-covered garden where as a child he had played and sunbathed and built snowmen stretched endlessly towards the black, tree-lined distance.

Michael opened the house door and entered the precious sanctuary that had been the kitchen of his childhood. His dad, known to his sisters as Yankul, had left a bowl of chicken soup on the table; he received it every Friday from the meals-on-wheels kosher dinner service, along with a loaf of Challah bread and a small tub of chopped liver. The kitchen was where the family of four – Mum, Dad, Michael and Jacob (three after his mother had died) - had eaten all their meals and drunk endless cups of tea with biscuits, using the warmth of the gas oven to make this the cosiest room in the house. His dad would stand by the oven, smoking a cigarette whose ash periodically cascaded onto his trousers and then the floor, roasting his backside till it smouldered.

"Who's that I hear downstairs?" purred his father from the bedroom, "is that our Michaelinsky?"

Michael climbed the stairs where he and his brother had once pretended to climb Mount Everest and where they used to slide down the banister, and entered Yankul's bedroom. He turned on the light to reveal the ecstatic smile and watery eyes of an old man sitting up in bed, dressed in a thick Scandinavian pullover and a red woollen pompom hat that covered his bald head. Michael approached the bed and embraced his father, kissing his warm forehead and holding his frail body tightly.

"Steady on lad, you're crushing me," squealed the devoted father for whom his children were his life. "Your hands feel cold. Come on lad, scratch my back."

Michael performed the ancient ritual that gave his father most pleasure. "It's started to snow dad, it's a couple of inches thick. How are you keeping; are you managing to keep warm?"

"Is it really?" replied Yankul with the amazement of a child experiencing snow for the first time. "How about a nice cup of you and me? By the way, I've left you a bowl of soup on the table. Just warm it up."

The best day of the weekend is Friday, because you've got the prospect of the whole weekend in front of you, stretching endlessly into the distance like a winding mountain path disappearing into the mist. The journey is the goal. And so it was when visiting his dad in Leeds. Standing there next to his father's bed, Michael felt the womb-like security of being home, insulated from the restlessness that would inevitably set in on Saturday, when the metaphorical mountain mist would clear, revealing Sunday in the valley below and Monday Bloody Monday beyond. In spite of his abject loneliness and physical infirmity, Yankul was always cheerful, looking forward to his sons' visits like nothing else in life, never complaining or indulging in recriminations about his isolated situation and failing vision, or the injustice of his living alone while his two healthy sons lived their separate lives elsewhere.

Michael returned to the kitchen, where he warmed up the "Jewish penicillin" – chicken soup – and brewed his dad a giant mug of sweet milky tea.

"That's just the job lad," said his dad loudly, slurping his warm cup of you and me, spilling the obligatory percentage onto his pullover, and crunching on a Crawford's custard cream with the few remaining teeth left in his mouth. "Champion!"

Yankul was a man of few words and simple pleasures, and drinking tea and crunching biscuits like his father Louis before him ranked highly in his pantheon of out-of-body experiences. His smile was one of immense pleasure as he performed this sacred Zabinskian rite in front of the person he loved most in the world, his own flesh and blood, his son.

"Sleep well dad, see you tomorrow," said Michael, kissing his father once more on a slightly warmer tea-infused forehead, and removing the cup from his thick-fingered carpenter's hand. "It's good to be home again dad."

"Sleep well Micho, it's good to see you again," replied Yankul as he lowered his wool-covered head onto the massive pile of pillows that he'd arranged for himself. "Don't forget to drink your soup."

Michael once more returned to the kitchen and poured the steaming broth into a large soup bowl. Blowing each spoonful to prevent the incineration of his mouth and tongue, he broke off an irregular lump of Sabbath bread, covered it with lashings of chopped liver, and chewed it greedily between mouthfuls of delicious, golden, kosher serum. Although he had long since stopped celebrating the Sabbath, this ancient Jewish ritual of bread, chopped liver and soup, like the bread and wine of the Christians, provoked an almost Pavlovian response of spiritual salivation and the most exquisite sensation of pleasure. He even managed to conjure up his mother lighting the candles in "the room", scarf on head, reciting the prayer "*Lehadlik ner shel Shabbat*"; the blessing for the candles.

Next morning he awoke to the sound of his dad shuffling around downstairs on his Zimmer frame and the smell of fried eggs and burnt toast. In spite of his infirmity and failing vision, Yankul was cooking Michael his favourite breakfast.

"Come on Michael, rise and shine," sang his dad chirpily from the kitchen. "Grub up!" Morning was always the best time for Yankul and the worst time for his son, the source of many a conflict between them.

Michael entered the kitchen and embraced his dad, whose cigarette was hanging Andy Capp-like from his lips, ash covering his pullover, red pompom hat perched at an angle on his perspiring head, warming his *tochas* on the stove and listening to Terry Wogan on the radio – with both hands.

"It looks like it's been snowing," said Yankul excitedly, unable to clearly see the snow, but recognising the unmistakable wintry stillness and intense light.

It had indeed been snowing. Wiping the condensation from the window, Michael saw that everything was white. The branches of the lilac trees, the privet hedge, the garden and the houses beyond were all covered in a thick layer of pure, fresh snow radiating its own unique bluish whiteness. And it was still snowing. A swirl of tiny flakes cascaded out of an orange-grey sky that typically accompanied heavy snow.

Michael sat at the table and wolfed down his fried eggs and burnt toast, helped along by a mug of sweet and milky you and me. "That was champion, Dad," he said.

"Now you can wash up lad," declared Yankul, slipping effortlessly into the long-practised banter that always developed when these two were together, each anticipating the other's lines.

As he opened the house door, a blast of freezing cold Siberian air muscled its way into the kitchen, dumping a vortex of dancing snowflakes onto the linoleum floor for good measure. Michael negotiated his way through deep snow drifts up to his knees into the pristine white, glistening garden. It was just like the winter of sixty-three. He opened the snow-covered door of the Stevenson Screen which housed his childhood collection of thermometers. Taking care not to breathe a hot cloud of exhaled air onto the meteorological instruments, he studied the thread of mercury: minus five degrees Celsius.

As he marvelled at the incredibly low temperature – twenty three degrees Fahrenheit – the snow pirouetted around his head, sticking to his curly black hair and eyebrows and making him look like a character from *Doctor Zhivago*. His father had built this beautiful weather station with his own loving, carpenter's hands. When other kids had been reading *Oliver Twist* or *The Three Musketeers*, Michael had been reading advanced weather books. For reasons unfathomable to his family, from an early age he'd had a geekish fascination bordering on an obsession with the weather, and would study detailed meteorological maps on the back page of *The Guardian* from papers supplied to him by Veronica Middleton at school. He used to sit on the toilet and pray for thunderstorms and snow. So when his father offered to build him a proper Stevenson Screen like the Met Office used, it was the equivalent of a normal child being promised a new bike with derailleur or 'double clanger' gears.

For what seemed like many weeks and months, Yankul worked every evening after work, patiently making his son's dream of a weather station come true. It was a labour of love, cutting the thin wooden ventilation slats on the table and gluing them together, then painstakingly assembling them in the shape of a rectangular Stevenson Screen. Stilts were erected in the garden so that the screen could stand the required four foot six inches above the ground to ensure internationally recognised accuracy of measurement. And so to the day when the screen was finally attached to the base, painted brilliant white to reflect the sun, and the instruments installed – a maximum and minimum thermometer to measure temperature, a hygrometer to measure humidity.

Michael had been overwhelmed by this beautiful piece of craftsmanship, created by the skilled hands of his own father. It was his pride and joy and by far the best present he'd ever received – better even than a train set from Father Chanukah. He remembered holding Yankul's still strong body tightly in the garden, kissing his bald head, and saying, "Thank you so much dad, that's great," and his dad replying in typically modest fashion, "I hope it's OK Michaelinsky, perhaps now we'll get some decent weather." It was a priceless gift, like Jacob's coat of many colours to his favoured son Joseph, a demonstration of unconditional human love.

But that was in the summer of sixty-four, when he was still at school and his father was still fit enough to work. Now it was the winter of seventy-six; Michael taught in a violent London comprehensive and Yankul was a housebound semi-cripple.

"It's minus five dad!" exclaimed Michael excitedly, as he re-entered the cosy capsule of the kitchen, stamping the snow off his shoes and onto the mat as he did so. Yankul was as thrilled as his son at this hot-off-the-press revelation of the incredibly low temperature, and he shook his head and smiled contentedly. As the ash from his cigarette once again cascaded down his pullover, he gave his backside an extra dose of compensatory heat from the stove.

As always, Saturday and Sunday flew by and it was once again time to leave. Parting is such sweet sorrow. Michael collected the plastic bag containing the chopped liver bagels and an apple that his father had prepared and insisted that he took with him for the return journey.

"You'd better go early love, in case you get delayed by the snow," said Yankul, as selflessly as ever. "You never know what might happen."

Michael looked at his dad tearfully. The bright glow of his eyes on Friday had been replaced by the clouded but defiant Sunday eyes of a man who once again bravely faced the solitude of a house without the most precious thing in his life.

"Take care Dad, and don't do anything crazy. And thanks for the no-expenses-spared hospitality."

The two men embraced, father and son holding onto each other, separating again because of the cruel necessity of life to go on.

As he tramped down Cedarwood Avenue through the ever-deepening January snow, Michael turned round, as he always did, to take one last look at his house. The orange glow of the bay windows struggled to penetrate the driving snow in the street. He always had a pang of heart-wrenching sadness and guilt at this point. But what could he do? His job and his future life were, like so many of his generation, in London.

As always on the return leg of a weekend spent away, the atmosphere was dire. The euphoria of the outward journey was replaced by a profound sense of sadness and trepidation at the rapidly-approaching new week ahead, signalling a return to work and the rat race.

The faces of the passengers on the Sunday evening express from Leeds City to King's Cross were pale and tense. No one spoke, no one made eye contact with the person sitting opposite, no one shared cans of beer or crisps or the story of their life. The train was once again packed with baggage-laden travellers, who stood in the corridors or crouched on their cases and rucksacks by the cold carriage doors. There seemed to be an unspoken rule of reverential silence, as at a funeral, which the English with their propensity for the stiff upper lip did well.

For once, central Leeds looked tranquil and peaceful in its winter shroud of virgin snow as the train meandered its way through the desolate southern suburbs of the city. But by the time it reached Stevenage, the dark, wet, sleety blackness of the outward journey had been restored, adding to the sense of gloom and foreboding on board the inter-city. On arriving at King's Cross, the travel-weary, darkly-clad passengers, heads hung low, trooped along the platform like refugees fleeing a war zone and dispersed defeated into the anonymous labyrinth of the London Underground.

Chapter 6

The summer of 1976 started badly. May was, as it so often is, cold and dull, with what seemed like heavy rain every other day. Michael got soaked on his way to school. The plane trees were in leaf and the grass was lush and green, but the roses were finding it hard to bloom in the dingy light, and those that took a chance soon regretted their impatience, for their delicate petals were battered, their fragrance dissolved and diluted by the incessant rain. And then suddenly on June the sixth, the skies cleared, the sun came out, and the scorching hot summer of seventy-six began.

Weather determines mood, the way people think, and their ability to be creative and productive. It explains why the English are reserved and why the Enlightenment occurred in temperate Europe, rather than the sweltering Congo basin or the steamy Amazonian rainforest. So when the weather in London became like the weather in Botswana, it was perfectly natural for Michael to discard his winter coat and put on his shorts, sandals and Pula shirt to go to school in.

London exploded into a luscious paradise of summer scent and colour as thousands of hitherto dormant or reluctant buds burst into life, completely transforming the city and the mood of its inhabitants. And with the flowers came the insects – bees, butterflies and moths, whose metamorphosis had been suddenly triggered by the heat. It was already twenty-five degrees at eight in the morning when Michael left his squalid flat and boarded the West Ealing line to school.

And with the hot days came the sultry nights. Young women suddenly appeared in sexy see-through blouses and short skirts, the heat seeming to swell their fecund thighs and breasts, which like the opening buds of June roses, fertile and erotic, invited pollination from hopelessly hypnotised males who dreamt only of squeezing and ravishing them. They were irresistibly, ball-burstingly pretty.

And so it came to pass that our young and iconoclastic hero, dressed only in brown sandals, orange shorts and a bright blue Pula shirt, disembarked the Central Line tube at Greenford, and strolled confidently down Watersplash Lane. He imagined he was back in Botswana on the daily trek from his mud hut through the village to the school campus. But the local response was different: instead of "*Dumela rra*," wolf whistles and jeering from the bawdy inhabitants of the concrete jungle; "Get em off," or "Zabinsky you perv," but also "Nice legs sir," and "Like the Bermudas". Michael wallowed in all this attention, playing shamelessly to the invisible gallery of admirers hiding in their cracks and crevices.

In the staff room teachers smiled, deputies rolled their eyes and Doug Barratt quipped "No woman no cry," in his best Mancunian Bob Marley accent. Although there was no formal dress code at Somersby, Michael's Caribbean costume was clearly off the Richter scale of acceptability, no one having ever turned up like this before except on Mufti Day. He looked condescendingly at his sad colleagues, who were unable to break out of their straitjacket of conformity despite pretensions of being hip and radical. Sammy Bell wore the same shiny grey suit every day, as if there were no seasons. Bob Schofield never changed his navy pullover. Even that great hedonist John Levin turned up in his usual linen jacket and Paisley tie. Michael felt the self-righteous sense of superiority that only those who know they are right can appreciate. In a school without air conditioning, he would surely be the coolest swinger in town; the rest could go sweat themselves to death, drown in their own salty bodily fluids.

When he turned up to register 4X4, his fun-loving pupils descended immediately into uncontrollable laughter and showered him with a barrage of paper airplanes and freshly minted pellets as a show of their appreciation.

"You've lost your marbles sir," opined the ever-complimentary Stuart. "You just come from Carnival sir?" chortled Eric, his impish face glowing with delight at the prospect of winding up his teacher.

"Zabo! Zabo!"

"Enough already," retorted Mr Zabinsky, appealing in vain to the class's non-existent sense of fair play. "Haven't you ever seen a science teacher in shorts?"

"No sir!"

In spite of their youth and their punk-inspired rebellious nature, the children were in their own way as conservative as their parents. Children always were. Spitting, shouting, farting in class was OK, but not science teachers in shorts. Hurling abuse and chucking missiles was fine, but not science teachers in shorts. Setting off fire bells or blocking toilets was cool, but not science teachers in shorts. Children simply replace the conservative traits of their parents with their own set of equally conservative traits, and we describe this as rebellion. Sociologists had long since noticed that the most anti-social kids were the ones most likely to join the police force or the army if they were lucky, or end up in prison if they were not. Or become PE teachers. Either way they craved order and discipline: Very conservative.

After a couple of days, the kids, as they always do, got used to Michael's summer collection. But the teachers did not. On the third day of defiance, with the thermometer nudging thirty-two in the shade – ninety degrees in old money – the impressively presented deputy head, Bruce Trimmer, whose straitjacket-tight senior management suit made him walk like the repressed puppet he was, informed Michael discreetly that Mrs Barnes would like to see him in her office.

Michael knocked on the head's door and entered. Mrs Barnes sat at her desk, her auburn hair perfectly permed, her face covered in a thick layer of clown's makeup, her eyelashes painted blue.

"Do sit down, Mr Zabinsky," said the headmistress, her trademark smile and little-girl voice reminding one of a doting mother addressing her baby. It was the voice Brenda used to address teachers in staff meetings and sixth-formers – "her little lambs" – in assembly.

"How are you Mr Zabinsky, how are things?" she continued in her faux-posh voice.

"Excellent Mrs Barnes, and nice of you to ask," said Michael, taking in the sickly-sweet perfume of the eccentric middle-aged woman who sat before him, her watery always-on-the-verge-of-tears eyes staring at him maternally. He wanted to cuddle up to her bosom and drink her milk.

"And how are you coping with the hot weather?" continued the slightly batty Mrs Barnes wearily, her head cocking to one side, as it often did in moments of confrontation with bolshie teachers.

"Very well Ma'am" replied Michael, "I manage to keep cool."

"Now here's the thing," continued Brenda, a slight frown appearing on her powdered pink forehead, "I've heard a rumour from one of the parents that a certain member of Somersby staff has been seen dressing rather flamboyantly. Do you have any idea who that might be?"

"It sounds like an art teacher" obfuscated Michael. "Mrs Shakespeare is always wearing Moroccan beads and flower-power dresses."

"You see Mr Zabinsky," explained the head, now staring apoplectically at Michael's blue Pula shirt, "Somersby is a very conservative area and parents feel threatened by change. Do you see what I'm getting at?"

The next day Michael turned up in long trousers and a Pula shirt. He didn't want to annoy Mrs Barnes, but he had his principles.

Chapter 7

The scorching hot summer of seventy-six unsurprisingly awakened dormant memories of Botswana, which although still fresh in his mind and indeed impossible to forget, had been utterly swamped and overwhelmed – blown out of the water even – by the whirlwind of new experience that was Somersby High and the sheer thrill that was seventies London.

And the weather really was just like Botswana in December before the rains; thirty-two by day, twenty-four by night. Hot weather massively affects the way we think and behave. And it wasn't just Michael's primeval urge to wear Pula shirts and Bermuda shorts to school: it was the effect that heat had on the human psyche. Hot nights meant difficulty in sleeping, windows wide open, the noise of traffic and low-flying planes coming into Heathrow, impossible-to-catch mosquitoes buzzing around the room as well as the exhilaration of sitting in beer gardens, taking in the perfumed air and the sexy fragrance and laughter of highly-available, scantily-clad young women. There was something hugely primordial and erotic about the sights and scents and noises of a balmy, starlit, moonlit summer night. On the urban streets of Haringey and Lewisham, there was a palpable sense of long hot summer-style racial tension as bands of black youths roamed the suburbs, venting their anger on property and passers-by.

Hot days meant slowing down; drowsy thinking; feeling sleepy; a sense of lightness and timelessness; the caressing and soothing sensation of sunshine on the skin. And a general optimism that life was not quite so shit after all.

In Botswana, Michael would be sitting on the veranda of the village bar, surrounded by all those colourful characters he once knew. In London it was the beer garden of the Red Lion, or nearer to his flat, the Sussex Arms. In Botswana it had been the kids whose lives had fired his life. In Somersby it was the teachers. In Botswana he would visit the houses and rondavels of other volunteers and enjoy entertainment in the school hall; as a jolly he'd go to Gaborone. In London he would visit Willy's wine bar, go to gigs in seedy pubs with his buddy Tony Finkelstein who he'd met in Israel, or go to the casino and Windsor races.

The teaching experience was so different. Pupils in England were wild and carefree and in your face; education was peripheral to their lives. In Botswana children behaved like angels; education was their only hope of a future and survival. Teachers were far less driven and dedicated than in Botswana. There was so much going on in the metropolis; school was peripheral to their social lives.

There were as many seriously odd teachers at Somersby as there were pupils. Jon Dale, of eponymous racehorse fame, was a roll-your-own, chain-smoking Brummie art teacher who stank of smoke and whose spindly fingers were coated in nicotine. He resembled the archetypal penniless artist from nineteenth century Rive Gauche Paris, a self-styled bohemian with shabby paint-stained clothes he never changed and a dazed worse-the-wear-for-drink look on his dishevelled flaky face. He cycled every day from Hanwell, often arriving fashionably and so artistically late, splattered with muddy spray, with sixties cycle clips he often forgot to take off and wore throughout the day. He believed in free love, and transport, and accommodation. He loved the kids, who in turn reciprocated by mercilessly taking the piss out of his oddness. He felt stifled by "the system" which most regarded as being incredibly liberal and laissez-faire, and entertained the fantasy of one day telling Mrs Barnes to fuck off and going freelance, selling his own work in the galleries of trendy Islington. The rest of the art department thought he was a tramp, a hopeless charlatan whose artwork was as unimpressive and outdated as his charity-shop clothes.

Will Ferris was an uptight French teacher who wore red braces and brogue shoes and lived with his elderly mother in Perivale. Although only a prematurely balding thirty-two, he was of the old school, spoke like a proper schoolmaster and believed in strict discipline and academic excellence. And therein lay the seeds of his problems. Except for the high-flyers of the L-band, the pupils at Somersby favoured indiscipline and academic mediocrity. The very words 'strict' and 'excellence' were anathema to their culture. He had a neurotic twitch in his right eye, whose frequency was inversely proportional to the intellectual calibre of his class. He resented having to teach French to bottom set pupils, whom he regarded as uncouth yobbos undeserving of his refined mind. The children for their part regarded him as a pompous dickhead who couldn't teach. As with Jon Dale, they mercilessly lampooned anyone who did not fit their narrow conservative stereotype of a proper teacher.

Every few weeks, Will took French leave to recover from stress and "look after his mother". As is often the case with morally superior types who bang on about professionalism, he was gloriously unaware of the irony and crass unprofessionalism of his own actions. On the other hand, his old-fashioned politeness towards other teachers meant that Will was admired by his colleagues, who regarded his eccentric idiosyncrasies as both amusing and endearing. And when he wasn't twitching he was bloody good at soccer and badminton. Like Jon Dale, Will Ferris dreamed of telling Mrs Barnes to fuck off – politely of course – and getting a job in a small private school where polite middle-class kids would appreciate his unique talents.

To end the sultry summer term of seventy-six, Michael organised a trip to Battersea Power Station for bottom set year four science. Although they caused havoc in school and were totally undeserving of any favours or sympathy, cynicism had not yet corrupted his still-youthful sense of altruism, which believed in the educational value of giving children another chance. It seemed a nice end-of-term idea to get these so called "disadvantaged kids" out of the asylum and into the real world of the city. And likewise the teachers.

On the last Friday of term, fifty academically and behaviourally-challenged fourteen-year-olds took the Central Line from Greenford, accompanied by Michael, the octa-armual physics teacher Harry Knowles – known for his extreme touchy-feeliness after a few bottles of Diat Pils – and the voluptuous young English teacher Daphne Blower, whose tight designer clothes, erotically-perfumed body and faux-vulnerability activated the testosterone of every male teacher, and the irresistible John Levin in particular.

Tube journeys were a convenient nightmare for school parties, because it was impossible to control the kids. Though specifically instructed to stay together and travel in the same carriage, as soon as the automatic doors opened the group scattered like leaves in a storm to the four corners of the train, with only the softies remaining behind with the teachers. This was bad because the rowdiest kids would be doing God knows what, to God knows who, God knows where, but good because the teachers who were supposed to be looking after the pupils were spared the embarrassingly hopeless task of having to control and discipline them in public.

Changing at Oxford Street for the Victoria Line and their final destination of Vauxhall passed without too much rape and pillage, the pupils being still half-asleep and not fully operational. And then on down the depressingly soulless Nine Elms Lane in single file – made bearable by the blue sky and exhilarating summer warmth – to the iconic, four-chimney skyline of the Grade II listed building, Battersea Power Station. They were met by a nondescript, elderly looking gent in glasses and wearing a bright yellow workman's jacket, who gazed incredulously at the sea of cheeky faces staring at him indolently.

"Mr Zabinsky, Somersby High School," said Michael, "nice to meet you."

"You in charge here?" interjected Ron Quigley, a deceptively benign-looking lad from the back.

"Don't be rude, Ron," retorted Ms Blower, her flushed face and heaving chest only adding to her faux-vulnerability and rendering her more desirable than ever.

"Sorry, banana man," said Ron, squeezing the last drop of confrontation out of the moment and playing to the gallery.

The workman dejectedly escorted his fourth group of unappreciative school kids of the day to reception in the magnificent art deco marble entrance hall. After registration and a pep talk on how to behave in a power station, they were collected by a middle-aged man in blue overalls and an orange safety helmet who took them through a featureless labyrinth of corridors to a large, glass-walled control centre. Through the wide double-glazed windows one could see but not hear the massive turbine hall, which at its peak had generated one fifth of London's power. The stern-faced guide introduced himself as Gerald.

"First things first, I don't want no trouble. Just listen to me and don't touch anyfink. There'll be time for questions later." Very strict.

The control room was staffed by about ten almost certainly married men in their fifties, also in blue overalls. But what struck Michael straight away was the in-your-face display of colourful, highly-explicit photos of big-busted nude women in various states of sexual arousal that adorned the "notice board" above each man's desk. Harry and Daphne gazed on agog. As Gerald droned on about the power station's illustrious history, the children's already non-existent attention span was tested to destruction by the wall of porn.

"Battersea power station is the largest brick building in Europe," continued the yellow-helmeted guide, in that nerdishly monotonous style so typical of English officialdom and so mercilessly lampooned in television sitcoms. He was oblivious to the growing absurdity of his situation. "It was used as the backdrop for the 1965 Beatles film, "*Help*!" Gerald would shortly be in need of all the help he could get.

To the muffled background radiation of the guide's soporific monologue, the behaviourally-challenged, under-educated and over-sexed pupils of Somersby High warmed to the finer points of this unexpectedly edgy exhibition of power-station art. The teachers looked on in mounting horror. The urge to squeal uncontrollably with laughter at the increasingly farcical drama unfolding before them was suppressed by the horrible realisation, witnessed so often in the classroom, that the situation was rapidly getting out of control and would shortly erupt in the traditional Somersby way – abusively. Once they got started there was no holding them back.

"That your girlfriend mister?" inquired the congenitally cheeky, tight-skirted Mavis McAllister, deliberately winding up the by now profusely sweating guide. She was pointing at a tarty-looking girl in black knickers with unnaturally large breasts and huge red nipples,

"If I worked here, I'd be jerking myself off all day," opined the congenitally vulgar Ricky Robinson, a guy whose brother was doing time in the Scrubs for GBH.

"I wouldn't mind giving her one!" shouted the congenitally coarse Billy Hagan, who had been living with his nan since his parents split up.

"Oh God," moaned the sweet-smelling Daphne nervously, totally freaked-out by the speed at which children degenerated into savages, *Lord of the Flies*-style.

Gerald pretended not to hear; in fact he was so enthralled by the sound of his own voice that he probably didn't care.

The control room workers in their blue overalls observed the school group with contempt. This behaviour simply reinforced all the deep-seated prejudices they held about schoolchildren in particular and the state of education in general. In their day things were different. They had respected their teachers and knew right from wrong. This explained why they had turned out to be such decent law-abiding model citizens, veritable pillars of the community and purveyors of moral rectitude; their only vice being to cover their office walls with grotesque, degrading, misogynistic porn. Except that they didn't regard explicit photos on the walls of their workplace where cleaning ladies would certainly enter as a vice at all. It was something that normal red-blooded English blokes did.

Michael saw that they were utterly oblivious to the irony of their situation and completely unaware of how pathetic they looked and the part they played as role models in the corruption of the young people they were so quick to condemn.

Then the lights went out. Fifty unruly X-band children, three apoplectic teachers, ten sad workers and a resentful guide were plunged into partial darkness, trapped in a poky room somewhere inside Battersea power station. The fire bell went. Panic. Everyone shouting and swearing, pushing and shoving; silhouettes against the orange glow of the turbine hall, filtering through the double-glazed windows.

"Let's get the fuck out of here!" shouted the unmistakably hysterical voice of Donna Wells.

"Bloody perverts!" shouted another. Complete pandemonium. "Fucking kids!"

Then the sound of tearing, ripping, pornographic paper. Harry fumbled his way along the wall and located the switch.

The door flew open and a mob of highly-agitated science students piled out of the office, through a never-before-opened fire door and onto the sweltering courtyard outside. With their teachers now in hot pursuit, St Trinian's-style, the mob headed for the sturdy metal gates of the power station and onto the road.

"Wait at the gate!" cried the by now frantic and dishevelled figure of Daphne Blower, her perfectly applied makeup now streaked with running beads of perspiration, like the dendritic drainage on a steep Alpine slope.

To the receding sound of the fire bell, the invading horde from Somersby wound their way noisily down the hot and still desolate Nine Elms Lane towards Vauxhall tube, like a still-rampant but retreating army. As before, a group of well-behaved softies stuck close to the teachers for protection, laughing nervously among themselves while the mutinous majority bolted down the road towards the tube, hurling power-station literature in the air and the remains of once erotically-configured women now reduced to ripped fragments of their former selves like grubby pieces of a porno puzzle, a breast here a buttock there. Within a few minutes, Nine Elms Lane had been turned into a rubbish tip, strewn with white paper and coloured crotches, like a street that had never been swept.

The sound of a police siren could be heard coming from the direction of the power station. Michael, Harry and Daphne laughed out loud. They were past caring.

"Jesus H Christ!" exclaimed Harry, giggling uncontrollably like a naughty child at the scene of desolation before them. A wanton act of vandalism, gratuitously committed with gay abandon and swagger.

"Why do they behave like this?" wondered the naive, straight-out-of college, green-behind-the-ears but still gorgeous Ms Blower. Why indeed? And yet instead of feeling guilty or ashamed that the pupils had somehow let themselves and the school down, or feeling responsible for their antisocial behaviour, the teachers felt only relief. Freedom was just another word for nothing left to lose. In a Carry On sort of way it had been entertainment in the best tradition of Ealing comedy; tits, bums and innuendo.

When the exhausted army reached Vauxhall, it dawned on

them that they couldn't board a train without a teacher. Michael had deliberately held onto their tickets in order to exert at least some control over his control-averse charges. After taking the register to confirm that everyone was there, Michael led his group onto the platform. The artful dodger Greg Papadopoulos and his simple-minded disciples, being both dense and rebellious, missed the changeover at Oxford Circus and continued along the Victoria Line in the direction of Kings Cross. The remainder disembarked and propelled themselves like sewer-rats down the connecting tunnel to the Central Line, frightening the life out of terrified tourists and horrified commuters who were unfortunate enough to be coming the other way.

Five were now missing in action, but Michael was in no mood to wait. If Greg wanted to play silly buggers, so be it. He wasn't going to allow a few gormless idiots to derail the journey home. He didn't give a monkey's about Greg. In fact he fantasised about him being arrested for not having a ticket and thrown in jail.

As before, when the train to West Ruislip arrived, the softies loyally stayed with the teachers while the anarchists allowed themselves to be dispersed along the platform by the powerful headwind that preceded the train. The depleted party arrived at Greenford a little earlier than expected, due to their premature ejaculation from Battersea. A sort of *visitus interruptus*.

The children were dismissed from the station, even though it was only three o'clock. The last thing they wanted was to unleash forty-five high-as-kites kids back into the school before the last period of the day had finished.

As they walked along the dusty and strangely deserted Watersplash Lane towards Somersby High, the intrepid young trio of happy-go-lucky teachers were assailed by the ninety-degree oven heat of that scorching afternoon before the end of term. What a day.

Chapter 8

In his local pub that evening, Michael reflected on the day's events over a pint of Fuller's ESB. The Sussex Arms was one of those huge suburban ale houses so typical of London, with its black-beamed facade, a massive high-ceilinged lounge, a separate public bar with dart board and pool table and a spacious beer garden decked out with country-style wooden tables and chairs. He sat in his usual corner observing the packed room of summertime drinkers exuberantly celebrating the joys of being alive on such a lovely night. There were elderly married couples who'd been coming there for years, quietly imbibing a glass of gin or port, not needing to say much, having said it all years before; and beautiful young things getting high on each other and the elixir of youth, drinking in each other's company, the ever-present frisson of sexual energy and the pregnant possibility of passion to come.

The air was fragrant with the decadent musty smell of Kentish hops. Fuller's ESB was undoubtedly one of Western civilisation's greatest achievements. Extra special bitter was like no other beer; sweet honey-flavoured nectar, a powerful aphrodisiac that always made you feel good and left no aftertaste or hangover. It was like rocket fuel and was rumoured to have powered the Apollo Eleven mission to the moon. "The Eagle has landed, one small step for man, a giant step for Fuller's ESB." It was Michael's favourite tipple, infinitely more desirable than marijuana, and legal: extra strong, extremely sensual beer.

The ESB worked its magic, instantly refreshing his parts and crystallising his thoughts. How to make sense of the day? On one hand it had been an exhilarating experience, bordering on the surrealistic. How many professionals were paid good money to spend their time visiting the sights of London in the company of congenitally carefree children who were overflowing with a zest for life and an unquenchable craving for a good time? What he had experienced that day was better than any film or play, any novel or sitcom. Art was great, but never as great as the real thing with its spontaneity of performance, ad-libbing of lines, playing to the crowd utterly unscripted. What a day; travel, fun, chaos, laughter, confrontation, farce, a fire bell, porn, a chase, losing pupils. Priceless entertainment, even better than the Bash Street Kids. What a day.

On the other hand, he was supposed to be teaching these kids. He was responsible for their education, their future, their chances of getting a job. What had they learned today? Maybe how to negotiate the Tube and travel into London? But most were already streetwise. Maybe how to behave in public? But most already knew how to behave in public; they just chose not to on school trips. Maybe they had learned how a power station works and the historical importance of Battersea? But with all the distractions and disruption, that was highly unlikely. Michael thought back to his own childhood. Yes, he had mucked around on school trips and that youthful craving to have a good time was always present. But his class had instinctively known when to stop, and he could remember to this day the geology of Arran and the marine biology of Robin Hood's Bay, as well as the blue eyes of Diane Mapplethorpe and the scent of Anthea Macintosh.

He remembered the children of Botswana, still vividly clear in his mind. Again they had that universally youthful drive to have fun and play pranks and enjoy life. But my God, with none of the material comforts of suburban London kids, they had a passion for learning that infused their every waking action.

What would become of year four bottom set science? Would they somehow muddle through life, using their natural savvy and *chutzpah* to get a job? Would they go into their uncle's dodgy building businesses as many had imagined, or get an office job in one of the many international companies springing up in the capital? Or would their refusal to listen, their outlandish behaviour and their inability to learn, render them unemployable and consign them to the scrapheap? What would become of Greg or Donna or Ron Quigley? Was this really what he had come into teaching for? In Botswana he had wanted to change the world. Here the world was changing him.

Michael wandered up to the brass-banistered bar and ordered himself another pint of ESB. Through the corner of his eye he noticed the lovely smile of a blonde-haired German girl staring at him.

Chapter 9

Under the 1944 Education Act, every school was required by law to perform a daily act of collective Christian worship, although in keeping with Britain's tradition of religious freedom, there was an opt-out clause for those of different faith. In post-war Britain this was a largely uncontroversial issue, since virtually everyone was either a practising Christian or considered themselves to be nominally so; morning assembly was the norm. Even in Michael's day, the Jewish kids at Abingdon Grange were exempt from what they regarded as the corrupting influence of Christian worship, and instead of attending Gentile assemblies, they either mooched around noisily in a designated room until the preaching and hymn-singing was over or had to endure their own parallel Jewish assemblies in which the comical figure of Rabbi Kirschbaum tried unsuccessfully in an unintelligibly thick German accent to inspire his largely disinterested co-religionists.

By the mid-seventies, this law was being increasingly flouted in urban schools, where the rising number of immigrants or the children of immigrants from the Indian sub-continent made the plugging of the same old Christian message increasingly untenable. At the same time, the death of religion among the indigenous white population meant that fewer teachers had the heart or soul, or indeed the knowledge, to continue participating in a practice which they regarded as both irrelevant and outdated in a so-called multi-cultural society. So assemblies gradually morphed into "be-a-good-person" sessions, in which a teacher or group of children, often accompanied by music, would stand on stage and tell a story with a message. Moral fibre was good for you; it was the cure for spiritual constipation.

Each teacher interpreted the requirement for a daily act of worship in their own way. Some related a personal experience; others quoted a relevant passage from the scriptures and ended with a prayer.

Stuart Goldblatt, or "Stu the Jew" as he was affectionately known by his friends, was a special needs teacher who wore a black toupee that looked about to slip off his head. He was a political animal, a committed socialist and member of the Labour party, who believed, like Freud, that a child's behavioural problems were the result of insufficient love during childhood. He was convinced that kids who fucked around in class must be given the freedom to express themselves, because they had been deprived of the chance to play when young. This was typical of the muddled, wishy-washy thinking which was fashionable in his department at the time. As a result, the kids ran riot in his lessons. It was not unusual to see his pupils literally climbing out of the windows of his grubby, prefabricated special needs hut in a desperate attempt to escape his caring clutches.

"Michael," explained Stu philosophically, in his caricature of a Jewish wheeler-dealer Alf Garnet accent, gesticulating theatrically with his chubby hands, his large moist trouble-laden eyes peering through his thick myopic glasses, "they need more space than a conventional classroom can provide."

So it was no surprise that Stu, oblivious to the reality of classroom teaching and life as we know it, should give an assembly of unparalleled surreality. As he clambered on stage, a ripple of laughter spread through the crowd of two hundred restless thirteen-year-olds gathered in the hall.

Head of lower school Doug "fruit fizzer" Barratt had introduced Mr Goldblatt, who would be talking about this term's topic-citizenship. But Stu had other plans, or more precisely, no plans at all.

"I don't know whether you're familiar with Monty Python," said Stu with a supercilious grin on his over-confident face, turning to the staff at the side of the hall for approval, " but I'd like to play you an excerpt from my favourite episode, the "Dead Parrot" sketch. It's really funny."

Turning his back on the audience, Stu proceeded to fumble with a portable black tape recorder and cable, which he attempted to connect to a power point at the back of the stage.

"It won't take a minute," mumbled Stu obliviously, as he fast-forwarded the tape in order to get to the right place. It had not occurred to him to set the tape up in advance, and as he pressed play and then fast forward in order to locate the track, the increasingly impatient pupils became irritable and started to talk and muck around.

"Can you hear it at the back?" enquired Stu, still not sure where the parrot sketch episode was, or indeed whether he'd brought the right tape. He piddled around as if he were at home in his own room alone.

"No!" screamed the back row, warming to the mounting confusion. They could sniff out a cock-up with all the promise of chaos from a distance of ten kilometres, like a shark detecting a molecule of blood in the ocean. He had forgotten to connect the recorder to an amplifier, so the assembly had to rely on the machine's own, pathetic, inbuilt speaker.

Eventually Stu was ready. He pressed the play button, sat down next to the tape recorder facing the assembly, and said: "Just listen to this."

The restive crowd continued to talk and giggle amongst

themselves, as the barely audible crackly tape started up. It was like listening to Radio Luxembourg under the pillow.

John Cleese: "I wish to complain about this parrot what I purchased not half an hour ago from this very boutique."

Michael Palin: "Oh yes, the, uh, the Norwegian Blue. What's, uh... What's wrong with it?"

Stu began to chortle, with that knowing look of someone in the possession of a superior truth who's seen the light. The kids continued talking.

John Cleese: "I'll tell you what's wrong with it, my lad. 'E's dead, that's what's wrong with it!"

Michael Palin: "No, no, 'e's uh... he's resting."

John Cleese: "Look, matey, I know a dead parrot when I see one, and I'm looking at one right now."

Stu chortled uncontrollably to himself, barely able to suppress the urge to laugh out loud, tears running down his pleasurably contorted face. Doug shuffled uncomfortably on his chair, but kept a straight head of year's face. Michael looked on incredulously, barely able to suppress his own need to scream with laughter at the surreal spectacle unfolding before him. Did Stu not realise that the children had probably never heard of Monty Python, never mind the 1969 Dead Parrot sketch? Barney grinned at Sammy Bell, whose normally watery doggy eyes were on full flood alert.

Michael Palin: "No no he's not dead, he's, he's restin'! Remarkable bird, the Norwegian Blue, idn'it, ay? Beautiful plumage!"

John Cleese: "'E's not pinin'! 'E's passed on! This parrot is no more! He has ceased to be! 'E's expired and gone to meet 'is maker! 'E's a stiff! Bereft of life, 'e rests in peace! If you hadn't nailed 'im to the perch 'e'd be pushing up the daisies! 'Is metabolic processes are now 'istory! 'E's off the twig! 'E's kicked the bucket, 'e's shuffled off 'is mortal coil, run down the curtain and joined the bleedin' choir invisible!! THIS IS AN EX-PARROT!!!"

Doug tapped his watch nervously, trying to alert Stu of the need to finish; but too late, the bell went. Two hundred thirteen-year-olds simultaneously stood up and began to leave the hall. The chant of "Goldblatt's a wanker," emanated from a mob in the vicinity of young Billy Keanon and his twin brother Kieren.

"What a knob," mumbled John Levin into his hand, "what a fucking knob."

So much for citizenship.

At the other end of the assembly spectrum was Mrs Barnes. As the headmistress of this august exemplar of Western civilisation, Brenda Barnes was expected to lead by example and give weekly assemblies. Like most heads, she was fired by a combination of religious conviction and the vocation to create a better world in her own image-like God. She had a mentally-handicapped son and had recently lost her devoted husband Henry, who had in every sense been the centre of her life and the person who had given it most meaning. As is so often the case, personal loss and misfortune can strengthen one's resolve to get immersed in society, either as a means of forgetting or as a means of replacing unrequited love or the love of the deceased with the love of others. It was a therapy to dispel loneliness through doing good, and like most do-gooders, she meant well.

Her Church of England upbringing had taught her that there is good in everyone, and as a consequence, she fostered a benign view of the children at Somersby High, who she referred to as her "little lambs". Like Jesus, she believed that every individual could be redeemed and saved from his sins; but if not, her loyal deputy Bruce Trimmer, would slipper them. Brenda was a rather sad and lonely middle-aged lady, who needed the adulation of both teachers and pupils. School was her life.

She stood up to address the sixth form. They were like an island of sanity in a stormy sea of madness; in her eyes beautiful young adults. At least here were a group of relatively sane and intelligent students, who had actually chosen to stay on and do their A-levels, with a view of going to university; in stark contrast to the rebellious, bloody-minded riff-raff that populated the nether regions of the school and made everyone's life hell. Her face was, as always, heavily made up to paper over the cracks of sorrow that life had dealt her. She looked like a giant cuddly toy in her thick tweed skirt, high leather boots, and a fluffy light blue lambswool pullover on which was pinned a brooch she had inherited from her grandmother.

"My little lambs," she began, her warm motherly face surveying a hundred pairs of seriously bemused sixth-form eyes. "It's so lovely to see you all looking so smart and well turned out." Brenda believed in praising her flock.

The rustle of amused but non-confrontational shuffling rippled across the school hall. It was a bit like being hugged by your granny, being suffocated by one of her slobbering kisses; you knew that she loved you.

"As I was driving to school this morning, I thought to myself, like Louis Armstrong, 'What a wonderful world.' After a spring shower, the sun was once again shining on the wet glistening streets, like a painting from Constable but with houses instead of oak trees. My car radio was playing the fourth movement of Beethoven's Pastoral symphony, which exquisitely depicts the beauty of nature and its endless capacity to renew itself after a storm cleaner and fresher than before. You can smell the blossom and hear the birdsong in his music."

The pupils were silent now, unsure how to react to this touching but strangely disturbing performance by their headmistress. Mrs Barnes's moist eyes and rapturous smile revealed a solitary messianic figure in a trancelike state of quasi-religious otherworldliness. She lovingly stared at the field of little lambs in front of her, blissfully frolicking in the sunshine of her imagination.

"As Jesus said to the crowd," continued the head, quoting from the Sermon on the Mount:

"Blessed are the poor in spirit,
for theirs is the kingdom of heaven.
Blessed are those who mourn,

for they will be comforted.
Blessed are the meek,
for they will inherit the earth.
Blessed are those who hunger and thirst for righteousness,
for they will be filled."

"God loves us all my little lambs, and we in turn should love *Him* and each other. There is so much good in the world. When you leave today's assembly, I want you to feel the power of the Lord and how good it is to be alive."

Like a Shakespearean actor after delivering a gut-wrenching soliloquy, Mrs Barnes silently left the stage, a frail, tortured figure carrying the suffering of mankind on her shoulders like Jesus of Nazareth, immediately followed by her trusty servant and bodyguard, Mr Trimmer.

The assembly was over. The sixth-formers filed out of the hall in their smart suits and tasteful costumes to face another day of learning at the Somersby academy. All this talk of God and religion and the wonderful world we live in – was she a bit simple or just plain bonkers? Nobody believed this guff about God anymore. There had been race riots at the Notting Hill Carnival, Arabs and Israelis were busy killing each other, and the unions were holding the country to ransom. Where was this mythical world?

Michael reflected. What influence did Mrs Barnes have on the sixth form? How effective were her assemblies in strengthening moral fibre and relieving the spiritual constipation of savvy, streetwise, seventeen - and eighteen-year-olds? Did they dismiss her as a batty old eccentric, an irrelevance, a sad and senile throwback to another age whose wishy-washy ideas were utterly out of touch with their world? Did she have no effect whatsoever on them, her heartfelt words going in one ear and out the other? Or did her childlike faith in humanity, her smile, her simple kindness, make them feel better about themselves? Was it the age-old problem of the preacher or teacher or loving parent trying to save the young from themselves, hoping against hope that they will choose the right path in what they know from experience is a life riddled with temptation and danger?

In spite of Mrs Barnes's commitment to the now fashionable forces of progressive, more liberal teaching, the school could not function without a strong, no-nonsense old-school deputy like Alan Stills. He was a salt-of-the-earth working-class east Londoner who had risen from the modest confines of a Barking council estate to achieve his ambition of becoming a deputy head. He was always clean shaven, and wore a dark suit and tie as the professional working classes always did – a sign of respect for traditional values and common decency. And it was this sense of decency and fair play that made him so unique and indispensable.

He had the air of the local bobby, a *Dixon of Dock Green* character whose mere presence and stature reassured everyone from the headmistress down to the most insignificant pupil and helped diffuse conflict, present or intended. In spite of his natural tendency to rebel against authority and men in suits in particular, Michael was immensely grateful for the calming, father-like influence of old Stillsy. How many times had he bailed him out of hair-raising situations in the classroom? He had the common touch, and was equally at ease talking to teachers and pupils alike. He even joined in staff cricket matches. Like so many school deputies, Stillsy was an ex-PE teacher, but unlike some of that persuasion, exercised a compassionate rather than an authoritarian control. Virtually everybody liked and respected him. Even the serial truants and trouble-makers had a grudging admiration for Mr Stills, much as petty criminals have a grudging respect for the policeman who shopped them. "Fair cop guv'nor." Only irredeemable swine, scumbags like Dave Short, hated him; although they too would probably view him fondly when older – if they ever got old.

And so it was the greatest of catastrophes when Stillsy was killed in a motorcycle accident. Mrs Barnes called a staff meeting to announce his passing, and as she stood there, eyes swollen and red with sorrow, streaming tears cutting deep gorges through thick layers of makeup on her contorted face like rivers slicing through ancient geological strata, flanked only by her Swiss Guard of Bruce Trimmer and Maureen Blundell, but not Alan Stills, she resembled a bereaved child unable to comprehend the loss of a parent. It was a truly moving sight, like a newborn lamb bleating and abandoned by its mother. It was hard to believe that this crushed, lifeless shadow of a woman was the headmistress of a London comprehensive school.

"Alan would have wanted us to continue without making a fuss," said Brenda in a quiet, pathos-ridden voice, appealing for visual support from the sea of salt-stained eyes in the staff room. "Lessons will run as normal as a tribute to his dedication to this school. Alan never had a day off in his life, and nor shall we."

Michael was saddened by Brenda's stoical, martyr-like, stiff-upper-lip response. How could we just carry on as normal? Just because Stillsy didn't like making a fuss it didn't mean that we should passively accept his death as if nothing had happened. If you couldn't make a fuss about such a man, a titan who had held the school together and was loved even by those who had never loved before, what was the point of having feelings at all? The British stiff upper lip had its limitations; carrying on as normal was the last thing we should be doing. Mrs Barnes's innate inability to break down, rend her clothes asunder and shout "Alan why have you forsaken me?" should not be the yardstick by which we determine our own emotions.

In the Red Lion that evening, Michael sat alone with only a pint of bitter and a packet of cheese and onion crisps for company and reflected on the life of Alan Stills. How could a man spend his whole career at a place like Somersby without going crazy or becoming deeply cynical? How could a man get up each morning for thirty years in the full knowledge that each day would be a never-ending circus of disturbed and unruly kids whose adolescent antics and outbursts he was meant to diffuse; classroom incidents, fire alarms, hoses, fights, teachers who couldn't cope, rape and pillage, gratuitous violence and vandalism? Or was that the attraction – the thrill of the chase? Had it always been like this, or had he become stranded like a beached whale at high tide, in a school whose original ethos had been decimated by the ravages of great social upheaval, that no longer resembled the one he had joined as a young man? How did he cope with the wishy-washy, new-age vision of Mrs Barnes, so different to his own, and her high-octane emotional demands and inherent instability? And what drove him? Was it religion, altruism, a sense of social responsibility, a wish to create a better world – or just habit? Where would he, a young idealistic teacher at the beginning of his career with a zest for life and a love of children, be in thirty years' time?

One thing he knew for sure: a man like Alan Stills gave him hope rather than despair; he was the very antithesis of cynicism and hopelessness. He showed that brave warriors can still make a difference to the lives of ordinary suburban children. Michael raised his half-empty glass of beer, which now seemed strangely half full, and toasted the deceased but never forgotten Alan Stills: "Stillsy, I knew him well."

Chapter 10

Michael's time at Somersby High was coming to an end. He had spent five years of his life – more time than in any previous job – at the same school. When he had first arrived on that dull pre-Christmas afternoon in 1974, he had never imagined he would spend five years there. In those days five years was an eternity; you lived your life in short bursts – a year in Israel, two years in Botswana – making sure you didn't get tied down in one spot or with one person. You didn't want to restrict your options, have your style cramped, have your escape routes blocked by committing yourself to anything or anyone, and getting stuck in a rut like all those other sad bastards who had left university at twenty-one and were now unhappily married with babies, slaves of the rat race. The "c" word was not for the likes of a passionate lover of freedom like Michael. Looking back, it was amazing how fast those years had gone; the old adage that life goes faster as you got older – something to do with Einstein's theory of relativity, he thought – certainly seemed to hold true. Why was it that so many familiar adages seemed to come true, despite being old, and therefore surely crap? He was only thirty, so there was still lots of time and exciting new people and places ahead of him. But for the first time in his life, he could sense the clock ticking.

Teaching had been so different in London. He had flown in from Johannesburg full of third-worldly wisdom after two of the most exhilarating years of his life in a picture-book African village, and been thrown like a Christian into the lion's den that was Somersby. He had been seriously mauled at first, and it had been touch and go as to whether he would survive. But once he'd learned how to tame the beasts, ingratiate himself with them, do a deal with them, it became possible to control them and even teach them.

At first he had been overwhelmed, like a naive country boy unable to cope with life in the city. He had never met such wild kids before. He had read about them, seen them on telly, encountered them and tried to avoid them whilst walking down the Headrow in Leeds, been in fear of them at football matches, on the buses, on trains; but never in his wildest dreams did he imagine he would one day have to teach them, tame them, spend every working day for five years with them.

But as he tamed them they tamed him, and in a perverse kind of way he started to like them. After the shock of that first week when they had rampaged in and out of his science lesson, stolen his dinner money, graffitied his desks and called him a wanker, his initial despair and cynicism had given way to the sort of rapport that develops whenever people are together long enough and get to know each other; Stockholm syndrome. True, Michael still resented the sheer bloody-mindedness of the "unteachables", the crooks, the liars, the petit-thieves that made up the lowest caste of Homo *somersbyus*, but gradually he had learned to like them. He would certainly miss their cheeky little faces, just as he had done in Botswana – although because of their greater worldliness and lesser dependence on him for their survival, perhaps not as paternally.

Clearly Botswana had been the exception, not the rule, like a secure and loving childhood that could never return. Teaching in

British state schools was a hair-raising experience, but real for all that. There was no use looking back at the good old days or living in the past. The laws of natural selection determined that it was the survival of the fittest. You had to swim or sink, kill or be killed, adapt or face pedagogical extinction. He had certainly got through to some of these streetwise west-London kids. As in Botswana, he had enriched the quality of their lives, as they had his. That's what happens in teaching; kids are kids wherever they are. With others he had failed to penetrate their teacher-resistant carapace of blag and bluster and sheer white working-class indolence and bloody-mindedness.

But Michael had the impression that they would survive in spite of him. There were enough money-up-front, cash-in-hand, no-questions-asked jobs in the London underworld economy to absorb these chancers, these wheeler-dealers, these Jack the Lads.

In Botswana, his youthful idealism and unquenchable zeal to change the world had propelled him through each day; if a man is not a socialist by the time he is twenty, he has no heart. He had subconsciously set out to dispel the negative myths of the "white man's burden" by engaging with Africans as equals. His mission was both political and humanitarian. He was clear in his own mind that he could play his part in breaking down the centuries-old barriers between black and white and in some way compensate, assuage his guilt for the years of European exploitation and discrimination and slavery. He was even convinced that he was doing his bit to help undermine apartheid by showing that not all whites were arrogant, race-obsessed bastards like those over the border in the Republic of South Africa.

These were the stratospheric moral aspirations that only a starry-eyed young idealist with no experience of life could ever dream of entertaining. But at the time he was in no doubt that his teaching science to black children at Moketse would enrich their lives and give them a better chance of survival, a greater sense of self-worth. He had set out to improve the lot of the underdog – the black man – and believed that he had largely succeeded. Only time would tell whether his fleeting two years in their midst had made any difference, whether fate would give life a sporting chance of working out well. We have a limitless capacity to delude ourselves that we are more important than we really are. The important thing was that Michael had been motivated to making a difference, and the feedback from the eyes of those loving children told him that he had. His love had been requited.

The situation at Somersby had been more complex. In Africa, the gentle, barefoot, mud-hut dwelling Batswana, had craved education, had loved learning, had come back for more. Here the descendants of slaves, taken to Jamaica in the nineteenth century and returned on the *Windrush* to the land of the slave trader – the black West Indians – were extremely difficult to teach. This was unrequited love, which on its journey through sadness and despair had morphed into cynicism – as it does. Luckily the fun-loving camaraderie of his sport-playing, beer-swilling, piss-taking colleagues had rescued him in time: the social life of the staff room had become more important than the teaching. In truth, Michael had never been a natural cynic or a pessimist, and unlike some of his contemporaries who wallowed in their own sense of impotence and hopelessness, he had adapted and still managed to salvage some of the passion that had driven him into teaching in the first place. He would not be so easily ousted.

But equally he was not the same as when he had flown out of Gaborone on that hot and sultry December afternoon in 1974. Whether it was the acid test of reality or just age, he had, like many teachers before him, become more right wing. His views on such issues as discipline had become less "enlightened" and he was increasingly suspicious of what he now considered wishy-washy views on multiculturalism and the deification of the working classes. For the first time he wondered whether he would still be voting Labour in the next election, and what the exact point of the increasingly Bolshevik, solipsistic and irrelevant NUT and NAS/UWT teaching unions was.

Michael still liked being a teacher, but he had taken a knock, had been wounded in battle; for the first time he questioned whether he was in the right profession. Either way it was time to move on. He had applied and been accepted for a job at a relatively new, purpose-built comprehensive in the west London borough of Hestwell; the Beechwood School.

PART 3

Beechwood

Chapter 1

The Beechwood School stood at the edge of Hestwell Heath, next to a golden-domed mosque, and was in the direct flight path of a never-ending stream of planes landing at Heathrow, just a couple of miles away. You flew over it on your way to the airport. From the outside, the school looked like a giant lump of concrete that had been dumped by some extra-terrestrial fly-tipper when no one was looking. It had a South Bank look about it, as if a concrete iceberg had broken off London's flagship arts centre on the Thames and somehow drifted westwards into Hestwell, leaving the Royal Festival Hall and National Theatre behind; whether it embodied the same rarefied cultural values was another matter.

Rumour had it that the school had once been used as a set for an episode of *Dr Who*. Some said it resembled one of those hideous conceptual art installations that regularly win the Turner prize at the Tate; others mistook it for a new factory or a prison even. It was impossible not to notice it or have an opinion about it. To Michael, it was like no other school he had ever seen, and it was the wacky, in-your-face appearance of this emporium of knowledge that had made him want to teach there.

And the headmaster, Godfrey Burns. Burns was like no other headmaster he'd ever met. A pain in the local authority's arse, he was a short, spectacled, impeccably-dressed man in a suit with penetratingly intelligent eyes, who looked as if he'd been born fully formed without ever having to go through the somewhat unsavoury business of childhood and adolescence. He exuded Jewishness, and looked like a cross between Bernard Levin, Henry Kissinger and Groucho Marks. Godfrey was an Oxbridge man through and through, whose loyalty to his alma mater, Jesus College Oxford, was like a nineteenth century hussar's allegiance to his regiment.

At his interview, Burns had introduced himself with the maxim inscribed on the forecourt of the Temple of Apollo at Delphi, "*Gnothi seauton*"; know yourself. He described himself as an ancient Greek in modern clothing, a student of the school of Athens to whose classical values he was unflinchingly committed. He probably had pictures of Plato and Socrates on his wall at home, if such people did such mundane things as decorating their walls. Michael could see why Godfrey was regarded by many in Hestwell as an eccentric crank. His razor-sharp views on education were diametrically opposed to the woolly, wishy-washy educational establishment of the day, espoused by well-meaning characters like Mrs Barnes. He used words like "intellectual rigour" and "academic excellence", which sent many of his contemporaries scurrying for the nearest copy of *Bloom's Taxonomy* and a swig of chardonnay, lest their anti-elitist, half-baked theories on pupil-centred learning and inclusiveness, be exposed as so much utopian ephemera. Uttar Pradesh.

Michael admired his *chutzpah*. How refreshing to meet someone who was so unashamedly intellectual, who actually had a profound view on education that embraced the great philosophers and thinkers of ancient Greece, who talked freely about such mind-bogglingly interesting subjects as the human condition and the state of our civilisation. He was probably the only state school head teacher in London who unapologetically relished the election of Maggie Thatcher – regarded by the left as Satan – to Number 10 in 1979, and admired all she stood for. Godfrey obviously enjoyed his pariah status in the borough, taking great delight in dismembering philosophically inferior opponents, who he contemptuously described in public as intellectual pigmies. And this included the whole leadership of the local authority. The man had gravitas. In so many ways Michael had found a kindred spirit: Burns was a classically educated version of himself.

The intake of Beechwood was overwhelmingly Asian; although Hestwell was quite a mixed borough, it looked like a ghetto school. This was not helped by the presence of a huge mosque next door, which attracted a continuous stream of pious-looking bearded men in white shrouds and prayer caps attending worship five times a day. On Fridays or on holy days like *Eid*, the approach roads to the mosque and the shared access with the school were completely blocked by throngs of devout worshippers coming to pay their respects to Allah. After prayers, zealots defiantly distributed leaflets by the radical Islamic group Hizb ut-Tahrir, who regarded all infidels as *haram*, and yearned for a return to the golden age of the Islamic caliphate, when *sharia* law ensured an equitable allocation of beheadings and the total subjugation of women. At such times, Barrington Road was more reminiscent of downtown Karachi than a suburb of west London.

In spite of this, race relations at the school were allegedly good. There were approximately equal numbers of Muslims, Sikhs and Hindus, with a small percentage of indigenous whites holding the balance of power. The whites consisted of two types: working-class kids, increasingly referred to in the tabloids as white trash, whose attainment was very low, like those Michael had met at Somersby; and white middle-class kids, whose parents had deliberately sent them to Beechwood as an act of faith in the comprehensive system and the philosophy of multiculturalism. They attained high grades and often ended up at Oxbridge.

In comparison to Somersby, the teachers at Beechwood were overwhelmingly young, well dressed and disturbingly high-powered. At his first staff meeting at the beginning of term, Michael was amazed by the calibre of debate that took place and the quality of the questions asked. He got the distinct impression that these feisty, overtly ambitious teachers, were vying with each other to impress their guru Godfrey Burns, who smiled and nodded his head knowingly when a point to his liking had been made, mouthing the word "exactly". Were they a sad set of sycophants, shamelessly trying to ingratiate themselves with the head and kiss his Jesus College Oxford arse, or were they genuinely interested in exploring the finer points of education and pedagogy? A staff meeting where stimulating discussion actually took place and the audience didn't die of boredom? This was not something he'd ever experienced before – but it did excite him.

The school building was like a giant labyrinth, consisting of three floors and a colour-coded system of corridors and rooms. In those first days of the autumn of nineteen eighty, when Michael got lost several times a day, the pupils and staff seemed to be wandering around in a state of perpetual Brownian Motion, which was obviously the best way of getting about. Eventually, according to the laws of thermodynamics, a random particle would go where you wanted it to go and enter or leave a classroom. Michael was amazed by how civilised the place was; kids waiting patiently outside doors, walking, not rampaging, up or down the stairs. At no time did he feel he was going to get mugged or abused. There were no shouts of "Zabinsky, you wanker", no high-risk, no-go areas like the Bermuda Triangle, or endless corridors where pupils could run and scream and let off fire extinguishers at will. What a strange place.

When the children finally arrived in school the day after the staff meeting, Michael was allocated his new tutor group; Seven Engels – in contrast to Somersby, a year seven to thirteen system operated here. Each tutor group was named after a famous person who had supposedly once lived in Hestwell. Apparently the great

Thomas Gainsborough used to walk his pet poodle on Hestwell Heath, no doubt seeking inspiration for his next masterpiece. Other groups were named after Einstein (Albert), Shelley (Percy) and Constable (John); all very different from 3X4 or 5L1. There was no messing around here, as the school mission statement, "The pursuit of excellence", proudly declared. It appeared on every official notice and publication, at the school gates and even on the headmaster's backside, it was said, and was mercilessly lampooned at every prize giving.

Chapter 2

From the moment he first stepped into a classroom at the Beechwood School, Michael realised he was somewhere special. At interview he was only interested in getting a new job on a higher pay scale, and only vaguely aware of what he was letting himself in for. He remembered being asked some politically-loaded question by Ms Loads, one of the many deputies who seemed to inhabit this place, on how he proposed to teach female pupils, and a question by Mr Burns on what he thought about cricket. But in the surrealistic atmosphere that inevitably surrounds a day being interviewed in a strange place by slightly odd people he could have no idea just how different, and in many ways unique, this place this really was.

For a start, the science department occupied the whole third floor of the school, so there would be no more traipsing along miles of desolate corridors pursued by hunting packs of feral children in search of their daily diet of grilled teacher and sautéed potatoes. When he arrived outside the door of his new lab, 300P, his general science class, 9B1, a top set of thirteen-year-olds, was waiting quietly outside the room in a straight line. This struck him as strange, a bit formal even. Since when did pupils wait quietly outside a classroom? Why weren't they fighting or letting off fire extinguishers, or farting loudly and having a laugh? Michael walked to the front of the lab and invited his class to come in and sit down. Except that they didn't sit down, nor did they rampage around the room committing gratuitous acts of vandalism. They remained standing.

"Good morning everybody," said Michael surveying the array of young faces staring respectfully at him. "I'm your new science teacher, Mr Zabinsky. Please sit down."

This was almost like being back in Botswana, Michael thought. There must be a catch; children don't behave like this in Britain. He began to call out the register.

"Mohammed, Sanjay, Kuljit, Cheryl, Jason."

"Yes sir." "Here sir." The faces were overwhelmingly Asian; clear brown-skinned complexions, a few turbans, a few hijabs, the occasional jet-black African face, an embryonic Rastafarian mop of Bob Marley dreadlocks, a few blonde girls and ginger boys. Michael reckoned that most of the children were of Pakistani or Indian origin; the Africans could have been from Somalia (tall and thin, a hint of Arabia) or maybe Nigeria (very black); he couldn't tell. There were also a few mixed-race, lighter coloured, freshly minted golden complexions. Another strange thing was the smart nature of their school uniform – very different from the crumpled, went-to-bed-in-my-clothes, so-what-if-I-did style of the Somersbians.

"Knowwhatamean?"

"Who knows why we study science?" asked Michael tentatively, a question which he thought was a good way of getting to know the pupils and gauging their knowledge of, and interest in, the subject.

An immediate forest of hands.

"It's to help explain the universe sir," explained Rajesh, a precocious-looking boy with a bad case of acne on the front row.

"It's to help us go to university and get a good job sir," opined

Saira, a plump girl on the middle row wearing a black hijab and radiating a kindly smile across her huge oval face.

"It's to do experiments and invent things and learn about Einstein and Charles Darwin," suggested Grace, an attractively presented West Indian girl at the back.

Michael nodded his head and exaggeratedly pursed his lips to show that he was well impressed by the enthusiasm of the class and the quality of their answers. Respect! This was unlike Somersby, where he'd have received a barrage of wise-guy remarks alluding to the male or female genitalia; but also unlike Botswana, where for reasons of cultural deference, the class would have been reluctant to readily volunteer their opinions. This was good stuff. He felt a frisson of excitement at the realisation that he might actually be able to do some teaching here. How strange.

Chapter 3

Every school has its local pub, a watering hole where teachers gather to drown their sorrows, have a nibble or chat up members of the opposite sex. For some the pub was a means of delaying going home to an empty flat or a nagging spouse; a sort of sanctuary, a departure lounge for a later plane.

From the outside, The Plough looked like a bog-standard suburban local, with an olde-worlde facade, poky car park and adjoining beer garden. But there was nothing ordinary about this pub. It was a house of freaks, a club where only those covered in grotesque tattoos and with a previous or preferably current criminal record need apply. And in an overwhelmingly Asian neighbourhood, its clientele – a pompous word if ever there was one for the misfits who drank and fornicated here – were overwhelming white. They belonged to the burgeoning white underclass, that rump of uneducable freeloaders left behind by the Thatcher revolution, for whom the ladder of social mobility – if it had ever existed – had not only been withdrawn, but vindictively cast aside, chopped into firewood and burned on the funeral pyre of a welfare dependency they were unable to escape. They sat in family groups, clans of toothless no-hopers, fag-ends of society, drinking themselves into oblivion, chain-smoking themselves into an early grave which the state would have to pay for. They were usually accompanied by a slobbering, flea-infested dog or two and feral children, Dickensian throwbacks from *Oliver Twist*, who chased each other between the tables, scavenging crisps and pork scratchings from the filthy floor. In summer they would sit outside in the beer garden, women with children by four different boyfriends and their itinerant feckless menfolk, while their wild uncouth offspring urinated on what remained of the grass and smashed up the hanging baskets of flowers. Nice people.

At the end of his first week at Beechwood, Michael sat observing the squalid scene from a vantage point near a window overlooking Barrington Road and the school beyond, like an anthropologist marvelling at the behaviour of a species hitherto believed to be extinct. The ceiling and walls were nicotine yellow, being liberally coated in a thick layer of carcinogenic tar that had accumulated over the millennia and long since obliterated the original Etruscan frescos. The "naff seventy-five" upholstery was similarly decrepit, torn and faded, bearing the ancient stains of cheap beer, saliva and other bodily fluids too disgusting to mention.

There was a "Functions Room" where up to fifty dysfunctional dropouts could celebrate family gatherings at the taxpayers' expense, and a public bar where wild-looking Neanderthals with earrings and long hair shouted abuse at each other and cursed the day they were born to the sound of billiard balls crashing into each other like rocks against skulls. "Chelsea, you cunts!" "We are the West Ham, wankers!"

Michael approached the bar and ordered a pint of Fullers' London Pride from the grotesquely tattooed barman Darryl, whose broken nose and black eye told its own story of human degradation and depravity. He was on probation after being sentenced to eighteen months at the Scrubs for throwing a brick at a policeman down Millwall, as you do. Like many pubs, The Plough sold amazingly cheap pub grub, cooked in the twice-condemned kitchen for "unhygienic practices" – mice, cockroaches, dog excrement – to pull in the punters, and for two pounds fifty you could get a giant burger and chips with mushy peas, fried, it was said, in the bodily fluids of the landlord's wife Tracey. Nice. "You awroyt Darryl?"

Being surrounded by all this filth and squalor made Michael feel superior, like standing with the working classes on the football terraces of Elland Road in the Sixties. And this was the attraction of the pub – one felt a messianic calling to save these people, like a prophet, like Jesus, put on this earth to save the needy, the destitute, society's rejected human flotsam, so that the meek could inherit the earth. He was the "chosen one", put on this earth to teach the illegitimate issue of their loins. He was their saviour. "Hallelujah brothers!"

And yet, just as the first mammals scurried around furtively in the Jurassic undergrowth, biding their time until the dinosaurs became extinct and they would have their day, so a family, the Peacock family, could be seen on Friday evenings with their daughter Elizabeth and little boy Mathew sipping beer and coke, eating crisps, stroking their dog, fraternising even with the great tattooed unwashed in The Plough. Mrs Peacock had the classical features of a women whose husband beat her for a laugh when he got bored, as you do; flat face like the back end of a bus, prematurely thinning wiry hair, cigarette hanging from a spittle-encrusted lower lip, wide vacant eyes, looking every bit like Andy Capp's wife Flo. Mr Peacock, like most of these underclass types, resembled one of the Mitchell brothers from *East Enders* – bald as a coot, muscular tattooed arms protruding from a skin-tight Iron Maiden T-shirt, the look of a man looking for a fight imprinted on his thickset, square, ape-like face.

It is easy and indeed hugely satisfying to wallow in the exaggerated caricatures or stereotypes of identifiable groups of people, which more often than not have a ring of truth about them and form the basis of the characters that populate most comedy, theatre and literature. Indeed we couldn't survive without creating stereotypes. If a couple of tattooed drunkards approach you on a Saturday night, the odds are they're going to kick the shit out of you. But we all know of exceptions. What we object to is not stereotypes per say, but *negative* stereotypes. It's fine to admire a Welshman's legendary, that is stereotypical, ability to sing, but uncharitable to describe him as a "Welsh windbag". Mr and Mrs Peacock were in fact, loving, caring parents, whose daughter Elizabeth would become one of the brightest girls Beechwood had ever produced, winning an international debating competition in Salt Lake City and ending up studying English and American literature at Harvard. On closer inspection Elizabeth's parents had kind, considerate eyes and a certain working-class beauty; like most of us, they couldn't help being the way they were.

Chapter 4

Michael knew that the best way to win over a class and enthuse them with a love of science was to stage a spectacular, hands-on lesson in the first week of term. And he knew from his days at Moketse that looking at leaf litter – the annual dump of leaves beneath a tree – was a sure way of doing this. As a teacher he had never lost his drive to take risks, try out new things, go where no man had gone before, even if it meant failure and looking a complete ass in front of the class. That was the only way you grew and developed and became exceptional. And he knew that this lesson worked on every age group and with all abilities – you were never too old or too clever to look at a pile of rotting leaves.

In his first week at the school, Michael had noticed that the playground and the vast school fields were bordered by trees – oak, hawthorn, sycamore – whose annual shedding of deciduous leaves produced a thick carpet of organic matter. Rummaging under the trees at seven-thirty on a still warm September morning in his first term, Michael collected a bin liner full of debris, ripping his hands on bramble thorns and tearing his trousers as he did so.

So when his new bottom set year seven group, 7S4, turned up for their second lesson of term, they were greeted by empty plastic trays on their desks. Miriam, a huge Somali girl wearing a loose black headscarf-cum-shawl, with giant glasses projecting at an ungainly angle from her invisible ears and big enough to be mistaken for a sixth former if it weren't for her round makeup-free baby face, looked disappointed. She loved science but could not see the point in plastic trays. Michael explained that trees were the world's biggest litter louts, always had been, and that the children were going to play at being detectives. Instead of looking for criminals, they would be looking for creatures.

The class split up into groups of four and were supplied with a hand lens and forceps – tweezers to you and me – and a key to identify the creepy-crawlies they might find. They were also given a choice chamber in which to impound those creatures unfortunate enough to be captured until they could be brought before a court and charges preferred. Michael came round with his sack of leaf litter, playing to the gallery like Father Christmas distributing his presents and giving each group a huge helping of leaves, twigs and assorted invertebrates.

It took precisely two seconds before the first squeal of excitement. Khadijah's group had discovered a giant, wiggly, amber-coloured centipede, which proceeded to wriggle its way irregularly across the table and plunge recklessly to the floor. "Heeeeeeeeeelp!"

Almost immediately after, Alfie's group discovered a spider and a woodlouse. Everybody discovered a woodlouse – they were as common as the muck they lived in. Michael, now in his element and in full theatrical mode, wandered through the class visiting each group and subjecting the bamboozled children to rigorous Socratic questioning.

"What's an invertebrate, what's an arthropod?" "Why is the litter so full of creatures?" "What's in it for them?" "Why is leaf litter so good for the soil?" "What does biodegradable mean?" "What happens to the leaves once they drop off the tree?" "What do we mean by mean?" The kids didn't get the Monty Python joke, but he did and thought it bloody hilarious.

Michael stood back and watched the class's reaction to the leaf litter. As always the boys reacted differently from the girls, each fulfilling their preordained gender stereotype. The boys – loud and raucous, mucking around, conflating learning with play – left no leaf unturned but never once used their key to classify a creature or recorded anything in their books, preferring to pick up spiders with their bare hands and put them on girls' jackets, or wander around visiting other groups and stealing their lenses. The girls by contrast, sat down, meticulously placing each animal in the choice chamber and using the key to identify it, making notes and drawing diagrams, some screaming and screeching and becoming hysterical. Were these differences nature or nurture? Was there any point in trying to change them? Were all attempts to socially engineer them to be otherwise doomed to failure?

But the greatest thrill was seeing the sheer joy and excitement in their eyes – every child was actively engaged. Some were scared, but none were bored. And the fact that this was a bottom set mattered not a jot; the immaturity often associated with such groups enabled them to use their as yet unsuppressed childish inquisitiveness. Education = more curiosity squared, and young children are the only true scientists. Discuss.

When the bell went for break, 7S4 didn't hear the ringing above the cacophony of cognitive chatter. They could have gone on forever. Every kid had learned something. Even the semi-literate Alfie Pinkerton, whose parents spent more time supping ale in The Plough than looking after him, and whose utter frustration at being unable to read or write often erupted into anger and violence, learned that leaf litter is heaving with invertebrate life, connected by something called a "food chain". Little Sara, who was usually too shy to ask or answer a question in lessons, was able to explain to the class – yes, the whole class – the difference between a mollusc and an insect. Once again Michael wondered who got more pleasure out his lessons; the kids who learned so much, or the teacher who experienced the satisfaction of seeing them learn. It was just like being back in Botswana.

Chapter 5

The "Thank God It's Friday" club met, as you might expect, every Friday, and was an excuse for members of the science department and their guests to celebrate the weekend over a glass of wine or three and put the world to rights. In winter the club was held in one of the labs, where beakers that only an hour before had been awash with sulphuric acid or cyclohexane were used to sip Pinot Grigio or whatever cheap plonk was on offer that evening. Sometimes Laszlo and Brian played chess. In summer the club was held *alfresco* on the science department roof.

Normally locked during office hours to prevent stroppy pupils or suicidal teachers hurling themselves onto the playground three storeys below and getting their names in the *Hestwell Times*, the roof was an absolute gem of a location with fantastic views of the school grounds and beyond. On a warm evening in the summer term, one could watch carefree children with their whole lives ahead of them playing cricket on the field or tennis on the courts, and see the endless stream of planes coming in to land at Heathrow to the west, as if joined by an invisible thread, bringing people from every corner of the globe to London, the greatest city on earth, the "new Athens". After coming in to land over central London with those spectacular views of Westminster and Buckingham Palace, one often flew over the slightly less well-known architectural masterpiece that was Beechwood just a few seconds before touching down at Terminal One. There weren't many teachers who were able to fly over their own school. Until that fateful day in July 2000 when that once-great feat of British and French engineering fell out of the morning sky in a ball of flames killing everyone on board, Concorde could be seen at exactly four-thirty every evening, thundering its way across the heath to Heathrow like a giant, gleaming silvery bird. You could set your watch by it. To the east one could see Twickenham rugby stadium and the twin towers of Wembley, and on a clear day the skyscrapers of Canary Wharf protruding through the city mist.

Michael loved these roof gatherings. There was an unofficial rota for supplying the booze and nibbles, and if that failed Brian would produce a bottle of his "special reserve", which he stored in the chemistry prep room in the section marked "oversized apparatus and glassware". Michael was usually the first to arrive as soon as the kids had evacuated the building – which on a Friday evening took about five minutes – and set out an assortment of chairs and lab stools in a semi-circle facing the heath. Protruding through the roof was a ventilation pipe from the staff toilets below, which on a warm day emitted the stench of raw sewage whenever someone took a crap, and could only be blocked with the help of an inverted fire bucket.

By four o'clock most club members had arrived, placing their refreshments in the centre for communal use. Every member of the department was a character, each flawed in his own way but loveable nonetheless. Alex Dimbleby, a Wimbledon fan and unreconstructed male chauvinist pig from Bristol who genuinely believed that women fancied him and for whom no act of self-publicity was too vain, opened the first bottle of *vino* and munched greedily at a packet of tomato flavoured Doritos. "Red" Len

Lightman, a rampant leftie from up north somewhere, a staunch union member and a passionate believer in comprehensive education – until he had reluctantly had to send his own daughter to an exclusive grammar school more suited to her special educational needs – sipped a bottle of Newcastle Brown Ale while opining about the evils of Margaret Thatcher's Britain. He was a hugely generous and loveable human being and an inspirational teacher, but like all good socialists, he believed in the redistribution of wealth in his favour, and was unable to see the contradiction between the comfortable middle-class lifestyle he enjoyed and the humble working-class utopia he aspired to and actively persuaded others to believe in. He was unable to see that his high principles never withstood the acid test of reality. Alison the feminist, Dermot the born-again Christian and the voluptuous NQT Anthea made up the runners and riders.

Sometimes people popped in on their way home after an end-of-week slash in the science toilets. Joseph "Stalin" Rooney, a Jimmy Tarbuck lookalike from Wigan and lifelong Labour Party member, was head of sixth form. He was famous for his Soviet-style discipline and a penetrating stare which frightened the life out of staff and pupils alike. Like "Red Len", he believed in the redistribution of wealth through the medium of horse racing – the poor punters robbing the rich bookies, so that they themselves could become rich. No contradiction there. He was a colossus whose commitment to gender and racial equality and passionate belief in a fairer society infused everyone who met him.

Sometimes the head walked by in his stunningly well-tailored suit and tie and sneered condescendingly at the debauch goings-on in front of him, usually accompanied by some quotation in Latin or Greek that no one understood. It reminded him of his undergraduate days as a student of philosophy and politics at Jesus College Oxford. He never accepted a drink, unless it was his favourite tipple, Chablis – which it hardly ever was.

Laszlo Liszt – allegedly related to the great composer Franz – was a larger than life, free-spirited bohemian from Budapest who ticked every Hungarian stereotype known to man, with extra lashings of goulash plus VAT. He was the very antithesis of the stiff-upper-lip, two-faced Englishman. He was loud and eccentric, "The Mad Hungarian", and it was rumoured that he had fathered at least four children with three different women, two of whom were his wives. Every one of his children was an off-the-wall social misfit. And of course he was called Laszlo: everyone in Hungary was called Laszlo – even the women and the dogs and the budgies. He had allegedly fled the Russian invasion of fifty-six, and been running ever since. As with most Hungarians, nothing was quite as it seemed, and it was unclear whether he'd actually escaped the advancing tanks of the Red Army or been thrown out as a troublemaker by the Hungarians. He lived with his long-suffering mother in a small flat near the Barbican – the father was never mentioned – where walls covered in sepia pictures from the turn of the century, revealed a family of wild-looking bearded extroverts. He had never fulfilled his mother's hope that he would become a respected man, a great poet or musician like their illustrious though in all probability fictitious relative Franz. Laszlo was a professional Hungarian, and like most Central Europeans lived and relived history as if it were yesterday, never getting tired of recalling, proud patriotic eyes filling with tears, voice cracking with emotion, the mythical "Battle of Mohacs" of 1526, in which the Magyars had "single-handedly" defeated the Muslim Turks – allegedly; in fact it was the Hungarians who were defeated. He loved his football and constantly reminisced, eyes watering this time with that greatly overrated central European sentimentality, about the legendary Ferenc Puskas and his role in Hungary's 6: 3 defeat of England in 1953, and repeatedly pointed out that the Rumanian striker Gheorghe Hagi was an ethnic Hungarian.

Laszlo dressed like a vagabond. He was a massive man, with large fleshy ears, a long waxy nose that looked as if it could melt at any time, and a tuft of unkempt brown hair protruding from his huge head like a bird's plumage. He had an unhealthy grey complexion, which with his large sunken doggy eyes and always moist spittle-encrusted lips, made him look like a cross between a gangster and Count Dracula. But everyone loved him. The teachers never tired of listening to his fantastic stories: it didn't matter whether they were true or not, they were bloody good stories. They loved his childlike, very un-English openness, and the ease with which he opened up his heart and expressed his emotions. Like his fellow Danube-dwellers, he wore his feelings on his sleeve – if he was happy he laughed, if he was sad he cried. They enjoyed hearing about his chaotic life, the weird and wonderful people he knew and the even stranger things he got up to. He was cultivated and relished talking about literature and politics. He loved talking period; sitting quietly was never an option. Michael's East European origins enabled him to instantly connect with the "Mad Magyar" from Budapest, and they became close friends. Laszlo never lost his thick Hungarian accent, and addressed Michael as "Zabo you bastard".

And the pupils loved him. Although he was in the conventional sense of the word a hopeless teacher who never met deadlines or marked books – totally disorganised, unable to control a class, ill-prepared for lessons – his charisma and the sheer warmth of his personality meant that the children loved being around him. He launched rockets on the school field to the applause of his many disciples. He launched rockets from the science department roof. He invited the English chess champion, Nigel Short, to challenge the school team and staff and recreate the bohemian milieu of his childhood – filmed by the BBC. He organised chess competitions with other schools.

On one occasion, after driving a group of chess players to a Jewish school in Mill Hill, Laszlo invited the whole group for fish and chips at the local Chinese chippy afterwards. He was a man of the people, if not the headmaster and his deputies. When their minibus arrived at the Beth Chaim School for Boys, the high iron gates were locked and guarded by a sickly man in a blue uniform whose job it was to protect the school from anti-Semitic attacks. They were met by a cool-looking, yarmulke-wearing student in an open shirt and grey flannels, who escorted them through shabby bare corridors to a classroom where the competition was about to take place.

Over the classroom door hung a picture of Rabbi Akiva, one of Judaism's greatest scholars who lived in the first century Kingdom of Israel. A bearded rabbi in a dark woollen suit, religious tassels dangling over his trousers, scuttled down the corridor on his way to somewhere else. Although Michael had long since renounced Orthodox Judaism, it was impossible to ignore the sense of calm spirituality that pervaded the school and infused its pupils, who exuded a quiet confidence and understated intelligence. It was palpably a place of warmth and learning, in which the torn wallpaper and peeling paint of the corridors and classrooms, impinged not one iota on the education of the pupils who studied there. For the mostly Muslim students from Hestwell, this was their first ever encounter with their arch enemy, the Jews. And because they were in essence so similar, they got on just fine.

Brian Rees was one of the original founding members of Beechwood when it began in the 1970s as a cluster of prefabricated huts. Like all pioneers, he constantly looked back – back to the days when as a young chemical engineer working in industry he had retrained as a teacher and helped build a New Jerusalem. Those were heady days, when, like the first *kibbutzniks* in Israel or the Pilgrim Fathers in Plymouth Massachusetts, he was fired up by the messianic zeal of the pioneer and the optimism of youth. Those were the days when everyone had a common purpose, when like-minded social reformers and rampant socialists like himself could paint on a fresh canvas – a tabula rasa – and put into practice their progressive teaching methods to create a school in their own image. In those days even Godfrey Burns voted Labour, before the Winter of Discontent forced him, like so many others on the soft left, to move to the right and straight into the seductively-outstretched arms of Margaret Thatcher. But not Brian Rees; he remained true to his roots as the son of a Welsh miner and in the spirit of Keir Hardie. Those were the days before Hestwell changed from being a white working-class suburb on the edge of Heathrow to an Asian ghetto. That was also PM – pre-mosque.

Brian looked like Mr Bumble from Oliver Twist – a Dickensian character from another century, long sideburns, plump ruddy face, with the stocky build of a rugby player who had gone to seed. Like most portly people, he was outwardly jolly, always joking and laughing out loudly, but inwardly he was a moody rebel. His *schtick* was wandering the corridors and the classrooms whistling the theme tune from *The Magnificent Seven*, every bit the school eccentric, the mad scientist in a white coat on day release from the asylum. Like most people he was a mass of contradictions – a socialist who read the *Daily Mail* "for the sport", an atheist who believed we were all a mass of meaningless molecules yet loved the spirituality of Welsh male voice choirs and the choral music of Bach.

And believing we were a mass of meaningless molecules didn't stop him loving his two boys. He talked endlessly about them and had a picture of Gareth and Mervyn – both named after Welsh rugby players – on his office table below posters of his twin heroes, Albert Einstein sticking out his tongue and a fuzzy-focus image of Bob Dylan looking cool and forever young. He would get up every morning at five to take his sons swimming down the local pool before putting in a full day's work at school. He had no inhibitions, and talked authoritatively about his recent vasectomy, complete with all the gory anatomical details; it was his contribution to saving the world from overpopulation.

But he was also an intellectual who loved poetry and drinking, much like his countryman Dylan Thomas. Which meant he was good company to argue the toss about anything and everything, and good to get totally pissed with. They talked metaphysics and metachemistry. Michael was just the same, so they got on like a lab on fire. They watched the same sitcoms and shared the same humour. When they met in the corridor, Michael would say "Morning Fawlty," to which Brian would reply "Morning Major." As if to emphasise his eccentricity, he kept two large snakes at home which kept escaping. Like all Welshmen, he loved rugby and Michael would goad him about the barbaric nature of the game and the uncanny resemblance of the players to orangutans and Great Apes. Brian feared the imminent collapse of the world's financial system. He drove a vintage Messerschmitt KR200, which he only just managed to get into and which apparently helped save the planet by covering one hundred miles to the gallon. Every summer was spent with his wife, kids and the father-in-law, camping in the Spanish Pyrenees. At staff meetings he was notorious for criticising the minutiae of every policy proposed by SMT – like it mattered.

And so it was with these colourful characters that Michael spent Friday evenings on the roof of the science department in summer. They would sun themselves in the still-powerful insolation pouring in from the west, like big shots in a penthouse, watching the kids playing cricket and tennis below, their youthful exuberance wafting up on a convection current of laughter and happiness to the third floor. They gazed in awe at the lush expanse of the heath, stretching out towards the horizon like the Serengeti. They watched the never-ending stream of planes landing at Heathrow and wondered who was on board and what stories they had to tell.

As the wine flowed, so did the conversation. The more they drank, the more they listened, the more they talked, the more they laughed. The quality of their conversion improved accordingly – or so it seemed. They talked about the Middle East with Michael *le Juif errant en résidence* defending the Israelis, maths teacher Kenny defending the Palestinians. The Left were predictable because they had a fixed take on everything. They viewed the Israeli treatment of the Palestinians as being uniquely evil in the world, yet another example of American, Zionist, neo-colonial repression of defenceless Muslims – the Left's *cause célèbre* – conveniently ignoring the daily butchery taking place throughout the Arab world. They lampooned the latest wheeze, the latest *fatwa* or "fat one" from the Department of Education, and told alcohol-fuelled stories about the crazy things that the pupils of the Beechwood School had got up to during that week. Material for a dozen plays, a hundred sitcoms, a thousand films. They discussed the existence of God with Dermot and the absurdities of feminist thinking with Alison, whose views were as predictable as those of the left – ossified, inflexible, not remotely interested in open dialogue. They discussed the Battle of Mohacs with Laszlo, and like everywhere else on earth, the utter stupidity of senior management.

By five-thirty, when the school caretaker's appearance signalled that it was time to go, only Michael, Laszlo and Brian remained sitting on the science department roof, clutching their last stale glasses of Rioja or Merlot and surrounded by the debris of an evening's drinking; empty wine bottles, crisp packets, the remains of a box of samosas that sixth former Jatinder had brought in as a quid pro quo payment for the private tuition she received. They resembled the last stragglers on the beach enjoying a Sundowner, looking out over an ocean of green, listening to the waves of aircraft landing at Heathrow, completely relaxed, utterly sozzled. A few stray seagulls from Southend or Bognor Regis glided over the school fields to complete the alcohol-induced illusion. The three friends had once again put the world to rights. There was nothing like drink and good conversation to unite men. They had communed with each other, as only men can.

As Michael took a precautionary piddle before hitting the road, he mused at the "Tide Tables" that some joker had put up in response to the propensity of the staff urinals to overflow. He looked in amazement at a piece of Wrigley's chewing gum that had been there for at least ten years and had stubbornly refused to biodegrade. He marvelled at the chewing gum's resilience and sheer will to survive against overwhelming odds.

As he drove along the M4 that evening he felt marvellous. There was no better feeling than this. He knew intellectually that he shouldn't drink and drive, but that would have precluded attending the Thank God It's Friday Club. You couldn't spend two hours drinking orange juice.

As he crawled along the motorway in the usual bumper-to-bumper Friday evening traffic, the windows of his Ford Escort wide open to let the warm evening breeze caress his face, Michael gazed at the other motorists and wondered what sort of a week they'd had. They certainly looked happier than they had at seven o'clock on a Monday morning.

Chapter 6

Being confined to the classroom didn't suit Michael at all. As if he was a caged bird it cramped his wings, his need to fly, his craving for space. And likewise his restless children, who like him needed to expend energy and commune with nature. He realised that virtually every lesson started in the classroom could be enhanced by going outside. On sunny days he'd take the kids onto the playground to study solar energy. They never got tired of using a hand lens to burn pieces of black paper, and like good scientists, using the very same principle to burn holes in each other's trousers. The thrill of seeing an exercise book going up in flames! They loved watching the solar fan spinning, driven by the sun, and the solar buggy trundling along the asphalt like a lunar explorer. Everyone wanted to have a go, even those normally too shy to participate in science lessons.

You could teach the principles of kinetic theory in the classroom with polystyrene balls, but how much better to go out on the field and pretend to be moving molecules in a solid, liquid or gas. The children zoomed around simulating the three states of matter, shouting and shrieking, enthusiastically crashing into each other in simulated Brownian Motion, colliding with great gusto. They could let off steam and have fun, but they undoubtedly enjoyed learning that way. Science was great. On other occasions they played the predator-prey game in which "foxes" – usually boys – hunted "rabbits" – usually girls – and tried to tear them limb from limb. Their natural animal instinct to kill or be killed readily transcended their gossamer-thin veneer of civilisation – as happens to soldiers in war – the ruthlessness of nature in which only the fittest survived. Natural selection. Or he would hide a hundred sweets outside and the pupils had to forage for them like real herbivores. Whatever you got, you ate. If ever one needed proof that the natural world was unfair, then this was it. Nature favoured the strongest, usually the males, who thought nothing of pushing the weak out of the way, or stealing their sweets in order to "stay alive".

One could study rusting in the lab in the traditional way, by exposing iron nails in test tubes to different variables such as air, water and oil, and leaving them for a week. But how much better to take the children on a "rust field trip" in the school car park, pointing out that every exhaust pipe was rusty because hot, moist, iron reacts readily with the air, and every painted car body was not. That is with the exception of Lazlo's vintage Beetle – the one he had probably used to escape from Hungary in 1956 – untaxed, a crumbling piece of scrap metal, a rotting rust box. The doors no longer locked and the radio aerial, no longer able to pick up Radio Budapest, had long since sunk into the bowels of the car and now just protruded through a brown rusty hole. "Is that your car, sir?" the class joker would usually ask, pointing to Lazlo's pile of scrap.

In these outdoor lessons Michael could release his inner thespian, his need to show off, to give a performance – his need to make others laugh as well as himself.

But why stop at augmenting inside lessons with an outside visit? Why not take the whole lesson outside? Michael had spotted the potential for this during his first year at the west London comprehensive on Beechwood's own heath, the vast expanse of pristine land on the school's doorstep. The heath was a nature reserve extending almost to the perimeter fence of Heathrow, which had been used as a military airstrip during the war. It was rumoured that highwaymen such as Dick Turpin used to stalk the heath in the eighteenth century, roaring "Stand and deliver!" and terrorising the locals. These days it was a protected area of grassland, Hestwell's own Serengeti, bursting with wildlife, through which people could walk their dogs and commune with the quasi-natural world.

So on warm days in the summer term, Michael would ditch his planned lesson and under the all-encompassing guise of "ecology" lead whichever group he was teaching, like the Pied Piper of Hamelin, across the school fields to the locked gate which marked the entrance to the heath. He would always stop here and make a big show of entering Narnia, The Secret Garden.

"Are there any paedophiles out here, sir?"

"Stay close together and watch out for snakes."

As the children passed through the gate, they really were entering another world. The closest most had been to nature was their own back garden or a park, and they knew next to nothing about wildlife and how to deal with it. Kings of the road in the streets of Hestwell, they were utterly ill at ease here, like ducks out of water having strayed from the comfort of their pond. Everything was strange and unfamiliar. They experienced for the first time the high-pitched staccato of crickets, so well camouflaged in the long grass they were invisible, as they rubbed their little wings and legs together, trying desperately to attract an unsuspecting mate. They were amazed that the grass was so long – taller than them. Why?

They shrieked as they stumbled and brambles tore into their flesh, and laughed nervously at the strange sounds and smells of the heath and the plethora of weird and wonderful insects that whizzed by. Every now and then a girl would scream as a boy, in that age-old attempt to show his love, tried to push her into the bushes or throw grass and seeds at her. "Ho, bloody ho!"

They assembled at "base camp", a clearing bounded by logs

and frequented by druggies and dropouts, who left the paraphernalia of their addiction and dead-end, fucked-up lifestyle strewn on the floor – needles, cigarette papers, empty bottles of cider, used condoms – testimony to the utter hopelessness and uselessness of the sad, fag-end of a fucked-up life they had chosen, or fate had chosen for them. Every junkie's like a settin' sun.

Before the kids were let loose on the "savannah", Michael would stand on the highest log, like Ralph in *Lord of the Flies*, or Robin Williams in the *Dead Poets Society* – "Oh captain, my captain" – loving his position of power and the chance to give a performance, and explain what the pupils had to do. Their "safari challenge" was to collect as many animals and plants as they could in order to win the game. Each organism had a value – one for an ant, five for a snail, ten for a ladybird – and unable to resist the temptation to be absurd, five hundred for a giraffe, and a thousand for an archaeopteryx. "Sir what's an archaeopteryx?" Sandeep would ask. "Sir, how do we catch a giraffe?" Mohammed would wonder aloud. Absurd challenges thrown in just for the hell of it to entertain both himself and the pupils, but also to make them think.

They were given fifteen minutes to collect their specimens. This was one of the best and most enjoyable lessons he'd ever devised. Michael watched with satisfaction and pride as the children, *his* children, scurried through the long grass – as he used to do with his brother as a child in a field behind their house in Leeds – collecting living things. There was something for everyone, something to appeal to every ability and temperament. The shy ones – mostly hijab-clad Muslim girls – stayed close to the teacher for protection and stuck to collecting leaves and flowers worth one point each. The more extrovert – mostly boys and naughty girls – ran around catching insects or each other, or disappeared behind the bushes for a more secluded experience.

Michael would gaze around him in awe. The grassland extended as far as the eye could see, in all directions lush and heaving with life. There were hundreds of wild flowers – cow parsley, ragwort, vetch, thistles – and patches of lupins or sweet peas that had somehow been transported by birds from neighbouring gardens and dumped on the heath courtesy of their faecal pellets. There were giant "toilet brush plants" or teasels, protruding a metre above the grass, and brambles bearing blackberries. There were insects of every shape and size, thousands of them – caterpillars, bees, butterflies, ladybirds, ants, grasshoppers – as well as birds and snails. It was like the Garden of Eden must have been before Eve ate the apple and was forever banished. It was like the African Savannah. And hundreds of dogs of every breed, each beautifully turned out, paraded by their owners like at Crufts.

The summer sun would beat down from a milky-blue suburban sky as a few fair weather cumulus clouds floated by on a gentle south-westerly breeze. The perfume of a million scented wild flowers would intoxicate his senses, and Michael hoped that the children would be similarly exhilarated by this out-of-body experience. He wanted to instil in these city kids a love of nature and a love of learning about nature by being part of it. Looking out over his flock, he saw the happiness that only the young, unencumbered by the cares of adulthood can experience, radiant faces enjoying the thrill of being alive, the joy of being in this paradise, freed from the constraints of the classroom, free at last, free at last, to throw off their shackles and run as freely as nature intended.

It was inconceivable that the children were not learning. As they chased a bee with a plastic beaker, they understood what it was like to be a predator, how tiring it was, how much skill and patience was needed, how much energy was consumed. And they understood for the first time perhaps, that a food chain was an energy chain, and why energy was lost at every stage, and why a food chain was really a food pyramid. The primordial thrill of the kill – that moment when the prey is caught, food is secured, and survival of the fittest ensured. The ecstasy of seeing a bee so close, marvelling at its pollen-coated, hairy, always-quivering, always-moving body, its bright colours, how the buzzing sound was amplified by the beaker, understanding why it was an insect, marvelling at its desire for freedom – like them – and the speed with which it escaped captivity, almost catapulting itself like an arrow towards the sky when the beaker was uncovered, its insurmountable will to survive driving its every action and reaction.

They watched the flowers being pollinated by bees, butterflies and lacewings and marvelled at the relentless industry of these six-legged arthropods in their never-ending quest for nectar. They saw thistles covered in aphids and ants and ladybirds – a food web – the feeding chain of each creature criss-crossing that of the other, food being shared around, energy being recycled. They noticed how the heath changed over time, how the grass grew tall and green and then gold like corn, just like wheat and barley, and that grasses were thus related to our crops. They saw the cycle of nature unravelling over real time, everything making its allotted entrance. Every week new flowers appeared like a floral firework display, carefully choreographed to bloom and fade at the right time and in the right order. Flowers became fruit, bramble blossoms became blackberries, food for birds and humans. Orange tiger moth caterpillars in June gave way to the black Peacock butterfly caterpillars of July. And in the same way Michael saw his pupils grow and develop, metamorphosing before his eyes, gaining in knowledge, gaining in confidence.

The children would come running back to him at base camp, like returning lovers, out of breath and delirious with excitement, to reveal their quarry and cash in their points.

"Look sir, we've caught two bees – one hundred points," squealed the usually shy and reserved Seema and Paramjit from 10R2.

"That's marvellous girls, two bees, or not two bees – that is the question," said Michael, relishing the chance to discharge one of his favourite if not somewhat corny play-on-words Shakespearean gags.

"How much do I get for collecting four black caterpillars, sir?"

enquired little Jonny Bowen from 7X4, a semi-literate, bottom-set kid who never did his homework and always came last in exams.

"That's fantastic Jonny – four times ten equals forty, and ten bonus points equals fifty for being Top Predator."

Like the father of a large family, Michael wallowed in the adulation of his many children, swollen with pride at their wide inquiring eyes and their zest for living. Every kid learned something, irrespective of his age, ability or gender. Muslim girls in hijabs, Sikh boys in turbans, cheeky white kids without a tie who would have fucked around in class and ruined everything, came to life on the heath. It was a great leveller. Being top in science was no guide to your ability to catch a bee or find a snail, or your ability to cope in the hostile environment of the heath. In their natural habitat outside in the fresh air, the able could excel, while the less able who would talk nonsense in class and muck around could shine like never before, often revealing previously untapped knowledge gained through fishing or camping, or on holiday with their families in the New Forest or Cornwall. Like giraffes, they felt taller than the grass – ten feet tall.

As they traipsed back to the school after a session in the "Secret Garden", the kids were hot, tired and sweaty, but fulfilled. They would laugh and joke and talk loudly, and drag their feet so as to be late for their next lesson. They didn't care, and nor did Michael. Like the first men on the Moon condemned to returning to a mundane life on Earth, the prospect of an hour's maths or English literature could never compete with the exhilaration of roaming the heath.

Chapter 7

As so often happens in life, one thing led to another. Michael had noticed the huge number of snails on the heath and how easy they were to collect. While the more extrovert pupils warmed to the thrills and spills of the chase and were able to catch bees and butterflies, the shy ones could still collect points by collecting sedentary creatures like snails, which were sitting ducks. Their dry shells made them easy to pick up, they didn't run away and they were unlikely to sting or bite. Michael loved horse racing, so why not race the snails?

So on a sunny day in June or July, when the heath was lush and verdant and the snail population had expanded exponentially with the supply of its food, Michael would take a class – any class – into the Secret Garden to look for the common or garden snail. Armed with only a plastic beaker to collect the molluscs, the children would follow the intrepid explorer their teacher had become along a densely overgrown track to "Snail City", where thousands of the slimy invertebrates could be found munching away at their favourite food-giant horseradish leaves. Instead of using the easier, well-trodden path, Michael had deliberately chosen a wilder route covered in deep grass and scratching thistles, to create a sense of danger and excitement, to help simulate what it must have been like for the great explorer Dr Livingstone on his voyages of discovery through the Dark Continent.

Once again Michael couldn't resist dramatising a mundane event for his own entertainment and he hoped the entertainment of his children, getting carried away and substituting Snail City for Victoria Falls. As he strolled through what he conjured up to be the African bush, he smiled at the sound of yelps and screams from the by now strung-out line of pupils as the thistles and brambles tore into their freshly laundered school uniforms and cut the tender young flesh below.

Snail City was like any city – busy. Huge clumps of giant horseradish leaves, some a metre in length, grew out of the ground like Manhattan sky scrapers. On the upper leaf surface huge holes indicated the presence of the voracious gastropods feeding on the surface below, hidden from the stereoscopic vision of would-be predators. Ladybirds and ants scurried up and down the stems while the warm humid air above was filled with the perfume of summer flowers and the sound of a thousand insects flying above the city, like aircraft on their way to JFK. For snails, horseradish was the most delicious food on the planet. It was like bamboo shoots for giant pandas, nectar for humming birds, ice cream for the children of the Beechwood School. If their rudimentary brains would have been more developed, the snails would have had wet dreams about horseradish, longed for a horseradish house in the country, fantasised about having sex with a horseradish leaf.

There were two types of snail on the heath; the larger olive green *Helix aspersa*, and the smaller more colourfully striped, *Cepaea hortensis*. Because they only had an hour, the kids were given just ten minutes to fill their beakers with the booty. As always, the introverts timidly stood around unsure how to proceed, while the extraverts dived into the clumps of horseradish, turning over every leaf, catching the snails *in flagrante* and overcoming the powerful suction that held each snail in place by picking them off the leaves like removing magnets from a fridge. A third group mooched around doing nothing, too cool to dirty their hands, too indolent to get involved, and as always wishing their lives away, waiting for the lesson to end before it had begun.

But for most of the pupils this was more exciting than any computer game or action video. Engaging with nature always was. Some had never seen a snail; most had never picked one up. None could have conceived in their wildest dreams or nightmares that so many creatures could be concentrated in one spot. It was like watching a slow plague of locusts decimating a crop. There must be millions of them on the heath, a hundred tonnes of voracious herbivores foraging off a thousand tonnes of juicy plants, each photosynthetically replacing the consumed matter as fast as it was eaten.

For speed, they took the easy way back to the school. As they wandered along the return path, the children laughed and joked. Some screamed as the snails, desperate to escape the clutches of some grubby schoolkid, began to climb out of the beakers, their huge slimy heads and alien-like stalk-eyes protruding over the rim, wondering whether they'd live to eat another leaf. Every so often an airborne snail came flying through the air, narrowly missing Mr Zabinsky and bouncing off some poor unsuspecting pupil's head – usually a girl's.

Once back on the school field, the pupils were sat down in a circle on the grass and divided into groups. Those who couldn't stand the heat – like the snails hiding under the leaves – sheltered below a sycamore tree. At the centre of the circle lay an upturned plastic tray which would become the racetrack. Each group was given a stop-clock to time the race, asked to select their "fittest" mollusc, give it a funny name that wasn't obscene and place it at the start of the track. The track was aligned with the sun to make the snails race, with a large juicy horseradish leaf at the far end to further motivate movement. Time and distance would be recorded and the speed calculated.

"And they're under orders and they're off!" Zippy, a hugely overweight olive green *Helix*, glides into the lead, closely followed by the spritely Zabo, an orange-striped *Cepaea*. Sadly, not all the contestants are in the mood. Some move sideways, some move backwards. Others fall off the edge of the track, hurtling relentlessly towards the grass some five centimetres below. The indolent ones do nothing, their performance reflecting the nature of their owner by some kind of mimicry by association. The children are getting hysterical, cheering on their charge, crowding the track like gamblers around a roulette wheel in a casino, blocking out the sun with their bobbing shadows.

At the halfway point, Zippy is overtaken by Banksy, while Zabo decides to have sex with Loopy, climbing on top of her sensuous exoskeleton at the ten-centimetre mark, "Why don't we do it in the road?" style. The kids can hardly control their excitement at this display of erotic acrobatics, shrieking and leaping in the air, like fleas – uncontrollably. "Look sir, they're having it off with each other!"

As the finishing line approaches, it's neck and neck, with another huge *Helix*, Mahindra, crossing the line first in a late surge of lubricious bodily fluid. The winning mollusc has a speed of 0.2 centimetres per second; slower than Daley Thompson, but faster than an overweight twelve-year-old on Sports Day.

Michael loved horse racing, and the ecstatic celebrations surrounding Mahindra were reminiscent of those on a Monday night at Windsor or a Saturday afternoon at Ascot, if he was lucky enough to have a winner. There was something universally thrilling about racing. From the Greeks racing each other on the plains of Olympia to the Roman chariot races in the Coliseum, man's need to race things and watch them race was ancient, satisfying some primordial need of the human condition. The reaction of these children to the racing of soporifically slow slimy snails was exactly the same as grown-ups watching a thoroughbred winning the Derby or an athlete winning an Olympic medal; both satisfied the need for speed, the need to compete, the need to have a wager.

Once again Michael felt a surge of enormous pride and satisfaction at having used his imagination and creativity, his sense of the absurd and the ridiculous, his powers as a director and a pedagogue to enthuse and thrill and educate his pupils. Michael had never had teachers like this when he was at school.

Chapter 8

Michael was on a roll. He was at the peak of his powers now, and felt able to expand his range of lessons in any direction he chose, think endlessly out of the box and satisfy his increasing appetite for innovation and the giving of a performance. It was time for the closet thespian within to be outed. After spreading his wings outside, it was time to sex things up indoors. The reality was and always would be that most teaching takes place inside the classroom.

Michael was aware that certain topics were difficult to teach, even to the most able, because they were intellectually demanding and abstract. And one of these was the menstrual cycle, which both boys and girls needed to know, not just to pass their biology GCSE, but so that a woman could understand her body and a man could avoid getting sucked into the vicious PMT-fuelled arguments which are the biggest single cause of marital tension and breakdown.

He was convinced that everything could be dramatised, and decided to test this out with 10R1. Like most top sets, they were intelligent and precocious, but crucially they were able to appreciate the nuances of a fun lesson without missing the point completely, or confusing it with mucking around and going crazy. The class were theatrical at the best of times, full of drama queens, populated by wonderfully wacky and imaginative off-the-wall characters who would relish a bit of entertainment.

When the pupils tumbled into his lab, like eavesdroppers falling through a suddenly opened door, talking excitedly and greeting him affectionately with the usual "Hello sir, what we gonna to do today?", in addition to a large diagram of the menstrual cycle on the white board, four stages, like the Stations of the Cross in a Catholic Church, were set up around the perimeter of the lab. After explaining the theory behind what he genuinely believed was a mind-bogglingly interesting cycle that should stimulate the brain of any intelligent being and including the usual anecdote about the origins of its name in the twenty-eight day phases of the moon – the "moonstral" cycle – Michael introduced the class to his menstrual "Via Dolorosa".

At station one – day one of the menstrual cycle – a plastic brain represented the pituitary gland – the master endocrine gland that fires the starting gun for the process to begin – and a lavender air-freshener canister marked FSH, which when squeezed simulated the release of Follicle Stimulating Hormone into the blood. Station two – day seven of the cycle – contained a plastic model of the female reproductive organs complete with ovaries and a canister of lemon-scented air-freshener, which when squeezed simulated the release of the hormone oestrogen. The FSH activated the ovaries. At station three – day fourteen of the cycle – was another model of the female organs representing the thickened lining of the uterus, a spray canister marked "P" for progesterone and a beaker containing two large Tesco free-range eggs to simulate ovulation. Like oestrogen, progesterone causes the womb lining to thicken. And finally station four – day twenty-eight of the cycle – contained a pot of red food dye, fake menstrual blood for when fertilisation didn't occur, and a series of plastic foetal stages if it did. And in the event of birth, a bag of Waitrose mozzarella cheese represented the amniotic sac.

A frisson of excitement rippled through the class, like a peristaltic wave forcing newly-released eggs down the Fallopian tubes into the womb. As expected, 10R1 were really up for this, chomping at the bit as they sensed the potential for fun and games and the chance to give their flamboyant natures free rein. Their bright eyes and grinning faces exuded precocious, theatrical intelligence.

"Who wants to be part of the menstrual cycle?" asked Michael. A forest of hands shot up from a class eager to please and participate, straining every sinew to be picked. He tried to select a balance between girls and boys, extraverts and introverts. Enter Kieran, Penny, Kwame and Aisha.

Believing himself to be suitably cerebral, Kieran Walsh volunteered. He was the court jester, the class comedian who never stopped talking or did any homework, yet somehow managed to be incredibly knowledgeable and continually asked the sort of questions that only a bright mind could ask – a naturally intelligent white working-class boy, in short. He was game for anything. As he approached the station, Kieran raised his hands like an Oscar winner, his long straw-coloured hair flopping over his cheeky acned face, milking the moment for all it was worth as the class cheered and applauded. "Goo on Kier!" "Kieran! Kieran!"

Kieran lifted the model brain above his head like a trophy, then held it in front of him, effortlessly playing Hamlet, skull in hand: "To be or not to be, that is the question." He was rapidly warming to his subject.

"At the beginning of the cycle, the pituitary gland – the top gland like me bruv – squirts FSH into the bloodstream and tells dem ovaries to get laying dem der eggs," recited Kieran in an increasingly Deep South, black-American cotton worker's accent, squeezing the lavender spray high into the air, then above the class, then at the pupils themselves, picking out his mates and Darshana Patel in particular, who he fancied. Coughing and spluttering, screams and yelps of joy from the class. If there was one thing you could rely on, it was that Kieran Walsh would go OTT. It was in his DNA, it was his specialist subject.

"OK Kieran, enough already."

Penny O'Leary was one of those typically shy girls, always smartly dressed, always quiet and polite, who did her homework, did OK in exams, but never asked or answered a single question in class. But she had volunteered here. She stood by station two holding the plastic womb and the lemon-scented can marked "O", her wavy ginger hair covering the left corner of her freckly forehead, her bright blue Irish eyes shining through a flushed rotund face. She smiled self-consciously and stared at her feet.

Kieran shouted, "Goo on Penny, in for a penny in for a pound!" Penny chuckled.

"On day seven, after receiving the message from Kieran the pituitary gland, the ovaries secrete the hormone oestrogen into the blood, which thickens the uterus lining in preparation for a baby." Her face creased up in an exaggerated witch's smile, screwing up her nose, mouth and cheeks as she sprayed the back bench with gay abandon. *Et tu Brute*? Even nice little goody-two-shoes Penny, who never misbehaved or asked questions in class, could not resist the lure of the spray can. A huge cloud of "oestrogen" hung in the air as it diffused through the class's bloodstream infusing the mesmerised members of 10R1. More coughing and spluttering and rubbing of eyes. They were beginning to enjoy this piece of bizarre biological theatre. Being part of the menstrual cycle wasn't so awful after all. It had been given a bad press.

Penny had to be surgically removed from the oestrogen spray can, so determined was she to meticulously perform her assigned task as if it were a piece of important coursework. Like a madman with a gun, she had to be carefully approached and cajoled into putting down her weapon and quietly led away to her seat, her eyes still bulging with menstrual madness as if the *ersatz* hormones had gone to her head and made her go a bit funny. Huge applause and whooping as she sat down, the sham of her shy personality shattered forever, the real, raunchy Penny revealed at last.

Next up was Kwame Boateng. The son of Ghanaian parents, he exuded the innate confidence of an African prince. Polite, snappily dressed and charming, he was hugely popular with the girls, who swooned over his good looks and infectious personality, and with the boys who respected a guy who had a way with the ladies and hoped that some of his black magic might rub off onto them. He was a natural performer, who took the lead role in school plays and thrilled everyone with his wit and rhetoric in assemblies. It was impossible not to like Kwame.

He ambled towards his station – day fourteen – with a self-assured theatrical gait that excited his adoring audience. He lifted up the plastic organs showing large pink ovaries, and then a glass beaker containing a large Tesco free-range egg.

"On day fourteen, one of the ovaries produces a mature egg, which enters the Fallopian tube and passes down into the womb," said Kwame with a knowing smile on his face. "This is called 'ovulation' and it's the time in a woman's cycle, her fertile period, when she is most likely to become pregnant. No sperms today folks."

He cracked the egg dramatically against the rim of the beaker, gesturing with his head, splattering some of its slimy contents onto the table, and pouring the remaining yellow and white liquid, along with some fragments of shell, into the vessel. Thunderous applause from the spellbound audience, egging him on after every action.

He now passed the ovulated ovum to Aisha, who was already waiting at day twenty-one. Aisha, a precociously intelligent child with long black hair and a lovely smile who Michael had "rescued" from set four in year seven when her bright eyes had bewitched him, held up the progesterone canister marked "P" and proceeded to direct the spray enthusiastically towards the ceiling and into the air and the hair of the rows of cowering classmates, who were by now getting tired of being doused in the choking fragrance of *ersatz* female hormones.

"After ovulation the ovaries secrete a second hormone, progesterone, which like oestrogen continues to thicken the womb lining in preparation for a baby and stops the pituitary gland producing any more FSH – like a contraceptive."

Aisha then carried the unfertilised egg to the sink, added a squirt of red food-dye "blood" to the beaker, and poured the lot down the sink, turning on the cold tap to flush it away.

"On day twenty-eight of the menstrual cycle, if no fertilisation has taken place, the lining of the womb detaches and the woman has her monthly period – menstruation." Aisha took a bow and returned to her seat to the sound of loud clapping and the banging of tables.

"Was it real blood?" enquired Sameer, finally breathing normally after three bouts of hormone warfare and still unsure what to make of the amateur dramatics he had just witnessed.

The class was now buzzing like a hive of worker bees just returned from a successful forage for nectar on the heath and waggling their quivering bodies in the direction of the food as they performed their primordial waggle dance. "This is the menstrual cycle Jim, but not as we know it."

Michael was loving this, watching his cunning plan take shape, seeing his vision unfold, witnessing his creativity and imagination acted out by others, bearing edible fruit. He felt the buzz of the director, seeing his new play going down well on the opening night at The National.

Act Two: Fertilisation. The old cast were dismissed and replaced by new actors selected from the forest of still desperately-waving hands, like corals swaying on a reef, filtering nutrients from the warm ocean currents, begging to be chosen: Karan, Sally, Ranjit, Sanjeev. Even those who had performed in act one had their hands up, hoping to get their old jobs back, hoping that Mr Zabinsky wouldn't notice. How many teachers could claim that their pupils begged them to be taught?

So Act Two was played out; Karan FSH, Sally oestrogen, Ranjit ovulation and Sanjeev progesterone. But this time a sperm was needed to fertilise the ovulated egg. Enter Ashley.

Ashley was a mixed-race lad with a white mother and a Jamaican father. He sat at the end of the front bench so that he could entertain Fahreen, whom he fancied, and bolt out of the door when the buzzer went for break – on the rare occasions when he wasn't detained for mucking about. He had thick wavy black hair and a light-brown cheeky complexion. Like Kieran, he fancied himself as the class comedian. In short, he'd make a good sperm.

Waiting in the wings like the Black Swan in Swan Lake, Ashley the giant sperm, ran into the classroom as Ranjit released her ovum, making swimming motions with his arms, and grabbing the beaker affected to fertilise the now scrambled egg, to the hysterical laughter of the class.

"Goo on Ashley you great big spermatozoa!" shouted Kieran.

Ashley, readily warming to his new role – he had played a good sperm, he was born to be a sperm and he knew it – carried the beaker towards the sink, passing and holding up the developing foetal stages lined up on the table as he did so, and finally, holding up the bag of mozzarella, cut it open with a scalpel to let the waters out, and producing a plastic foetus from between his legs, gave birth to a bouncing baby boy or girl.

10R1 erupted in applause. The proud "mother" Ashley, bowed appreciatively, cuddling his first born maternally to his breast and spontaneously yelling "Goo on my son!"

Chapter 9

As the months passed by and his he confidence grew, Michael cast his educational net ever wider. There were to be no limits; nowhere would be out of bounds. Just as it was absurd to restrict his lessons to the laboratory, it was unthinkable to confine his teaching to the school. He began to view London, the greatest city on earth with a cultural heritage second to none, as a natural extension of Beechwood, a giant classroom where anything was possible.

Just because these kids were working-class and the sons and daughters of immigrants it did not mean they should be cosseted or protected from the ways of the city. In fact exactly the opposite: in order to integrate and compete with those privately-educated, well-heeled kids from Totteridge and Kensington, they should be immersed in as much highbrow culture as possible. Virtually every institution had special rates for schoolchildren, so he started taking his sixth-formers to the theatre, the opera, the ballet, and to art galleries and concert halls. There would be no no-go areas, nothing would be out of bounds, nowhere would be too posh or too refined. They saw *Swan Lake* at the Royal Opera House, *Hamlet* at the National Theatre and Caravaggio at the Royal Academy. They watched *La Bohème* at the Coliseum and saw Pinchas Zukerman playing Beethoven's violin concerto at the Festival Hall. They mixed with arty types, luvvies and classical music *cognoscenti*, as well as beautifully-spoken Oxbridge graduates and members of the chattering classes, media types and politicians. Michael was not only branching out from the school, he was now dabbling in the arts and the humanities. He was becoming a self-styled polymath.

And then there were the science lectures at the Royal Institution and Imperial College, lectures on quantum theory and nanotechnology by prominent scientists and researchers. He took coach loads to watch England play and usually lose at Wembley. He escorted groups to appear on BBC *Question Time* and watched with the swollen pride of a parent as his children quizzed government ministers and eminent movers and shakers of society. Democracy in action, on the telly.

As well as going out and about, he invited people to bring their expertise into the school; scientists, musicians, politicians, authors. He celebrated the centenaries and bicentenaries of famous people; Chopin, Liszt, Einstein, Darwin, Dickens, Freud. He had eccentric concert pianists playing Chopin and Liszt on stage and the great-great-great-great granddaughter of Charles Dickens talking about her illustrious ancestor and showing off her lovely, most un-Dickensian legs to a hall of salivating sexually-repressed students. During every election he invited in local candidates to debate the great issues of the day with each other and answer questions from the floor.

Then there was science week. Using local expertise, he organised an annual bonanza of fun science events given by the science teachers of his department; DNA extraction, volcano making, rocket launching, heart dissections. As a finale to the week, visiting scientists would perform spectacular experiments and blow things up on stage, and a falconry expert would fly barn owls and peregrine falcons across the main school hall.

But why confine oneself to London? Michael's universe was still expanding; he was becoming a producer and a director – an impresario already, a big *macher*.

The Cheltenham Science Festival was held every year in early June and attracted schools from across the country as well as TV scientists like Robert Winston, Brian Cox and Alice Roberts, who flaunted themselves unashamedly wherever and whenever they could to satisfy their craving for exposure, their need to be seen, the need to sell their latest book, and of course the adulation that comes from appearing on stage in front of a large crowd. They were science pop stars; science had become fashionable among the chattering classes, sexy even. That's not to say they didn't have a genuine commitment to science – they did. They were all involved in, or had been involved in, cutting-edge research until they became famous. But appearing in public was better than being stuck in a stuffy lab and appearing on mainstream television was irresistibly addictive, the most ego-enhancing aphrodisiac known to man.

So on a lovely summer's morning in June 1995, a coach full of fifty year nines and four teachers left the school car park for the spa city of Cheltenham. In some ways the children were well-travelled, having almost certainly visited their relatives in India or Pakistan for a wedding or a funeral, and in some cases an arranged marriage, as well as visiting family in Asian-friendly cities like Birmingham, Leicester and Manchester. When they were old enough, many of the Muslims would have the pleasure of being taken – usually in school time and against their wishes – on a pilgrimage to Saudi Arabia for the *Hajj*, to that delightful monument to medieval civilisation, Mecca, where they could witness the fully "unplugged" version of their bizarre religion, swirling around the *Kaaba*, throwing stones at the devil and imbibing the undiluted opium of the people with millions of other intoxicated worshippers clad in white. But apart from a few northern cities, their knowledge of England was restricted overwhelmingly to London and their beloved Hestwell; it was reasonable to assume that Britain consisted of brown-faced ethnic communities like their own. For most, this was their first trip to Middle England: they felt more at home in the narrow streets of Lahore and New Delhi than they did in the country lanes of Gloucestershire and Somerset.

The coach made its way through the monotonous suburbs of west London and hit the M4 westbound at around seven-thirty in the morning. Like Michael, the sun had been up for hours and now brightly illuminated the motorway and surrounding fields with its powerful light, blazing through a clear blue midsummer sky. The forecast for Cheltenham was a sweltering twenty-five degrees, and as is always the case when the sun shines in summer, the world looked pristine and perfect. The atmosphere in the coach was similarly upbeat, with the kids laughing and joking with each other and gazing out of the windows. Michael remembered vividly the excitement of going on school trips to the Lake District and Scotland, the thrill of travel, the youthful yearning to see the world, the limitless possibilities, the great expectations of an unknown journey.

Michael was in his element in charge of a coach, the main actor on a moving, hermetically-sealed capsule of a theatre, from which there was no escape. Power and control; he could use the microphone and intercom system to address his captive audience. He began by welcoming everyone on board flight FXZ 05HJN to Cheltenham, which would be flying at an altitude of two hundred feet above sea level and travelling at a speed of sixty miles an hour. No eating or drinking on board or wandering around the coach; no obscene gestures at passing motorists; no standing up or shouting, seat belts fastened at all times. Anyone mucking around would be punished with a detention after school and banned from all future trips. But they *were* allowed to breathe – quietly.

Michael sat next to Munira, opposite Reg the coach driver and in front of science technicians Doreen and Malcolm. Like most coach drivers, Reg, a sickly-looking, overweight man in his mid-fifties, needed constant cajoling and ego-boosting conversation to keep him awake and in good spirits, and reduce the chances of his latent misanthropy erupting into outright warfare with the kids. The rear seats were as always occupied by the school miscreants, who thought that just as in the classroom being at the back would enable them to hide: *au contraire*. The quieter, more timid kids sat at the front for protection and reassurance, near teacher. Munira was great company, always game for a laugh but ready to help out; unlike some teachers she was not just here for a jolly, and was certainly not here for the beer.

After negotiating rush-hour traffic on the network of motorways to the west of London, the coach finally joined the A40 which would take them to Cheltenham. The June countryside was stunningly beautiful, with lush green wheat fields stretching as far as the eye could see, bordered by hedgerows heaving with bird life and copses of verdant trees in full summer leaf. They travelled deep into Middle England through the rolling chalk hills of Berkshire and Oxfordshire and on to the oolitic limestone slopes of the Cotswolds in Gloucestershire. Cows lazily grazed the succulent meadow grasses, while sheep roamed freely on the higher drier ground.

For the children, this was a world they had read about in geography or seen in Agatha Christie films or rural costume dramas, but never experienced themselves. It was every bit as exotic as the Amazon rainforest or the Atacama Desert. Their discovery of Middle England was like Columbus discovering America: it was in every sense a New World.

As they travelled deeper into Gloucestershire, they passed through breathtakingly picturesque picture-book Cotswold villages with funny names like Bourton-on-the-Water, each with an ancient stone village church, an old inn, a duck pond and clusters of stylish thatched-roofed cottages made of cream-coloured local limestone. Opulent villages were surrounded by ripening wheat fields and apple orchards. No mosques, no Gurdwaras, no Hindu temples. Everyone was white, English and Anglo-Saxon. Villagers with ruddy complexions, crooked teeth and bloodshot eyes pointed and stared at the coach load of exotic turban-headed, hijab-wearing brown people, like caged animals in a zoo, while the children, equally bemused by the sight of such odd-looking country bumpkins by the wayside, waved and laughed and pointed back in return, like tourists in a safari park; no blacks, no Asians, no Chinese. Don't feed the natives. Like two alien tribes meeting for the first time, Navaho and Apache, each suspicious of the other, each unsure how to react or how to behave.

They drove past exquisite country pubs by the roadside, each made of Cotswold stone, each with spacious beer gardens, magnificently manicured rose beds and colourful hanging baskets of geraniums and scented petunias. The Dog and Gun, the Flower Pot, the West Country Wench. In a few hours' time the car parks of these pubs would be brimming with four-wheel drives, Jeeps and Land Rovers; the beer gardens would be heaving with country types in tweed jackets supping pints, beautiful women in expensive silk summer frocks sipping cocktails, perfectly-mannered privately-educated children with confident accents, drinking lime cordial, dining on pheasant or *duck a l'orange*.

As the coach approached the salubrious outer suburbs of Cheltenham, the children became quiet. They stared in awe at the sumptuous mansions and villas that lined the wide and bountiful streets and boulevards, the huge gardens filled with clematis and lavender and highly-scented red and yellow roses, the posh German cars, the beautiful tree-lined pavements, the utter other-worldliness of it all. It was difficult to imagine a place less like Hestwell.

After the discovery of mineral springs in 1716 and because of its patronage by King George III, Cheltenham became a fashionable spa town for the rich and famous. And although people still come to take the waters, the town's beautiful Cotswold setting, stunning Regency architecture and legacy of magnificent buildings like the Pittville Pump Room and the town hall have enabled Cheltenham to rebrand itself as Britain's premier festival town with an international reputation for jazz and literature, and more recently, science.

As they neared the town centre, they saw that the streets were festooned with festive banners proudly announcing the Cheltenham Science Festival, each with the hallmark logo of an atom surrounded by a cloud of orbiting electrons. At nine-thirty, the coach finally arrived outside the festival venue, the town hall, and disgorged its cargo of exotic Hestwell residents opposite the main entrance. Reg, looking forward to a few hours' relief from the depressingly happy and cheerful coachload of kids, drove off to the coach drivers' car park, after agreeing to pick them up around three.

They were met on the imposing steps of the town hall by two smart ladies of about forty brandishing clipboards, their short skirts and leather boots emphasising the sexuality of a mature woman with nice thighs in a position of authority. The warm sunlight made Poppy and Molly look even sexier. Their pretty, powdered, lipsticked faces brightened as they suddenly recognised the odd-looking group stood on the pavement.

"Beechwood School, I presume?" asked Poppy, her blue-green eyes lighting up, her pale face flushing at the sight of this handsome, suntanned teacher from the big smoke who had until now been just another email correspondent. "You're the only group that's come from London. We've been so looking forward to seeing you." They embraced affectionately as old cyber friends do – pouted lips, rubbing cheeks, feigning an aerial kiss.

They were directed through the sumptuous building, past the main hall with its huge Corinthian columns and ornate ceiling to a huge white marquee where the first session would begin at ten. On their way through the town hall, they had past the unmistakably pompous figure of IVF pioneer Robert Winston, holding court with a group of journalists hanging off his every word, pipe in hand, wise glasses perched on his ample proboscis, thousands of years of Jewish learning etched on his kindly face like the Ten Commandments, opining on something or other, it didn't matter what.

Cheltenham Town Hall had been built in 1902 as a venue for social events. Situated next to the neo-classical Imperial Square, its brown limestone facade dominated the surrounding buildings and spacious gardens. The Central Spa dispensed the waters from all the pump rooms of Cheltenham Spa. Today the town hall was clad in colourful flags of the town and the science festival.

The children were given the chance to assuage the hunger of a two-hour coach journey with a quick snack and a swig of coke. As they queued alongside the marquee waiting for the first show to begin, giggling and joking and munching a sandwich or a Mars bar in the morning sunshine, they gazed at the odd-looking collection of students milling around next to them. Virtually everyone was white; they seemed to be the only non-Caucasians at the festival. Standing nearby was a group of blue-eyed blonde girls – probably year nines like themselves – wearing the distinctive kilt skirts and green blazers of Cheltenham Ladies' College. The girls, whose parents – surgeons, diplomats, farmers – could afford to send them to one the country's most prestigious independent schools with fees of £30,000 a year, looked disarmingly composed and confident as they talked quietly and politely to each other in refined middle-England accents. They had beautifully fresh, smiling complexions and exuded an air of natural superiority. A group of younger pupils wearing the red-rimmed blazers and red-striped ties of the equally prestigious Beckhampstead School waited nearby with their Eton-educated teacher. It was all quite intimidating.

At ten to ten, the long queue of excited young people was let into the marquee. As they entered the tent, they were struck by the enormous size of this man-made space as their eyes adjusted from the brilliant light outside to the dimness within. It was like being inside the Big Top at the circus – dark and stuffy, with rows of improvised seating rising high towards the rear, the smell of warm canvas – but instead of a ring for performing animals and clowns, there was a rectangular stage for performing scientists. Teams of young volunteers dressed in orange science festival shirts kept the masses moving and directed them into the auditorium.

Michael sat his group about ten rows from the front, centrally placed for a good view and near enough to the stage to participate in any action that might spill over in their direction. The marquee was now filled to the rafters with hundreds of increasingly impatient children, each school identifiable by its uniform, sitting with their long-suffering teachers, each trying to keep their group under control. There were the immaculately-behaved private schools in their posh uniforms; state schools like Beechwood, which had been vetted for trouble-makers and shit-stirrers before leaving London; and other groups of local comprehensives where the teachers had opted for a day out with their uncontrollable bottom sets rather than having to babysit and suffer with them back at school.

The lights dimmed, the hubbub subsided, and a spotlight revealed a stage decked out with the accoutrements of a spectacular science show; an assortment of tubes, balloons, flasks, pumps, bottles of colourful liquids and strange-looking gadgets.

The first act, "Slap, bang, wallop chemistry", was presented by a couple of Geordies who went by the name of Bill and Ben, the chemistry men. Sam Copperthwaite and Archie Ramsbotham were a couple of university science technicians from Newcastle who had teamed up to indulge their innate Tyneside need for fun and farce to tour the country like a parody of Simon and Garfunkel, giving science shows to schools and festivals and anyone who would have them. They were available for weddings and bar mitzvahs, asking only workman's wages when they got offers. Archie, a twice-divorced fifty-year-old father of three with a pocked face like the surface of Ganymede, chunky tattooed arms with pictures of Marilyn Monroe and a pony tail of coarse brown hair cascading down his equally chunky neck, was Sam's sidekick. Sam, a spritely fifty-five-year-old with a broken nose, a broken family life and a huge pot belly that protruded from his baggy, shiny trousers like a wobbly jelly-the result of a lifetime supping brown ale and stuffing himself with nutritious pork pies and fried Mars bars-looked like a cross between Eric Burdon and Joe Cocker in their twilight years. It was not unusual for him to burst into a verse or two of "I'll get by with a little help from my friends", or "We gotta get outta this world" during his shows. They were the Morecambe and Wise of the comedy science circuit scene.

Sam and Archie came on stage to huge applause from an audience which was glad of the chance at last to let off steam, like a couple of mad scientists wearing white coats and oversized goggles.

"Hello boys and girls and welcome to the Cheltenham Science Festival," shouted Sam in a voice reminiscent of Bobby Charlton. Thunderous applause and whooping from the crowd.

"Is there anyone down here from Newcastle?"

"Nooooooooooooooooooh!" screamed the kids, warming to the duo.

"I've got three balloons here filled with hydrogen. Is there anybody out there who would like to burst them?"

"Yeeeeeeeeeeeeeeeeeeeees!" yelled the crowd in unison, a hundred straining hands temporarily blocking out the stage.

"Get me a few punters from the floor, Archie," said Sam to his sidekick.

Being short-sighted, Archie could only focus on the first few rows. He pointed towards Michael's group strategically seated directly in his line of diminished vision. Nasira, Chad and Sarbjit traipsed onto the stage for their moment of glory amidst more whistles and yelps from the increasingly effervescent audience. Michael was immensely proud of his children as they looked out on the expanse of eager, mostly white faces, smiling and holding their heads up high. There was Nasira, in her black hijab, Sarbjit in his white turban and Chad, looking as cool as you like, his long ginger hippy hair flowing over his shoulders like a Seventies rock star. Each child was given a pair of safety goggles and a lighted taper to burst the balloons.

"You're not from these parts are you pet?" said Sam addressing Nasira.

Laughter from the audience.

"No, I'm from Hestwell," replied Nasira

More laughter.

"What do you know about hydrogen, Nazeeyrah?" inquired Sam.

"The sun's made of it and it's the lightest element in the universe," retorted little Nasira, nodding her head confidently, milking the audience for applause. She was gaining in confidence.

"That's right, Nazeeyrah. Now burst the red balloon."

Nasira cautiously approached the balloon and theatrically plunged the lighted taper deep into it, like a sword. BANG!

"Didn't she do well boys and girls?" asked Archie, putting on his best Bruce Forsyth imitation. "Good game, good game; noyce to see you, to see you NOYCE!"

Bill and Ben continued their show with a spectacular display of fiery chemistry interspersed with crude Geordie humour, and of course the obligatory liquid nitrogen which every science show on earth includes and of which the punters never tire. The children were well pleased by the first event of the day. The pyrotechnics had fired their imagination, with the humour and humanity of the two chancers from Newcastle enjoying a late flowering of their career in showbiz, greatly enhancing their hugely enjoyable learning experience. If only school could be like this. But unless they had free-thinking teachers like Michael, prepared not only to think but to live their lives outside the box – which most schools did not – it could never be like this. Nor did it have to be. Shows like this certainly stimulated the kids, and for many made an otherwise unintelligible subject fun. They were like catalysts for greater learning. But no teacher could give a performance like this every day. The understanding of science still required deep thought, quiet reflection, study and hard work. There was no way of getting around that.

The atmosphere in the marquee had become uncomfortably hot and sticky, like a tropical rainforest or the Palm House at Kew, as the heat from the sun outside was compounded by that generated by the chemistry on stage and the audience within. You could smell heat, feel it, taste it even; and sensations bring back memories. It reminded Michael of his youth, when as a scout he would go camping every May half term at Langbar, an isolated farm somewhere in the Yorkshire Dales, with Lionel Hurwitz, Jonathan Galinsky and other childhood friends. The smell of heated canvas and the warm succulent grass on the floor of the marquee reminded him of this.

So it was a relief to file out of the steamy tent for a breath of fresh air before visiting the exhibition in the main hall. Universities and science-based companies from all over England were displaying their wares in this ornately-decorated, high-ceilinged space at the very centre of the town hall. The kids spread out and visited each stall, asking questions about careers, having a go at all the gadgets and collecting free pens and colourful brochures from every display. Michael watched proudly as the kids wandered around in groups, trying everything out, getting stuck in and mixing easily with the dense crowd of schoolchildren who didn't look at all like them. Many he hoped would go to university, get good jobs with some of these high-tech companies, integrate and become good citizens. Why not? They were every bit as good as the well-heeled, well-connected sons and daughters of toffs treading the boards at the fair. This was the dream he had for his children; it was why he had become a teacher.

At twelve-thirty came the part of the day everyone had been waiting for – lunch. No matter where you took school parties – the Alps, the great cities of Europe, the Dorset coast – the bit they enjoyed most was eating, and spending money. Lunch would take place in the Imperial Square Gardens which bordered the town hall. The kids were told to stay in the square and given an hour.

Imperial Square was, as its name suggests, imperial. It was like one of those delightful squares that make up central London – Portland Square, Berkeley Square – the sort of square featured in countless period dramas, exuding class, opulence and decadence and bordered by imposing Regency buildings made of Cotswold stone, lovingly-tended flower beds and horticultural show-standard rose gardens interspersed with beautifully-maintained stretches of lush verdant lawn. It oozed money, unashamedly flaunted its wealth. And on that sunny day in early June, it had never looked better.

Michael left Munira and the technicians on a bench and as teacher in charge, wandered around keeping an eye on things. The Beechwood kids were scattered around the square. Some sat in groups on the grass and others sat on wrought iron benches, while a few stood around looking cool. They were all lovely children; the sun had obviously gone to his head. But in that warm summer sunshine they looked even lovelier, their smiling happy faces bathed in light and made to look holy, like the Virgin Mary or Jesus in a Renaissance painting by Raphael or Caravaggio. Sunlight causes our body to release the endorphins that make us feel happy. Not so clever as photosynthesis perhaps, but worthwhile nonetheless.

As always on school trips, and in spite of decades spent challenging gender stereotypes, girls sat with girls and boys with boys. Natasha, Parveen and Sherry sat on a bench consuming vast piles of sandwiches, cakes and fizzy drinks. Ahmed, Jason and Sandeep, who being boys had forgotten or couldn't be arsed to bring a packed lunch, begged and scrounged scraps from the girls, combining feeding with courtship as they'd been genetically programmed to do. The lawn was strewn with groups of children from local schools, each with their distinctive uniform, some lying on the grass sunbathing, their jackets removed, the girls revealing their irresistibly soft white thighs for the titillation of the staring, salivating-like-dogs-on-heat boys, powerless to resist. A group of bored and indolent-looking city kids from Bristol stood out from the more genteel children gathered on the lawn, not wearing uniforms, fighting and swearing loudly to attract attention, flicking food around and giving their hapless teacher a hard time. They stood out like an angry working-class sore.

Michael's attention returned once more to the sheer majesty of Imperial Square. Imagine living in one of those imperial buildings, looking out each day at those colourful flower beds, professionally designed, planted and maintained by the gardeners of Cheltenham Council for your personal delectation, changing with the seasons; pansies, primroses, daffodils and tulips in spring, giving way to roses, petunias, lobelia and geraniums in summer. And looking out at the ever-changing demographic of festival visitors who gathered on the lawn between sessions to talk and drink and flirt, or give interviews to the press-white, sophisticated, middle-aged and middle-class to a man for the jazz and literature festivals, young, naive and full of youthful life for the schools' science event in June.

The lunchtime peace was shattered by a noisy crowd of boys that had gathered in the north-east corner of the square, and the sudden surge of children streaming in that direction meant only one thing – a fight. Like a policeman at a football ground, years of playground duty had conditioned Michael to instinctively recognise the first signs of mob conflict and react accordingly, like Pavlov's dog salivating at the sight and smell of food or the ringing of a bell. Without a moment's thought, he headed straight towards the disturbance, stepping over reclining picnickers as he did so, pushing his way through the mob as he had done so many times before. He was a closet hero. Two boys stood eyeballing each other, face-to-face like two animals vying for territory or females in the wild, sizing each other up, neither side wishing to show fear or weakness.

Myron, a tall, dark-eyed lad, the result of an illicit liaison between his Sri Lankan mother and Jamaican father in the Paradise Hotel in Kingston, sporting an aggressively combed mop of black afro hair like the American civil rights icon Angela Davies, faced Simon, a blond, blue-eyed, wavy-haired boy with acne from St Bartholomew's Cheltenham, wearing a purple school blazer with the Latin inscription "Carpe Diem". They were about to exchange blows. Michael had warned his pupils beforehand not to get involved in any nonsense, especially the hot-headed Myron, whose propensity for easily-provoked physical engagement was legendary. Once he deemed himself to have been insulted, he could not step back. Michael gallantly stepped between the two combatants and separated the warring factions. Like the Montagues and the Capulets, the two clans of Beechwood and St Bartholomew's were involved in an age-old feud, each attracting an angry following of jeering supporters scenting blood and guts.

According to Myron, the posh white kids from Cheltenham had been goading the brown-skinned kids from Hestwell; that most ancient of conflicts between tribes of different colour or religion or culture. Each viewed the other as a threat, as alien, as "the other". In all probability both sides had been guilty of demonising the other. This was not simply a case of racism. When two herds or clans met on the great plains of Africa, there was always the potential for territorial conflict. To the children of Hestwell, the white kids of Cheltenham looked every bit as strange as they did to the children of St Bartholomew's. Enough already!

After lunch alfresco, the pupils attended two further afternoon sessions, on human evolution and making polymers, and then returned to the coach, once the miserable misanthrope Reg had driven his vehicle round to the front of the town hall. As they boarded the bus, many were laden with free pamphlets and posters, while others had bought festival memorabilia from a shop stocking plastic dinosaurs and three shelves of atheist Richard Dawkins's latest book, *The God Delusion*. As the coach left the front of the town hall, Poppy and Molly waved them goodbye. It was three o'clock.

The journey back is always more subdued; school trips are always more tiring than a routine day in the classroom. The pupils were pleasantly tired if not exhausted, the sense of excitement at going somewhere new having dissipated. As the coach retraced its route along the A40, some talked, while others closed their tired eyes and slept. The early evening sun was shining outside, still warm although its position was now lower in the sky. They sped through Gloucestershire, with its lambs and cows and fields of wheat, interspersed with quaint Cotswold villages, each with its funnily-named pub and ancient church. As they passed Oxford, they saw university students waiting for buses and doddery lecturers cycling into town.

By five o'clock they were back in their natural habitat of *ersatz* Islamabad, Calcutta or Mogadishu. The green fields and strange white people of Middle England were now a distant memory as the bus threaded its way through the suburban semi-detached streets of Hestwell, thronged as always with cheerful, swarthy-looking people in turbans, saris and hijabs, with lots of children, but not a cow or sheep in sight.

As they entered Barrington Road, they recognised their friends on the pavement and waved and cheered and jumped for joy. Against the backdrop of the reassuring sight of the school and the mosque, tearful parents greeted and embraced their most precious possession – their children.

The pupils would never forget this day, and nor would Michael. It had been so rich in experience and newness and knowledge, like nothing they had seen before. As they disembarked from the coach almost every child said, "Thank you sir, that was a great day." Michael once again knew why he was a teacher – the most satisfying job in the world.

Chapter 10

༄ ⋯⊛⋯ⓒ⋯⊛⋯ⓜ⋯⊛⋯ⓢ⋯⊛⋯⊛

On the morning of September 11th 2001, an event that would become known as "9/11" occurred in New York City that would send shock waves around the world, changing it forever and affecting even the Beechwood School.

They say you always remember where you were when terrible events like the assassination of President Kennedy or the shooting of John Lennon occurred. The answer was that you were usually on the sofa watching television. On Tuesday September 11th, Michael was carrying out his usual end of school duty in the main hall, cajoling waves of excited children just released from six hours' imprisonment in the classroom, to leave the school premises and go home. Just before his duty ended at 15.35 GMT – 10.35 East Coast Time – the little Aussie science teacher Charlie Reaves zoomed past him in his usual frenetic fashion and whispered, "Have you heard what's happened in America? Terrorists have attacked New York." Before Michael could respond, Charlie had disappeared into the bowels of the school like the Mad Hatter on his way to the tea party.

The first thing that came to mind was that it must be the Palestinians – al-Fatah, Yasser Arafat's PLO – who had developed a perverse penchant for attacking Western targets and the murdering of innocent civilians in the name of their fight for a Palestinian state. If true, it was an action guaranteed to alienate them ever further from the international opinion they so desperately craved to win over, an action guaranteed to make ordinary, fair-minded people distrust and fear Muslims even more than they already did. After the last stragglers had left the building, Michael made his way upstairs to Resources on the first floor, where he knew the television was always on to relieve Jane and her team from the tedium of daily business. As he entered the photocopying room he was confronted by a crowd of about ten wide-mouthed teachers, huddled around a large screen and staring at reruns of the day's surrealistic events in America. The video showed a plane crashing into a huge glistening glass skyscraper and exploding, and then a second plane doing the same thing into another building. Then the skyscrapers collapsed like a pack of cards, throwing dense white clouds of dust through the streets of lower Manhattan, like a winter blizzard, an avalanche, a *nuée ardente* cascading down a horizontal mountain, enveloping everything in its way, covering everything and everybody in a layer of thick white ash. It was like watching the sort of gratuitously violent video games one saw at seaside amusement arcades or that young kids played on their Nintendo Game Boy Christmas presents.

As they watched the ashen face of the BBC's North America correspondent, Matt Frei, trying to make sense of a scene that resembled the computer-generated horror of a disaster movie like *Independence Day*, those gathered around the television were palpably shocked. The attacked buildings were identified as the Twin Towers of the World Trade Centre. English teacher and consummate atheist Lydia Paynter put her hand over her mouth and cried "Oh God!" "Jesus H Christ," gasped the lapsed Catholic and geography teacher Chris Jennings, a look of utter incomprehension radiating from his dilated pupils. Unreconstructed Marxist-Leninist history teacher and part-time *Socialist Worker* salesman Jerry Ledbetter smiled with the satisfaction that America was finally reaping what it had sown. As more teachers dropped in to photocopy tests and lesson plans for the next day, the crowd around the box swelled.

Over and over again the television screen showed replays of the by-now-assumed-to-be-hijacked planes smashing into the two glass superstructures and exploding into orange fireballs. An Islamic terrorist group calling itself al-Qaeda was being blamed as the probable perpetrator of this most ungodly of acts. Tearful New Yorkers were shown embracing each other, pointing to the sky in disbelief and crying, "Oh my God!" Others could be seen running away from the approaching dust cloud in fear of their lives, but as in that most common of nightmares, being unable to run fast enough to escape and being enveloped by it. White zombie-like figures crouched in doorways like ghosts as the tsunami of debris washed by. The flashing blue lights of the NYPD and FDNY could be seen trying to reach the stricken skyscrapers in downtown Manhattan. As the flames consumed the upper part of the buildings and thick black smoke bellowed out of broken windows, the silhouettes of matchstick people – stockbrokers, Wall Street traders, office secretaries, mothers, fathers, masters of the universe – could be seen jumping out of windows on the eightieth floor to a certain death below. A guy called Osama bin Laden was increasingly being mentioned.

Michael left the stunned crowd in resources and clambered up the stairs to the science floor to have a slash and prepare himself for home.

"Have you heard what's happened?" shouted a happier-than-usual Munira Masood, as he stuffed some documents into his leather bag and prepared to leave.

"I've been watching it in resources," said Michael. "Terrible isn't it?"

"The Americans had it coming," Munira replied, her normally

kind and caring face exuding a disturbingly ruthless messianic zeal. "It's about time they got a bloody nose."

Michael was shocked at his colleague's response.

On his journey home along the M4, Michael tuned into "Five Live" to get the latest update. He noticed that other motorists too were glued to their radios, listening intently to the horrible news. How could Munira, a decent and westernised Muslim, a Brummie for God's sake who harboured no hatred or vindictiveness towards anyone and supported Aston Villa, react like this? It wasn't just the absurdity of her having enjoyed several holidays in the States with her brother and his family. But if such a lovely, kind and gentle friend could react like this, what hope was there for the fundamentalists? Just how much power did her religion hold over her and her co-religionists?

The events of 9/11 changed the world for ever. The Big Apple, that hitherto impregnable beacon of freedom, that custodian of the Enlightenment, had lost its innocence. As the hijackers smashed into the Twin Towers, murdering their terrified and screaming passengers and obliterating the lives of nearly three thousand innocent employees in the World Trade Centre from every country and every religion on earth, they did not only destroy the World Trade Centre – they destroyed the credibility of Islam itself. The planes that desecrated the sanctity of New York on that fateful September morning as they appeared like vultures from the clear blue Manhattan sky, that haven for millions of ragged refugees escaping persecution and poverty who had sailed past the Statue of Liberty and been given sanctuary on Ellis Island, heralded the clash of civilisations between the West and Islam. The Statue of Liberty shed a tear on 9/11, ashamed that it had in some way let down the huddled masses yearning to breathe free, the wretched refuse of Europe's teeming shores seeking the American Dream. There could be no greater contrast between the liberal, tolerant, life-giving city of New York and the hopeless nihilist death cult of fundamentalist Islam.

Back in Britain, the world was changed forever as well, but in unexpected ways. For an indigenous population that had lived through the book burnings of Salman Rushdie's *Satanic Verses* in 1989, the 9/11attacks confirmed their worst fears about Islam and intensified their distrust of Muslims. Except for those on the left who were congenitally programmed to identify with any cause that is anti-American and that involves the perceived persecution of anyone that is not white, the terrorists' aim of gaining sympathy for their jihad spectacularly backfired. But for the Muslims themselves, it was different. When a community's faith or identity is challenged, the initial response is to close ranks and enter into a state of denial. And so it was at Hestwell. Instead of feeling ashamed of the atrocity carried out by their co-religionists in their name and questioning the teachings of a faith whose holy scriptures preached jihad, Muslims became even more pious.

At the local mosque, attendance at Friday prayers increased dramatically. People whose faith had waned in the face of the much more agreeable, easy-going British way of life, suddenly "saw the light" and turned up to prayers in white Islamic costumes, Koran in hand, that far away messianic look in their eyes that believed in one God, Allah, and his prophet Muhammad, to the exclusion of all else, and that non-believers or apostates were *haram*, unclean, who should burn in hell. Skull caps and beards were once again essential Islamic accessories. Outside the mosque, the virulently anti-Western Islamist group, Hizb ut-Tahrir, "the party of liberation", banned throughout the Islamic world and responsible for the radicalisation of vulnerable young worshippers, high on the indoctrination of Friday prayers to join the jihad and commit acts of terror in the name of Allah, continued to distribute their insidious literature condemning democracy and preaching the resurrection of a mythological Islamic caliphate somewhere in the Middle East. The organisation that embodied the very mindset of the 9/11 terrorists, instead of feeling remorse for the barbarism of their co-religionists, continued to peddle their hate-filled, anti-Semitic, homophobic filth just a stone's throw from the school, poisoning the minds of Beechwood children – Michael's children – as if 9/11 had never happened – or maybe *because* of it.

In times of war or natural disasters when friends and loved ones are wiped out and cities are reduced to rubble, instead of condemning the God that allowed this to happen, the churches are filled with people praising the Almighty and asking for forgiveness. Religion: the opium of the people, where belief is inversely proportional to evidence. After an earthquake, the houses of worship are filled with peasants praying to the very same God that stood by while their houses were flattened and their children and parents were crushed to death. Michael remembered as a child being taken to the Louis Street synagogue by uncle Israel on Rosh Hashanah or Yom Kippur. It was overflowing with worshippers, many of whom had lost relatives in the war. How could they believe in a God that allowed six million Jews to be gassed in the concentration camps? What sort of a God would allow this to happen to his chosen people? A God that didn't care, the vengeful and vindictive God of the Old Testament who so loved to smite sinners? Or a God that didn't exist? If God did exist, why did he allow the Holocaust? If he ever existed, God died in Auschwitz: he was either gassed along with the chosen people he'd led out of Egypt with an outstretched arm or committed suicide when he saw what man – *his* creation – was capable of, that the creation of man with the free will to do evil, was a catastrophic error of judgement.

At the Beechwood School things were changing as well. As their faith became temporarily strengthened by the perceived Islamophobic backlash following the 9/11 attacks, more and more Muslim girls started wearing the hijab headscarves previously worn only by a pious few. Sixth-form girls who had discarded the hijabs of their childhood, liberating themselves from the conservative clutches of their claustrophobic religion, celebrating the feminine beauty of their lovely hair and face like other girls, capitulated under relentless pressure from misogynist male relatives and so-called community leaders – imams, fathers, uncles, brothers – and became once again desexualised and shackled by the medieval dress code of their Pakistani ancestors. They were like colourful butterflies being forced back into the confinement of the cocoon from which they had just escaped after briefly tasting the freedom and the feeling of sheer exhilaration that comes from emerging as a fully-formed imago, spreading their wings for the first time and tasting the ephemeral sweetness of life's nectar.

Ramadan was celebrated with renewed vigour. At the entrance to the mosque, traffic was brought to a standstill as ever more worshippers attended prayers five times a day. Children took more time off school or arrived late for lessons, temporarily convinced that their religion took precedence over their education.

Then sixth-formers started appearing in niqabs, black Islamic costumes common in those bastions of enlightenment and human rights – Saudi Arabia and Iran – covering the whole body except for an eye slit, protecting defenceless girls from the lecherous ogling of crazed, sex-starved boys. It started in a tutorial a few weeks after 9/11, when Michael noticed an amorphous-looking, ghostlike shape, like a black Dalek, hovering near the back of his sixth-form tutor group. There was no way of recognising who she/he/it was apart from the register, which indicated that she must be Yasmin Ahmed – a quiet, polite, not particularly clever girl with jet-black hair and a lovely smooth face that was always smiling.

"Is that you, Yasmin?" Michael asked in a worried voice, like a parent trying to identify a child hiding behind a tree in a game of hide and seek.

"Of course it's me sir," Yasmin replied with mock surprise, "who did you think it was?" As always happens in these circumstances, the students closed ranks and stood in solidarity with their classmate, irrespective of what she had done.

"But *why*, Yasmin?" asked Michael, trying tactfully to defuse the situation.

"I just feel the need to dress more modestly sir, as instructed by the holy Koran and commanded by Allah, peace be upon him. I have become more devout recently and feel the need to express more fully my faith in God." Yasmin, the attractive, black-haired younger sister of the very cool and highly westernised high-flying Oxbridge hopeful Irfan, had previously not shown the slightest interest in religion, preferring instead to giggle and chatter with her mates rather than answering questions in science or discussing the meaning of life.

Michael immediately reported Yasmin to the head of sixth form, Joseph Rooney. He warned Joseph that unless we acted quickly others would follow. And sure enough, the very next day her friend Salima turned up wearing a niqab to assembly. Joseph excluded both girls and told them not to return until they were wearing normal school uniform.

And Michael began to change as well. Until 9/11 he had trod warily with Muslim children, preferring to placate or appease their heightened sensitivity to any criticism of their religion, like most, not wishing to confront them out of fear. He recalled the emotional reaction of an anxious year ten boy named Osman when he had jokingly referred to the story of Adam and Eve as being a myth, a fairy tale invented by man to explain creation. They really *did* take the Koran literally. He had witnessed the hysterical reaction of Muslims – not just in Pakistan but on the streets of Bradford – to the publication of the *Satanic Verses* and the ensuing book-burnings. The Ayatollah of Iran had issued a *fatwa* on the author, Salman Rushdie, sentencing him to death for apostasy. He had identified the Rushdie affair as an attack on the very fabric of British society, free speech, but was unsure how to deal with it. 9/11 changed all that. Michael realised that the existential threat posed by Islamic fundamentalism to British society and everything he held dear was too great to ignore. As often happens after a defeat, a disaster or a personal tragedy, the catastrophic events of 9/11 gave him new strength to confront the Muslim question, the enemy within.

So instead of treading carefully for fear of causing offence – which meant any criticism of Muslims or Islam – he went on the offensive and embarked on a campaign of proactively confronting the problem. Michael believed in his heart of hearts that the overwhelming majority of Muslims were decent people who wanted their children to do well at school, go to university, get a good job and integrate into British society. As a teacher he *had* to believe this. His Muslim pupils were as enthusiastic as everyone else, the vast majority being delightful, caring children. But he owed it to himself and to them, to be honest.

So he ordered a set of giant colourful posters from the Open University, showing the evolution of man from a single cell to *Homo sapiens*, and displayed them prominently on the walls of his lab next to posters depicting the periodic table and the Big Bang. Muslims overwhelmingly believed in the Adam and Eve creation story, so it was essential to make it unequivocally clear, once and for all, no ifs or buts, that science believed in the theory of evolution, for which there was overwhelming evidence and for which the existence of a god – a First Mover, a supernatural being – was superfluous to requirements. This didn't mean being openly hostile to a child's religious belief or making fun of it; of course not. Freedom of religion was an essential part of the tolerant, pluralistic, democratic society in which Michael passionately believed. But indulging religious superstition was not doing the children any favours either. In order to integrate into a secular society like Britain, they had to understand that their irrational religious belief was an anomaly.

The theory of evolution was the basis of modern biology in the same way that the periodic table was the basis of modern chemistry and the Big Bang was the basis of modern physics. Michael would refer to these posters as often as possible so that evolution became a normal part of everyday conversation rather than some wacky show-stopping hypothesis. The idea was that it would become as self-evident as a map of the world or the alphabet. With his newly-acquired confidence, Michael began to teach the theory of evolution with renewed vigour, exposing his knowledge-thirsty children to a hands-on array of preserved animal specimens, skeletons, fossils and embryos. In spring he brought in tadpoles from his own pond to show how aquatic creatures could "evolve" into terrestrial ones. Pupils built their own DNA models and extracted DNA from kiwi fruit. Live maggots were brought in, not only to scare the living daylights out of the pupils but to ram home the idea that the concept of adaptation which everyone used to describe the way in which an organism was well-suited to its environment was a *de facto* acceptance of evolution. Fun lessons, but with an unbending message. Like a barrister in court, Michael wanted to present enough evidence to convince the jury – the pupils – that evolution had occurred beyond reasonable doubt.

After the initial shock of 9/11 and the coming to terms with its implications, the number of Muslims attending his extra-curricular trips actually began to rise. Sixth formers increasingly wanted to demonstrate that although they were still proud Muslims, they did not share the closed mindset of Bin Laden and wanted to expose themselves to the new ideas and experiences that London had to offer. And this despite an increase in hijab wearing and regular mosque attendance. Taking kids to see the overtly Christian images of Raphael, or plays like Schiller's *Don Carlos,* which exposes the hypocrisy of religion and the church and by implication Islam, were no longer off limits.

Friday prayers had long been used as an excuse for lateness by scoundrels who shamelessly misused religion for their own selfish ends. But after 9/11, Michael challenged every pupil who tried it on, and punished those who persisted. During Ramadan, misbehaviour by Muslims unable to cope with the absurd demands of an ancient religion in the twenty-first century obliging them to fast every day for a month from dawn till dusk was punished rather than tolerated. In a secular school, it wasn't fair on the others. Room 101, the sin bin, was overwhelmed by children unable to deal with the mediaeval dictates of the Koran, which had become an anachronism to their everyday lives. With the exception of a strong-willed few, instead of transporting one to a higher plane of spiritual consciousness, the absence of food and drink makes one tired and irritable, and one thinks only of food and drink.

Bottom sets were always a pain in the backside, and by year eleven, they were virtually impossible to teach. One had to humour them and hope they didn't wreck the place, and would stay in the room until the bell released them from their penal servitude. These classes overwhelmingly consisted of Muslims, who felt trapped between a strict and backward-looking religiously conservative culture and a modern, secular, liberal Britain. And a sprinkling of white working-class children. Instead of pretending not to hear the never-ending tirade of virulently homophobic and anti-Semitic remarks, Michael challenged the pupils – not just because it was offensive, but because it would be doing them no favours, and it would be irresponsible even to allow them to leave school thinking that such comments were acceptable in polite society.

Outside the mosque, bearded men in white Islamic dress and skull caps and that far away other-worldly look in their glazed dark-brown eyes continued to distribute *Hizb ut-Tahrir* leaflets after Friday prayers to the vulnerable children of Beechwood, undermining everything that the school stood for. A house of learning next to a house of book burning. Michael made a point of collecting these flyers calling for jihad and the undermining of Western democracy, as well as the overthrow of Middle Eastern states to create a caliphate, and passing them on to the new headmaster, Damien Bickerstaff. For some reason Tony Blair refused (or was unable) to ban this insidious organisation that not only radicalised young people but nurtured jihadists who went on to blow themselves up in public places, maiming and murdering innocent civilians. Michael put pressure on Damien to express the school's concerns to the imam of the mosque. These guys were corrupting our precious children.

But *Hizb ut-Tahrir* kept pumping out their poison, so Michael collected yet more leaflets, mingling with the worshippers after Friday prayers, his swarthy Semitic looks rendering him invisible to a crowd high on the unassailable certainty of their belief as they greeted him with the peaceful Arab greeting "*Salam Alaikum*".

Once again he petitioned an increasingly reluctant headmaster who did not wish to rock the boat and was unable or unwilling to accept the danger on his doorstep and talk to the imam.

Michael had joined the "war on terror". Most of his colleagues with their unshakable commitment to multi-culturalism and their fear of how Muslims might react thought he was mad, over-sensitive and probably prejudiced because he was a Jew. Like a biblical prophet mocked as a crank and a doom-monger by the Children of Israel, his words were ignored, his message unheeded. He was a one-man army fighting an enemy that others couldn't or wouldn't see – like the little boy who saw that the emperor had no clothes. A paranoid delusionalist who thought too much and took life too seriously.

Meanwhile, on the streets of Hestwell, more and more niqab-wearing Daleks began to appear. After the 9/11 attacks, the world, Hestwell and the Beechwood School itself would never be the same again.

Chapter 11

Like a parent, one of the greatest joys of being a teacher, as the one *in loco parentis*, was watching your children grow up. Assuming of course you stuck around in the same school for long enough – which Michael had noticed was becoming increasingly a thing of the past in the post-Thatcherite world of the twenty-first century. Like everyone else in the "modern world", teachers, although still driven by a sense of vocation and altruism, were increasingly focused, high-powered technocrats, ambitious for status and rapid promotion and the material wealth that this could bring. They aspired to wear expensive clothes, eat out in fashionable restaurants and see the Seven Wonders of the World before they were thirty. Gone were the carefree days of the Sixties and Seventies when teachers like himself – motivated solely by a naive idealism to change the world and create a more equal society, and for whom materialism was a dirty word – could simply drift into teaching without any detailed game plan for the next twenty years. They were definitely not focused.

Little Anastasia Kanowski arrived at Beechwood in September 2008. Like an increasing number of children in London, her parents had taken advantage of Poland's recent accession to the European Union – that rich man's club, that high-speed gravy train travelling first class from Brussels all the way to the bank – and sought a better life in Britain where the streets were paved with gold, jobs grew on trees, and welfare payments were the most generous in Europe if not the world. She had grown up in a small provincial town just outside Krakow, where everyone was white, Catholic and Slavic, and her first language was Polish. She now found herself in an enormous comprehensive school in darkest Hestwell, where most of the children originated from the Indian subcontinent and spoke a mixture of Hindi, Urdu or Gujarati at home with their grandparents and the never-ending stream of recently-arrived members of their extended families from Delhi and Lahore.

For an adult this could have been a huge, possibly insurmountable culture shock. But kids see the world differently. They take everything as it comes without the ingrained prejudices and misgivings of their parents, without their own cultural baggage, and adapt effortlessly to their new environment. It seemed perfectly natural to Anastasia that her new friends would be Khadijah and Simranjeet and that within a year she would be speaking almost perfect accent-free English. When she arrived in year seven she was shy, extremely deferential and well-mannered, as gentle as a Chopin sonata. The inherent language problems of new immigrants mean that they start life in a lower set so they can get extra ESL help.

As soon as Michael walked into his first lesson with 7S3, he noticed this beautiful child on the second row, not confident enough to sit at the front, not naughty enough to sit at the back, a vast lion's mane of blonde frizzy hair emanating from every follicle in her ever-attentive head, her big intelligent blue eyes fully open and craving for knowledge. The eyes of a child reveal its inner soul, the soul of an angel. Like her Polish-speaking parents, Michael was immensely proud of her.

Michael had watched as this shy little child from the ancient forests of Poland had metamorphosed like a voracious leaf-munching caterpillar into an exquisite nectar-drinking ballerina of a butterfly with white gossamer wings, like an ugly duckling becoming a swan, into a confident but still modest sixth-former who was now on track for Oxbridge. She was every teacher's dream; industrious, helpful, laughed at his jokes. She loved communing with nature on the heath, where her natural curiosity and inquisitiveness flourished like no other.

As the years went by her exam results improved along with her English, and with this came the confidence to ask and answer questions and perform experiments. By year eleven she had worked her way up into the top set and had lots of friends, all of whom loved her. It was impossible in the purest sense of the word not to love this child of God. Anastasia means 'resurrection' in Greek – everyone around her was born again.

Shakeel Hussein was a devout Sufi Muslim whose parents had arrived in Britain from Pakistan in the late Eighties. He had an almost meditational calmness about him, so characteristic of the Sufi tradition which fashioned his very being, and was active in the mosque. Michael only met him in year ten, when for once he had been dealt a decent GCSE biology set in the annual lottery of class allocations that his prematurely balding and hopelessly disorganised new head of science, Ray Milburn, passed off as a fair and equitable timetable.

Shakeel had been raised to be a good Muslim, kind and polite and instilled with the Prophet's love of learning and enquiry by his equally humble parents. They turned up every parents' evening, his mother in her black Islamic costume and headscarf, his father in his best off-the-peg Marks and Spencer suit, to hear the good news about their most precious possession and life insurance, their eldest son. Sometimes a pupil stands out because of his brashness or cheekiness; Shakeel stood out because of his self-effacing modesty. He sat on the front bench so that he could be as close to the teacher as possible with his friend Mathew, spotlessly turned out, long flowing jet-black hair like a throwback to the psychedelic flower-power days of *Sergeant Pepper*, when free love and peace were in the air and The Beatles dabbled in eastern mysticism under the auspices of the colourful conman guru Maharishi Mahesh Yogi. He looked like an Asian Paul McCartney.

Shakeel was a joy to teach because he was intelligent enough to understand the things that Michael found interesting and most enjoyed teaching, like genetic engineering, biotechnology and evolution. In the aftermath of nine-eleven, Michael wanted to instil – was increasingly *driven* to instil in his students, especially the Muslims – that science was the key to knowledge, not the woolly musings of religion, and that it was only through science that disease could be cured and man's supply of food and energy assured. He had long since stopped pussy-footing about the veracity of the Big Bang and evolution, for fear of offending the Muslims for whom such thoughts were heresy and anathema. These were no longer alternative explanations to the scriptures, which one could take or leave; they were theories, like gravity, for which there was overwhelming evidence. The days of sitting on the fence, of pandering to the antediluvian mindset of these backward-thinking people, were over, because they gave credence to the very Islamists who had robbed Manhattan of its innocence and wanted to bring our enlightened civilisation to its knees. Teaching had always been political. Back in Botswana it had been the insidious influence of apartheid South Africa on the black children of Moketse; in Somersby it had been the stifling effect of politically correctness on freedom of speech and the teaching of Afro-Caribbeans. But never so urgently as in post nine-eleven Beechwood.

Shakeel had no intention of relinquishing his religion – why should he? But his enquiring mind, possibly activated by a study of the Koran in the same way that Jewish minds are stimulated by studying the Torah, loved science, and he could appreciate its uniqueness in solving mankind's earthly problems, if not its spiritual ones. He relished asking and answering questions. His brand of Sufi Islam had never recognised a contradiction between the two antagonistic philosophies, unlike the fundamentalists who were in danger of taking over the asylum. Each had its role to play in leading a full and honourable life. He was also receptive to the second of Michael's politically-driven arguments: that science generated thousands of interesting well-paid jobs, which would not only provide a worthwhile career, but would liberate students from the grasping tentacles of their increasingly ghettoised communities, and provide them with a pathway into mainstream society and the best insurance against alienation and extremism – integration.

Shakeel got straight As at GCSE, and went on to study chemistry, physics and biology at A-level. Although Michael was no longer his teacher, his continued commitment to Michael's mantra, $E=mc^2$ – Education = more curiosity squared – meant that he attended virtually every extra-curricular trip organised by his mentor to broaden his education, and increasingly to reveal the richness of British society and give him a reason to be part of it. Shakeel attended lectures at the Royal Institution on Xenotransplantation and Quantum Theory, and asked questions at both. He attended an exhibition of the sculptor Antony Gormley at the Hayward Gallery and was gobsmacked by the display of life-sized bronze human figures perched on buildings across the London skyline. He was the first to volunteer to be part of the audience on BBC Question Time at the London Oratory School – alma mater of Tony Blair's son Euan – and, reverting to modest Sufi mode, allowed himself to be enthralled by the televised debate between government ministers, eminent journalists and the Great British Public. Which included a question from Michael himself – as always leading by example and not at all averse to the possibility of giving a performance, of hearing his own voice and appearing on the telly. Just think of the adulation he would get back at school tomorrow. Wallowing in the fame – ooh yes, I don't mind if I do.

On the tube back to Hestwell, Michael experienced possibly the high point of his career: his pupils, his beloved pupils whom he had tried so hard to enlighten and educate, arguing excitedly about the evening's debate, confidently discussing education and the health service, while the passengers looked on in amazement. Elizabeth Peacock, the cleverest girl the school had ever produced, who had herself asked the Minister of Health a question that evening on cancer treatment, sat opposite, quietly reading Maigret – in French. Michael apologised to a passenger sitting nearby for his students talking so loudly about politics on a train. The passenger replied, "You're kidding pal, I love politics and I love seeing your beautiful students talking politics with such passion." Utter pride welled up in Michael's lachrymose eyes.

When Shakeel left to study biochemistry at Cambridge, he presented Michael with a copy of Darwin's *Origin of Species* and the Koran. And he kept coming back to the school that had so willingly nurtured him, to help out at open days and talk to the children about life at university. He had taken and now he was giving. He had greatly enriched the school and the lives of the teachers, like Michael, who had had the pleasure of teaching him.

Seema Kaur Kholi was an Afghani refugee whose family had escaped the terror of the Taliban just before the invasion of that country by the Allies, following the attack on the Twin Towers. Being Sikhs, her parents had suffered discrimination and intimidation by religious fanatics, who wanted to create a medieval Islamic theocracy in a country where Muslims, Sikhs and Hindus had once lived in peace with each other. Several of their close friends had been brutally murdered by the warriors of God, the *mujahideen*, so they were forced to leave Kabul, where their community had lived for generations, and their beautiful house with its spacious jasmine-scented verandas with spectacular views of the Hindu Kush, and flee across the border to Pakistan and then on to India, where they had boarded a plane to Heathrow and requested asylum.

Seema had been only a little girl when this had happened, but she still had recurring nightmares of being chased by crazed, Kalashnikov-toting men in tribal robes with long Islamic beards. When Michael first met her in year nine as a cover for the perpetually-menopausal Mrs Chakraborty, she was a shy, pale-looking girl, whose traumatised eyes reflected the suffering of her people and their war-torn country. Seema belonged to a growing number of refugee children at the school whose families had escaped the horrors of war in Iraq, Somalia and Afghanistan – the flotsam of an Islamic world descending into barbarism and chaos in the name of their faith. Many had witnessed first-hand the deaths of friends and loved ones and the bombing of their homes and villages back to the Stone Age.

But refugees can achieve great things. Thousands of Jews escaping the pogroms of nineteenth century Russia had arrived in New York with nothing but the rags they wore and the hope for a better future and become great musicians, entrepreneurs and intellectuals in the "Land of the Free". It is often this very status as the outsider with nothing to lose, the new kid on the block, which motivates the immigrant to excel and outperform the indigenous population. It was Seema's good fortune that she had ended up in Britain and the Beechwood School in particular, where teachers were sympathetic to her predicament and prepared to go the extra mile to help her.

In year nine Seema was like a frightened mouse, a girl whose faded and torn clothing reflected the poverty of her parents, a weather-beaten flower that refused to open. But all that changed in year ten when she found herself in the top set for chemistry. Like a cherry tree coming into blossom in spring in response to the sun's warmth and refreshing April showers, so Seema responded to the stimulation of her bright and lively classmates and the life-enhancing charisma emanating from her new teacher, Mr Zabinsky.

Her eyes were now alive with interest, her face glowing with the joy of learning and being taught by a teacher who understood her. With the innocent flirtatiousness of a teenage girl with a crush, she constantly asked questions to get the teacher's attention, and to show the world that she had arrived. "Hey guys look at me, I'm no longer the Cinderella from Afghanistan, I'm just like you." She began to smile and laugh and make jokes. As her petals slowly opened she exuded the heady scent of confidence, the bright colours of intelligence, the sweet nectar of success. The harsh Taliban winter was over. She produced reams of meticulous homework, carried out every assignment given, and showed an interest in everything from mitosis to the fractional distillation of crude oil. Her favourite element was potassium, because when it reacted with water it was just like her-effervescent, brightly glowing, precocious.

Seema volunteered for everything and had decided meanwhile to become either a doctor or a biochemical engineer – whatever that was. She fitted in well with the rest of the class, who could not believe she was the same shy girl who used to sit dreamily, day after day, lost in her own war-torn world thousands of miles away. She had started to think big. She wanted to make the world better and maybe one day go back and help her people. Such are the dreams of the young, who in their youthful optimism see an infinite lifetime of opportunity stretching out in front of them as far as the Hindu Kush. She was like Khaled Hosseini's "kite runner", who comes to life when flying his simple kite high over the alleyways of 1970s Kabul. Only here it was the chance to fly her newly-discovered confidence and her gift for science over the heads of her peers and out over the streets of Hestwell and beyond. She was free at last.

She had escaped from a primitive country that would never be at peace, where the unchanging conservatism of the tribal, male-dominated clans would never allow the likes of Seema, or indeed any woman, to succeed. Her life expectancy would have been low. She would have been condemned to a life of domestic servitude and treated like a farm animal to be milked and exploited, a breeding machine to be discarded when she had outgrown her usefulness. If she had been allowed to attend school, she would have left at the age of thirteen.

She chose English Literature and German in the sixth form – which was not a rejection of science or Michael, but rather proof that she was mature enough make up her own mind. Or maybe it *was* the vengeful act of a young girl who on realising that she could not marry the teacher she loved – who had all along been treating her in loco parentis as his own daughter – tried to hurt him.

The truth was, she was good at everything. She went on to study politics at university and joined the United Nations.

Chapter 12

❦❦❦❦❦❦❦❦❦❦❦❦❦❦

The news of Khalid Khan's death while on holiday in Dubai shocked everyone. The head made the announcement to a stunned staff room in a meeting at the start of the new term. Apparently Khalid had been riding a quad bike in the desert, when his vehicle flipped over on a dune and catapulted his young carefree head and frail gangly body against a rising pile of Arabian sand. He had not been wearing a crash helmet. There were gasps of horror, mumblings of "Oh no, poor Khalid – I can't believe it." Tears were shed; people sobbed and shook their heads in disbelief.

Damien Bickerstaff, in typically deluded senior management jargon, described the unfortunate boy as a diligent student who had been expected to get good A-levels and study nanochemistry at Imperial College. There would be a service at the local mosque on Friday, where staff could pay their respects.

Khalid was a lovely lad, but Michael, as his form tutor, knew better than most that this unfortunate victim of circumstance was a complete piss-head who had a reputation second to none for being the sixth-form joker. And for this reason he was loved by his fellow students, who always like a joker, a rogue, a rebel. He always arrived late for registration, never completed his subject assignments on time and had managed to scrape into the upper-sixth by the narrowest of margins. After virtually every set of tests, his parents were sent a "letter of concern" threatening to expel him from school unless he mended his ways. Each time he would promise and each time he would revert to type; like most people over a certain age, he was unable to change. He had the ability to make everyone laugh with his funny gestures, his eccentric mannerisms and the pranks he would get up to. Amongst the teachers he was known for his outrageous excuses for not delivering the goods; his dog ate his homework, his alarm clock went off late, he was abducted by aliens. He seemed to perpetually wander the corridors, greeting everyone with a supercilious gesture or wisecrack, like a hyperactive bird nervously moving its head from side to side, Manchester United scarf thrown around his neck like a French intellectual. His *faux* remorse and endearing smile – head cocked disarmingly to one side, eyes wide with confected contrition, eyebrows raised in resignation, the sad pursed lips of a clown – meant that it was impossible to get angry with him. And if you did he would just make an exaggerated "I'm sorry Ollie" face, or put his hand over his mouth and giggle; which made the teachers giggle as well. You wanted to pull him to your bosom and give him a hug, suckle him, cuddle him like a baby, console him – but that could be construed as professionally inappropriate. End of career.

The service at the local mosque was in keeping with Khalid's life – a piece of surrealistic theatre. Droves of worshippers turned up as usual for Friday prayers, some dressed in traditional Islamic costume while others came in ordinary work clothes. A constant flow of Muslim humanity streamed through the shared mosque-school entrance from Barrington Road, mostly dark-skinned pious-looking men of Pakistani or African appearance and a smaller number of shawled, hijabed or niqabed women walking deferentially in accordance with ancient custom, several paces behind their menfolk. Others arrived in flash cars – Mercedes,

BMWs, Audis – blocking the entrance from Barrington Road, hooting impatiently, showing off their un-Islamic material wealth.

The Beechwood contingent – the head, Michael, head of science Ray, Jay, Munira, new head of sixth form James Bollinger – entered the mosque together at around midday, safety in numbers like a posse of gangsters entering a Wild West saloon. Michael had always wanted to enter this mosque, this hotbed of Islamist indoctrination, this corrupter of rational thought, to see what really went on there. Just as in an orthodox synagogue, the women had to wear a shawl or head scarf for reasons of modesty and general female subjugation, and prayed separately from the men – in this case in a side room. In accordance with Islamic tradition, everyone had to take off their shoes at the entrance to the mosque – hundreds of identical shoes, what were the chances of ever seeing them again?

The only mosque Michael had ever visited before was the Dome of the Rock in Jerusalem back in 1971, with its iconic golden dome, one of the holiest places in Islam. It was completed on the site of the Second Temple to wind up the Jews, as has happened so often throughout history, one religion asserting itself over another, a church built on the site of a mosque, a mosque built on the site of a church, after the Second *Fitna* in 691 AD, on the rock where the prophet Mohammad was said to have ascended to heaven. As a young man of twenty-one, dabbling with the idealistic Zionist notion of settling in the Holy Land before realising the absurdity of that dream, Michael remembered visiting that mosque on a searingly-hot September day, seeking shade from the merciless sunlight, the pure blue Israeli sky framing the golden dome that brilliantly reflected the Middle Eastern sun. He remembered rows of shoes outside that entrance too and the fear of never seeing his grubby Marks and Spencer sandals again.

They were met by the reassuringly friendly and gentle face of Michael's old protégé, Shakeel, still on leave from Cambridge, who seated them in the overflow corridor like guests of honour, just outside the full-to-the-brim main prayer hall. Michael watched how new arrivals raised their open hands to their face in prayer, gazing upwards towards Allah, and then prostrating themselves on the ground in submission. He observed through an open door how the all-male congregation periodically prostrated itself and uttered the words "*Allahu Akbar*", God is great. Michael recognised some familiar Beechwood faces – members of Khalid's tutor group who greeted him respectfully. Like a Catholic crossing himself on entering a church, or a Jew touching and kissing the mezuzah, a holy scroll on entering a synagogue, every religion had its own entry rituals designed to humble its worshippers in the presence of the Almighty. It was just like being in synagogue. The constant coming and going and never-ending conversation, reminded him of the Chancery Lane synagogue in Leeds, on a Saturday morning in the mid-sixties, where he recalled laughing and joking with Raymond Fleischer and his brother Harvey, and being constantly told to "shush" by some old fogey sitting nearby. The head was surprised by this apparent lack of respect, which would be unthinkable in a Sikh Temple. It was the same in church – you had to keep *schtumm*.

The internal simplicity of the building and the complete absence of icons or human images which might tempt the weak-minded to take the Lord's name in vain or indulge in a spot of idol worship was just like a synagogue. Even the drone of the imam's prayer as he recited the Koran and the occasional discordant response of the congregation sounded exactly like a rabbi reciting the Torah in the synagogue. How ironic that a religion that had in almost every sense evolved from Judaism and adopted so many of its customs lock stock and barrel – circumcision, kosher/halal food, separating men from women – should be so viscerally anti-Semitic. And yet inside the mosque, Muslims, looked far less threatening than they did outside their natural habitat, far less like crazed jihadis. They looked quite normal in fact – just like you and me.

As the imam said a prayer for the dead, the body of Khalid emerged from the prayer hall, carried by sobbing friends and family in an open coffin. The box was laid down on a row of chairs and immediately attracted a crowd eager to get a last glimpse of their deceased friend. Michael joined the queue of mourners and finally got a look at the boy who never did his homework but made everybody laugh. As with most dead bodies, Khalid seemed to be sleeping. It was impossible to believe that he was really dead; that he was no more; that he had ceased to be. He was dressed in white Islamic clothing, hands folded on his chest, and seemed, like Victor all those years ago in Botswana, to be peaceful and smiling. One half expected him to suddenly sit up and burst out laughing, his feigned death turning out to be yet another of his crazy stunts. But he didn't. His happy made-up face gazed calmly out of the satin-lined coffin, looking smaller and younger than in real life. It was difficult to comprehend that only a few weeks before, Khalid had wandered the corridors making funny faces at everyone, proffering his endless repertoire of fantastic excuses to bemused members of staff.

Michael shed a tear and embraced two of Khalid's distraught classmates, their eyes red with mourning; his tutees Tariq and Osman.

Once again the big existential questions reared their head. If there was a God, why did he let this happen, and to one so young? If God gave us free will, then he must have expected this to happen even if he didn't cause it, just as he can't have been surprised when six million Jews were exterminated in the Holocaust. He had created a fatally-flawed being in his own image, a faulty model that like its creator, could not help fucking things up. How come all this pious behaviour, this endless praying and chanting five times a day, the fasting during Ramadan and the utterance of so many "*Allahu Akbars*", had not saved Khalid, taken in the prime of his life, or spared his loving parents their grief, the sleepless nights, the recriminations that they should never have taken him to Dubai in the first place? If Allah was so Akbar, why did he let this happened to a good Muslim, albeit a Muslim who worshipped Michael Jackson and Manchester United?

Michael was glad that he'd finally entered this mosque and mourned with others his former pupil. He was glad that he'd finally attended Friday prayers; they no longer seemed quite so alien and threatening. It had felt good communing with Khalid's friends; he felt he had gained their respect. He had a better understanding of Islam. He had broken down barriers.

Outside the mosque, worshippers gathered in the autumn sunshine. The women emerged from their *purdah*, many crying openly, some inconsolable with grief. And as he returned to school for the afternoon session, he spotted a group of bearded men in white Islamic robes and prayer caps, obliviously distributing *Hizb ut-Tahrir* leaflets to his children.

Chapter 13

꩜⊶◉◑⊷◉⊶⊶⊘⊶◉◑⊶⊙⊷◉⊶◉

On the first day of the autumn term in 2012, Michael decided it was time to retire. Over the years, all the original members of the school and the science department in particular – like a body replacing all of its cells over a lifetime – had either retired, left, or in the case of Laszlo, left and been killed in a car crash. That was typical of Laszlo: he couldn't just die like everyone else; he had to live his death as he had lived his life – chaotically and dramatically. His life had been one huge car crash waiting to happen, or more precisely a series of car crashes. From the moment he crashed out of Hungary in 1956, to the moment he crashed into the new head of science and the senior management team at Beechwood in 1995 and been "relocated", sacked for gross incompetence and un-Beechwood-like Hungarian behaviour, living life in the fast lane, a car crash had been the perfect metaphor for his life.

An enigma till the end, Lazlo had apparently suffered a heart attack whilst driving his clapped-out uninsured rust-bucket of a Volkswagen Beetle to visit his daughter, and crashed through the high stone wall of the very graveyard in which he would later be buried, saving his best performance till last. You couldn't make it up.

Brian had taken early retirement in 2007 when his ninety-five-year-old mother had suddenly snuffed it during an episode of *East Enders*, leaving him and his brother a tidy fortune. That was closely followed by the departure of Joseph "Stalin" Rooney a couple of years later because of "irreconcilable, philosophical and existential differences" with the new head and his merry band of sycophants. Red Len had gone into teacher-training, where his rampant socialism would be better appreciated by the lefties that ran the educational establishment. The visionary founder of the school, Godfrey Burns, who had massively influenced Michael with his free-thinking intellect, had been replaced by the "steady-as-she-goes" Damien Bickerstaff, who would take five years to emerge from the shadow of his former mentor, tormentor and boss.

Somehow and without realising it, as the years passed by as they always do, each year faster than the last as life hurtles through space-time, Michael had become the oldest surviving member of the school, the oldest swinger in town. The *ancien regime* had been replaced by a new order. Teachers like himself, forged in the white hot furnaces of political ferment in the Sixties and Seventies, when social revolution was in the air and anything seemed possible, had been replaced by a new, quieter generation of ultra-ambitious, twenty-and thirty-somethings. Carefree, hedonistic, hippy parents had given rise to straight, risk-averse conservative children, every action having an equal and opposite reaction in accordance with Newton's third law of motion. Thatcher's children dressed in smart suits who were too busy watching their backs and seeking promotion to risk challenging the system; internet-savvy executive types, conditioned to implement rather than question every harebrained, half-arsed wheeze handed down by the Department of Education.

Although his hair had begun to turn fifty shades of grey, like Dustin Hoffmann, Michael looked distinguished. And even though his midriff was showing the first restless signs of wanting to leave home, of escaping the confines of his size thirty-four waistline, he still felt young and strong and full of vigour. And yet somehow, when nobody was watching, he had reached the age of sixty-three. When he first arrived at the school he had assumed, as he had always done before, that he would stay a few years and then move on to the next thrilling adventure. At first he had applied for exotic jobs abroad – Hong Kong, Vanuatu, Ascension Island – but somehow fate had conspired to keep him where he was, so he stayed. Thirty-two years in the same school. For a young person this would seem like an eternity. Thirty-two years was a lifetime. But he had long understood and accepted philosophically – from books, from plays, from real life – that most people eventually end up and stay for longer than expected, in what turns out to be their last job. Even the most ambitious and creative types; pop stars, doctors, journalists, artists, musicians, teachers. You couldn't keep running for ever. People married, had kids and settled down. Stuff happened. The problem was, it was not possible to know in advance which job that would be.

Michael had been dabbling with the idea of retirement for a while. But on the morning of that autumn term in 2012, he knew that the right moment had come. People often ask, "How did you know that the moment was right?" The answer is that one just *knows*. Michael had watched others retire, heard their witty, tear-jerking retirement speeches, got pissed at their retirement dos. He had felt the hubris, the sense of superiority that others had succumbed, shown weakness, got older, while he was still going strong. Age would not weary him. Like the guilty feeling of quiet satisfaction one gets at the funeral of a contemporary, a sort of *schadenfreude*, the knowledge that you had survived them, that you had outlived them.

As he drove down the motorway on that lovely September morning, the leaves just beginning to turn, the wheat fields harvested, the long grass dry and golden, Michael knew that he couldn't face this "new start" again, face arriving at school for yet another interminable staff meeting, face yet another session haggling over the implementation of a new course with the science department, face yet another in-service day preparing for yet more lessons with yet more lesson plans. It wasn't that he was tired, or ill, or no longer able to enjoy teaching: the last year had probably been his best ever, his reputation among pupils and fellow teachers at an all-time high. At the very peak of his powers, he was able to combine a voracious appetite for innovation and originality with nearly forty years of classroom experience. He had eked out his own little unassailable niche, which virtually no one could challenge, and was allowed more or less to get on with doing what he wanted to do. He did not have to worry about promotion or impressing his colleagues, and was unafraid of any of the senior management team, all of whom were younger and less wise than him.

He could not go on teaching forever, especially in the frantic *milieu* of a London comprehensive where the threat of rape and pillage was ever present. It was best to get out on top. Like an actor preparing to play Hamlet for the last time, he was simply no longer prepared to face the hassle, the rehearsals, the daily pumping-up of adrenaline required to give a great Shakespearean performance each day, live on stage. He would of course miss the adulation of his ever-youthful audience. An audience of Peter Pans who would never grow old had kept him forever young. But he would not miss the stress, the getting up at six each morning, the having to reinvent the wheel every few years as one education secretary was deposed and replaced by yet another wet-behind-the-ears Oxbridge zealot determined to create an education system in his or her own image. The maniacal Ed Balls being replaced by the messianic Michael Gove. Nor would he miss being observed for the umpteenth time by Ofsted inspectors who knew about as much about education as a remedial streptococcus. As he drove along the motorway, he knew it was the right time to go.

Once the decision had been made to retire, he was able to relax and enjoy his last year like no other. Like a weary traveller who finally sees the silhouette of his home village rising out of the mist in a distant valley, he felt instantly revitalised and energised for the last stretch of his long journey.

By the time his final year at the Beechwood School was over, he had been there for thirty-three years. That's a long chunk out of anyone's life; nearly half of his life in Michael's case. In fact it was the longest time he'd ever spent anywhere. Eighteen years in Leeds, three years at university, fifteen months in Israel, two years at Moketse, four and a half years at Somersby. But it wasn't just the end of his time at Beechwood; it was the end of his career as a teacher. In its own way, each chapter of his life had seemed like a long time – until it was over, when in retrospect the time had flown by. As one gets older time seemed to accelerate and pass by more quickly, even though the standard SI units of time have not changed. A second was still a second, a minute a minute, an hour an hour wherever one was in the universe. But Einstein had shown that time was relative, $E=mc^2$. As a body approaches the universal constant – the speed of light, three hundred million metres per second – its mass increases but time slows down relative to the time back on Earth or elsewhere in the universe. A man travelling at almost the speed of light through space would find on returning to Earth, that although he had aged by only a few hours, those he left behind had aged by many years. The astronaut had stayed young, while his contemporaries back on Earth had become wizened old men and women. Some may even have died of old age. Michael was not quite sure how this related to Einstein's theory of relativity, but as one got older the speed of life increased; the speed of life was directly proportional to age. So time is relative to age, just as time is relative to the speed of light. How were the two equations related? When his mother had died prematurely on that fateful July day in 1960, his grieving father had lamented that their twenty-two years of marriage had felt like a dream, so quickly had it passed by. This must be how it is at the end of one's life, no matter how old one becomes. A human life passes by like the blinking of an eye, like the flapping of the wings of a fly.

Michael did not wish to become too philosophical – which usually meant heavy. Comparing retirement with life and death and the universe, was perhaps taking things too far, a little OTT. But at great turning points in life or history, the human mind is apt to wax philosophical as well as lyrical. Indeed the former often leads to the latter. As his final year elapsed, Michael, with the freedom that comes with having nothing left to lose – as Janis Joplin so aptly put it – increasingly did what he liked and ignored the things that he didn't. Attendance at the tedious and increasingly pointless after-school briefings in the staff room each Monday became superfluous to requirements. The half-termly updating of utterly meaningless pupil data in order to generate equally meaningless interim reports that consisted of vacuous statement-bank comments that few parents could understand – was treated with even more contempt than usual, care being taken only to ensure that every grade was the same as last time plus one, to satisfy senior management and Ofsted and nobody else that the child was making "progress". He was the last to arrive at meetings and the first to leave when they had finished. On Sports Day, he would slink off into the bushes like a naughty pupil, the moment the last race was over. He declined invitations to attend the annual Oxbridge mock interviews held on freezing cold Saturday mornings in November. He disappeared early on those interminable "Ofsted-friendly" inset days which made one lose the will to live. But for things that he enjoyed, or things that were important for the kids, he devoted *more* time. As on so many occasions before, he was the last person to leave on parents' evenings, often waiting behind for late parents he had been unable to see earlier; a lonely martyr-like figure, gathering up his crumpled, dog-eared notes long after the circus had left town. He loved parents' evenings; the thrills, the spills, the sheer theatre of it all. He loved causing a stir in meetings, and with an increased sense of confidence and audacity, he never missed the chance to ask a probing question or make a pithy comment. He wallowed in the adulation of his peers. He organised ever more trips, flamboyantly marketing his events like a street vendor in sixth-form assembles. He spent ever more time outside or on the heath, often inventing the most spurious of excuses for abandoning the classroom. That last summer was hot and sunny, so that by the time it came for him to leave, he looked like a sunburnt film star. Because he knew this would be his final curtain, his last hurrah, he was motivated to create and deliver some of his best and most imaginative lessons ever, with wit and panache, like an actor in his last season in the West End.

To make things more exciting, Michael decided to keep his little secret to himself for as long as possible. It was better that way. If he revealed his hand it would be a distraction. He didn't want a whole year of interrogation: "Why are you leaving sir?", "How long have you been here sir?", "How old are you sir?", "What will you do when you retire sir?" Like a good playwright, he wanted to keep the dénouement of his story till the last scene. The head had been trying to replace him with a "younger model" for some time, so when he was asked at his annual evaluation when he was thinking of retiring, he had replied that according to Teachers Pensions, he could technically work until he was seventy-five, just to wind him up, as you do, and see that look of despondency on his face. Not that the head wanted to get rid of Michael; it was just that younger teachers were cheaper and easier to manipulate and bend to your will.

Michael enjoyed the thrill of leading a secret life, like a double agent in a Bond movie. It was fun. He hoped that the spring in his step and the glint in his eye didn't arouse suspicion. But apart from the head, who knew the score once he'd handed in his letter of resignation at Easter as required by the local authority, nobody suspected a thing. Not even his trusty technician Smita, an *ersatz* mother who was young enough to be he daughter, became suspicious when for the first time in recorded history he began to clear out his typically cluttered and close to collapsing "male" cupboard, stuffed full of ancient documents and lesson plans, some of which dated back to before Magna Carta. He was so relaxed that even his worst class failed to wind him up. These were the virtually unteachable but in a strange way lovable 11B6, a dozen or so sons and daughters of semi-literate Somali refugees who were unable to stop talking and arguing and fighting and shouting and chasing each other around the room for a single nanosecond. The knowledge that he would never have to put up with them again was tempered by the thought that their life chances in this alien culture were slim and that they would find it really hard getting a job. Adil, a typically tall and handsome Somali boy with a smooth black complexion, tribal markings on his face and narrow but intelligent eyes, would ask: "How come you never get angry with us sir?" "How come you never lose your temper?"

"It's not for want of trying," Michael would reply.

He felt like a polar explorer who knows that he must spend just one more season in the freezing cold wastes of Antarctica before going home to the warmth and comfort of his centrally-heated cottage near Saffron Walden.

But there was also a growing sense of nostalgia. It would be the last time he appeared as the eccentric Italian on the teacher's panel of "Strictly Come Bhangra" during Charity Week. It would be the last time he took his sixth-formers to a science lecture at the Royal Institution, or a ballet at the Royal Opera House. It would be the last time he took his kids to Question Time or the National Theatre, or accompanied them to the National Gallery or Royal Academy. He began to wonder what life would be like without the daily exposure to the young, funny, beautiful faces of the children of Hestwell in all their racial and religious diversity and perversity. The laughter, the arguments, the daily miracle of seeing his pupils *learn*. He tried to imagine a world without children, a world without their constant zest for life, a world without their hopes and dreams. He tried to imagine an empty school hall with just the echoes of a hundred assemblies and the thousands of youngsters he had seen there slowly changing from children into adults in front of his eyes, and then leave; like summer flowers that bloom and grow and then go. After his last visit to the Royal Institution in Albemarle Street – that beautifully preserved neo – classical Grade 1 listed Georgian building at the heart of Mayfair – he had wondered what it would be like after he had gone. He had stared tearfully into the now empty and strangely silent lecture theatre where Michael Faraday had once thrilled Londoners with his weekly science lectures and demonstrations and wondered whether any of his working-class, multi-racial students would ever return. Or would this hallowed lecture theatre revert to its all-white, middle-class and middle-aged audience, with only the ghosts of Gurprit and Ahmed and Karishma and Elizabeth and Cyrus communing with those of Michael Faraday and Sir Humphry Davy?

In fact Michael's decision to retire was discovered, like so many secrets, by accident, about six weeks before the end of the summer term by the head technician, Siobhan, whose job it was to draw up the following year's science timetable once teaching allocations had been passed onto her by the congenitally indecisive and hopelessly organised head of department Ray. Even Siobhan, a bonny Irish Catholic girl with a roaming eye who had married a Pakistani and converted to Islam, and who like most women was an amateur sleuth – a closet Miss Marple continuously monitoring the "gossosphere" for rumour or scandal on her highly attuned female antennae – had failed to pick up so much as a blip about Michael's retirement on her radar until she noticed that his name did not appear on Ray's list. She came rushing down to Michael's lab, a huge grin on her cheeky Irish face, brandishing a draft copy of the timetable.

"What's this?" she exclaimed. "Are you leaving?"

Michael lifted his hands and opened his palms, lips pursed, eyes closed, and pushed his head forward in that age-old admission of *mea culpa*.

"Fair cop, Siobhan," he said, still pursing his lips, his guilty face slowly breaking into a sheepish smile.

"But why didn't you tell us earlier?" gasped the technician, shaking her head admonishingly and going red. "What are we going to do without you?"

Michael looked into those kind blue eyes. He knew he would miss them. "I didn't want to cause you too much anguish," he said, in his usual melodramatic, self-effacing way. "Please don't tell the others."

Within ten minutes, all the technicians knew his secret and came piling into his lab excitedly, one by one, an astonished smile on their faces, shaking their heads incredulously and asking, "Why Mr Z, why?" "How are we going to live without you?" "I don't believe it!" "What about Herbie?" "Who will burn all the magnesium ribbon?" "Who will take the children out on the heath?"

Now that the cat was out of the bag, Michael felt relieved. It was strange to think that his name was no longer on the list. Like a deposed Soviet leader during the Cold War, he had been disappeared; he was no more, he had ceased to be. For the first time, Michael realised that he was utterly dispensable.

Chapter 14

And so, after thirty-three years at Beechwood, Michael's final week as a teacher arrived. He had not told his year eleven GCSE classes or his A-level tutor group that he was leaving before they went on exam leave, so as not to destabilise or worry them, or sadden them – he hoped – with the news that he would not be returning next term, that they would not be seeing him again.

Michael left it to the last week of the last term he would ever teach at the school to tell his remaining classes – years seven, eight, nine and ten – one at a time, that he was retiring. He was moved by the overwhelmingly sad expressions on the young and innocent faces of his dear pupils – the response he had secretly hoped for. Everyone craves to be loved and therefore missed. Michael put on a brave face, played the martyr; the consummate professional who does not get emotionally involved with his students or show weakness, the hard-as-nails adult who like a jilted lover, cannot show that his heart is breaking at the prospect of never seeing those lovely children, *his* children, again. There would be plenty of time for that later.

And since the weather in that glorious summer of 2012 was so good, he took every class onto the heath for the last time; one last holy communion with nature; one last walk together through the deep and golden wheat-like expanse of waist-high grass and flower-covered, insect-heaving, bee-buzzing hot grassland. Every pupil received a "goodbye sweet". Outside on the heath the usual suspects – boys, naughty girls – ran and laughed and chased butterflies, while others, mostly girls, sat reflectively on the logs at base camp, contemplating life without Mr Zabinsky.

Little Aishwarya Sandhu – Michael's most diligent student from 10B2 biology – sat mournfully alone, her normally happy and cheerful face and bright intelligent eyes darkened by the knowledge that the favourite teacher who had so inspired her to love biology and learning in general with his witty, wacky, always thrilling lessons would not be teaching her next term. Michael felt her pain and yearned to put his arm around her, console her and kiss away her tortured tears as a father would a daughter about to leave home for university. He wanted to tell her that everything would be all right. But such normal touchy-freely human behaviour would be construed as "inappropriate" and result in certain dismissal from the profession for gross misconduct.

As they trooped out of his lab for the last time, he told them how much he would miss them and wished them well.

"Bye sir."

"Love ya sir."

"See ya sir."

"You're the best sir."

"We'll miss you sir."

"I'll miss you too," said Michael bravely. "Take care and behave yourselves."

On the final day of the summer term lessons finished early as always, and the children went to lunch. Michael mooched around upstairs in the science department, which had become his natural habitat over the years and the power base for so many pedagogic campaigns, twiddling his thumbs, pretending to clear out his cupboard or surf mindlessly on the Internet, as was becoming the norm in an increasingly digital and atomised society.

After lunch came the usual end-of-term assemblies in which the achievements of each year group would be celebrated, sports day certificates awarded and the pupils instructed to have a restful holiday and return next September ready for the new academic year. Such was the endlessly repeated life-cycle of a school. Michael could have attended all the assemblies, but it would have been vain and self-indulgent to wallow in the adulation of every kid and teacher in the school, although it was tempting. Instead he decided to attend the year seven and eight joint assembly, because he loved the vitality of the younger kids and had probably made fewer enemies amongst them. As with being a parent, one's own children were more lovable when they were young and more likely to love you unconditionally in return before their hormones transformed them, Jekyll and Hyde-like, into bolshie and ungrateful rebels without a cause, as they gradually matured into young adults with their own bloody-minded personalities.

Michael stationed himself at the rear of the lower school assembly in a packed school hall. The teachers sat around the edge, while the smaller year sevens sat on the floor and the larger year eights – "the senior pupils" – sat facing the front on elevated rows of seats. The senior management team walked into the hall to the pompous sound of Beethoven's Ninth, giving the headmaster and his deputies a quasi-regal aura of great importance and reverence, like a Roman emperor appearing on stage at the Forum with his senators. The school choir sang a lovely song by Lennon and McCartney – *All You Need Is Love* – and the headmaster delivered his end of term review of the year's events.

Then came the announcement of the teachers who would be leaving. Damien Bickerstaff surveyed the rows of attentive young eyes staring at him from the well of the hall and the teachers perched on stools around the perimeter, ostentatiously blinking every few seconds, as if to photograph selected members of his audience.

"This year the school will be saying goodbye to a number of

teachers – Ms Kerridge, Ms Singh, Mr Patel... and Mr Hall, who will all be taking up promoted posts in other schools." Each teacher got a generous round of applause. "And finally to Mr Zabinsky, who is retiring from teaching after thirty-three years of loyal service to the Beechwood School. Many of you will have benefited from Mr Zabinsky's passionate and energetic lessons and his unmistakable style. And he's here today at the back of the hall."

The pupils turned their heads in one synchronised movement, like iron filings being drawn towards a powerful bar magnet. When they spotted the familiar features of their beloved Mr Z – the silhouette of his mop of wild curly hair, blue linen jacket with buttons undone, colourful tie draped over the backdrop of a blue M&S shirt – emerging from the shadowy recesses at the rear of the hall, they started to clap. Michael stood up and raised his hands high in appreciation. Over four hundred children rose to their feet and started to clap more loudly and cheer, like a concert audience applauding a Russian pianist at the Barbican, or a standing ovation at the Royal Opera House after an exquisite performance of Puccini's *Tosca*. The cheers got louder until the hall erupted into spontaneous and ecstatic applause. Through the dim assembly hall light, Michael could recognise the cheeky face of little Alfie Pinkerton, that illiterate scoundrel from 7S4 who never did his homework but loved experiments. He could identify the endearing face of the hijabed Khadijah Begum, who never stopped putting her hand up to answer questions in class. He recognised so many of his pupils – Maryam, Kabir, Louis, Aqsa, Mohsin, Anju, Cheng, Anouska, Charlotte, Kulvinder, Jagjit – whom he'd taught, watched develop and grow from being weedy year sevens on the first day of term into confident, bubbly, vibrant members of the school. He had tried so hard to inculcate them all with the love of science and the joy of learning.

The noise of the children was now deafening, an impenetrable wall of cheering and yelping and clapping uncontrollably. This is what it must feel like to be a pop star; the adulation that ultimately drives every performer on stage or in the classroom. The need to be appreciated and loved is that most basic of human cravings, the motivator that keeps us going and inspires virtually all positive human activity. The need to be rewarded for giving of oneself – a parent by its child, a child by its parents, a pupil by its teacher, a teacher by its pupils. More gratifying than money or fame or material wealth, more powerful than Viagra, more satisfying than oysters; an asexual aphrodisiac that leads to the consummation of the purest love between two people.

Michael stepped forward onto the illuminated edge of the hall, opened his arms wide and blew kisses at his beloved audience. "Thank you," he mouthed quietly, "I love you all." He was beginning to sound like a vacuous actor at the Oscars. "I love you all" – did he really say that? He put his hands together and bowed reverentially. "*Namaste* my children." More thunderous applause. He had become Gandhi.

The applause went on for what seemed like several minutes, increasing in intensity and now accompanied by a rhythmic chanting and the stamping of feet. "Zab-in-sky! Zab-in-sky!" The sense of love and affection that he felt from the children in the hall moved him profoundly. An actor never knows for sure whether his performance has been appreciated until the show is over. This was better than he had dared to hope for, the sweetest of dreams, a vindication of everything he believed in, his constant striving to try out new things, his determination to innovate and take risks, to give his kids the most enjoyable lessons possible. This was a fitting end to a lifetime in teaching, the delayed gratification of a marathon runner, the feeling of exhilaration of a man who has conquered Everest. And he returned the love and affection. "I love you all." "Thank you." "*Namaste*."

His teaching career was now over. All that remained was the end-of-term lunch in the dining room and the after-dinner speeches, of which his would be the last. He couldn't face standing at the school gates and wishing every pupil farewell. That would be too much of a performance, too vain, too ostentatious, although the temptation was strong. Instead he looked out of the window of his lab, room 300P. To the left he could see pious looking worshippers dressed in their white linen costumes for Friday prayers, filing into the mosque from Barrington Road.

To the right he could see an endless flow of kids drifting out of the school gates for the last time that term – Abdi, Scott, Kamaljit, Slavic, Kwame, Muhammad, Ahmed, Raj, Melanie, Sandeep, Amy, Krishna, Priti, Mark, Suhail, Sara – free at last. How often had he stood at that gate during break time or on an after-school duty? Trying to stop pupils escaping, checking those coming in late, moving on the undesirables who always turned up brandishing a really cool cigarette, trying to reason with unreasonable kids and their designer dogs who'd been expelled for violence or drugs, returning to the scene of the crime to parade their utter uselessness to impressionable girls or to intimidate the younger pupils as they had so loved to do in their day, the leopard never changing its spots.

The children's idea of heaven was the freedom to be themselves, to play cricket or relax in front of the telly without the threat of schoolwork or the watchful eye of teachers. They skipped and pirouetted and ran out of the school like spring lambs high on the prospect of six weeks' holiday, a time span that seemed infinite when one was young and the speed of life was slow. The hot sun burned from a cloudless July sky, pale blue in the summer city haze. The streets of Hestwell looked uncharacteristically friendly and welcoming bathed in the life-giving sunlight. The children had removed their jackets and consummated their release from bondage by ripping off their ties and deliberately flaunting their white shirts which hung rebelliously out of their trousers like a flag of defiance. Up yours mate! "Free at last, Free at last, Thank God almighty we are free at last."

As he watched the young people piling out of the Beechwood School, Michael reflected on his long life as a teacher. What had he achieved? What had his pupils achieved? Had his successes outnumbered his failures? How had he changed over the years? How had education changed? Had he on balance been a force for good or evil? Had he helped create a better world? Had time made him a better or a worse teacher? Had his youthful idealism stood the test of time?

In Botswana he had genuinely believed that he could change the world, take a sad song and make it better. He was convinced that his presence as a white man in 1970s Africa could help redress the injustices of racial discrimination and alleviate the pain of apartheid. As a young man who both looked like and sang like Cat Stevens, his enthusiasm for life and his idealism had been boundless; he had not had a cynical cell in his body. There was no doubt in his mind that he had opened his pupils' minds to the thrill of science and helped liberate many of them from the monotony of village life by enabling them to pass exams and obtain jobs for life in the civil service or go to university. But he also knew that this meant depleting the village of its brightest sons and daughters – much as apartheid had taken a whole generation of young men to the gold mines of the Witwatersrand. They would probably not return, preferring instead the relative luxury of living in a concrete cube in the capital that had running water and electricity. They would probably forget their roots and become middle class. Although he loved his pupils dearly, he had learned, as parents learn about their own children, that they were not quite as sugar and spice and all things nice as he had at first naively imagined. But naivety is the bedfellow of idealism. The idea that the poor and the dispossessed were necessarily morally superior to us wealthy Westerners was blatantly not the case. But his teaching had improved from the wet-behind-the-ears hippy he had been, and he hoped that they remembered him as fondly as he remembered them.

Coming to Somersby had been a severe shock to the system, like a bolt of forked lightning from the firmament. He had never encountered such wild and unruly kids in his life. It was like the planet of the apes, like Dante's inferno, and that experience – as so often happens when idealism confronts the acid test of reality – had made him cynical and right wing for a time. He had even dabbled with the heresy of voting for Margaret Thatcher. It had taken him many weeks to figure out how to teach those cheeky, urban working-class kids, and he was in little doubt that he had failed to teach some of them anything. He felt guilty about that, even though he knew that some children were quite simply unteachable in a classroom situation. But this baptism of fire had strengthened him as a human being and as a teacher, even though it had partly been at the kids' expense. He consoled himself with the knowledge that they all seemed to get jobs and showed no sign of malice when they met in the pub – quite the opposite in fact. His days in Africa seemed more and more like a childhood memory – beautiful and pure, but of another time. Although much of his youthful idealism had remained intact – he still believed in creating a better world for his children – the daily assault on his sensibilities and the sheer stress of survival had made him grapple for the first time with the heretical possibility of leaving the profession.

Beechwood had restored his faith in teaching, but it had been a close call. In the early eighties, Milton Friedman's book *Free to Choose* had seduced him and many of his contemporaries to the temptations of monetarism, and he had seriously considered becoming an entrepreneur. He applied for some of the enticingly highly-paid jobs in insurance which had started to appear in the TES – "Double your salary in a year" – and even considered setting up his own business selling horse paintings to race courses. The lure of these jobs was a release from the shackles of the classroom, from the daily abuse and violence, and the chance to earn big bucks along with what seemed like everyone else at the time. Teachers were leaving the profession in droves. Beechwood had saved him from Mammon.

PART 4

The Reunion

Chapter 1

⟶∞∙◎∙◇∙∞◎∞◎∙◎∙◇∙∞∙◎

On a glorious September morning in 2013, Michael boarded the eleven-thirty South West Trains service from Windsor to Waterloo. It had been a typically lousy summer in which it had rained or seemed to have rained continuously for forty days and forty nights, a bit like in the Bible where for some reason things tended to occur in units of forty; Noah's flood, Moses' journey to the Promised Land. However the September sun, still as strong as in April, had the power to warm this godforsaken strip of temperate terra firma to a balmy twenty-four degrees Celsius. It was amazing how often the best weather occurred in September, the so-called "Indian summer", the German *Altweibersommer*, when this land of mellow fruitfulness was bursting with the unmistakable signs of autumn-ripe fruit, yellow leaves, longer nights, misty mornings – yet still reserved the right to incubate Mother Nature in its womb-like warmth. As a child, his dad had always taken off the first week in September for their annual holiday to Bournemouth, where it had always seemed warmer and sunnier than in Leeds. Even the rain had seemed warmer. He would always come back with a fantastic tan after spending the whole day on the beach, come rain or shine, and show off to his much richer and more sophisticated classmate Tony Harrison, who could afford to go to some posh resort in Italy that he'd never heard of.

It was almost two months now since his retirement and Michael felt relaxed and calm in the half-empty carriage, staring out of the window in his green M&S California surfers T-shirt with matching M&S blue floppy linen trousers. Having recently boosted his summer tan in a seasonal act of consummate vanity designed to emphasise the look of youthful vigour that he liked to cultivate, he looked disgustingly healthy and handsome. His smooth-shaven face, trimmed grey beard and still long and wavy flowing black hair with silvery-grey highlights gave him the air of a Hollywood film star. "Good morning Mr Bond." A year ago he would have been teaching the nitrogen cycle to one of his many GCSE classes in a stuffy dark suit and tie.

He was on his way to a reunion with Paul and Josh who'd just flown in from America, forty years – that biblical number again – since they last walked the sandy tracks of Mochudi, Botswana together. Michael had suggested they meet in Richmond, a beautiful suburb of west London he knew well. He wanted to look his best for these guys, to give the impression that the intervening years had not wearied him, that he had defied the ageing process and that in short he still looked the same as the last time they had met. The problem was that because they were forty years older a whole lifetime had elapsed – instead of being in their twenties they would now all be sixty-four. After weeks of preparation for this reunion – tracking people down, emailing everybody, getting people on board, fixing dates – he was seriously excited about the prospect of seeing these two again, but also nervous and apprehensive. He had heard bad things about reunions, having read about Philip Roth's alter ego Zuckerman going back to New Jersey to meet the decrepit relics of his high school class; once beautiful girls looking old and haggard; once sexually virile boys who'd had prostate operations; guys who'd had triple bypass open-heart surgery; school mates who'd died of cancer or been killed in a road accident. Would they have anything in common? Would they have anything to talk about? How would they look? Like childhood acquaintances one hadn't seen for years or old school friends, one always remembered them as they were when you last met, when you and they were still young. He had studied their photos; Josh was a long-haired, easy-going Rocky Mountain hippy without a care in the world, with forever smiling blue eyes, while Paul was a more cerebral neurotic type, a thin-haired portly New Yorker with trouble-laden eyes who loved smoking dope. And yet when you spoke on the phone you always sounded the same – one's voice didn't change.

As the train pulled into Richmond-upon-Thames, Michael rose to leave the carriage, along with half a dozen other passengers, and made his way up the stairs, past the ticket office and out onto the pavement in front of the main station entrance on Kew Road. They had arranged to meet at twelve, and he was five minutes late. He felt once again like one of those characters he'd seen so often in the movies where the hero waits for the girl to arrive, usually in a station – *Brief Encounter*, *Casablanca* – and the high sense of drama and emotion, the unbearable longing that goes with it. Heartrending music, soft-focus artistically enhanced close-ups of the leading characters, the man standing waiting, the woman frantically fighting her way through the throng, panic-stricken eyes, wide shots of the station, the back of someone who looks like the girl but turns out to be someone else, close-ups of the hero's face as the meeting time passes and she hasn't turned up, the watery sadness in his missing-her eyes, the palpable sense of disappointment, of dreams not realised, of a future together shattered. What is it about stations and tear-jerking moments? Who will ever forget that moment – perhaps the most emotional in cinema history – when the father appears through the steam in *The Railway Children*, and Jenny Agutter shouts, "Daddy, my daddy!"?

It is so much easier to express one's emotions in the movies. But this overwhelmingly surrealistic moment was not a film, it was for real. Michael scanned the crowd scurrying along the pavement like ants foraging for food on the forest floor, a never-ending bustle of myrmecological humanity. He looked around him at the commuters entering and leaving the station. What exactly was he looking for? In his mind he saw Josh and Paul as he had known them forty years ago, young twenty-somethings, fresh-faced wet-behind-the-ears American kids with their whole life in front of them, unattached, unmarried, all of life's possibilities still invitingly open to them, beckoning them to come on in.

He looked again, and suddenly noticed two old men sitting on the low wall surrounding a huge plane tree in the middle of the pavement. As their eyes met, the two figures stood up and slowly walked towards the advancing Michael. They embraced passionately in broad daylight on a bustling lunchtime pavement in Richmond. There were no soft-focus camera angles, no rising crescendos of sweet mellow violins; just the sound of gas-guzzling traffic passing by. The three sexagenarians embraced like lovers reunited after a lifetime of separation, or triplets separated at birth, holding each other tightly, unashamedly, hands greedily clasping the other man's shoulders like rugby players in a scrum beneath the effusive light of the midday September sun.

The heavy-set guy with the glasses was Paul, his older, paler face looking like a rock hewn from the granite cliffs of Mount Rushmore, his fuller greyer visage revealing a hard life lived on the mean streets of New York, his sad sunken eyes that knew the meaning of suffering peering out through pink, thin-rimmed glasses, his thinning, straw-coloured hair flopping over a creased worried forehead, much as it used to do. The tall, lightly-built man with the short-cropped hair and bald patch was Josh, his stubble-covered face only partly papering over the tortured cracks in his Rocky Mountain face, his long nose now protruding between two much sadder and duller, life-weary eyes. Three fully-grown men showing their emotions in public on a crowded London street.

"Hey guys, it's so good to see you," said Michael, clasping his two friends more tightly, his eyes beginning to moisten.

"It's good to see you too man," said Paul, in a slow, emotion-laden voice.

Josh mumbled, "This sure feels good." The body had changed, but the voice had not. Michael had noticed this many times before. When long-forgotten acquaintances from the past had phoned him out of the blue – Alan Turner from university, Tony Rosen from Leeds – without the older face to confuse him, Michael had immediately recognised that person as if time had stood still. It was uncanny but true that unlike the body, the voice didn't age.

So this was what forty years of a man's life looked like. In the blink of an eye two youthful faces became old, like one of those computer-generated pictures on *Crimewatch* predicting what a missing person or wanted criminal might look like today. It was that relativity thing again. Michael felt like the proverbial astronaut who, having completed a round trip through space at almost the speed of light, returned a few days later to find that everyone had grown old. He still felt young, but did Paul and Josh see him in exactly the same way? Did he seem like an old man too?

Of the two, Paul was the easier to recognise. His voice and manner of speech had not changed; it was the same slow, clear, New York accent. He had the same short stature, the same stocky body, the same troubled eyes peering through the same thin-rimmed spectacles. Age had simply exaggerated those features and made him look older. What he saw in front of him was essentially an older version – heavier, paler, balder – of the Paul he had known.

But with Josh it was different. He would never have recognised him from a photo or walking down the street. Gone was the flowing, golden-brown hippy hair, his freak flag, which used to cascade over his shoulders and down his back like a waterfall, tied together in a ponytail. Gone were the carefree, world-unwearied spaced-out smile and the dreamy light blue eyes. Only his voice, his slow, gentle, Rocky Mountain voice, had stayed young. What remained of his hair was short and coarse. He wore a baseball cap to cover his balding scalp and his complexion was dull, his sunken eyes emitting only the cold light of a dying star. He looked as though he had suffered. Michael wondered how accurately a person's face reflected their life.

Michael led his old friends to the White Cross, a riverside pub on the Thames he knew well and had deliberately chosen to showcase the style and opulence of Richmond. Paul and Josh seated themselves in the main lounge, facing the river, while their host bought them both a pint of traditional English ale – Young's Bitter.

As the trio sipped their beer and conversation ensued as it always did with Young's Bitter, the familiarity of their voices, that unsullied link with the past, seemed to override the absurd sight of each other's ancient weathered faces. As always happens in such circumstances, the old faces rapidly morphed into the new as each adjusted easily to the new reality and conversation flowed as if it had never stopped. They talked about life and politics, just like in the old days. They reminisced about those magical days in a far away African village where their lifelong friendship had been forged, the kids they'd taught, the people they'd known, the things that went on. Two pulsating years in the prime of their lives, that had happened so long ago – *forty years ago* – and yet seemed like yesterday: relativity again. How strange time was; two shared years that had bonded them forever, an eternal link between the past and the present.

Michael was surprised by how little Paul and Josh remembered when compared to his vivid and detailed recollections of faces and names and events and feelings. Was that simply memory loss with age, or had those two years at Moketse affected him more profoundly, meant more to him, than them? Ever since childhood he had been more nostalgic for the past than his contemporaries – like Raymond Fleischer, who delighted in remembering nothing. When he was at school he reminisced about his childhood, when he was at university he reminisced about his schooldays.

As alcohol anaesthetised the senses and dulled the inhibitions, and one pint led to another, each man told his story. Josh had gone back to the States, and being at a loose end and finding nothing else to do, had dabbled in teaching disaffected kids at some special school in Washington State. He had stuck it out for a couple of semesters, trying to come to terms with the coarseness and uncouthness of the delinquents he had to teach, until he realised what he had known in Botswana – that he wasn't cut out to be a teacher. Unlike Michael, he had no burning ambition to change the world or take a sad song and make it better, and had got into conservation in what was always his natural habitat; the outback of Oregon. And amazingly, this simple child of the Rockies, of the Washington coastal trail, who ate raw potatoes and dried jerky and bivouacked in the wilderness under the stars and eschewed all vestiges of materialism, had started his own forestry business and become the rich entrepreneur, the capitalist pig he had sworn he would never become. Yet another beneficiary of the American Dream. And with land ownership came conservatism; he now had something to lose, and detached from the city with its deprivation and the politics of the chattering classes, he had become a Republican – a fucking Republican! How was it possible that a guy who had witnessed the ravages of apartheid, taught village kids with torn clothes and no shoes, listened to the music of Neil Young and Joni Mitchell and lived in a mud hut with no running water or flushing toilet had become a Republican?

He had married and had two children, and adopted two more from his wife's first marriage. He had loved them all, treated his stepchildren like his own kids. But now he was embroiled in an acrimonious divorce – his wife wanted half his estate; she was trying to ruin him. One of his children had been involved with the police; his elder son was at a rehab clinic for drug addiction. Life had made him bitter. He talked about expelling kids who misbehaved in school, slinging hoodlums and drug pushers in prison and throwing away the key. He had even discovered Jesus for Christ's sake, become a fucking born-again Christian like so many before him, and had sought solace in the Lord. There but for the grace of God go I. In the end we are all victims of circumstance, like a rocky coastline battered and sculptured by the tides of time and the stormy seas of life, at the mercy of the elements. No wonder he looked so old. And yet as they talked, Michael realised it was still the same Josh beneath this battered exterior. Flashes of his old humour stirred as his eyes lit up and fleetingly recaptured their old blueness and kindness. And his gentle Washington voice had not changed either.

The friends ordered another pint, their third, and a burger and chips. The Americans were certainly enjoying their pints of Young's Bitter. Getting quite sloshed even. Michael gazed at them and still couldn't believe that they were really there. He pinched himself; it was so surrealistic, Paul and Josh from the US, his old friends from Botswana here in England.

The pub had started to fill with lunchtime drinkers, mostly middle-class Richmond luvvies, a few tourists, the spindly and sunburnt form of Gordon, a guy of indeterminate age who always propped up the bar and held court with his coterie of disciples. Through the large bay window, one could see Old Father Thames rolling, still rolling along, bearing the occasional pleasure boat coming up from Kew or sailing down to the Embankment. The September sun was still shining strongly and glistening on the river like animated diamonds. Beautiful women strolled by, their summer dresses flowing seductively over curvy hips and smooth white thighs, full breasts pressing on deliberately-tightened blouses. The pub beer garden was filling up with drinkers basking in the sun, taking in the last of the summer wine.

Paul had returned to New York after taking in Europe and returned to his family home some fifteen miles upstate along the Hudson River in Riverdale County. His parents had never got over the death of their precious daughter Jody, Paul's younger sister, so tragically killed in the prime of her life in a road accident in Queens on her way back from the wedding of her best friend Selene. The culprit was some manically-depressed Vietnam veteran, drugged to the eyeballs, rejected by his peers, unable to cope with being shunned by the very society he thought he'd been fighting for, protecting them from the evil and ever-present forces of communism, killing the Vietcong, maiming innocent women and children for Uncle Sam. He'd rammed his 1960s Chevy into Jody's Volkswagen Polo at high speed, giving her no chance of survival and taking her with him to the oblivion he yearned for, punishing America for treating him like a leper and not a hero.

Unable to stand the tension, the ever-present sadness, the endless recriminations and surges of guilt, Paul had moved into a flat in Brooklyn where he tried his luck as a businessman – something every American is genetically programmed to do – selling "office accessories" to high-tech companies in Manhattan. Having no business acumen to speak of, he'd gone bust within five years and filed for bankruptcy. Like Josh but unlike Michael, Paul had never seen his time in Botswana as anything other than an adventure, a stopgap after college while he figured out what to do with his life. That and avoiding being drafted into the army and being sent to Vietnam to die for a cause he didn't believe in. Unlike Michael, he had never been fired by the higher purpose, the vocation, of teaching in Africa as a means of saving the world and making it a better and fairer place.

By one of those strange twists of fate that life continually conspires to throw at us in its infinite wisdom, Paul now realised that teaching – something he'd got into purely by chance straight after college – could save his world by offering him a well-paid job for life. So he'd gone back to school and retrained as a maths teacher at Columbia University on the Upper West Side. The catch – and there's always a catch in matters of divine intervention – was that his new job entailed teaching trigonometry to rebellious black teenagers in the blackboard jungle that was the Bronx. It was to become his own West Side Story, a civil war between two disparate tribes; Montagues against Capulets, Jets against Sharks, teachers against students. Mirroring exactly Michael's blood-curdling experience of being crucified by the wild kids of west London but to the power of ten, Paul had rapidly discovered that his experience spent teaching the polite and gentle black children of Mochudi was of no use whatsoever in teaching the indolent, work-shy, black kids from the housing projects of New York, with all their hang-ups, one-parent fatherless families, drugs, prostitution, crime – the legacy of slavery still very much alive and well and calling the shots over a century after its abolition in 1865. Paul had suffered over twenty-five years of abuse and goading, daily challenges to his authority as a pedagogue, assaults on the very essence of his sentient humanity, and it had taken its toll. By the time he had retired he had become a burnt-out shell of the man he used to be, a hollowed-out husk. But at least he had a good pension and the time to travel the world.

In 2006 he had revisited Botswana and discovered a barely recognisable country. They say you should never go back to the places of your youth, the places where you experienced life more intensely than at any other time, because as an older man or woman it can never be the same; it can never recreate the rapture of those carefree heady days. It will always be a disappointment, a wallowing in nostalgia searching for a lost world. Better to leave the past unsullied by the present, leave it as an unassailable memory, a dream, a myth that cannot be debunked, a fairy tale that cannot be exposed as a fraudulent fantasy, a confected figment of your imagination. Better to let the past rest in peace, preserving its sanctity. Returning to the scene of your childhood or university days was always painful, because everything looked smaller, the buildings more faded, the people shabby and old like the survivors of an apocalypse searching for scraps of food in the rubble. Or the old streets had been demolished and replaced with brash, modern, inhumane developments erasing all vestiges of the past as if it had never happened: relativity again.

Michael remembered the heartbroken look on the pale, tearful face of his ageing father just before he died. On a joint holiday to the Lake District, he had insisted on taking a day trip to Blackpool, where he tried to locate the hotel, or more likely the boarding house, where he had spent his honeymoon, enjoyed those first blissful days of married life with his darling wife Hannah. The seafront had changed beyond recognition, the once-proud Victorian facades looked shabby and neglected, the boarding house had been replaced by an amusement arcade, the most cherished memory in his whole life defiled and desecrated. He remembered the look of utter bewilderment on his father's face when he showed his two sons the bulldozed remains of what used to be Trafalgar Street, the street he had grown up in and played in near the centre of Leeds, the street that evoked his most intense memories of childhood reduced to an ugly building sight, the memory of his father's history demolished along with that of Nelson's greatest sea battle. And yet the lure of the past is often too great; like eating fruit from the tree of knowledge, we cannot resist.

Paul had visited Gaborone, that sleepy embryonic town where he used to do his Saturday shopping courtesy of Cedric's truck, take in a movie, or down a pint or two of ice cold Lion lager at what seemed in those days to be the opulently-stylish President Hotel. Like all African towns, "development" had transformed Botswana's capital into an ugly urban sprawl with litter-filled streets, beggars on every corner and heavily made-up ladies of the night with artificially whitened skins and wavy-black wigs parading outside every bar. Everything looked tacky. A giant shanty town had grown up on the outskirts of Gaborone, populated by peasants from all over Botswana seeking to "better themselves" in the filthy dog-infested streets of the squalid township. The President had become a decadent relic of its former colonial self, the old guard of white expats and well-to-do blacks, having long since been replaced by the perpetually inebriated riff-raff of Gaborone's not-so-polite society.

But the biggest shock was reserved for Mochudi. Paul had rented a car and travelled up the newly-constructed "motorway" to Francistown, which was lined with the rusting carcasses of a hundred drunken road accidents, resembling the untouched relics of a desert war. Pilane, once a few crumbling rondavels and a concrete village store on a hill, now presented an unsightly landscape of breeze-block prefabs, a huge sign and a giant gas station marking the turn-off to the Bakgatla village. Even the rutted dustbowl of a track to Mochudi which used to be shared with goats and donkeys in the winter and impassable in the rainy season had been replaced by a state-of-the-art metalled road.

In the thirty-five intervening years since he had last graced this patch of holy ground, Mochudi had been completely transformed, "modernised" and "developed" into a huge concrete conurbation that was well on the way to becoming an outer suburb of Gaborone. All those pretty rondavels, in the sentimental minds of the mekgowa, all those painstakingly and skilfully-thatched African mud huts, the like of which he had once lived in, had been replaced by a desolate sprawl of soulless breeze-block dwellings, cubes of monotonous grey concrete, like a cubist painting by Picasso, boasting their own supply of running water, electricity, inside toilets and satellite TV aerials. Progress. It had resembled a low-rise version of downtown Chicago: ugly as hell.

The dusty patch of desert in front of the old bar, the "Library", long since "upgraded" to a two-storey knocking shop with proper windows and flashing neon lights advertising Coca Cola, had been transformed into a paved piazza bordered by newish shops and sleazy shebeens servicing the needs of an ever-growing population. Bleary-eyed drunkards in shabby suits and reversed baseball caps danced in the street, bodies thrust forward, bums protruding exaggeratedly backwards, clutching cans of beer and smoking simultaneously to the *gumba gumba* music blaring loudly from the drinking houses. A bronze statue of Sir Seretse Khama, Botswana's first president, stood incongruously in the square, his green weathered verdigris eyes looking out towards the Kalahari desert, dreaming no doubt of those vast open spaces, "the lands", where his family still farmed vast herds of beef cattle, Botswana's top export after diamonds. At the base of the statue the word "PULA" was engraved in huge letters. Flash, turbo-charged American cars driven by the Mochudi *nouveau-riche*, gangsters dressed up like film stars, cruised through the village at breakneck speed, hotting and hooting, screeching their brakes and tooting their horns. Graffiti was everywhere.

Paul felt uneasy sitting in his open-topped Toyota outside the "Library". In the old days he had never felt fear walking along the dusty village tracks, even at night on his own. But things had changed. People stared threateningly at the white interloper as if he didn't belong. It was like Harlem. He had toyed with the idea of leaving his car in the piazza and wandering through the village towards the old *kgotla* and Papane Hill. But his instinct had said "no, don't do it – your car will be stolen and you'll get mugged." He had felt ashamed; frightened of his fear, saddened that he now felt the same paranoia of "the other" that he did back home in the States. So he drove across the river and up to the school.

Moketse Secondary School, once a cosy place, a sanctuary with its clean white classrooms and a population of five hundred children, was now an ugly sprawl of new prefabs, a random assemblage of vulgar new buildings bulging in all directions with no discernible pattern. Paul tried to locate his old classroom, but couldn't. Graffiti was everywhere, some of it personal: "Fuck Masire", "Matron is a cunt", "Seretse sucks" as well as graphical renditions of the male and female genitalia. Just like back home in New York, it looked like a rundown school in the Bronx. Instead of the soothing hum of the generator and the purr of children learning, the place was noisy and tense. He could hear shouting from one of the classrooms, a vicious argument punctuated by jeering kids and the bawling of a teacher screeching, "SHUT UP AND SIT DOWN!" Every so often a pupil wandered past him, heading towards the gate and left the premises, obviously bunking lessons. A group of lads smoked weed behind the assembly hall, giggling as they did so; a boy and girl kissed and groped each other desperately outside the kitchens. None of this had happened in his time.

As he surveyed the silhouette of what used to be his home, a peaceful place of learning, of loving, of laughter, of music and fun, a place where he'd spent two of the most fulfilling years of his life

– which was why he'd come back – a band of gun-toting police suddenly burst into the compound and headed for the science rooms. A few seconds later they emerged dragging a screaming girl apparently suspected of practising black magic and a boy believed to be a drug trafficker.

Paul noticed that some of the windows had been smashed, some of the door handles vandalised. Moketse looked like a slum, a sink school in the projects. How could a place go so far downhill in just thirty years? He thought he saw the ghosts of Mr Seretse and Jo Maktum, he thought he heard the laughter of Batsile, saw the podgy face of his favourite pupil, Pius. Where were they now? He thought he could hear the sound of Matron conducting the school choir and the perfect African harmony of children singing the national anthem for the umpteenth time. Paul got back in his car and drove out of the compound, passing the faded sign announcing the entrance to "Moketse Secondary School, People's Republic of Botswana" as he did so. He drove slowly back towards the village and was flagged down by what looked like a stooped old lady holding a stick, by the roadside. He pulled over, opened the driver's window of his air-conditioned vehicle, and stared at the face before him.

"*Dumela,* Mr Winkelman," said the gaunt woman in a broken voice, her sad sunken eyes like those of a concentration camp survivor bearing witness to unimaginable loss and suffering. His mind whirred into memory recall mode as he tried desperately to identify the frail specimen beside him whose weary smile implored him to remember her. With those for whom the passage of time has been unkind the younger face is always recognisable through the eyes, those portals into the human soul that never lose their identity. The eyes were dull, tired and bloodshot, and from the colour of the iris, undernourished. But these were unmistakably the eyes of Naledi Gaopalelwe, that once-beautiful, full-of-life child Paul had taught maths to in 1974, the one who always put her hand up to answer questions, whose lovely face and joyous mood had lighted up every room and touched every heart.

"Naledi?" asked Paul incredulously.

"*Ee ticheri*," replied the stooping woman deferentially, bowing her head in shame and avoiding direct eye contact.

Paul stepped out of his rented car and thrust forward a quivering hand.

"*Dumela mma*," he said, taking Naledi's small hot hand and squeezing it with intense emotion.

The two figures embraced each other tightly, like father and daughter by the hot sandy roadside, as a Toyota truck drove by throwing up clouds of brown dust; teacher and pupil; man and woman; black and white.

Paul stared into Naledi's still lovely eyes, sunken into her hollowed-out face, barely holding back the tears, recognising instantly that evocative scent of sweat and smoke, the African e*au de Cologne* that every villager has impregnated into his clothes and skin.

"How are you?" asked Paul in a voice cracking with emotion. "What's happened to you? Where are the others?"

Naledi pointed towards a barren strip of land to the south; the village graveyard. The teacher and pupil – now a woman of perhaps fifty but looking eighty – walked together along a hot stony track, winding its way through a cluster of dilapidated rondavels where the homeless still squatted, past a stunted *motlopi* tree bearing the wizened remains of last season's succulent orange fruit, to a fenced-off compound with the name "Phitlong" painted onto a rusting metal sheet at its entrance.

The cemetery consisted of what looked like a hotchpotch of graves stretching as far as the eye could see in every direction, a vast landscape of death, each plot marked out by a gravestone and a cross. Some graves had photos of the deceased, and the more recent ones were covered in the desiccated remains of funeral flowers. Like all graveyards, and indeed all human enterprises, the rich could afford the best – spacious plots housing classically-crafted granite headstones with gold-painted inscriptions and an ostentatious stone cross, while the poor had to make do with simple, sometimes pauper's graves, often just a rectangle of collected rubble and bricks and a simple wooden cross. In death as in life, segregated by differences in material wealth.

Naledi explained that AIDS, the disease that had long since been brought under control in Europe and North America through education and anti-retroviral drugs, had decimated Botswana like the ten plagues of Egypt, but instead of taking the first born as the tenth plague had done, it had infected forty per cent of the adult population – the second highest infection rate in the world after neighbouring Swaziland. The average life expectancy had plummeted from sixty-five to just thirty, taking some of the most virile and productive members of society with it and massively undermining Botswana's economy. Like the Black Death in medieval Europe, every family had been affected. Families were left without parents; older children had to look after the young; frail grandparents had to undergo the humiliation of doing menial work to support fatherless and motherless grandchildren. There was no state welfare. The natural promiscuity of the population and the tribal superstitions surrounding the use of condoms, endemic throughout Africa, or the belief that it was a punishment from God, had enabled the HIV virus to gain a foothold before reason and government action could intervene. When the first case of AIDS had been identified in 1985, the nation had reacted as many do when confronted with an inconvenient truth; they had gone into a state of denial. Only Mandela's influence in South Africa had brought that country to its senses.

"I was one of the lucky ones," said Naledi in that quiet dignified way so common amongst the naturally gentle Batswana. "I got AIDS but recovered. God had mercy on me. But my husband and three children were taken by the Lord to be by his side."

Like most Africans, Naledi was deeply religious and therefore fatalistic, Christianity having only partially superseded an ancient tribal belief in ancestor worship. Paul had wondered what sort of a deity would inflict so much misery on the God-fearing citizens of Mochudi. Why was it always the poor and the defenceless that had to be punished? Didn't Jesus say that the meek shall inherit the earth? Didn't he wash the feet of the poor and the dispossessed? Why, if it was easier for a camel to go through the eye of a needle than for a rich man to enter the kingdom of heaven, did so many rich people in the developed world keep squeezing through that needle here on earth? God must be either indifferent to man's suffering or a cynical sadist, someone who took a delight in the degradation of the very people he had created – it is alleged in the book of Genesis – in *his* image. Or was this yet more proof that God did not exist? Another nail in the coffin of those who continued to believe in the supernatural. As in war or famine, adversity seemed to strengthen the belief in a merciful, omnipotent, omniscient and omnipresent God. Belief was inversely proportional to evidence.

"I look so old because I have been ravaged by disease and lost everything. But at least I am alive," said Naledi stoically. "My school friends – your pupils – were not so lucky."

They wandered a little further into the *phitlong*, past crumbled, derelict graves with no names, the original inscriptions no longer legible on the weathered sandstone headstones from the mid-eighteen hundreds, when the London Missionary Society first brought Christianity to Botswana. Near the southern perimeter fence, row after row of gleaming new graves appeared like a newly-built housing estate for the dead. It looked like one of those endless cemeteries in northern France for the soldiers cut down in their prime, not by AIDS, but by German bullets.

"Molefe Molefe, died June 4th 1990, Aged 34. May God bless him and cause his face to shine upon him. *Go Itse Morena* [may your soul rest in peace]".

Molefe squared had been one of the school's best kids, good at everything, an all-rounder who had been good at sport, good at academic work, and had the best voice in the multiple-award-winning school choir. He had been head boy and exuded an air of confidence and grace like no other. Paul had taught him maths and identified him immediately as a talented student, someone with leadership qualities who would go far.

"Oh my God!" cried Paul, shaking his head slowly from side to side as he always did in moments of despair, "why *you* Molefe, why did they have to take you?"

"I loved him too," said Naledi, sobbing uncontrollably into a crumpled handkerchief, "we used to sit together in school, he was my best friend. May God have mercy on him. The Lord giveth and the Lord taketh."

A few yards further on, they stopped again. "Nkomeng Matlapeng, died August 17th 1988, Aged 32. *Tsamaya Sentle*."

Paul's mournful eyes filled with warm salty tears as he cried openly and unashamedly as he had not done since childhood. Even the death of his sister had not elicited this response. He had rented his rondavel from Nkomeng's mother, Habile, for the princely sum of two rand a month and had visited them on their "lands". He had helped Nkomeng with her homework while Habile had looked after him like her own son, bringing him water, tidying his hut, and giving him massive portions of *bogobe* and relish when they could hardly afford to feed themselves.

"Why oh why did they have to take Nkomeng? I loved her like a father loves his child, unconditionally and unreservedly. She was so kind and loving and full of life, kept me going in my darkest moments, hugged me when my own sister was killed in America."

Paul fell to his knees, clutching the sand, running his hand along the rough surface of the gravestone as if it were Nkomeng's face.

Naledi hung her head, and covering her face with both hands, wept uncontrollably as well. She had shed so many tears for so many of her childhood friends, for her husband Mandrise and her three darling children, the very meaning and epicentre of her life; Sophie, Tebogo, Moses. Her hollow eyes were a testimony to that. How many tears could a person shed? Did the lachrymal river ever run dry?

Naledi helped her portly maths teacher rise to his feet with her left hand while supporting herself with the stick in the right, and as he stood unsteadily trying to regain his composure, she lovingly removed his tear-stained, gold-rimmed glasses – the type he used to wear at Moketse as a younger man – from his reddened, grief-stricken sweaty face and dried his swollen eyes tenderly with her crumpled handkerchief, like a mother tending her son. They embraced again, holding each other tightly as the sun beat down mercilessly on this arid desert of death.

They walked on a little further, this time holding hands as close friends do in Botswana, passing the tombstones of other Moketse children; Boitumelo (happiness), aged thirty; Bontle (beauty), aged twenty-eight; Dikeledi (tears), aged twenty-five. Like fallen soldiers in the Somme, a one-sided battle against an invisible enemy, rows of young conscripts to the lottery of death, cut down in their prime like lambs to the slaughter by a sub-microscopic virus. How defenceless the poor were against microbial attack, without the heavy weapons of modern science. Where were the African Louis Pasteurs and Edward Jenners? There were even younger victims of Africa's Black Death – for they were all black these days after the advent of anti-retroviral drugs and treatments in the West – whose names Paul did not recognise because they had started school after he had returned to the sanctuary and guaranteed longevity of the United States. Kagiso (peace), aged twenty; Kgomotso (comfort), aged eighteen – probably a child catching the deadly disease on her first covert night of sexual pleasure after leaving school. Like the first man to go over the top in the trenches of Flanders, she would become one of the many whom age would not weary. Many of the graves were inscribed with the word "*Pula*", rain.

Naledi led Paul, still holding his hot stubby hand, to the graves of Nicodemus and Cornelius Tau, two brothers who had taught with Paul in the 1970s. Tau meant 'lion' in Setswana. Nicodemus had been banished to Francistown after an affair with a pupil, and returned to his home village in 1995 to die of AIDS at the age of forty-four. He had an infectious zest for life, a boyishly carefree attitude which endeared him to everyone, and had taught Paul the few words of Setswana an American was capable of learning. His older brother Cornelius "Marapo" Tau had succumbed to the plague in the same year, aged forty-seven, cheating lung cancer and cirrhosis of the liver – the result of his chain smoking and alcohol addictions – out of killing their man first. Beneath their combined headstone was the inscription "*Ditau di Tshwerwe ke Tlala*"; The Hungry Lions.

They say you know you are getting old when your contemporaries start to die. Nicodemus and Cornelius were his contemporaries all right, but having drawn the short straw of life by being born in the wrong place at the wrong time, and black, they were destined to die prematurely from a disease for which there was no known cure. Why did God rub the noses of the poor in their own excrement? Or were they just created that way for his own sick delectation?

The Tau brothers, the two Mochudi lions who had played hide and seek near the *kgotla* as kids and drunk the milk of a wildebeest, had carried the hopes of their poverty-stricken parents and their village for a better future. But even a majestic beast like a lion that has no natural predators other than man, even the king of the jungle, had been no match for an invisible virus like HIV. Nicodemus and Cornelius had died of AIDS, while Paul and Josh – the *de facto* brothers who had trained together with the Peace Corps – had returned to the States, made money, got married and had kids, and were now free to travel the world in their opulent retirement. Where was the justice, the equal opportunity in that? The problem with living too long was that you saw too many people die.

As they were about to leave the cemetery through the "eastern gate" – a gap that had been ripped out of the flimsy wire fencing by vandals – a tall and emaciated, once handsome and proud man with a stubbly beard, dressed in a shabby raincoat, dirty shorts and without shoes on his bare lacerated feet, shouted across the graveyard like a ghost from the past; "Mr Winkelman, Mr Winkelman, *O tsogile jang*? *O kae*?"

The sickly man shuffled his way slowly towards the two

visitors, tripping over some graves and stepping into others as he did so. He was drinking *chibuku* from a one-litre carton and looked distinctly Brahms and Liszt. When he finally reached Paul and Naledi they could see his yellow cracked teeth and smell the sickly stench of fermented sorghum on his hot rancid breath.

It is easy to recognise a teacher from one's childhood. Whereas a child undergoes massive changes as it metamorphoses into adulthood – boobs, beard, complexion – like a maggot turning into a fly, the teacher changes very little by comparison, the old familiar face fixed in the classroom eyes of the pupil, staying old, and instantly recognisable when the two meet later in life. Noah had immediately recognised his teacher, but Paul had not recognised his student. Observing that Paul had not the faintest idea who the pathetic stranger in front of him was, Naledi introduced the man as Noah Kefilwe.

Noah was a loner. After getting up each morning at five to fetch water for his elderly grandparents – his mother had died giving birth to him and his father had gone looking for work in Johannesburg and had never returned – he always looked tired and neglected. He had few friends because he was so different from his classmates – children will always shun an outsider – and smelled strongly of smoke. But in spite of his immensely disadvantaged start in life, he had somehow managed to remain cheerful and sit attentively at the back of the class trying desperately to concentrate, until sleep overwhelmed him in the heat of the afternoon. Paul had always had a soft spot for the boy – it was in his nature to empathise with those less fortunate than himself – and had tried to help him. He had given Noah extra tuition after school to help catch up on missing work – he was frequently "ill" – and as well as secretly giving him money to buy food for his family, had bought him a new pair of sturdy leather shoes from Gaborone to help mitigate the suffering of two tender feet destined by fate to walk ten miles a day through the hot dusty tracks of Mochudi.

Paul stared intensely into the sickly but still cheerful eyes of his ex-pupil, trying hard to match what he saw before him to the child he had once known. Logging onto his photofit recall, he could see that beneath the dense undergrowth of wiry stubble and face fungus there was the same boy he had tried to rescue from abject poverty some thirty years before. As always it was the facial expression and the smile, and those eyes – those windows into the body disclosing the deeper recesses of a man's soul – that had stayed roughly the same, while the flesh had succumbed to the vagaries of time and the vicissitudes of life, like a nail that had rusted, like a rock that had weathered, battered by the raging storms of adolescence and the setbacks and disappointments of adulthood. He looked very much like his biblical namesake after the flood, tired and hungry, in search of dry land after being trapped in the Ark for forty days and forty nights with a load of smelly animals and his wife Naamah. And older.

"*Dumela* Noah," said Paul, shaking his head from side to side in disbelief, lips pursed, sorrowful eyes. "How've you been man?"

"*Dumela* sir – not so good."

It turned out that having left school with five O-levels, Noah had turned down the chance of a cushy job for life with the civil service in Gaborone, unlike most of his classmates, and had instead felt himself duty-bound to look after his ageing grandparents and younger siblings in their *kraal* on the other side of Papane Hill. Tending their modest flock of goats and farming a couple of acres of semi-arid land three miles to the north of Mochudi had provided just about enough meat, milk and corn for their survival – in a good year. After his grandparents had died of "old age" in 1985 he had got himself a job as a teacher at Molefe primary school and worked there until his two siblings, Mogomotse and Basimane, had contracted AIDS and been taken by the Lord some five years later. In his despair he had succumbed to the temptations of drink and become an unemployable alcoholic. He had never married – who would marry a drunkard? Today he was visiting the graves of his grandparents and siblings.

THE PEDAGOGUE

Paul was struck by the fact that Noah looked older than him, as if relativity had once again played its tricks and caused the pupil to age faster than his teacher. How sad that the loner was still alone, that the tragedy of his birth should accompany him until the tragedy of his death, to curse him to his grave, as if there was someone out there determined to rub his nose in it, to atone for a crime he hadn't committed, the crime of being born black and poor. Where was the justice in that? Was there such a thing as fate? Why was it that some unfortunate sons of bitches seemed destined to suffer from cradle to grave, relentlessly, mercilessly, as if they'd deserved it? What sort of a God would condone such a thing? And yet somehow he had managed to stay cheerful.

Teacher and pupil, the two men – for they were both men now – embraced clumsily in the baking hot graveyard, as hot as hell, self-consciously clasping each other like lovers still unsure of the other's response, Noah smelling of smoke, Paul smelling of aftershave. Maybe this was hell.

"I still remember how to calculate the hypotenuse of a right-angled triangle sir," sobbed Noah, his desiccated bloodshot eyes temporarily soothed by the salty water of his tears. "Pythagoras's theorem: that the square of the hypotenuse is equal to the sum of the squares of the other two sides."

"Bravo Noah," cried Paul, "at least my lessons didn't go to waste."

But if his lessons had not gone to waste, what use had they been? Like so many of his milieu – white middle-class New York kids, the sons of immigrants who read books, who dreamed the American Dream and aspired to be professionals – he used to believe that knowledge was of itself worthwhile, that it had intrinsic value, that it expanded the mind; that the mere possession of it somehow enriched a man, made him a better person. But that was a purist's view, a view that imbued knowledge and education with a sacred, quasi-religious power. But what use was knowledge that didn't change one's life, that didn't transform one's life-chances or improve one's social mobility –

327

knowledge that didn't enable one to break free from the shackles, the lottery of one's birth?

They parted as they had come together, suddenly and without warning, Paul and Naledi looking out over the village graveyard of the damned, Noah, that quiet gentle boy from the back of the classroom, still smelling of smoke, returning to the wretched graves of his perished family, the ghosts of his life.

Where have all the soldiers gone?
Gone to flowers every one
When will they ever learn?
When will they ever learn?

They left the "house of peace", the *Friedhof*, and wandered through the sun-baked streets of the village, over the dried-out river bed, past the old *kgotla* and the Naomi Mitchison primary school to what looked like a shanty town on the other side of Papane Hill. Naledi unlocked the door of a small wooden hut with cracked windows and a corrugated roof and invited Paul into her pauper's house.

The hut consisted of a main room furnished with an old sofa, a few wooden chairs and a flat-screened television in the corner, and a bedroom hidden behind a zebra skin curtain, which also doubled up as a kitchen. A few faded photographs hung on the crumbling walls. She offered him a cup of tea and a piece of homemade sorghum cake. It was oppressively hot and dingy in the hut, the only ventilation coming from the wind which blew in one window and out of the other.

Paul looked at the photos. One was obviously Naledi and her family in better times – well dressed, well fed and happy. How does one cope when one's own spouse and children, the *raison d'être* of one's existence, are suddenly taken away without warning? Like loved ones apprehended by the secret police for questioning and never returned. A more faded photo showed "the class of seventy-four" with thirty happy, carefree faces sitting in rows in orange-brown Moketse uniforms and Mr Seretse, the headmaster, sitting at the front with a typically proud but caring smile on his face. Paul recognised many of the children.

"He died in eighty-four, just before the plague," interjected Naledi matter-of-factly. "Like an absent father, he was spared the ignominy, the heartbreak, of seeing his children die and get buried before their time. There was a quasi-state funeral in the cemetery reserved for dignitaries and those who could afford it, near the hospital. Everybody turned up – Chief Matlapeng, councillors, Catholic priests, doctors and nurses, village elders, Sam the barman, Sandy Coombes, 'local royalty' – and hundreds of Moketse pupils, past and present, come to pay their respects to a head teacher they had both loved and respected."

Naledi paused in front of a third photo taken at the funeral. "Look *ticheri*, that's me."

Paul saw a young woman in the prime of her life, sombrely dressed in black, her tear-stained face only accentuating her vulnerability and stunning beauty as funerals so often do. But that was BP – before the plague. The scene reminded him of one of those sepia photographs of Tsar Nicolas II and the Romanov family before the revolution, utterly unaware of the fate that awaited them, their expectation of life making their imminent death all the more horrible and poignant.

At the far end of the room, Paul's attention was drawn to a huge photo of Chief Matlapeng as Paul remembered him when he taught at Moketse, and below the inscription '1935-2005'. "*Et tu* Matlapeng?" The final nail in the coffin of Paul's memories.

"Kgosi was taken from us last year," said Naledi noticing the source of her teacher's gaze. "He suffered from diabetes and died of a brain tumour in a Johannesburg hospital."

Paul stared at the stunning picture of the chief. How could that youthful, handsome, fresh-skinned man he had known, holder-of-court at the Mochudi bar, who could drink everyone under the table and still remain sober, how could that cultivated conversationalist and lover of beautiful women be dead? He tried to grapple with the death of this once magnificent human being who had treated all the volunteers at the school as his equal. His eyes once again reddened as yet more fluid poured out of his lachrymal ducts, warm salty secretions of sadness bathing his uncomprehending eyes, a seemingly inexhaustible hot spring of sadness. Under the photo were the words: "*Robala sentle Kgosi-e-kgolo* Matlapeng II". Sleep well Matlapeng.

"Kgosi was a great man," whispered Naledi, visibly moved by the heartbroken state of her tearful teacher. "We all loved him like a father. As our chief he reconciled the warring factions of the Dutch Reform and Zion churches and enabled women to attend the *kgotla* and set up a refugee camp for the exiles of apartheid. He was a maverick visionary and conservationist who wanted to bring his beloved people, the Bakgatla, into the modern world. But he was also a supporter of the House of Chiefs and the continuity with the past it represented. Like so many, he died a disappointed man, saddened by the loss of respect for elders and the selfishness that materialistic development and progress had brought."

That pattern of development and disappointment had been repeated throughout the continent. The new replacing the old, material wealth creating spiritual poverty. It had happened in the States as well.

As he sipped his lukewarm milky tea, Paul looked around the claustrophobic, dimly-lit room and wondered why so much sadness should be visited on such a lovely person as Naledi. What had she done to deserve this degradation, this humiliation, apart from having the bad luck to be born in Africa? As a black African, she had drawn the shortest of life's straws. While her contemporaries in Europe and North America enjoyed an ever-increasing standard of living and life expectancy, she was destined to suffer squalor and disease. Where was the justice in that? What sort of a God would allow this to happen? Weren't the meek supposed to inherit the earth?

"That's the best cake I've had in years," said Paul, desperately trying to inject something positive into their conversation.

"*Ke itumetse ticheri*," replied Naledi, fully aware of the thoughts swirling around her teacher's troubled, balding head, "The Lord's ways are not our ways." That get-out clause that explains everything and absolves the perpetrator, the creator, of all this misery, of any guilt or responsibility.

The two sat in silence for a few seconds and stared at each other. Paul felt an overwhelming urge to grab Naledi and make love to her there and then behind the zebra skin curtain. To comfort her, to ejaculate his white serum into her fragile black body, an act of love to unite black and white, to somehow atone for the guilt he felt, rightly or wrongly, for the obscene inequality between them. The White Man's Burden. But what use would that be? A gesture. The act of yet another guilt-stricken white man trying to assuage his conscience by giving charity to the poor. An act of pity. But downtrodden people didn't want pity. They wanted dignity.

"Let me show you something, *ticheri*," Naledi said as if reading his thoughts. She opened the door and led Paul out of the hut, locking up behind her, and along a winding track that led to the gates of a huge house on the edge of the village. They stood opposite the gates and marvelled at the colonial-style mansion perched on the hillside. A brass sign on the gate read; "Dr Emmanuel Menyatso, physician and general practitioner".

Paul's eyes brightened up. He recognised that name.

Naledi pressed a button to gain electronic access to the mansion, and at the end of a long gravel driveway with a silver Mercedes parked outside, rang the bell of the black mahogany front door. A pair of colourful garden gnomes guarded the entrance to the house, greeting newcomers with their cheeky gnomish smiles.

After a minute or two, a handsomely-dressed man in a blue linen safari suit, highly polished brogues and sporting an expensive Rolex on his left wrist, opened the door.

"This is my old classmate Emmanuel from 5B, the one who made it," giggled Naledi, her eyes at last glowing as she squeezed the hand of Dr Menyatso.

"Mr Winkelman, I presume," grinned Emmanuel, holding out his left hand towards Paul.

"Jesus H Christ Emmanuel, is that *really* you?"

Apart from a receding hairline and the expanding midriff associated with well-fed men of his age and status, Emmanuel was still recognisable as the suave but modest boy he had taught maths to in 1973 and 74. He was the guy who sat three rows from the back of the class, always deferential, never put his hand up, but when asked knew all the answers. He had been everyone's favourite student. If Emmanuel couldn't make it, nobody could.

"*Dumela rra*," said the doctor, clasping Paul's hand as if he would never let go, "*Dumela* Mr Winkelman, I've been expecting you. Dr Livingstone, I presume?"

Bush telegraph had evidently informed Emmanuel that Paul was in town.

He shut the door and led his guests through a tastefully-decorated lobby and into a beautifully spacious living room that opened onto to a sumptuous veranda and a tropical paradise of a garden. They were seated on colourfully cushioned rattan chairs next to a marble table, and served cold drinks and nibbles by two highly attractive young black servants who looked suspiciously as if they might have been Emmanuel's nieces.

Paul gazed in awe at the unashamed opulence that surrounded him. It was like something out of Hollywood, except that it wasn't kitsch. From the designer furniture and exquisitely crafted curios in the living room, to the exotic plant pots, vases and mosaic tiles on the veranda, no expense had been spared. It was definitely worth a pula or two. The garden was filled with luscious plants from which emanated the delicate perfume of ripe oranges and papaya and the subtle scent of bougainvillea and jacaranda. A brass fountain at the centre of the garden in the shape of a roaring lion sprayed crystal clear water from artesian wells deep below the Kalahari through its feline mouth, high into the air and down onto the miniature statues of antelopes and zebra basking in the coolness below. Exotic South African birds from the Tropic of

Capricorn perched amongst the dense green foliage and punctuated the hot humid air with a soothing birdsong, while colourful butterflies fluttered their iridescent gossamer wings silently as they flew from flower to flower, drinking in the cool refreshing nectar like Paul and Naledi sipping their passion fruit cordial on the veranda. It felt like the palm house at Kew, like some decadent nineteenth-century outpost of the British Empire.

"I owe my position and my wealth to the education I received at Moketse," said Emmanuel. "To your maths lessons, Mr Winkelman, that taught me how to think logically; to Mr Zabinsky's biology lessons that opened up to me the hidden world of the microscope and the majesty of the human body; to Miss Winterton who taught me the beauty of literature and the importance of language; to the eccentricity of Mr Fanshawe who made me crave for knowledge and learning. Praised be the Lord."

Emmanuel lifted his glass and toasted his good fortune.

"God has caused his face to shine upon me. He has protected me from AIDS and enabled me to devote my life to others, helping seek a cure for this terrible disease and treating those who have been affected."

Paul wondered how his protégé still managed to believe in God after all the disease and human degradation he had witnessed. He had lost his brother and sister and half his school friends to the plague, so how could he keep his faith in an omnipotent, merciful deity when everything around him contradicted that faith? How, after being taught to think rationally at school, could he still suspend all reason and seek solace in the supernatural? But these were very superstitious people, for whom life had no meaning without God. The empiricism of Darwin and Einstein was no match for the wisdom of the scriptures.

"God helps those who help themselves," said Emmanuel as if reading Paul's thoughts. "When I passed Cambridge I did a degree in medicine at the University of Botswana, and then a PhD in tropical diseases at the University of the Witwatersrand in Johannesburg. I'm now the senior registrar at the Princess Marina

Hospital in Gaborone, working on a vaccine to prevent AIDS as well as helping treat my own people here in Mochudi."

Emmanuel removed a leather-bound volume from the bookshelf in the corner of the veranda and handed it to Paul: "The ten plagues of Africa, by Emmanuel Menyatso PhD". He leafed through the pages, which were covered in dense text and illustrated by electron micrographs of malaria parasites and the mine-like structure of the HIV retrovirus.

"I've been invited to speak at AIDS conferences in Paris and Berlin, and addressed the United Nations in New York. I even met Clinton at the White House in ninety-nine," said Emmanuel, rolling his head slowly from side to side, lips parted in surprise, eyes fully open as if he still couldn't believe the hand, the full house, the royal flush that life had dealt him.

Naledi stood up and embraced the only living member of the class of seventy-four to survive the terror and make it. He carried not only the hopes of his country but the hopes of all those who had gone to school with him, sat in the same classroom, laughed and cried together, taken the same exams – Noah, Cecelia, Victor, Kgosi, Nkomeng, Olefile, Tscholofelo – and the hopes of those who had perished on the way, to carry the flame for those who would never see the promised land.

Why had Emmanuel survived? Was it luck or fate? Did his good looks and superior intelligence somehow protect him, make him invincible; confer on him a special immunity to the deadly disease? Or had he been chosen to survive by a higher power whose ways we could not understand? Like a survivor of the Holocaust who had cheated the gas chambers and the ovens. The Chosen One.

Paul leafed through the pages of the weighty tome again. It was seven hundred pages of scholarship, meticulously researched, beautifully illustrated, taking in the full magnificence of what his pupil had produced against all the odds, in a society where the dice of life was loaded against you from birth.

"Jesus Emmanuel, I'm so proud of you," blurted Paul, staring in awe through his thin-rimmed tinted glasses, his mouth half-open with incredulity, still trying to get his head around the celebrity of his former pupil. "How did you manage to write such a big book, you son of a bitch?"

They all laughed at that; Mr Winkelman was always calling people sons of bitches. His pupils never fully understood the subtleties of this mother of all Americanisms they'd heard in films, and more recently on TV, but they knew it was an endearing insult that had nothing to do with sons or bitches. When it came to catchy idioms, there was no one who could surpass the Americans; "son of a bitch", "son of a gun", "asshole", "motherfucker". Never was a language so expressive when it came to dispensing gratuitous insults.

As the afternoon took its leave and the fiery ball of a sun plummeted towards the western horizon, the orchestra of crickets and frogs commenced its evening concert, a gentle overture at first, followed by an ever-louder cacophony in the first and second movements like a piece by Stravinsky ratcheting up the decibels in *The Rite of Spring*, a relentlessly pulsating sound sweeping away the silence before it like a storm crossing the Kalahari. The Frog and Cricket Philharmonic playing the modern-sounding, but eternally ancient song of the night, the song that Adam and Eve first heard in the Garden of Eden.

The two nubile servants reappeared, carrying plates of cold meat and cheese and bottles of fine French wine, and placed them on the marble table as if they were guests in a five-star hotel. Cut crystal wine glasses and a huge bowl of tropical fruit harvested from the doctor's own garden followed, along with fresh guava juice and bread. Paul and Emmanuel were served wine, while Naledi was poured a glass of cold fruit juice.

"Let's drink to the future," said their host, raising his glass of vintage Chateauneuf-du-Pape as he did so. "Cheers."

"*L'Chaim*," retorted Paul, the first rush of alcohol already dilating his pupils and lightening his mood.

"*Botshelo*, to life," said Naledi, getting into the party spirit at last, the original freshness of her once lovely face returning for a few fleeting seconds as her wrinkles disappeared like evaporating clouds to reveal the school girl beneath.

As the three tucked into their Botswana banquet, evening turned to night. The orange sun was replaced by the silvery moon and the vivid colours of sunset gave way to a bluish-black night sky peppered with a million twinkling stars. The fragrant perfume exuded by the garden intensified with the darkness and intoxicated all who breathed her. Birdsong became cricket song and frog song, as day song became night song, competing only with the occasional bark of a dog, the crowing of a cock or the cry of a child and the humming sound of recently-installed air conditioning systems. In the distance the relentless beat of *gumba gumba* music and the unmistakable sound of the Mahotella Queens – still popular after all these years – began to assert themselves over that distant African village.

Chapter 2

Michael and Josh sat in stunned silence, trying to make sense of what Paul had just said. And what a story. A couple on the next table averted their gaze so as not to be caught eavesdropping on this humdinger of a good yarn.

"That's what happened guys," laughed Paul nervously, downing the last dregs from his pint of Young's Bitter, searching for signs of a reaction in the eyes of his two friends. "The whole fucking village wiped out by AIDS."

"Jesus H Christ!" exclaimed Josh, still unable to comprehend the enormity of what he'd just heard.

"The moral of the tale guys, is don't go back – you never know what you'll find. Let the past stay the past. Don't dig too deep. Don't desecrate those precious memories, the illusions, the myths of childhood and youth which give you comfort in middle age. Leave the skeletons in the cupboard."

The three friends finished their drinks and walked along the river, each lost in his thoughts, each trying to reassess his life. The Thames footpath was crowded with Londoners and tourists taking in the warm autumn sunshine, drinking in the last hours of the day. The river was full of action as rivers always are, with a constant stream of small boats and the occasional canoe powered by muscular types from some posh school or other practising for their annual regatta. Flocks of white swans and portly overfed geese paddled effortlessly through the water, sometimes with, sometimes against the current, oblivious to the huge steamers which constantly threatened to mow them down but somehow never did. Young couples sunbathed on the grassy banks, girls showing off their silky legs, boys holding onto their girlfriends for dear life lest they should be lured away by some passing stranger more handsome than themselves. The early autumn sun bathed the landscape in a warm orange glow, lightening every heart as a few fluffy clouds drifted across hazy blue sky.

They walked for a while along the footpath and then on Michael's insistence, climbed the densely-grassed slopes of Richmond Hill until they arrived at the Roebuck, described in the *Good Pub Guide* as "a gem of an English tavern, serving traditional cask ales and good pub grub, offering unique views across the Thames".

"Let me buy you both a pint of Taylor Walker," insisted Michael, relishing the chance to show the Americans yet another classy London pub, which by association meant that he too was a connoisseur of fine beers and a man of good taste. He ordered three no-expenses-spared packets of crisps as well.

They seated themselves on a stylish wrought iron bench outside the Roebuck, facing westwards and overlooking the shimmering course of the river Thames below and the whole of west London. A continuous stream of planes drifted by, descending relentlessly towards Heathrow Airport in the middle distance, and the familiar outline of Windsor Castle could just about be seen above the distant hazy horizon, with a bit of imagination. On the far side of the river and looking close enough to touch stood the ugly silhouette of Twickenham Stadium, rising from the ashes like a concrete phoenix, the home of world rugby.

The Roebuck was a classy pub which attracted classy people –

young and handsome, middle-class, privately-educated and well-heeled Sloane Ranger types quaffing Chablis and chilled champagne – and a smattering of tourists and foreign students marvelling at the all-pervasiveness and sheer audacity of the English class system; priceless anthropological entertainment, like a painting by Renoir. To the left a starry-eyed pair of newly-weds, fresh from the registry office in their pristine wedding attire, the bride's flushed cheeks looking gut-wrenchingly beautiful against her virgin-white bridal dress, posed for photographers on the happiest day of their lives, against the uniquely stunning sun-drenched panorama.

The three comrades sipped their beer and munched their crisps loudly and enthusiastically: the crisps made you thirsty for beer; the beer made you hungry for crisps. That marvel of marketing, that vicious cycle of thirst and hunger, like a pair of lovers complementing each other's kisses. The sadness of Paul's story had given way to the warm glow of friendship, aided and abetted by the alcoholic anaesthesia from within and the September sunshine from without. How different this all was from the acacia-strewn African savannah, where the young volunteers had last drunk together some forty years ago in Botswana.

"Those were great years," said Josh philosophically. "I don't think I've ever felt more alive than in that lovely African village. Those kids – we just loved them and they loved us back. Who could wish for more than that?"

"You're right Josh," said Paul, nodding his tipsy dense head up and down rhythmically, agreeing with his fellow American as he had so often done in the past. "That heady cocktail of idealistic youth and a complete lack of worldly cynicism."

Michael lifted his glass of half-empty Taylor Walker and toasted, "Botswana. Those were precious days indeed." The others raised their glasses. It felt so good to be communing with these guys again after so many years – FORTY FUCKING YEARS! There must have been some powerful bond, like the strong force in the nucleus of an atom between sub-atomic particles, which had pulled Paul and Josh three thousand miles across the Atlantic, and at great personal expense. There had been a love between them that dared not speak its name, that he'd never thought possible between three heterosexual men.

As the sun approached the western horizon, casting its red evening light across the Thames and bathing our heroes in a rich fiery glow, Michael led his two long-lost buddies to the station at the bottom of Richmond Hill. The three embraced as they had done on first meeting each other nearly seven hours earlier. But this was the embrace of farewell, not welcome. Parting was indeed sweet sorrow, like Romeo and Juliet, but without the expectation that the lovers would ever meet again. The station clock chimed melodically as large groups of people milled around the station entrance, some leaving, others coming in for an evening of drinking by the river, or to take in play or a film, or to have a meal. People stared as the three clasped each other as if their very lives depended on it.

"Thanks for coming guys," said Michael, his breaking voice betraying his inner emotion.

Paul's tear-stained face mirrored the heartbreak in the swollen red eyes of Josh.

"Take care Michael, it was great seeing you," spluttered Paul, now crying openly and unashamedly in front of a hundred passers-by.

"*Tsamaya sentle,*" croaked Josh in that spaced-out Rocky Mountain way of his, the words barely able to escape the emotional gravity within.

As Paul and Josh disappeared down the steps towards the District Line that would take them away from him, maybe forever, Michael waved his two dear friends goodbye and turned towards the corridor that led to his South West Trains connection to Windsor.

Chapter 3

✻✲✦✷✪✸✦✯✵✦✲✦✽

On the train back to Windsor, Michael once more reflected on his life as a teacher. Paul's horror story about his return to Botswana had shaken him deeply, made him feel unclean and unworthy. How could he justify those days at Moketse when huge swaths of his children – he still thought of them as his children – had been wiped out by AIDS? He felt like a grieving father. Was it just an indulgence, a white man dipping his wick into a black African village and then withdrawing when it suited him, *coitus interruptus*, no moral consequences, no price to pay? Was the pleasure too one-sided? Did the deaths of so many taint the survival of the few? Was it indecent to look back with so much love and affection on the best years of his life when so many had suffered? Or was he being too hard on himself, too self-critical, too masochistic? He could not have known what would happen after he left, any more than a father can know what will become of his sons and daughters when they leave home. You could still celebrate the life of a dead child – indeed you were morally obliged to celebrate that life if it were to have any meaning. You could still feel proud of the lessons you had taught and the friendships you

341

had made, even if the children would never grow old enough to use the knowledge they had acquired. Age would not weary them. The main thing was that you had done your best. And you had played your part in the incredible success of Dr Emmanuel Menyatso, a world-famous scientist whose work on the AIDS retrovirus could help save the planet from the eleventh plague of Egypt.

The train stopped at Twickenham. An old lady with a stick got off, and a boisterous group of rugby fans and a young woman with a baby buggy got on.

But what about his teaching career as a whole? What use had he been to mankind? What would be his legacy? Or was the whole concept of a legacy altogether too pompous? Who the hell did he think he was anyway, Winston Churchill? Had he on balance been a force for good or a force for bad? Or like most people, had his brief encounter with this mortal coil been of no consequence to anyone, instantly forgotten like a wave at the seaside, a breath of wind, a passing seagull? A *nebbish*, a nobody. What had become of those loveable rogues at Somersby? Had they become plumbers or con men, or were they languishing on the dole? Had they got married and produced yet more uncouth brats? What would become of his children at Beechwood? Would they go to university and become doctors and accountants? Or would they become enslaved by the customs of their tribe and the excesses of their religion? Had he taught them anything useful? Whatever became of the unteachables? Donna Huffington, Gary Withers, Peggy Weaver, Leroy Derby; kids he had been unable to control because of his aversion to their loutish behaviour and aggressive temperament. How responsible was he for the failure to educate those godforsaken sons and daughters of bitches? How much guilt should he carry? How much praise did he deserve for those that had done well? How would he be remembered; as a wacky, original, inspirational teacher who loved children, or as a fucking bastard? "Zabo you wanker!" Did the children succeed because of him or in spite of him? Michael knew from his own experience that a child never forgets its teachers. Would those he'd crossed bear a grudge against him, or like himself, remember even those he disliked with affection? Mrs Wright, Mr Mangold. Had he made a difference to people's lives – broken down barriers of race, religion, class and gender as he had always wanted to? Had he opened young people's minds to the beauty of nature, the majesty of ballet, the thrill of debate? Or had all those trips and visits been a waste of time, a means of collecting brownie points, enough credits to get into a good university?

The fact is, you can never tell. A pupil may not see the purpose of his education till much later in life, just as a child may not see the value of his upbringing until he is himself a parent. In his career he had taught literally thousands of kids, some of whom would now be grown up with children of their own.

The train stopped at Staines. Nobody got on; a family of four and three buxom girls tarted up for a night out at the Half Moon got off.

Did it matter whether one had made a difference? With so many thousands of people being born and dying every day, *who cared*? Who was taking notes? Would there be some kind of reward at the pearly gates, or would one be condemned to eternal damnation in hell? How had teaching changed over the years? How had *he* changed? Was he still the wide-eyed idealist that stepped off the train in Gaborone in 1973, or had he become cynical and sarcastic with age? He hoped not. Realism was not the same as cynicism. Michael had seen many a young teacher destroyed by unruly classes, dismembered by bloody-minded yobbos determined to wreck every lesson, the stuffing knocked out of them, their enthusiasm crushed, disillusioned and bitter before their time. Lefties become righties.

In truth Michael believed that he had helped many more kids than he had hindered, that he had been on balance a force for good. But that judgement was ultimately up to others. He could think of so many children – far more than those he had antagonised – for whom he had made a difference; Olefile, Tebatso, Itumelang, Kenny Wiggins, Yusuf, Jayshan, Roy Partridge, Sanjay, Emma...

the list was endless. He had broken down racial barriers in Botswana, enabled white working-class kids in Somersby to take pride and show off their prowess at angling and introduced the children of Beechwood to the world of art, science and debate. He had challenged Islamism, anti-Semitism, sexism and racism – black and white – in fact every kind of twisted "ism", prejudice or discrimination he had had the pleasure of coming up against. He had relished challenging the assumptions of pupils, teachers, parents, politicians, SMT. He had eschewed political correctness. He had resisted the forces of cynicism and with the exception of the occasional relapse, remained true to his calling as a pedagogue, had stayed motivated and innovative to the end. He had not sat on his laurels, preferring to continuously engage with new ideas and thinking, never allowing his brain to stagnate or atrophy. He had been a free thinker. He had asked questions at every staff meeting, had written letters on every aspect of education to the press. He had never been swept away by the educational fads that successive governments had tried to foster on him. He had never succumbed to the pressure to reduce teachers to the role of "facilitators of independent learning". And he had had fun; the price he had paid for being a pain in the ass for SMT – the failure to make it into senior management – had been well worth paying. He had maintained his integrity to the end, and like Frank Sinatra, he had done it his way.

PART 5

At the races

Chapter 1

Some find retirement easy. They simply replace their job with their hobbies – racing, golf, travel, gardening, flower-arranging, origami. For others, those with mundane boring jobs, retirement was what they had been waiting for all their lives – sometimes since the day they started work. Michael found it difficult.

He had heard so many retired people going on about how great their lives were now, so chilled-out, all that extra free time, how there weren't enough hours in the day for them to do all the things they wanted to. They were living proof that there was life after retirement. Or they were all bloody liars.

Obviously Michael didn't miss the hassle, the getting up early, the mind-bogglingly boring meetings, the marking, the putting up with the continuous reinvention of the wheel that passed for educational progress. But he missed the kids. He felt like an actor who, after a lifetime spent in the theatre, has just given his last performance and now stands on stage before an empty auditorium.

He misses the audience, the applause, the adulation, the warmth, the feeling of being loved. He misses the adrenaline rush before each show, the indescribable thrill of giving a performance. He felt like a parent whose children have just left home, isolated and lonely, still wallowing in the past, thinking about when the kids were small, missing being loved, missing loving. He felt like a widower who had just lost his wife. He was in mourning.

It was like coming off drugs, going cold turkey. The body takes time to come down from the daily fix, the daily infusion of adrenaline coursing through the veins increasing the pulse rate, enabling the body to perform. It took Michael more than a year.

He was haunted by faces from the past, the lovely smile of Anastasia, the cheeky face of Kieran. He saw ghosts of those he had taught when visiting the theatre, at an art exhibition, when watching *Question Time.* He continued to attend science lectures at the Royal Institution and looked around in vain for the faces of the hundreds of sixth formers he used to take there. He missed taking his kids on the heath, the thrill of seeing them discover the wonders of nature. He missed being surrounded by young people bursting with life. How he would love to teach just one more lesson on the menstrual cycle, burn one last piece of magnesium ribbon. He wondered what had become of those he had first taught half a lifetime ago. What had become of the plastic manikin Herbie?

But you can't turn the clock back. In spite of his withdrawal symptoms, Michael knew be had retired at the right time. Every week he read horror stories about teachers leaving the profession in droves because of the intolerable pressure, the worsening pension arrangements, the ever-increasing demand on teachers' time. He had got in at the right time when teaching qualifications weren't necessary and all you needed was a degree and the idealism to change the world; and he had got out at the right time when teaching was becoming too professionalised and teachers were becoming too accountable to the Secretary of State for Education and the omniscient, omnipresent and increasingly omnipotent Ofsted. For most of his forty-year sentence as a teacher, teaching had been a bloody good laugh. In which other profession could one laugh and joke virtually every day with the people one worked with, the pupils? In which other profession did one have so much freedom to be oneself and the chance to continuously innovate and try out new ideas? Not many. Whether his pupils would ever remember him with any fondness, or whether he had in the end made not a jot of difference to their lives or to the betterment of society in general, he would never know. It was impossible to say. Just because you influenced someone didn't mean they would make the world a better place. They could remember you fondly and still turn out to be complete bastards. And there was no telling what they would do with the knowledge you had so lovingly imparted to them. A bit of knowledge can be a dangerous thing. Knowledge of the atom led to nuclear power and Hiroshima. The Haber process led to the production of fertilisers and explosives. Cultivated people who read great literature and listened to classical music ran Auschwitz. An interest in politics could produce a Churchill or a Hitler.

Time is a great healer, and two years after retirement Michael had got over his bereavement. He had received an email from Ray Milburn asking him to organise a reunion with the Beechwood science department at Windsor races. So on a balmy Monday evening in July – one of those rare summer evenings when the heat of the day doesn't immediately dissipate when the sun goes down – Michael donned his "summer suit" of yellow M&S shorts and matching green T-shirt and leather sandals and walked across the road to the racecourse two blocks from his house.

As he approached the main concourse along the beautifully-landscaped pathway that led up to the track, like the Yellow Brick Road, he spotted a band of familiar faces in the heaving crowd of Monday night racegoers standing by the entrance to the Grandstand. He could recognise the smooth outline of Ray's bald scouser head glistening in the sun and the stocky features of Aadiya with her familiar jet black hair and short stubby arms protruding from a commensurately stubby body.

As he neared the group, he began to feel a frisson of excitement at the prospect of seeing these guys again. But as is *de rigueur* with the emotionally crippled English, they don't care much for the unnecessary flaunting of feelings, and just stared indifferently at an undefined point in space. That is of course with the exception of Judy, Beechwood's answer to Coco Chanel, fashionably dressed as always in an expensive-looking designer dress, ostentatious gold jewellery and colourfully matching shoes and bag, and Caitlyn, dressed as rebelliously as ever in a black leather motorcycle jacket and silk scarf – Beechwood's answer to *Easy Rider*. Both women embraced him warmly and affectionately, with French-style, full-on, cheek to cheek aerial kisses and pouted lips. "Ooh *Darling*." "Ooh *Luvvie*." "How lovely to see you again Michael; you look *marvellous*."

"Good to see you Zabo, you cantankerous old bugger," said Ray, a clapped-out northern smile spreading across his bewildered northern face, thinking up his next gag as he spoke. Like so many Merseysiders, he was a walking stand-up comedian for whom conversation was not possible without a constant stream of jokes and wisecracks.

"How wonderful it is to see you again Michael," said the ever-polite and deferentially mild-mannered Bernard.

Aadiya, as always, played the role of the shy little schoolgirl, too timid to speak, her sparkling black eyes lighting up her cheeky, dark brown Sri Lankan face.

"Why didn't you write to us Michael, why didn't you answer my emails?"

"You never sent me any emails Aadiya, and you know it. And I did write to you, but you never replied. I sent you all a box of mini-Easter eggs last year." Aadiya smiled that smile of mock surprise.

Michael greeted the rest of the gang who self-consciously reciprocated – Don, Lindsey, Salma, Nicole, Lottie, Alison... it really did feel good to be with these guys again, each a couple of years older. It felt like a family reunion.

Inside the racecourse, the atmosphere was filled with the sound generated by a huge crowd of excited punters having a great night out with their friends, and the prospect of winning big money on the gee-gees. All of humanity was there: young couples, families with kids, groups of diamond geezers getting pissed on Fosters and groups of nubile young ladies dressed to the nines to attract a bloke, see-through cotton blouses showcasing ripe and succulent young breasts just waiting to be harvested, colourful linen dresses revealing the outline of their underwear and emphasising the curvature of their hips and the satin softness of their lovely legs below. Summer was all about fillies and sex.

Rows of bookmakers shouted out the odds displayed on their electronic screens, pulling in long queues of gullible revellers hoping to make a fortune. Tonight would be the night. As always before a race, the mood of the gambler was upbeat and optimistic. Master of the Universe, he couldn't lose. Honest Joe, Dishonest Sam, Charlie Reed, Barry Duncan, Ziggy, Victor Locksmith; bookies, mostly older men and their long-suffering wives who travelled the country from racetrack to racetrack – Cheltenham, Towcester, York, Ascot, Epsom, Market Rasen – trying to earn an honest penny or a dishonest pound from unsuspecting racegoers who were genetically programmed to bet their hard-earned cash on an animal that didn't even know it was a horse. Racing was a substitute for the thrill of the chase enjoyed by their Neolithic hunter-gatherer ancestors; the thrill of the kill. The one certain bet – apart from the bookies always winning – was that given a moving horse or dog, or raindrops on a window pane, the great British public would have a bet.

Drinks were bought and downed and bought again and downed, and Beechwood got merry. For the first time in his life, that canny scouser Ray Milburn, who hailed from Liverpool and wore his accent and his working-classness on his sleeve like a badge of honour, and had the uncanny knack of never buying a round of drinks, bought a round of drinks. Alcohol inhibits the inhibitions and loosens the tongue. It wasn't long before the latest goss from school was being broadcast to the drinkers in the Shergar Bar and meticulously analysed. Mabel, the school resources manager, was having an affair with Janek, the Polish caretaker. "Who would have *thought?*" Apparently they had been filmed by the school CCTV system having it off in the gym after a parents' evening. The deputy head, Audrey Morgan, was retiring after what seemed like at least a lifetime of dedicated service to the school, but because she was so widely disliked by SMT – who were sick to death of her backstabbing and overweening sense of moral rectitude – she would not be getting a proper "do" at the Richmond Hill Hotel as befitted a person of her seniority, and would instead have to make do with an all-expenses-spared buffet in the staff room. There she would be able to enjoy for the very last time the wide selection of polystyrene sandwiches she had so enthusiastically foisted on the staff last year by awarding the school meals contract to a "value for money" caterer whose taste buds had long since been surgically removed.

A record thirty staff would be leaving the school this year, many capitulating under the impossible workload to quit teaching altogether, including a mass resignation from the music and drama departments, the self-styled faculty of "performing arts" who were being asked to actually get off their pompous behinds and put on a play and a concert three times a year. The highly-strung luvvies in the music and drama suite didn't like that. There had been an end-of-term spate of bogus fire alarms going off, which until the culprits were spotted on CCTV cameras running into the loo was causing disruption to lessons. Every day an alarm going off; everyone herded on to the school playground for registration; the local fire brigade turning up and being dismissed; the school being charged for wasting the fire brigade's time. There had been trouble at the school gates when a group of pious-looking, thobe-wearing bearded Islamists on their way to mosque for Friday prayers had attempted to intimidate three white girls by calling them "*kuffar* whores" and "*haram* infidels". The police had been called, but under pressure from "community leaders", no arrests had been made. Posters demonising Israel and America and calling for an Islamic caliphate in Syria and Iraq had started to appear outside the mosque. A group of three delightful girls who Michael had taught in year ten – Salima, Ifza and Naila – diligent students who always did their homework and behaved impeccably in class – had disappeared to join Isis. More and more women in niqabs and burkas could be seen wandering the streets of Hestwell. Rizwan Shah, one of Michael's star students from the 1990s who had got a degree in biotechnology at Imperial College London, had become a professor of genetic engineering. Krishna Patel, the girl who had gone on every trip Michael organised, had become the Labour MP for Brentford and Isleworth. Philip McCormack, the boffin who never missed a lesson or failed to ask Michael an obscure question in chemistry lessons, had got a first in microbiology at Cambridge and been offered a place at the Columbia University College of Physicians and Surgeons to do his PhD. Gurpreet Sandhu had become a newsreader at Sky TV. Alfie Pinkerton, that affable little crook from year nine who once stole the small intestine and pancreas from Herbie the Human, was doing time in the Scrubs for burglary.

Michael felt a pleasurable twinge of *schadenfreude* on hearing that the school's GCSE results had slipped back to their traditional level of 65% A-C passes, after briefly peaking in 2013 at 75% – the year he left. A clear case of cause and effect there.

"The kids still talk about you, Michael," said Bernard in his distinctively deferential way. "No one organises those trips any more."

"Joey sends his regards," said technician Don, referring to the greyhound Michael used to enthral his classes with every summer. "He wonders when you're coming back to visit him."

The bar suddenly emptied as the time of the first race, the six-thirty, approached. The group spilled onto the crowded racecourse packed with hopeful punters trying to get a last minute bet on and studied the runners and their odds. Diamond Geezer, 3/1; Ocean Current, 9/2; Mansoor, 6/1; Thimblenimble, 10/1; Whatalady,

20/1... ten horses in all. As "Man on the Spot", Michael advised his wet-behind-the-ears ex-colleagues to back the favourite, Diamond Geezer.

"It won here last week by three lengths," said Michael confidently. "It always puts on a good performance."

So, assuming that Michael knew what he was talking about, everyone dutifully put a couple of quid on the Geezer, except for Ray, who, being a clapped-out northerner with generations of racing experience under his belt and in his blood and bones, put a fiver on Thimblenimble. The teachers repaired to the Grandstand now packed with excited racegoers, and watched the horses being led into the stalls on the giant screen on the other side of the track. First in was Mansoor – in the meantime backed down to fours – with red and white stripes and ridden by Seamus O'Flaherty. Then came the rank outsider, Ferkerl, the chestnut horse at 25/1, in blue and orange hoops, closely followed by Whatalady and Thimblenimble. And lastly Diamond Geezer, in his unmistakable gold and pink diamonds and ridden by Declan O'Reilly. Virtually all the jockeys were diminutive Irishmen. "And they're off."

Watching the start of a race was always a thrill, with the eternal candle of hope still burning brightly, all to play for, all horses equal in the eyes of the Lord, the start of a new campaign, another throw of the dice, one more spin of the roulette wheel. In the mind of the gambler, which recognised no limit to its self-deception, anything could happen. The horses burst out of the stalls as if catapulted forward by a giant spring and raced the first few metres of the six-furlong handicap sprint. Ferkerl, described by the *Racing Post* as a horse singularly lacking in pace or the courage to win a race, which had never once finished in the first three, led the field, followed by Rotten Tomato, Whatalady and Thimblenimble, with the favourite, Diamond Geezer, bringing up the rear.

After the first furlong the horses settled down. Ferkerl continued to lead on the rails, with Mansoor and Ocean Current taking closer order on the stand side and Diamond Geezer still some five lengths adrift at the back. These were not Ascot sprinters trained by Godolphin and costing thousands of guineas, and after two furlongs some were already showing signs of distress. Thimblenimble began lurching to the left and ceded his position to Ocean Current, while Mansoor, whose head gazed inquisitively around him at his fellow horses – as you do if you're a 75-rated Windsor handicapper – fell back a few places. That eternal loser Ferkerl in his bright crimson top and white cap, continued to lead.

Michael took his eyes off the screen, looked at his ex-colleagues and smiled the smile of a father looking after his children. Apart from the seasoned northern gambler and self-styled midnight rambler Ray Milburn, the rest were as unsure as the horses about what was going on, and not fully focused on the race. Caitlyn and Lottie were looking in vain towards the wrong end of the track; Bernard was ogling a group of tarted-up fillies who partied below him, knocking back plastic glasses of Prosecco and laughing lasciviously. Alison continued to radiate peaceful vibes from her tranquil face. Don screwed up his face and studied his race card. At the halfway point of the race, the huge crowd, with the exception of the corporate drunkards below, were uncharacteristically silent, in a state of pregnant anticipation.

As the pack of horses approached the furlong pole, the previously dormant crowd began to erupt. The chestnut Ferkerl, whose head was now bobbing up and down uncontrollably and sweating like a pig as his jockey whipped him to a pulp, was being joined by Whatalady on the outside and the red and black colours of Rotten Tomato on the rails. The gold and pink diamonds of Diamond Geezer had started to make rapid headway from the rear and now effortlessly loomed up to joined the leaders.

"Goo on Diamond Geezer!" shouted the crowd, as the favourite hit the front with fifty yards to go.

"Goo on the Geezer!" bellowed Michael.

"Goo on the Geezer!" screamed the rest of the Beechwooders, jumping for joy as they emulated their mentor Michael, the man with the Midas touch. Except for Ray, who had elected to invest the small-change leftovers from Charity Week on the not-so-nimble Thimblenimble.

There can be few more pleasurable experiences in life than seeing your horse hit the front fifty yards from home and watching it power past the winning post. It's a feeling you can never get sick of, never have enough of, like an addictive drug the craving for which can never be satisfied. This is what keeps the gambler hooked – the thrill of seeing his horse win and the reward of winning money. He feels that his "judgment" has been vindicated, that he is the master of his universe. The compulsive gambler feels that he too is a winner, even though he is a loser who has done nothing other than place a bet to deserve such an accolade. He feels important, someone worthy of respect. He gets his kicks vicariously through the success of others. Until he loses.

What a great start. Judy and Lottie and Alison and Aadiya looked elated as they brandished their flimsy computerised betting slips – not the colourful cards of old that used to litter the floor like confetti with just the name and address of the bookmaker and no information whatsoever about your bet and how much you could expect to win – and embraced each other as women do.

"We won, we won!" cried Lottie, smiling ecstatically like a child who has just been given a huge ice cream.

"Gimme five!" said Bernard in what he imagined was a black Mississippi basketball player's accent, raising his right hand and smashing it into Michael's in that life-affirming American ritual which like so many of those irrepressible Americanisms, had become part of everyday life.

"Bloody donkey!" mumbled Ray, acting out the self-deprecating role of the sad northern bastard expected of him, his loser's *schtick* honed to perfection over the years. He was one of the Likely Lads bred from birth to be a student of philosophy in the university of life and hard knocks. The very source of his northern humour.

The winning teachers joined one of the long queues that had formed in front of every bookmaker to collect their winnings. Two pounds at 3/1, six pounds; ten pounds at 7/2 – THIRTY-FIVE

POUNDS! What a great sense of satisfaction you got fleecing the bookies. For your average teacher used to spending two pounds fifty on the *Big Issue*, this was big money.

Michael led his friends behind the Grandstand to a huge, well-tendered, luscious green lawn, surrounded by pots of scented flowers encompassing the winners' enclosure and the parade ring and extending as far as the river. It was like a modern costume drama with hundreds of well-dressed, well-heeled and well-oiled Monday night revellers peacefully mingling with groups of ordinary punters. Perfectly-shaped young women with perfect complexions paraded their colourful summer costumes, like peacocks strutting their stuff; posh types genteelly sipped champers or Pimm's; the hoi polloi supped plastic pint glasses of cold Fosters, their women heavily made up with vulgar tightly-fitting cheap and cheerful dresses from *Top Shop* or *Next*, accentuating their ample buttocks and voluptuous let-it-all-hangout tits, their men clean shaven and dressed in suits and ties as if to emphasise their working-classness. A lone guitarist played songs from the Paul Simon songbook. It was like a sumptuous garden party to which everyone had been invited, with fashionable food outlets selling pizza, Chinese, pulled pork and seafood and bars offering exotic Caribbean cocktails, fine wines and beer. Owners and trainers emerged from "Members" clutching their race cards and wives with equal ownership and heading straight for the parade ring. The whole scene looked so civilised, so quintessentially English as the evening sun illuminated and warmed this most peaceful scene of *alfresco* summer merriment.

Drinks were bought and drunk and bought and drunk again. So enchanted were the Beechwooders by the sheer vitality of life on the lawn that they skipped the next race, preferring to get pissed and merry on their winnings. Ray bought everyone a round of chips – miscellaneous expenses from the science department allowance – doused in lashings of salt and vinegar, scouser style.

"It's so good to see you Michael," said Bernard for the second or third time that evening. Nobody was counting.

"We miss you so much," said the short and chunky Aadiya, hungrily sipping her fourth glass of red wine. The alcohol had gone straight to her head, reddening her cheeks, dilating her pupils and widening her smile. Tamils like a tipple. "I love your yellow shorts."

"It's so wonderful to see you all again," said Michael to anyone who was listening. "You feel like family."

The jockeys for the third race trooped by on their way to the parade ring, a line of tiny Irish dwarfs dressed in the silks of their owner, each wearing a cap and holding a stick, their weathered square Gaelic faces resembling wizened leprechauns. They were the size of the young children playing on the grass. Living Lilliputians. Once in the parade ring the jockeys deferentially doffed their caps – racing was all about doffing your cap, reinforcing the class system, kissing the backside of the upper classes, showing deference to one's betters – and exchanged pleasantries with the owners who were usually a syndicate of up to ten enthusiastic lovers of the turf. Next to each group of owners stood the trainer; always an ex-public school boy with accompanying straight back, healthy complexion, half-man, half-horse, confident in-your-face gaze, posh accent, Savile Row suit and trilby, disarmingly polite and able to bullshit confidently about anything at all and horses in particular until the cows came home.

The third and fourth races were won by rank outsiders, so no luck there, and the fifth was won by the odds-on favourite, "Royal Dancer", whose penny-pinching price of 1/3 was unbackable. There was no joy in betting three pounds to win one. And so it came to the sixth and final race, the nine o'clock. The sun was now low on the horizon, hovering above the tops of the willow trees that bordered the Thames and beginning to take on the orange and red colours of sunset as it shone through thickening bands of glowing cirrostratus. These were the best days of summer, when it stayed warm and light till late. In winter it was sometimes dark by four. For Michael, evening racing at Windsor was a deliberate way of squeezing the last drops of light from those endless summer days of June and July. He felt it was his duty. Like a starving man unexpectedly invited to a banquet, greedily feasting himself on the last scraps of food on a rich man's table, he was hungry for light. There was something magical, spiritual even about witnessing a summer sunset in your T-shirt and shorts, exposing your arms and legs to our nearest star; a quasi-religious ritual like those Druids at Stonehenge offering themselves to the sun god on Midsummer's Day.

The final race is often known as the 'getting out stakes', a last chance for the punters to recoup their losses. The spoils courtesy of Diamond Geezer had long since been reinvested in fish and chips and booze and bookmakers, so a win in the last would be an agreeable way to round off the evening. It was a one-mile handicap race and Michael had spotted a horse trained by Godolphin called Sharif. The Godolphin stable based at Newmarket and named after Godolphin Arabian – a horse that came from the desert to become one of the three founding stallions of the modern thoroughbred – was owned by the fabulously wealthy ruler of Dubai, Sheikh Mohammed bin Rashid Al Maktoum, a bit of a mouthful and better known throughout the racing world simply as "Sheikh Mohammed". He could often be seen disporting himself around the winners' enclosures at Ascot and Epsom, the very epitome of a super-rich Arab sheikh who uses the respectability of being part of the English establishment – the sport of kings no less – to give the impression of being modern and enlightened, and deflecting world attention from the alleged subjugation of foreign labourers back home and the bankrolling of God knows how many dodgy Islamist affiliates of Al Qaeda or Isis by some of his more unsavoury neighbours. Since money was no object, his horses had won most of the big races throughout the racing world including the Derby and the Arc de Triomphe, and his horse today was ridden by the top jockey, James Doyle. It was not unusual to get top jockeys at a poxy course like Windsor; Lester Piggott, Willie Carson and Frankie Dettori had all ridden there. Godolphin horses never lost at Windsor – or so Michael liked to believe.

Sharif had never won a race; hence its drop in class and its appearance at Windsor. But its breeding was good and its fifth and seventh placings at Newmarket and Kempton were in more prestigious company than today's encounter. Fortunately for the punters, the presence of three-times winner at Windsor Mr Blobby – now the evens favourite – meant that the odds on Sharif were a most generous 5/1. The market simply responded to the betting on each horse, and by far the most money was going on Mr Blobby. It was a case of form against class, unlike in society, where an Oxbridge graduate with a 2/2 will always be preferred over a student from the University of Bournemouth with a First. Prejudice, snobbery, stupidity.

When it came to racing and the possibility of winning money, an egalitarian like Michael was quite prepared to sacrifice his lofty principles and follow the "class" horse. Money concentrates the mind like nothing else. Even the most principled people know that wishy-washy theories don't always pass the acid test of reality. After his success with Diamond Geezer, it was not difficult for Michael to convince his disciples to put their remaining money on "Omar" Sharif.

"If we don't win we'll never speak to you again," threatened Judy affectionately.

"Oh Judy, you are awful but I like you," retorted Michael, playing along with Judy's coquettish faux anger.

Aadiya had a tenner, Don had a fiver, Bernard had a couple of quid. Even Ray, who had not had a winner since 1999, put a tenner on the Godolphin horse. Everyone was on board – Alison, Lottie, Ray, Don, Andy, Caitlyn, Lindsey, Bernard, Michael, Salma, Judy, Nicole, Aadiya. By the time they had gathered on the steps of the grandstand for the last time, the horses had started going into the stalls. A huge crowd waited patiently, buzzing like a hive of bees in anticipation of the race. First in was Micky Sticky, a grey with blue polka-dotted silks at 20/1, then Mr Blobby in yellow and red stripes, now at 4/5 the odds-on favourite, followed by Tamanaco, Fridgefreezer, Lord Larry, and finally the Godolphin horse Sharif, now backed in to 7/2 with late Betfair money online. As the sun set in a blaze of crimson glory over the Thames to the west, the last race of the day was about to start.

"And they're off!" A wall of horses tumbled out of the stalls like a colourful stampede of bulls charging through the streets of Pamplona. For the first couple of furlongs the pace was more a canter than a gallop, with no horse taking the initiative. But when the horses turned for home at the half way point, Mr Blobby suddenly quickened and opened up a commanding three lengths lead over the rest of the field, swaggeringly throwing down the gauntlet to his rivals. "Catch me if you can you punks!"

The red and yellow stripes of the favourite could be seen detaching themselves from the pack as he kicked for home along the rails. When this happens in a race it is very difficult for the other horses to recover, having been caught napping and taken completely by surprise, in the same way that an army which strikes first often gains the initiative and wins the battle. And this being Windsor, none of the horses had a known sprint finish to speak of.

Michael's heart sank. He knew that the game was up when Mr Blobby quickened again at the two-furlong pole and drew even further away. He'd seen it all before. The pack tried to respond but in vain, each horse being frantically ridden and whipped to within an inch of its life in a desperate attempt to catch the leader. Those in the crowd who had backed Mr Blobby became excited and started to shout their horse on. "Goo on my son, goo on my Blobby!" But for the others it was too little too late.

With one furlong to go, however, the gap started to close as the favourite began to tire. The bright yellow colours of Fridgefreezer and the orange chevrons of Lord Larry could be seen closing in on the front runner with the black and white stripes of Sharit just behind in forth. It wasn't that the challengers were quickening, it was the favourite who was tiring, bless him, after leading the field for nearly half the race. Suddenly there was hope for the Godolphin horse as Jamie Doyle finally managed to get a response out of the old nag. "Goo on Sharif!" blurted Caitlyn as if shouting at a pupil in her year ten physics class. "Come on Omar!" screeched Aadiya, the prospect of all that lovely loot causing her face to light up, restoring her faith in life.

With a hundred yards to go, Fridgefreezer, Lord Larry and Sharif effortlessly drifted past the rapidly-fading Mr Blobby, who had evidently shot his bolt and come too early in the equine equivalent of a premature ejaculation. The crowd erupted into a wall of Phil Spector-like sound as the line of three horses crossed the finishing post together in a dead heat. "Photograph!" announced the privately-educated, posh-sounding commentator from the shires, who had described the race as "all over" when Mr Blobby had hit the front four furlongs from home.

The longer the delay, the greater the uncertainty, they say. From the terraces it was impossible to tell who had won. The horses had shot by in an indistinguishable blur of shape and colour. Even the action replays could not unequivocally tell which horse had come first. Like that controversial goal from Geoff Hurst in the 1966 World Cup Final which hit the bar and bounced down onto the goal line, in spite of being shown a million times since on TV, its validity as a goal is still disputed to this very day.

The bookies were offering odds on the outcome of the photograph, with Barry Duncan offering 1/2 on Lord Larry and Charlie Reed offering odds of 4/6 on Fridgefreezer. Only Ziggy offered hope that the Godolphin horse had prevailed, with odds of 5/6 Sharif, 6/5 Lord Larry and 6/4 Fridgefreezer. The tension mounted as punters speculated on the outcome of the photograph finish. The TV cameramen, who generally know who has won, flitted from horse to horse, from jockey to jockey, as if to emphasise their uncertainty. It all depended on which horse had stretched its neck forward in the dying nanosecond of the race and pushed its gormless sweaty head over the finishing line first.

As the ex-army, ex-air force, doddering old bowler-hatted judges – looking every bit like little Homepride men in their black suits, straight out of an advert for plain flour, as short-sighted as they were long in the tooth, and as worse the wear for whisky as a

Glaswegian after a night out in Sauchiehall Street – deliberated over the result, the sun set over the Thames leaving a purple but darkening glow above the horizon. A flock of geese flew over the racecourse, squawking loudly as they flapped their weary wings along the river in search of an evening place to feed and rest, and a Qatar Airways Airbus made its noisy descent towards Heathrow. The crowd waited anxiously for the announcement.

"And here is the result of the final race. First number six, Sharif; second number four, Lord Larry; third number one, Fridgefreezer. The fourth horse was the favourite, Mr Blobby."

The Beechwooders exploded into a spontaneous roar of blissful relief and uncontrollable delight, like Vesuvius spewing out fiery yelps of joy and ejaculating gaseous screams of incredulity.

"We done it, we done it already!" shouted Michael, in what he imagined to be a downtown New York Danny DeVito accent.

"We're rich, we can all retire!" cried Aadiya, her chunky childish face radiating pure unadulterated happiness. "No more school, no more fucking school!"

The mob converged on the hero of the hour, Michael, purveyor of winning tips and oracle of all things racing, as if they were going to rugby tackle him. But instead of kicking the shit out of him or kneeing him in the groin, as is the way in a scrum or maul or ruck – or whatever the fuck those rugger-buggers called those conflagrations of gratuitous violence in the barbaric sport they call rugby – they embraced and kissed and cuddled and rejoiced. Michael and his friends, united once more: a lovely feeling of warmth and togetherness.

"Gimme fifty!" yelped Ray, a look of total disbelief on his bemused scouser face, holding his right palm to the sky to be thwacked by the fleshy sweaty hand of the irrepressible Alison. "A tenner at five to one equals fifty lovely smackers." How the socialist loves to benefit from the market forces that he so abhors in everyday life that govern the odds on a horse. How he loves to be a winner when others are losers. How he loves to embrace material wealth and the chance to get rich.

The beneficiaries of the getting out stakes collected their not inconsiderable winnings and repaired once more to the sumptuous setting of the lawn behind the grandstand. A huge crowd now surged towards the stage to the right of the parade ring, where a Cuban band was warming up to end this sub-tropical summer night with the music of the Caribbean.

The head of science, Ray Milburn, for the second time in his life bought everyone a drink: beers for the boys and Easy Rider tomboy Caitlyn; funny-looking cocktails for the girls.

"A Bloody Mary for me please Ray," demanded the fashionably-dressed Judy, her ostentatious jewellery glistening garishly in the evening twilight, a huge cheeky grin on her perfectly made-up faux suntanned face.

"Watch ya language ya pompous bitch," retorted Ray in his best John Lennon accent.

The sun had gone down before the last race, and the wonderfully warm and humid summer's evening, now fragrant with the scent of jasmine from the giant potted plants bordering the lawn, slowly darkened into night. Being mid-July, the western horizon continued to glow yellow, green and then blue long after the sky above had turned black for the few fleeting hours before dawn that high summer allowed. It was a truly sensual, perfumed, Caribbean night. It could easily have been downtown Havana, or Kingston Jamaica. As the evening twilight dimmed, the light from the bars and the food stalls seemed to brighten, and the stage lights stood out against the backdrop of the river. Pretty girls in cotton frocks stood sipping chilled champagne in groups, laughing and joking and flirting with their beer-swilling, tight-suited boyfriends. Just as in the tropics, nobody felt cold. With a million stars shining through a cloudless black sky, Michael could have been back in Botswana.

Bright spotlights came on – white, red, yellow, blue – punctuating the darkness, as the band started up with a medley of songs from the Buena Vista Social Club. Lovely swaying Cuban music, merging African slave and Spanish colonial melodies, the natural harmony of the female backing voices, the strumming guitars and Castilian lyrics of the male singers, complemented the incessant pulsating beat of the wooden drums and bongos. Like a steamy, sleazy club on the Gulf of Mexico, the sound of ocean waves crashing onto a pristine sandy beach just ninety miles south of Florida, mamba, rumba and flamenco rhythms blended into a heady fusion of Caribbean music. Piercing brass trumpets gave the music a jazzy full-bodied richness of sound that could be heard as far away as Heathrow and Havana. The whole racecourse rocked and swayed. Even the horses in their stables tapped their hooves, so infectious was the music.

The only thing one could do to this joyous, life-affirming music was dance. "*Vamos a bailar!*" And sure enough, within fifteen minutes of Los Cubanos appearing on stage, virtually every one of the five hundred or so punters that had congregated on the racecourse lawn had started to sway to the mañana rhythm of the Latin-American band. Near the stage, couples young and old materialised out of the black night ether and danced on a make-believe grassy dance floor, twirling and swinging with gay abandon and carefree exuberance, to the totally liberating tropical beat. Further back, groups of half-cut girls and recklessly inebriated blokes threw caution to the wind and danced where they stood, some facing the stage, others in quickly-convened semicircles, letting themselves go in the half-darkness where no one could see them – or if they could they didn't care – imagining they were on a Club 18-30 holiday in Benidorm or Ibiza. And all the time the harmony of the singers, the poetry of the trumpets, the primordial beat of the bongos. Tipsy girls danced with their wine glasses, occasionally stumbling forward as they temporarily lost balance, hardened gamblers and business types in fashionable Savile Row suits spontaneously ripped off their ties and their inhibitions as they gyrated wildly like born-again John Travoltas, flailing their arms as they succumbed to the Monday night fever. Lovers embraced. Older couples watched the scenes of uninhibited hedonism and were rejuvenated by their youthful vigour. Michael and the teachers joined in, high on their winnings on Diamond Geezer and Sharif, high on the heady atmosphere, high on each other. The crowd sang loudly with the band without knowing or understanding the words, swaying their bodies and clapping their hands to the rhythm. "*Arriba*! *Arriba*!" A full moon rose over the Thames, illuminating the racecourse like a celestial searchlight.

And as the crowd rocked, the ghosts of faces long gone but never forgotten began to rise upwards from the seething, heaving mass of humanity below, like floating Chinese lanterns, burning against the black summer sky:

HABILE,	SERAKI,	ANOUSKA,	CLINT,
MOENG,	RANJIT,	CHENG,	MMPHO,
CECELIA,	FAHREEN,	KWAN,	SUNITA,
KEITUMETSE,	RON,	MATHEW,	HERBIE,
IRFAN,	BOTSHELO,	PULE,	DARSHANA,
LEE,	JASON,	KARAN,	RAGINI,
MOHSIN,	PARVEEN,	PRITI,	ITUMELANG,
KIERAN,	KGOSI,	SANDEEP,	ROY,
AISHA,	SANJEEV,	KWAME,	KAMRAN,
ANASTASIA,	TSHOLOFELO,	PENNY,	MALALA,
ONTLAMETSE,	NOAH,	MOHAMMED,	CHANGWE,
BALJINDER,	VIOLET,	KEFILWE,	GREG,
EMMANUEL,	SUMMEET,	JAI,	SHAKEEL,
MANDRISE,	ALFIE,	BILLY,	CLARENCE,
TEBOGO,	MOENG,	AHMED,	KENNY,
SALLY,	GARY,	JASPREET,	KGOMOTSO,
SMITA,	OLEFILE,	SEEMA,	SHAHIDA,
OLLY,	DAVE,	NKOMENG,	ASHLEY,
MOTHUSI,	CHAD,	SHERRY,	NATASHA,
NASIRA,	MOLEFE,	BASIMANE,	DIKELEDI,
MAVIS,	SARBJIT,	TIRO,	SLAVEK,
NALEDI,	ELIZABETH,	BATSILE,	YASMIN,
DONNA,	BONTLE,	KHALID,	BOITUMELO...

24466668R00210

Printed in Great Britain
by Amazon